I0733201

The Dancer in Beirut

Thomas Edward Muller

Published in Australia by Sid Harta Books & Print Pty Ltd,
ABN: 34632585293
23 Stirling Crescent, Glen Waverley, Victoria 3150 Australia
Telephone: +61 3 9560 9920, Facsimile: +61 3 9545 1742
E-mail: author@sidharta.com.au

First published in Australia 2020
This edition published 2020
Copyright © Thomas Edward Muller 2020
Cover design, typesetting: WorkingType (www.workingtype.com.au)

Muller , Thomas Edward
The Dancer in Beirut
ISBN: 978-1-925707-39-7
pp430

About the Author

Thomas Edward Muller has travel in his genes and writes for travel magazines. Born in Kenya, he later migrated to Persia, then Canada, and now lives in Queensland, Australia. Raised by his Czech parents in a multicultural environment, he is fluent in six languages. For 25 years, he was a professor of economic psychology at universities in Canada, Australia and Japan, before retiring to writing and adventure travel on all seven continents. He is married to an aged-care nurse and their son is a mathematician aiming to be a research scientist.

The frog in the well knows nothing of the great ocean.

Japanese proverb

To
Bohuslav and Allegra

I was
gifted good genes
and they've been put to work for me.
In return, I pay them handsome dividends:
they get trained in the lessons of life and they will
reach the future, long after I am gone.

The future is embedded in the past.
History tells you what will happen next.
Will we ever learn—when will we ever learn?

We came whirling out of nothingness, scattering stars like dust.
The stars made a circle, and in the middle, we dance.

Rumi
13th-century Persian poet and Sufi mystic

for
Miyuki and Tommi

Acknowledgements

I would like to thank my editor, Barbara Ivusic, at Sid Harta Publishers for her ideas and suggestions for improving my story. Book designer and cover artist, Luke Harris, at Working Type Studio, brilliantly captured the theme of the story. The encouragement of Kerry Collison to turn my work into an historical novel was the inspiration I needed to finish the project and get it into print.

Sincere thanks go out to Lorie Badiyan and Fred Badiyan, in Minneapolis, Minnesota, for their insights into the Baha'i faith and for providing photographs of the Shrine of the Báb, on Haifa's Mount Carmel, as it looked in the 1920s and 1930s. These helped me envision the scene and keep the story accurate.

I am also grateful to my Czech friend Pavel Hajný, in Prague, for providing the published sources that helped me envision and describe the situation at the heavily guarded border between Czechoslovakia and Austria during the communist era in Czechoslovakia. I also thank my dear cousin, Rony (Aharon) Yifrach, at Israel Aerospace Industries, in Tel Aviv, who supplied insights into what life was like in British-ruled Palestine during the 1920s and 1930s.

I devoted countless hours refining my understanding of the epic Battle of Britain in 1940, so as to offer a clearer narrative: books, articles, videos and historical documentaries were my raw materials. Of course, the many years I had spent in Kenya, then Iran, under the Shah, and later in Europe, as well as the 22 years I had lived in Canada and the United States also helped bring reality into the historical saga of my characters.

For her help during my visits to the Czech Republic, in order to set the scenes and achieve historical accuracy, I sincerely thank Dáša Martinková, director of the Muzeum Tomáše E. Müllera, in Bohdalice, Moravia and am hugely grateful to my cousins, Jiří Trávníček and Martina Horníčková and their respective spouses, Eva and Vít, for giving me a home away from home in Vážany and Ivanovice na Hané, in Moravia while I was doing my research.

Readers will come across a very few words that look strange or are unfamiliar. I have taken these from *The Lexicon of Comicana*, by Mort Walker. They seemed appropriate words for what I wished to convey about a character's reaction to something, and I believe they will eventually find a place in standard English dictionaries. I am a firm believer in language evolution over time.

I close with the admission that I am heavily indebted to my family for their patience and support in giving me the freedom to complete this project. Such generosity and encouragement create a solid foundation for all inspired writers.

Preface

One writes an historical novel with a clear picture in mind of which global events would likely be turning points for the cast of characters in the story. My story covers an era that spanned the period between the end of World War I until shortly before the collapse of communism in Eastern Europe, two great turning points of mankind. Throughout my story, I aimed for historical accuracy and cultural balance, both Oriental and Western.

But there is more to it than that. Today's readers of an historical novel appreciate it when they come across major events they can clearly remember, and relate to, in an emotional way. Such reads endow their life memories with a connecting thread.

I still vividly recall where I happened to be, and how I had reacted, when the news reached me that Einstein had died, that the Soviets had launched Sputnik—the first artificial satellite, that President Kennedy had been assassinated, that the Arab-Israeli Six-Day War had ignited, that Bobby Fischer had beaten Boris Spassky to become World Chess Champion, that Margaret Thatcher had launched the Royal Navy to recapture the Falklands, that Space Shuttle Challenger had exploded, that Princess Diana's life was cut short in a Paris car crash, that two jet liners had flown into New York's Twin Towers, or that a monstrous 2011 earthquake and tsunami had struck Tohoku, Japan.

In a comparable spirit, I sincerely hope that readers of this novel will make similar connections between some of the events described and what was happening in their lives, at that particular time in recent history.

Chapter 1

A key turned in the lock and the house door swung open. He touched the prayer scroll nailed to the door frame outside and put his fingers to his lips.

'Papa!' she squealed. 'Did you win at backgammon?'

'No, I lost. A week of work, gone from my pockets. Why are you still up, so late?'

'I'm sorry you lost, papa. I was waiting for your story when I go to bed.'

Esther looked up; forehead crinkled. Darning socks worn thin was irritating in the lightbulb's sickly glow. 'You're late again! How much *arak* did you drink?'

'So? I was with friends. Business is slow. Clients don't want new suits. They wear the old ones longer. I closed shop early. And we played.'

'Until the money you played ran out. Lentil soup is cold. Heat it up. Eat what's there. We're out of chickpeas.'

'Papa, please tell me a story. Make me sleepy. Please, papa.'

She jumped into bed and curled up to where he was sitting on the edge.

'It was in the time of the King of Persia. He was the King of Kings, the great king, the king of countries. His empire was vast and his subjects many. He was a kind ruler to his people and showed them compassion and justice. They had great respect for their monarch because he had vision and honour and principles. They travelled from faraway lands to pay homage to the king they loved, and bring him gifts, gifts of sheep and camels and gazelle from Mesopotamia. And from Assyria, ahh yes, horses for riding and beautiful horses for racing. They brought shiny black stones carved into the king's image and polished with bird feathers by craftsmen in Egypt. They offered saffron, and spices, and nutmeg from Oman and dates from the palms of Arabia.'

She was smiling. Her eyes wide with wonder at this mysterious world, full of strange lands.

'The king would receive sparkling pearls from the Persian Gulf, or fine silk carpets woven by nimble hands in Parthia. They brought the king wine from Armenia, baskets of rice and the finest tea from Ceylon and India, embroidered silk cloth from Samarkand, goblets filled with rosewater from the gardens of Babylonia. And the honey the king received from the orchards of the Tigris River was blessed with the fragrance of spring flowers: jasmine, magnolia, lemon blossom, hyacinth. Yes, the offerings were many.'

He paused for effect. 'And, you know? There is a legend that from the mountains of Ecbatana, they even brought pure fire. It was found in a cave. They captured it and brought it to the king in a gold-encrusted ceramic vessel. The king was astonished at the brightness of the fire and said it gave the light of Ahura Mazda.'

Her eyes were closed. She looked asleep.

He moulded a forced smile and hoisted himself up on skinny legs. In hushed breath, he began his exit: 'Mm, she is tired, story is too long and getting boring.'

'No, it's not!' Her head sprang upright then sank again, denting the sweat-stained cotton pillow. 'I was beginning to dream of travelling to this magical land and bringing the king a gift too.'

'Heh, heh. And what would little you bring?' He caressed her cheek with a finger.

'A handsome suit, tailored by you, just for the King of Persia.'

He chuckled more. 'You continue your dream. Now sleep. I'll start working on the suit.'

She closed her eyes. 'Yes. It will be a magnificent gift.' Her head got heavy. 'A wonderful thing from Papa.' In the dim light, he could make out rapid eyeballs moving, darting to-and-fro under her eyelids. Dreamland was approaching on tiptoe.

She woke up early. Through the lace curtains of her room window, she could see the sun's first glow lighting up the hills. Papa was still asleep. Her dream had the incandescence of a Persian flatbread tannur. *I must tell Papa later about my amazing, amazing dream!*

The suit Papa had fashioned was magnificent beyond imagination. Fantasy had been created out of bolts of silk cloth and lamb's wool. The cut was meticulous in its hand-sewn detailing and proclaimed the work of a master artisan. The jacket was scarlet and its shiny, silk lapels were embroidered with brightly coloured beads. The buttons were glistening mother-of-pearl. It had gold-fringed epaulettes that seemed to give the wearer added stature. In her dream, she held the jacket close to her and caressed its front with her cheeks. She hung the suit from the ceiling light and danced around it a few times, imagining the king wearing it and herself bowing before him. She twirled like a whirling dervish full of joy at the creation of this royal gift, then pictured the king stepping forward and inviting her to dance with him!

Folding the suit over her arm, she flew to the king's marble palace on a tiny silk carpet, which she could pilot with ease by oscillating her hips and pushing down on the left or right fringed border with her feet, like pressing on soft pedals to bank and turn. The wind in her face turned her long hair into a fluttering, trailing hood as the fluctuating roar thundered past her ears. Holding tightly to the suit, she held her arms outstretched. The king lived in the domain of kings and the carpet knew the way.

Arriving at the palace, she was horrified to see an endless line of gift bearers waiting to see the king. The crowd milling about outside was greater than a thousand and one, and she tried to push and squeeze her way into the palace to where the king sat. But the crowd got rough. She was jostled, elbowed, pushed around. Frightened, she looked left and right to find a way forward, but the crowd pressed on, rude and aggressive. The beautiful suit fell to the dusty ground, and people began to trample on, and dirty, it.

They shouted at her, 'Who are you? Where did you come from? The king doesn't want gifts from girls! Are you a virgin?' In desperation, she tried to dust off the suit Papa had created, but it looked ruined.

Then, as if by jinni magic, the King of Persia spotted her and motioned to the people queued in front of her. 'Let the little lady through.'

She came forward. He showed great delight in this gift, delivered by a young girl with long, black hair. He was a tall king, with a kind nose and handsome moustache. His hair was shiny black and his eyes blue. But she couldn't understand his language. It sounded Slavic or Germanic, not Semitic, and his sentences were long and mysterious, yet she felt a bond of trust and humility that went beyond words.

Papa will be spellbound when I tell him about this jumble, bumble, crazy dream.

Puberty was now her companion. She was mature beyond her years. The clear sky and cool air stirred a familiar desire, deep inside, to climb to a secluded hideaway where only the sea breeze declares itself and a whole city reposes far below. She did this often, without telling anyone. It was her secret thinking place for dreams to play out in her teenage head. Dreams of escaping to a mysterious land of sultans. Or riding with a camel train deep into a king's domain and its shifting dunes, where the sun spat fire and the bone-chilling nights were starry wonders.

In the kitchen, Esther was preparing the evening meal. With the Sabbath approaching, she would not be touching any more work until the following evening.

Daniela got dressed, hurried into the kitchen and stuffed her cotton knapsack with a bread loaf and goat's cheese.

'Danni, where are you going?' probed Esther.

'To the market, ima, to buy some chickpeas,' Danni giggled. 'Ima, I need a bit more change. Can I please have five mils?'

'You're going to buy ice lollies, aren't you?' Esther dispatched her frosty look.

Late April, the old olive tree outside gave an abundance

of unripe, bitter fruit. Danni pointed a resolute finger at the tree. 'You make my mouth pucker, your vile olives! But only *you* know where I'm going.'

She took the familiar winding street that sloped upward, and the cobblestones soon gave way to a narrow dusty path that got steeper. It was a long hike to reach the secret place. She passed two donkeys descending towards town, one loaded with firewood for making charcoal, and the other with small rocks for stone masonry. The donkeys had large, rough turquoise beads strung around their necks, like good-luck charms safeguarding them from overload. The one in front wore a brass bell that tinkled as the animal's hooves sank into the gravel. It raised its head as if to bray, but only its thick lips parted and showed grinding, greyish-green teeth. A smell of donkey sweat swirled up behind, as though the animal perfume was hurrying to keep up with its owners. A gust of ill-timed wind picked up loose dust and shrouded the path ahead. A little way further, fresh donkey dung glistened yellow-green in the sun.

Their driver followed some distance behind. He wore a black and white keffiyeh, aged by the perpetual sun and its loose ends were wrapped around his lizard-rough neck. The years had given him deep grooves around the leathery eyes. His grey shirt was tattered. The worn-out trousers were fraying at the cuff, revealing slip-on shoes made from woven cotton string and stitched to rubber soles fashioned out of old tyre treads.

'*Ahlan wa sahlan!*' His gravelly greeting punctuated the air.

'*Marhabaan.*' Hello. The ring in her voice drew out the last syllable. Arabic danced without effort on her tongue.

Danni's complexion and translucent Mediterranean -olive skin radiated a confident youth. Her black hair, braided down to waist length, gave her a school-girlish, dutiful look. Huge, brown eyes dwarfed delicate features with a chin that appeared resolute. Her monthly periods heralded the prime season of life and, with it, shyness had somehow mysteriously vanished.

Up ahead, she saw tall, gnarled cypress trees fringing the path. Their branches were powdered with old dust and the moving air yielded a faint evergreen fragrance that underscored the morning quiet. The world of people seemed to disappear. Climbing higher, she passed a familiar feature: a simple, four-sided building made of local stone and containing nine rooms, the Shrine of the Báb, founder of Bábism, conceived in Persia and transformed into the Bahá'í faith.

Danni was spooked by thoughts each time she had gone past the shrine. Her mind would be taken over. *Why is this Shrine of the Báb troubling me; what does it want?*

No reply furnished, only silence. A disturbing hush. The stillness was immune to the rustling breezes of spring.

She reached her secret thinking place and sat on her favourite rock. High up, from her songbird nest on the mountain, she looked down at the busy cargo ships, loading and unloading. The city of Haifa stretched along the Mediterranean coast. As the ships came and went, Danni played imagination games. Where did this one sail from? Where is that one going? Secret thinking took over. *I want to go on one of those ships, anywhere it takes me.*

She picked up smooth pebbles and massaged them in one hand. They were warm from the morning sun. She began humming a tune, restrained at first, until the insistent, dizzying rhythm picked up the Hebrew words and urged her to break into a lively folk song:

Zum, zum, zum, zum;
Zum, zum, zum.
Zum, gali-gali-gali; Zum gali-gali.
Zum, gali-gali-gali; Zum gali-gali.
Hechalutz lema'an avodah,
Avodah lema'an hechalutz.
Hechalutz lema'an avodah,
Avodah lema'an hechalutz.
Zum, gali-gali-gali; Zum gali-gali,
Zum, gali-gali-gali; Zum gali-gali...

. . . and she faded the words back into a hummed tune like an audio technician at the voice controls.

World War I died the year Danni was born. The Ottoman Empire lay in ashes, cremated by forces beyond Danni's comprehension. Turkish rule in the Near East had ended. The Brits were now running Palestine. She knew the history. She had read it: The Great War stank of betrayal, useless sacrifice, hatred between eternal enemies. How could she fathom the stupidity of human affairs? Her mind was fresh, receptive, young.

In the distance, a cargo ship was leaving port and sounded one, long blast of its deep, throaty horn. It echoed its way up the hills. Like a Tibetan monk's lingering bellow, it reverberated for a moment, then joined the silence.

Where are you going this time? as though the wind would write down her question and deliver it to the vessel's master. *One day a ship like this will take me away to travel the world!* She sent the pebbles flying in the direction of the departing ship.

Starting back down, she passed that shrine again. She didn't want to look, but a cold and intangible hand turned her head. The shivers came back.

Then tell me. What is it you want?

Only silence. A disturbing hush.

'What is it!? You want to tell me something, don't you? My destiny, is that it?' She was hollering now, infuriated by the stony silence. 'Why are you frightening me?'

An old woman, her back hunched and body bent forward, was climbing up the steep path, panting and wheezing with the effort. She relied on the walking stick for support and held a small shopping bag stuffed with garlic cloves and onions. She spotted Danni.

'Who are you shouting at? Who is there?' She paused to catch her breath. 'Is someone there?'

'No, nothing. Nobody there. Did I frighten you? Sorry.'

'How old are you?' She cleared her throat and spat. There was blood in it.

'I'm almost fourteen.'

'Almost fourteen,' she grunted. 'What do you know about life? You are young and carefree and full of hope.' She trained a studied gaze at Danni. 'Um-hmm. You have a kind face, young woman. Who were you shouting at?'

'It's nothing, really.'

'You were shouting at the Shrine, weren't you? I do that too. *Ehhh, kheh*! Yes, I do that sometimes. *Ahurr, ahurr*!' Her voice was raspy, her throat dry.

'I'm so sorry. Are you Bahá'í?'

'I'm a Christian. What are *you*?'

'I'm Jewish.'

'Mah! Jewish, Christian, Moslem! They're all under the eye of one God, the same God. What's the difference? We don't need separate religions.' Her eyes widened, stretching the crow's feet and causing her forehead to pleat like the bellows of an accordion. She tapped her skinny, corrugated finger against her temple. 'It's all here, in the mind. Ha? Your beliefs. Ha? You keep them *here*.' Another tap. 'That's what I like about the Bahá'ís. They gather everyone under the same God. All of us children of the same God. Much better to worship that way.'

She steadied herself with the wobbly walking stick. Then, straightening out a little, she used the stick to point at the Shrine. 'That Shrine there. It talks to me. It's a voice full of knowledge about people's lives. It whispers to me.'

'Really!? What does it say?'

'You will find out, young woman. You have passed the Shrine many times. It knows you. It knows your life.'

Danni was bursting with curiosity. Now, she couldn't pull herself away from the old woman. 'You really hear a voice?'

'It doesn't answer your questions. It comes into your thoughts. But you never know when. Only *you* can hear the Shrine.'

'Can it tell my future? Does it warn me if there's danger?'

'You will hear when it happens. You are young. It has words of wisdom for the young. I am tired. I must go.'

Danni's heart tumbled. She wanted to hear more. But she could see that the old woman was in pain. 'Yes, yes, of course. Can I carry the bag for you until you get home?'

'No, young woman. You go. You have discovered what I have known. Do not tell what you know about the Shrine. Ha? Don't talk. It's yours, alone, to hear. Listen to it.' She began to cough, an abrasive ahurr, ahurr. 'Listen to it.'

'Will I see you again? May we talk more? Please, can we?'

The old woman turned and struggled up the trail, her walking stick scraping the gravel and leading the way.

'Please tell me your name,' Danni called out. Silence. Just the whispering breeze rustling the cypress branches.

Danni waited. Perhaps the old woman would change her mind and say something. Then she disappeared round a bend.

She waited more. Her mind was in a whirl. *Had the old woman hinted at predestination? The Arabs say, 'It is written.' Your entire life already is known. Allah has written it out. But you are forever barred from reading what Allah has scripted for you.*

As Danni continued her descent, she heard the distant wails of the muezzin, calling the faithful to noon-hour prayer. The loudspeakers fixed atop a minaret amplified his exhortations and carried them until they faded into the distance.

'Allaaaaaah u akbar ... Allaah uuuuu aaaaaaakbar ...'

Danni's mind wandered to the old woman: *It's so true. He is calling them to pray to the same God as mine. And her God, too. The same God of all worshippers. No difference.*

She repeated the Arabic words, so tame to her ears. '*La El-lah, hel* El-*lah,*' there is no God but *the* God. *So, if there's only one God, we all believe in that same God. What's the difference?*

The steep trail, plunging downward, quickened her strides. Gravity pulled. Danni braked in her tracks. She turned and looked uphill. Today's climb to the top of Mount Carmel was special. Her secret thinking place had yielded a secret. It was now her Mount Carmel secret. She held it in a tight grasp, squeezed the secret thought very tightly. *Maybe it will whisper my destiny.*

Danni made her way to the open-air market not far from home. She found her icicle man with his tiny cart. The flavoured ice lollies were moulded in the shape of a Royal Navy frigate and chilled in the cart with dirty chunks of ice. He chanted his familiar refrain in an Arabic rhyme:

> *'Telat el-shkal el-furgeta-a-a-a;*
> *Halib-u, limun-u, shukulata-a-a!'*
> And bending it into English:
> *'Three styles of ice frigate;*
> *Milk and lemon and chocolate!'*

Chapter 2

'You don't do your laundry on the Sabbath, and I won't do my laundry on Sunday. Do you hear? I don't want to have your clothes hanging from the wire, flying in my face on the Sabbath.'

Esther was talking to her Christian Arab neighbour. They got along fine, as long as Esther's rules were followed.

An arranged marriage had injected a sixteen-year-old Jewish firebrand into the life of Avram Meir when he was twenty-two. Esther was fat. In her best-dressed moments, she was an Icelandic whale stripped of blubber. Where she got her calories was a medical mystery: Avram's income was as unpredictable as his flow of clients. He was skinny, his dry skin firmly glued to his bones. How those two copulated was a topic that fuelled the occasional hushed speculation among neighbours and acquaintances. Backgammon and *arak* were his distractions from sex. Yet, by some physiological mechanism, they managed to have three daughters. All died after birth. When Danni came along, Esther feared the same fate for this one.

'Sell her to a virgin girl and she will survive,' Esther's Christian Arab neighbour urged.

Esther glared at her. 'What!?'

'Well, Abraham was prepared to sacrifice his son, Isaac, no? Are you afraid to sell your daughter to a virgin so she can live?'

In a superstitious and symbolic act, Esther sold Danni to the nineteen-year-old daughter of Jewish Russian immigrants who lived next door. She received one gold Turkish pound for her investment in Danni's survival.

Two sons came after that. Then a last one, at age forty-two. It died after birth and Esther blamed the hospital nurses for dropping the baby on the floor and killing it. She never saw that happen. Motherly fabrication made the loss more bearable. It died because Esther had a difficult pregnancy and the infant was born weak. Her accusation was a coping mechanism that girdled Esther's generous hips and buttocks like a corset stiffened with cursed whalebone.

The rowdy open-air bazaar, its smells and animated life, was Danni's hangout. It pulsed with an élan vital, a life force of its own, a local theatre staging a daily drama and turning Danni into the thrilled audience. The raucous vendors' cries, gossiping shoppers, and haggling taking place under sun-shaded stalls were the embodiment of boisterous scrambled merchandising.

Children and their parents posed in ridiculous costumes to have their black-and-white, grainy picture taken by the photographer and printed on a rough-matte card with serrated edges. Another photo-op stall had a World War I Sopwith Camel biplane painted on a plywood frame with a hole cut through, to reveal the subject sitting in the kitschy cockpit and posing with a leather flight helmet and removable goggles. The artist had blundered and Germany's Iron Cross was painted on the tail of the famous British biplane.

Camels and donkeys were everywhere, loaded with produce and saddled with wicker baskets that were stretched almost to bursting point with hay, olives, cucumbers, Jaffa oranges or watermelons. The bazaar was Danni's second school, offering free tutelage in street-smartness. She spent hours observing the behaviours of vendors and buyers, like watching an old woman shouting curses at the butcher because he had cheated her, or spotting a boy stealing oranges and escaping uncaught, or being amused by two vendors arguing about whose hawking space had been usurped by the other. She saw the beggars deploy their practiced schemes for generating sympathy, faking their misery by twisting an arm into a grotesque shape, or putting a bandage soaked in chicken blood over one eye.

She listened to the endless bargaining over the price of everything from goat's cheese and hand-woven place rugs, to kerosene heaters and hurricane lanterns. She studied how getting a good bargain works: the buyer overstates his demands and understates his offer. It's a bluff that marks the starting point of the haggling. Then the merchant and the buyer squabble back and forth, and the asking price comes down while the offer price grudgingly edges upward, until the two meet. To save face, there's a bit of grumbling about the final price, but the deal is made. Danni digested the strategy. She knew it would come in useful one day.

The daily drama staged various acts of deceit in its productions. One time, at the edge of the market, a private taxi driver was dumping his woman passenger short of her destination and refusing to take her any further. Danni heard the two quarrelling. Her husband had sent the woman to a downtown market with her infant and bag of wares, and had prepaid the fare. But the driver changed his mind, pocketed the money, and was about to drive off on another errand. Danni marched up to the car and planted herself in front of it.

'Out of my way, girl-brat! *Imshi!*' shouted the driver.

'I'm not moving until you return the fare to this woman.'

The driver tooted his bulb horn. Engine running, he

edged up to Danni, almost touching her legs with the bumper. She didn't budge. Indotherms radiated over his head. Two male bystanders watched the commotion. Time to decide the outcome of this spectacle. They pulled the driver out of the car. Danni strode up to him and donned her Arab persona.

'Shame on you! Is this what Islam has taught you? Is dishonesty what the Prophet Mohammed preached to his followers? Is that in the Qur'an, to cheat people!? Give back the fare she paid you!'

A scuffle broke out between the driver and the two men. They pinned him against the car. The driver was cornered. He began cursing as he dug into his pocket. He waved a sweat-stained banknote that made up half the fare. '*Khudh ha. Sha'ra min thiz el-khanzir!*' Take it. A hair from a pig's arse!

Danni snatched it out of his hand and gave it to the woman passenger. 'Now, the other half. Come on. Give back the other half.' The woman wept and the men began punching the driver until he broke free and squirmed in behind the wheel.

'*Kus ummak!*' Up your mother's cunt, he hissed, and blasted off in a puff of dust.

'May Allah, the Gracious, the Compassionate shower his blessings upon you,' the woman sobbed. 'We don't have much money. I need to sell these goods.'

'Why don't you sell them here, in this market?' Danni smiled at her. 'Maybe we can find you a spot. I know the fishmonger. Come, let me hold your baby. You have a lot to carry. In future, don't pay the ferry man until he gets you to the other side.'

The woman passed her baby over and touched Danni's bosom. '*Insha'Allah*, God willing, you will be blessed with many children. You are a kind lady.'

Danni was absorbing the smell of the street. It implanted a squirt of toughness and sharpened her intuition to know when opportunity knocked.

Her two brothers, Moshe and Yigal, would often follow her into the market. They wanted the company of an older sister, but they were full of tricks. One time, the boys played a joke on Danni. Moshe threw out a challenge: who could stay the longest under a standing camel? The boys pointed out that it was risky: the camel could move and they might get kicked. They would go under the camel's belly, between its front and hind legs, and count out loud. Ten seconds was their highest score before they ran out from under the beast, feigning panic.

Danni fell for the chicanery, boasting she could stay much longer than that. She maneuvered herself under the camel and began to count. Ten, twenty, thirty, forty seconds, a minute, two minutes. All at once, the pregnant beast began to urinate. Before Danni realised what was happening, her hair and clothes were soaked in camel urine.

The brothers ran home to escape their angry sister. When Danni got home, she stood before her mother, sobbing fake sobs.

'Ima, look what they have done to me.'

Esther smacked her across the head. 'You stink! Go wash your hair in the water bucket. And don't throw out the water. We need it for the vegetable patch.'

At mealtimes, economic management governed hunger abatement: the cost of the cheese battled against the cost of the much cheaper bread. Volume was important. Volume at minimal cost. Esther often screeched at the children: 'Don't eat cheese without bread. It will give you worms!'

Papa was sitting in the kitchen, peeling the papery skin off the garlic cloves. Danni came and sat on the table top close to him. 'Papa, why do flames dance?'

'They dance?'

'Yes, papa. Really. My schoolfriend took me to her Catholic church and inside, near the church door, there was a huge bunch of candles burning. And the flames were dancing! All the candles were together, they were short and almost melted away, and their flames were twirling and kissing each other.' She gave the movements with her fingers. 'They twisted around like they were holding hands and dancing. It was beautiful to see.'

'Well, you saw something special. Maybe it was a Christian ghost teaching them to dance.'

'Papa, I want to dance like those flames. I want to be a bright yellow-and-red flame dancing up to the sky.'

'And who will you dance with?'

'With you, Papa.'

'I'm not a dancer. Only the dice in the palm of my hand do the dancing when they hit the backgammon board.'

'Alright. A handsome king, like in your story.'

He put down the knife, looked up and smiled. Twirled his hand in a rising spiral. 'And someday, you will find the king of fire, and dance with him.' Danni put her palms to her cheeks and gave a hopeful giggle.

'Daniela.'

Danni looked up from her book. The librarian was pointing at the wall clock.

'Library is closing. You are the last one here, my dear.' That was Simone Mahfouz, a Coptic Christian from Egypt and librarian and teacher at the French-language girls' school Danni attended.

'Ohhh. What a pity. I was getting deep into the story.'

'Deep into the story,' she smiled. 'What are you reading?'

'Napoleon's Russian campaign of 1812. Could I please take the book home? Please?'

'Your parents must sign if the book is to be borrowed. But, just between us, you can take it until Thursday. Be sure you hand it back to me, personally,' she smiled.

Danni beamed a heartfelt, '*Merci*, Madame Mahfouz' and scurried home.

History was Danni's forte and she read a lot. She had a crush on Napoleon: idolised his military campaigns, his leadership skills and resourcefulness. She also admired Admiral Lord Nelson who defeated the French and Spanish fleets under Napoleon, at the Battle of Trafalgar. Lawrence of Arabia was another hero. He became her dashing figure, in linking himself with the Arab Revolt against the Ottoman Turks, and masterminding the surprise attack to capture Aqaba.

But geography would ignite her mind, too. Given a map, her finger would do the travelling and discoveries quickened her pulse. She saw it as a doorway to the mysterious and wonderful world beyond the shores of tiny Palestine. When her geography teacher mentioned the island of Spitsbergen, she made a fetish of the name and would repeat it, rehearse it, twist it, corrupt it:

'Sprrrritsbergen! Spits-berrrrgen! Shpeeets-berrrgen!' She liked the sound and knew the place was exotically far from home.

With algebra, it was hopeless. Her mathematics

teacher, Monsieur Lazare, laboured to make her understand that a negative number, multiplied by another negative number, would give a positive product; whereas a negative number, multiplied by a positive one, would produce a negative result. In desperation, he tried another way.

'Mademoiselle Meir. Look. It's not difficult. Really not difficult. Enemy is negative, friend is positive. Yes?' She nodded and he continued. 'The enemy of my enemy is my friend. The enemy of my friend is my enemy. The friend of my enemy is my enemy. The friend of my friend is my friend. Do you understand how it works?'

She didn't know what to do with that. 'But I have no enemies. I have only friends.'

'Then multiply them and you will always get a positive number!' he blurted.

Danni joined the Girl Guides. On Scout troop outings, she was the whistle master, making sure that the other girls were marching in step by synchronising with the whistle blows. But she couldn't swim: The Girl Guide whistle master, living on the shores of the Mediterranean, did not know how to stay afloat and propel herself through water. Her uncle was an officer in the French Navy and the thought of being unable to swim humiliated her.

Her brothers would fix that. They took her out to sea

in a row boat and when they were away from shore, in deep water, they pushed her overboard and shouted, 'Now, learn to swim!'

Danni was in a panic, struggling to stay afloat, thrashing her arms and gulping sea water as she tried to scream for help.

'Moshe, this is bad. Go get her!' Moshe dived in and grabbed her by the neck, kicking his way back to the boat. Yigal reached down to grasp her long hair, almost capsizing the boat. He held onto her hair and shouted, 'Moshe, swim to the other side and hold down the boat!' Then Yigal pulled in a gasping and spluttering Danni.

She was crying, shivering and coughing. 'I hate you! Hate you for this!'

It was a nightmare that gelled into a fear of deep water and never went away, even after learning to swim. Aquaphobia stayed on, like an unwanted guest, a hungry squatter in the soul, refusing to leave. *Water: danger! Sea: bigger danger! Ocean: full of danger, very deep, huge, black waves of drowning, widow makers!*

Papa hated his work. The tedious detail of hand sewing made-to-measure suits brought out an irritable temperament. Business was unpredictable: sometimes it was busy, at other times the orders dried up. Often, he would get lazy and leave his shop to sit in a cafe and play backgammon with friends and drink *arak*, aniseed-flavoured alcoholic spirit.

The ancient board game of backgammon had its addictive sounds. The whir-r-r-r of a pair of thrown dice rolling across the wooden board. The aggressive clack, clack, clack of the checkers being shunted around the board, then smacked into a slot or stacked on top of a checker by an opponent. The grunts of dismay when the dice throw was unlucky, and taunts from players teasing their opponent. All this, adding to the clink, clink, plunk of tiny cups of Turkish coffee being served by waiters wearing dirtied aprons.

At home, when his children got into quarrels, Avram lamented, *I have these three brats. What would I have done had I fathered six or seven kids?* He was the great storyteller but completely bald. As a child, he had typhoid fever and lost all his hair. He sported a generous handlebar moustache and, to cover his bald head, he wore a scarlet fez, which made him look taller.

Danni spotted her father wiggling into a cheap shirt, not ironed, and tucking the hem into threadbare pants. 'Papa, where are you going?'

'It's Friday, no? My scissors are dull. My tape measure is tired. My eyes are weak. Time to join my friends for backgammon.'

'Papa, don't forget your fez.' She ran and fetched it. Positioned it on his shiny head to minimise the reflective surface, then combed the black tassel on the fez with her fingers. 'Now you look just like a Turkish pasha!' She cradled his arm and rested her face against it. 'Papa, my dear papa. Today, you will win at backgammon.'

'Danni, life is like a game of backgammon. You get randomness thrown at your feet, and you create the best you can with what you got.' He chuckled and poked his finger into her chin. 'You are destined to be happy.'

'Really? You think so? How do you know?'

He said nothing and hurried off.

Danni was blossoming. Soon, she was attracting the attention of suitors. But Esther was not ready for these intrusions. When Danni was still thirteen, she asked her mother to take her to the synagogue on the Sabbath.

Esther, the captain on the bridge of the Meir family frigate, took over. Her passengers would go wherever *she* commanded. 'If I take you to the synagogue, they will think you have come to pray to have a man to marry. First, you must finish school. Then, we shall see.'

At sixteen, she graduated from high school and faced a world of uncertainty. Now, she needed a job in difficult times. Palestine in the mid-1930s was going through an upheaval. Stirrings of Zionist nationalism appeared on the streets and in the newspapers. The Arabs were getting restless and relations between Jews and Muslims were deteriorating. Violence between the two groups erupted in towns and cities.

Danni went through a succession of boring, menial jobs—barber's assistant, newspaper delivery, putting up event and campaign posters in the street, washing dishes at the railway station café. Occasionally, she would help Papa by shopping for suit-jacket lining fabric and the needed canvas, bargaining boisterously with the shopkeepers to get a good deal for him.

But Thursdays were special. Danni kept her spirits up by taking ballroom dance lessons in the evening. Her teacher, a Maronite Christian from Lebanon, loved jazz and played the trumpet. He taught her the Charleston, the samba, foxtrot, tango and quickstep. He was impressed with her natural sense of rhythm and fluid movement, and praised her often.

One evening, as she put away her dance shoes, her teacher said, 'Daniela, you have a gift for movement. Nice, smooth steps. You create ambiance with the tempo. Find a good partner and you will shine on the dance floor.'

Her outstretched arm and hand set the trajectory of her reaction. 'But *you* are my dance partner.'

'No. I am your dance teacher. You need a dance partner.'

'And where, do you suppose, I will find one?'

'Beirut has a lot of good dancers. Find a handsome man who'll sweep you off your feet and onto the dance floor.'

'Beirut?'

'Yes, Daniela. Beirut.'

'Thank you, dance master, but I don't know anyone in Beirut.'

He smiled. 'You'll find someone.'

She got to the door, spun round to face him. Her lips discharged an irritated, 'In Beirut.'

'Um hm. *C'est ça,*' he nodded.

She clenched her fists and growled. 'Beirut. *Quelle idée!*' What an idea!

Daniela spotted a job advertisement for an assistant store manager in a Kolo tyre outlet in Haifa. The ad was posted in Arabic, French and English. They were looking for someone smart who was fluent in these languages and would be a quick learner. The Kolo company, based in Brno, Czechoslovakia, made tyres for cars, motorcycles, bicycles and small utility vehicles. Kolo, the Czech word for *wheel,* was expanding into countries where these vehicles were popular and the market wanted cheap tyres that were service-backed. The Near East was an inviting target.

Kolo Haifa store manager, Nassim Malouf, was interviewing her. He sifted through her granular past and was swayed by Danni's apparent head for business. He gave her the job. Soon, she was adept at keeping the books, watching the inventory, placing orders, and talking to dealers about their tyre needs.

Kolo's Czechoslovakia-based store controllers oversaw their outlets scattered throughout Europe, North Africa and the Near East. The brightest of them, with a command of foreign languages, were dispatched to these foreign territories. They were the lucky travelling ambassadors who would be away for several months at a time, usually bachelors who didn't have families to worry about, and didn't mind travelling to faraway places.

Nassim Malouf received a telegram. He hurried to inform Danni. The store controller for Lebanon, Syria and Palestine was on his way by ship, from Trieste to Beirut, to visit the stores in his territory.

'Is that Mr. Novotny?' she asked.

'Yes, it is. From Beirut, he'll be coming to Haifa.'

'Umm. I look forward to meeting him. Do you know if he's a good dancer?'

Malouf kept it short. 'You can find out for yourself. Make sure everything is ship-shape in the store and the stock room, and see that the books are up to date. Let our customers know that Monsieur Novotny will be here soon.'

Chapter 3

Miroslav Novotny—friends called him Miro—was in his early-thirties. His shock of generous black hair, the deep-blue eyes, the tall, upright, self-disciplined poise made Miro very magnetic to young European ladies. He exuded the *savoir-faire* of a man who knew his way about the world and his confident, gentlemanly demeanour instilled trust in those around him. He was fluent in Czech and German and spoke a fairly good French.

He disembarked from his ship in Beirut. While in Lebanon, he spent several weeks visiting the Kolo tyre shops and canvassing the market for new opportunities. Beirut was clean, organised, well run and had a French flair that fascinated Miro. The 'Paris of the Middle East' brimmed with multicultural lures: exotic foods, inviting restaurants, magnificent hotels, and even more attractive nightclubs.

Virtually all educated Lebanese spoke French. There were Christian churches, synagogues, Catholic convents, mosques decorated in exquisite patterns, reflecting the influence of the Ottoman Empire, and a *laissez-faire* temperament he found infectious. He could see himself living here. Beirut's golden beaches on the Mediterranean were getaways for rich, sun-starved Europeans. *How far away, my landlocked Czechoslovakia.*

His work completed in Beirut, he headed eastward by bus. The road climbed into the Mount Lebanon Range, forested with cedars, then wound down into the Bekaa Valley before reaching Damascus. Syria, too, was influenced by French culture and he got around by speaking French. He sat with Kolo's agents around Damascus, catching up on market developments and checking on each store's business and requirements. Next stop was Haifa.

'*Enchanté de vous connaître, Mademoiselle Meir!*' Delighted to meet you. He gave a polite bow.

Danni looked up at his tall presence. *He is captivating.* She played with the thought. Around him, the air was infused with confidence. The practiced politeness kindled in her an instant feeling of trust. She hurried off to make a cup of Turkish coffee for him and Malouf.

The two men busied themselves with discussions about what needed to be done and how long Miro would stay in Palestine. There was talk about building a tyre plant, but the political situation did not bode well for such a move.

Danni made like she was busying herself. Every now and then, she would catch an unobtrusive moment to stop and study the man from Czechoslovakia. He looked a little like that kind king of Persia in her dream. *Yes, the hair was right, the eyes were blue. The nose was honest and could be trusted. He would fit beautifully into Papa's magnificent suit.* But his language was strange. A Slavic tongue was out of reach for her. She knew no one who spoke Czech. *Could he be the dancer in Beirut? Perhaps my dance teacher was onto something.*

A month later, when it was time to depart Palestine and return home to Brno, Malouf asked Miro about his next visit.

'I will cable you,' said Miro. 'It will depend on developments with the Tel Aviv people. There is unfinished business also in Lebanon.'

Malouf and Danni accompanied him to the bus station, where Miro booked a ride back to Beirut. Danni held out her arm to shake his hand. He raised her hand to his lips in the European taking-leave-of-ladies gesture.

'*Au revoir, Mademoiselle Meir. À la prochaine fois.*' Until next time.

Danny giggled out her embarrassment. He knew his manners. *She* was the innocent local in a land of different goodbyes.

From Beirut, he would take the ship to Trieste and

make his way to Brno by train. As the bus wound its way through the mountains, heading towards Beirut, Miro peered out the window at the passing scenery and thought about Danni. Her self-confidence and knowledge of the business aside, she had a vivacious manner that captured his admiration. He made a note of it in his travel diary:

Very impressed with Miss Meir. She is capable, efficient, and ... He left the rest blank. His thoughts continued the writing: *And she has a Semitic beauty, utterly different from the girls back home. The contrast delights me. Her eyes project an intelligent keenness, fuelled by enthusiasm, and, how to put it, she is gracious in the softest, feminine way.*

Before leaving Beirut, he sent Danni a postcard.

Dear Mademoiselle Meir,
Wonderful to have met you. Please continue your good
work. Kolo Palestine is fortunate to have such a bright
and pleasant employee. Regards to Monsieur Malouf.
Miro

Miro was seeing more than a few girlfriends living in Brno and smaller towns nearby. He took pains to ensure that they did not know about each other. Once, in an absent-minded moment, he over-extended himself and invited two of his girlfriends to the same dance gala. When both of them showed up, there followed a jealous quarrel between the two girls and Miro fled the scene out of embarrassment. From then on, he kept a more reliable diary of engagements.

Miro was back in Palestine.

'Mademoiselle, permettez-vous que je vous appelle par votre prénom?' Would Danni allow him to call her by her first name? He didn't speak English, Hebrew or Arabic and she drew a blank with Czech or German. They conversed in the diplomatic language of French. Two tongues kissing each other's ears, the French way. She didn't mind being called Daniela, but the sixteen-year age difference between them ensured that he would remain as *Monsieur Novotny.*

They were sitting at an outdoor cafe, on the palm-lined boulevard that mirrored the Mediterranean shoreline of downtown Haifa. He had invited Danni for an early-evening meal. More interested in her, than just as a Kolo employee, Miro's curiosity surfaced with the tactful questions about her life and background that filled the evening.

He spoke about the storm of uneasiness that was gathering in Europe in 1937. Germany was rearming at a hell-bent pace and her European neighbours were troubled by Germany's ambitions, spearheaded by a powerful man whose objectives were still unclear to them.

'Do you think there will be another war?' she asked.

'I don't know. It would depend on many things happening together. I am worried more about the situation here, Daniela. It does not look good.'

The British in Palestine were tightening their control amid the worsening situation between Arab and Jew. Jewish immigrants, especially from Eastern Europe, were pouring into Palestine and the resident Muslim population did not like what they saw. Hatred between the two groups was blossoming.

They switched topics and Danni told Miro about her parents and her upbringing.

'Mother is very strict and my parents are very religious. They have their own ideas about who I should marry. He must be Jewish and they must know his family.'

Miro smiled about this situation. He was gauging the robustness of this barrier. 'And are you very religious?' he probed.

She formed a polite smile. 'No, I cherish my precious freedom. But I'm so fascinated how different religions reveal differences in human culture and thinking. I want to understand why people come to believe what they do—Buddhism, Zoroastrianism, Hinduism, the Baha'is.' She felt a little self-conscious. 'But I'm boring you ...'

'No. Not at all.' His upturned palm urged her to continue.

'Do you like dancing?' she asked.

'Yes, I do.'

'And do you have a girlfriend in Czechoslovakia?'

'I have a few.'

'Then how will you choose which one to take out dancing?'

'Yes, that can be quite tricky.' His quiet smile boldened her curiosity.

'Um. I think you are a very good dancer,' she said.

'And how do you know this?' He offered a wide grin.

'I can feel it.'

A man passed by their table, playing an accordion. His hairy chest showed behind the unbuttoned, short-sleeved shirt he wore on beach walks. Behind him, a woman was selling flowers. Miro bought a single red carnation for Danni and she stood it up in her drinking glass.

'Do you play any instruments?' she continued.

'I play the mandolin. And you?'

'I play my books. And I love dancing.'

He walked Danni home, but kept a safe distance from her house. They stood beneath the old olive tree that knew of Danni's secret thinking place. His longing for her was flourishing. Modesty and polite reserve prevented any kissing.

'Do you think your parents would mind if they found out you were having dinners with a foreigner?'

It caught Danni by surprise. 'Does this mean you want to invite me again?'

Miro spent three weeks in Jaffa and Tel Aviv, studying a joint-venture proposal and connecting with old business acquaintances and store managers. When he got back to Haifa, he needed to file reports on how each Kolo store was doing and carry out a stock inventory of the store's merchandise. Sometime later, he was up on a ladder at Nassim Malouf's Kolo store, recording the count of tyres stocked on the top shelves when Danni came into the warehouse.

'Monsieur Novotny? Mr. Malouf needs to see you.'

Miro stepped down from the ladder, turned towards Danni, grasped her face in both hands and planted a kiss on her lips. Danni was thunderstruck. She had no inkling he felt this way. He left her standing there in an alien daze and went off to see what Malouf wanted.

Two weeks passed. Miro and Danni were walking along Haifa's Khayyat Beach, Palestine's scaled-down answer to the beaches of Nice on the French Riviera. Couples walked hand-in-hand and the young men came to ogle the local girls who dressed posh and wore makeup to impress them, while the older folk came to judge and question where today's youth were headed. Miro and Danni found a place to sit down.

'Mademoiselle Daniela, I want to marry you.'

'But you can't.'

'Why not?'

'Because my parents won't allow it.'

'Because I'm not Jewish, I know. So, let's elope. They

don't have to know until it's too late.'

'That would make my parents very, very angry, especially because you are a foreign gentile.'

'But a gentleman gentile, *un gentilhomme*,' Miro smiled. And Danni giggled.

Miro returned to Czechoslovakia and was back in Haifa three months later. It was March, 1938. Kolo was sending him overseas for the last time. He would be needed back in Czechoslovakia where the company was shifting gears and rethinking its priorities and strategies.

He asked her to marry him. She said she needed more time.

They continued dating, but Esther suspected that something was going on in Danni's life: she wasn't her usual self and less talkative when at home. Before long, Danni could hold it back no longer.

'Ima, I am being courted by Monsieur Novotny. I like him and he wants to marry me.'

Esther recoiled in disbelief. 'But he is a *goy*, is he not? What's his religion?'

'Ima, he's Roman Catholic.'

'You will do nothing of the sort. Do you understand?' Esther barked. 'Your father and I already have a husband for you.'

Danni's thoughts flashed to that Jewish businessman, Lev Gavish, who lived in Ramat Gan, not far from Haifa. As an acquaintance of the Meirs, he visited often and Danni disliked this obnoxious, slimy character, full of himself. He had fixed his eye on Danni and convinced Esther and Avram that he would make a good husband for her.

Miro and Danni returned from an evening walk and before she went inside, he stopped to kiss her underneath the old olive tree.

'Mademoiselle Daniela, have you been eating garlic?'

Danni went into shock. 'I'm so sorry. I really am. Please forgive me.' Raw shame smeared itself all over her, like a poisonous body lotion. She backed away and lowered her head.

'You put garlic in my food, didn't you?' she screamed at Esther. 'You know I don't want garlic in my food!'

One evening, when Danni came home a little late, Esther confronted her. 'You are not to see that *goy*, Monsieur Novotny, anymore. Do you understand me?'

'But, ima, he invited me for dinner. He is a kind man. I didn't want to—'

'You will *not* go out with him anymore. I forbid it! Outside of your working hours, you will not see him. You are my daughter and you obey my rules. Am I making myself clear?'

Esther sent word that she wanted to meet with her cousin, Isaac. When he showed up, she instructed him to visit his friend at the Notary Public. Esther issued her directive: Isaac was to get the legal official to issue a new birth certificate for Danni, putting her date of birth as one year later and making her not yet of legal age to marry. The official was to destroy any old certificates on file and adjust the records. Esther handed Isaac an envelope containing cash.

'This should be a nice incentive for our friend.' Isaac said he would do what he could.

A leisurely Friday morning saw the two of them together. Miro took Danni to the beach. He carried a picnic hamper. The chef at his hotel had prepared him lamb meatballs, falafel, hummus and *aish el saraya*—bread and cream pudding. Inside, Miro had sneaked a bottle of bubbly and two glasses. They sat on a mound of sand.

'*Chère Mademoiselle* Daniela, will you marry me?'

There was stillness. A torrent gushed from the fountains in her head. It did not announce itself, but it was the voice: the voice of the Shrine of the Báb. She knew it. A strange voice, yet unexpectedly intimate— transformed into her thoughts: *He is kind, gracious, well mannered. He can lead me to faraway lands like those cargo ships leaving Haifa. His loyalty will make him a good father—*

Her own thoughts interrupted. *He serenades his girlfriends back home on a mandolin and they go crazy for him. He's been called home and cannot return. He is offering you the world. Your parents' anger will subside. Forgiveness is the daughter of time.*

She reached over and touched his hand. 'I will marry you. I want to marry you. It will make me very happy.'

A tiny curl formed at the corners of her lips and, like a muted wave, spread into a smile. She looked down at the sand. 'Why me?'

'What?'

Her eyes lifted and roamed his face, studied his expression. 'Why did you choose me? There are a thousand girls who would say yes to you.'

'Because you are everything I want. And now that I've found you, dear Daniela, we are one.' He brought out a platinum engagement ring, set with a one-carat solitaire diamond from South Africa.

'Ohhh!' she breathed. 'It's divine perfection.' She held it up and gyrated it to point in all directions. 'It has a thousand mirrors of coloured light. It's like a million stars twinkling on a crystal-clear night.'

'Like the stars of the Andromeda Galaxy ...'

'Is this galaxy very pretty?'

'One day, I will show you. We will pick a clear night, high up in the mountains.'

'It sounds very romantic.' She couldn't hide her delight.

They kissed. She was nervous: he had stepped down

from the ladder in the warehouse.

'Moravian tradition dictates that I must not put it on your finger, you must do that yourself. It signals your acceptance. Your hand accepts my proposal.'

'Is it the same with the wedding rings?'

'No,' his face lit up. 'That's different. You'll see when the time comes.'

Danni threaded her finger through the ring and played with it with her thumb. The ring was a touch loose. She could have that fixed, later. Miro discreetly brought out the champagne and poured her a glass. 'Have you tried champagne before?'

'No, never!' She was beaming at this discovery. 'It's so fizzy. Tickles my tongue. I like it.'

They ate, and Miro became more serious. 'Mademoiselle Daniela, I need to say this. Europe is heading for big changes and they are not all good. Germany's Nazi regime is talking expansion and preparing for war. People are afraid that the face of Europe will be transformed. As you know, Germany is targeting the Jewish people in Europe.'

Danni hung her head and bit her lip. *What's coming next?*

Miro could see she had tensed up. 'My homeland is next door to Germany. My company is calling me home and my new bride will be in danger if she remains Jewish. I want you to convert to the Catholic faith.'

'But can I do that?'

'Yes, but you will need to undergo catechism, religious lessons, and then be baptized and take a Christian name.'

'Oh, my goodness.' Danni cupped her hand to her mouth. 'How do I do *all that*?'

'I have a very good friend in Beirut, a Czechoslovak. His name is Marek Svoboda, he is from my home town and he works for Kolo. He is in touch with the Convent of the Redeemer in Beirut. He will introduce us to the Mother Superior, and we'll take it from there. We will need to travel to Beirut for two or three weeks while you do your catechism studies and until your baptism and confirmation.'

'Am I allowed to talk to anyone about this?'

'No. We'll need to do all this in secrecy. We will treat the Beirut trip as travel for Kolo business.'

'And then?'

'And then we have our wedding.'

'In Beirut?'

'In Beirut, my dear. At the convent.'

'Monsieur Novot ...' She sensed the silliness of calling him that. 'Er, may I call you Miro?'

'No, you must always address me as Monsieur Novotny.' She looked puzzled and he came to the rescue. 'To you, Daniela, I will always be Miro.'

Her face brightened as though a prediction was about to fall into her lap. 'Miro, are you my dance partner in Beirut?'

'If you want me to be, I'll be your dance partner in Beirut.'

A smile came to her eyes. 'My dance teacher was right.'

'Your dance teacher?'

'He said to me, "You'll find someone."'

She was beginning to fathom the changes ahead. Things were becoming interesting, challenging. And now she was in the ballroom of love with the perfect Beirut dance partner.

Three weeks in Beirut was all the time available. Before leaving Haifa, they went to Khayyat Beach for a last swim in the sea. The afternoon was calm. The sea was peaceful. Lifeguards had planted two flags on the beach, one white, one red—a signal to bathers that the day was perfect for swimming and being massaged by the waves. Only white and white denoted a calmer sea. Two flags, both red, meant danger to those who were not strong swimmers. Two black flags planted in the sand signalled that nobody was allowed into the water at the patrolled beach.

Danni thought about the horrors of that day when she was pushed overboard into deep water by her brothers. Today was different. The sea was forgiving and inviting. It was white and red.

She ran down the sloping sand and into the surf, rolling with the gentle waves and paddling in the shallow water. Danni sprang upright. The ring was gone. It had slipped off the finger. In a frenzy, she groped with her hands, then feet, combing and raking the sandy bottom.

She ran out of the water and up to him. 'The ring! Miro, my ring is gone!'

Together, they searched for the sesame seed in a sand dune, the paper clip at the bottom of the bottomless ocean. The engagement ring had sunk into hiding, like a speck of dust inside a subterranean South African diamond mine.

Danni's voice quivered. 'It's a bad omen!'

Miro held her face in both hands, gave her a peck on the lips. 'There is no bad omen. We will be happy together. We will share a good life.'

'No, it is an omen. I know it.'

He took her to his hotel and they made love. Afterwards, she sat on the edge of the bed thinking about the ring. *It graced my hand so briefly and now it's gone—forever.*

'Look, I've got something even better,' he said.

He took out a small box with two gold bands in it. Danni removed them and placed both rings in her palm, then closed the hand and pressed it against her bosom. Tears welled up and a drop took shape until it could no longer hold itself from cascading over the edge and rolling down one cheek. Miro averted his gaze, effacing himself from her private moment.

Life would be very, very different for the nineteen-year-old girl with the long, black hair and the resolute chin.

Chapter 4

Danni said goodbye to her mother.

'Ima, I need to work in Beirut for a few weeks. The company is training me there to be a store manager. My future looks very bright. You will be proud of me.'

'And what about that *goy* Monsieur Novotny?'

'He's going home to Czechoslovakia.'

'He's leaving here and going back?'

'Yes, ima.'

'Well, well. That's a new chapter in your life.'

Danni threw in another decoy. 'Ima, I will try to visit Auntie Rosa, if I find time.' Auntie Rosa, Esther's sister, owned a small chicken farm in the mountains outside Beirut.

Nassim Malouf took Danni to the bus station for her ride to Beirut. Miro was waiting for her in Lebanon. Next day, they were picked up by Marek Svoboda. He knew Lebanon well and was based in Beirut to find market opportunities and engage new Kolo dealers. Marek and Miro were old friends from college days, dating girls and taking them out to dances. Marek was a little younger and saw Miro as a world-wise role model. They had similar tastes and interests—shared a common flair for languages and an enviable cultural adeptness.

Danni was taken aback by the parallel. He, too, was tall and handsome and had a lively manner that exuded confidence. Her mind travelled back to her first emotive encounter of Miro. She quickly absorbed Marek's demeanour. *Another Moravian edition of the consummate ladies' man.*

He spoke in fluent English. 'Daniela, we are going to meet Mother Angelica. She knows that you wish to convert, but that's all she knows.'

They arrived at the Convent of the Redeemer. Danni had never been inside a convent and the prospect of learning the Catholic faith and espousing it felt like an adventure into the unknown. Marek left them there and would return for Miro when the arrangements had been made.

'Daniela, my child, why do you wish to become a Roman Catholic?' That was Mother Angelica.

Danni turned to Miro. 'Am I allowed to tell?'

Miro nodded.

'Because, Mother Superior, I will be travelling to live in Czechoslovakia, and they don't like Jews in that part of Europe.'

'Is that all, my child?'

That wit, sharpened by the open-air bazaar in Haifa, jumped to the fore. 'But, more than anything, I want to become a Christian and my future husband is Catholic. It will be good for our children.'

'Very well, Daniela, I shall assign Sister Scholastica to you and she will be in charge of your catechism. You will be required to attend prayers three times a day. Are you prepared to do that?'

Danni smiled and gave animated nods. Mother Angelica took her on a brief tour of the convent. Later, M. Angelica took Miro aside. 'Your fiancée is a lovely girl and she seems so keen. You are a fortunate man, Monsieur Novotny. May your future be blessed with many children who grow up to be wise.'

It took two-and-a-half weeks. Her favourite part of the day was going into chapel with the sisters and singing the prayers of the mass—the *Agnus Dei*, the *Sanctus*, the *Kyrie Eleison*, and *Gloria in excelsis Deo*. Some of the sisters had magnificent voices. She immersed herself in the Gregorian-based intonations and the Latin words came home, as though they resided in one of her many tongues. With all the music, this religion was fun for her, even without the dancing that the whirling dervishes had, in their Sufi recognition of God.

'Monsieur Novotny, would you like to choose a godfather and godmother for the baptism of Simone Thérèse?' That was Sister Scholastica meeting Miro, at the end of Danni's residency.

'Simone Thérèse? I don't follow. Do I know this person?'

'Your fiancée has chosen those names.'

Danni was asked what name she wanted, under her new Catholic identity. She chose Simone, her beloved librarian at the French school in Haifa. When Sister Scholastica asked her to choose a middle name, Danni hesitated. A book of female Christian names was brought out, the page chosen at random and Danni was told to close her eyes and point somewhere on the open pages.

'The Lord will guide you, my child,' said Sister Scholastica. 'Now, open your eyes.'

Her finger was on *Thérèse*.

After Danni's baptism and Confirmation, came her First Communion. Then, they set the date for a very private wedding at the convent.

The July morning dawned clear and crisp in the early hours. There was a tender sea breeze that scented the air with iodine. Beirut was at its best. The azure Mediterranean glistened whenever a wave formed and spilled onto the sandy shore. It was ten o'clock. Marek Svoboda was there, as best man and witness. So were Sister Scholastica and Mother Angelica and two other nuns. Danni wore a plain, white silk dress and a lace head covering. Miro was in a dark suit with jacket lapels of black silk and a red carnation in one of them. Father Joseph Lapierre performed the ceremony and the rings were exchanged.

That evening, Miro, Simone and Marek celebrated at Beirut's acclaimed Restaurant Le Paris. The band that played was an East-meets-West combination of Maronite Christian and French musicians, and the polished wooden dance floor was peopled with shoes worn by European expatriates and the Lebanese upper crust. She smiled at everyone around her. They smiled back, including the waiter who served their table. She felt liberated and imagined herself as the galactic centre around which the lesser stars circled and danced.

Marek and Miro took turns partnering her in foxtrots, tangos and waltzes. They danced the night thin, sipping champagne in between countless, 'May I have this dance, m'lady?' overtures to the irrepressible bride.

Occasionally, Miro and Marek would take a break to chat together in Czech. Simone grabbed this chance to study them and compare the two. Tapping a finger repeatedly against the champagne glass she was holding, she easily could imagine either of them as her groom. *What if fate had switched them and Marek was the one who had dated me in Haifa?*

Marek turned to Simone. 'How do you like this atmosphere? Is this how you imagined your wedding night would be?'

'Shouldn't we have invited Mother Angelica and Sister Scholastica to celebrate with us?' she giggled.

'Daniela, nuns don't dance. They pray.'

'Simone, remember?'

'Yes, of course. Simone. Forgive me.'

'But they do sing, too, you know,' she reminded.

Just three days left before they had to sail. Miro visited the Czechoslovak embassy in Beirut and submitted an application for Danni's passport. The consular official checked over the details.

'Do you have proof of your wife's date of birth?' Miro showed him a copy of the Kolo employee records and the identification booklet she carried. Both gave her birthdate.

'Mister Novotny, your wife's passport will be ready tomorrow. Thank you, sir.' He stood up and gave a small bow as Miro left his office.

Danni held the brand-new passport in her hand, its navy cover embossed with the national coat of arms—gold lion rampant with two crossed tails. It was her very first passport. Inside, in bold lettering, was her new name: *Simone Thérèse* NOVOTNY and the document proclaimed, *Valid for all countries of the world, tous les pays du monde.* Her imagination began to roam and her eyes seemed to follow. She was on a rocket to the moon.

'I can travel anywhere with this!' and shot her arms high in the air in a gesture of victory.

Miro snatched the passport out of her hand and held it behind his back.

'A passport for your thoughts,' he taunted.

She turned her resolute chin upwards in a gesture of dare-me, then ran in circles around him to catch him off-guard and snatch back the passport.

'Come on then. Tell. Where will you travel?'

'Spitsbergen!' she yelled.

The next afternoon, Marek Svoboda brought them alongside their ship docked in Beirut Harbour. It would take them to Dubrovnik, in Yugoslavia, after stopping at the Egyptian port of Alexandria for a day, to board more passengers.

She received a tender hug from Marek.

'I'll have to get used to your new name. Simone Thérèse, so m-u-u-u-sical.' He continued as though reciting his lines in a play. 'It has a lovely r-r-r-ring to it. And a ring to go with it. How fortunate, that thou shouldst find thee a paramour, so grand and gallant, and single no more!'

Simone was giggling at this articulated display.

'I shall miss both of you,' he said.

'Marek, will I see you again, soon?' she insisted.

'I'll send you a postcard from Beirut.'

'Promise?'

'If I break my promise, you are allowed to shoot me in the right leg.'

'Your right leg. Why your right leg?'

'Because I am a footballer, and I can score only with my right leg. My left one is useless.' One more hug for Simone.

'Postcard promise?' she pressed.

He turned to Miro. 'Be well my dear friend.' They hugged like old school chums. 'You're a very lucky man.'

A short climb up the gangway, a dozen parting waves. Then the ship slipped its moorings and set off for Alexandria.

Danni had her ship at last, and it was taking her far away to a world unseen, a life unknown. She stood at the railing on the top deck to get a good view. As the ship left port and gave the traditional blast of the horn, she thought of Mount Carmel.

You granted me my dreams, Shrine on Carmel. She took in the iodised breeze and felt her past as Daniela slipping away. She looked once more at the receding wharf and saw Marek in the distance, still waving. She didn't wave back. It felt too much like a farewell forever.

After dinner, they went up to the ship's radio room and sent a telegram to Haifa.

AM MARRIED STOP TRAVELLING WITH HUSBAND TO CZECHOSLOVAKIA STOP LOVE FROM YOUR DAUGHTER STOP SIMONE NOVOTNY.

The cable was delivered to Avram Meir's tailor shop. He couldn't decipher the message worded in French, so he closed shop and hurried home to show it to Esther.

'Who is Simone Novotny? Is this for us?' He handed the cable to Esther.

She read it and let out a scream. She flapped the paper in the air, gripping it as if pulling someone's hair.

Grawlixes emanated from her mouth. 'Your daughter has gone and married a *goy*! *That* foreign goy!' she shrieked. 'She's taken his name and she's even changed her first name.'

Papa came to the rescue. 'But why is this so bad? She is a songbird. She has flown from the cage and up to the sky. At night, she sails free among the stars like a brilliant comet. Don't you want her to be happy?'

'You and your useless stories. Does it make you happy to lose her?' Her Daniela, sold to a young virgin in order to keep her alive, had sailed around her controlling fingers and vanished into destiny.

Chapter 5

Alexandria sank below the horizon. Now a dizzying constellation of settings and encounters awaited. The Shrine was silent. She heard no mind whispers. Simone and Miro disembarked in Dubrovnik and took the bus to Sarajevo. He took a week off work for their honeymoon. To Simone, Sarajevo was surprisingly reminiscent of Palestine. The Islamic influence was strong here, a holdover from the Ottoman Empire. The city's soul resonated with mosques, chanting muezzin, open-air markets and people speaking many languages.

Miro began speaking to her in Czech. Easy sentences, key words, important stuff. He knew that a few Czech words a day were not wasted on Simone: counting to ten on her fingers, salt-pepper, beautiful-ugly, hot-cold, up-down, chocolate ice cream. The word *kniha*, book. That one stuck. So did the Czech words for, 'Come here, give me a kiss.'

Leaving Sarajevo, they headed north by train, stopping

in Budapest and Bratislava, before the train rolled into Brno Central station. Miro had cabled his half-brother, Lubor, to meet them at the station.

Miro helped her down to the platform.

'Stay here with the bags,' he grinned. 'I'm going to surprise him.'

He found Lubor, and the two embraced.

'And where is the young bride?'

Miro turned around and gestured towards Simone. There, standing on the platform, with her head cocked to one side in a comical pose, she beamed back a radiating smile. They hurried towards her.

'*Pěkně vítám, Simonko!*' My warmest welcome, Simonko! Lubor gushed like a gleeful Viennese fountain.

He was delighted that his oldest brother, elder statesman of the Novotny family, had gone and found himself this exotic bride. He stretched out his massive welcoming arms and enveloped her in a farmer's embrace, then released her from countrified compression with a kiss on each cheek. He spoke nothing but Czech, a sign of things to come. But the gods gave her a head for languages. She would soon learn, and get accustomed to the diminutive of her name, '*Simonko.*'

Lubor took them to his apartment. They stayed the night. Miro moved out of his own bachelor flat and into larger company-owned lodgings. He caught up on developments at the head office in Brno. Simone was taken on a tour of the Kolo plant and discovered how the company treated its employees. The company village housed workers, rent-free. There was a company cinema and restaurant, a sportsground and library, and even a theatre where employees could put on their own shows. They had an airfield and a corporate twin-propeller aircraft, so that staff and executives could be flown to key locations.

Miro was assigned as store controller for southern Moravia, which bordered on Austria. He would be gone for a fortnight at a time.

Simone missed him but she never was lonely.

Her in-laws absorbed her as one of their own, and she was bombarded with questions about life in her native land. She became close to Milena, Miro's youngest half-sister, same age as Simone and not yet married. They were like cousins, eggs laid by different hens on the same free range.

Mastering Czech was far easier and more enjoyable than Monsieur Lazare's lessons in algebra: the mother of my mother is my *babička*. The brother of my father is my *strýc*. The son of my father is my *bratr*. And the enemy of my enemy is my *kamarád*. All very positive, no negatives to manipulate.

The months that went by were steeped in discoveries. Milena was visiting Simone and they were talking about Slavkov, where Miro and their father, Stanislav, were born.

'Do you know why Slavkov is special?' Milena asked.

Simone hesitated and Milena got the message. Rising from her chair like an ardent tour guide, Milena slapped her thighs in a decisive signal.

'Come, Simonko. Let me take you there and show you.'

They got to Slavkov Castle and Milena pointed to the hill across the valley from where they stood.

'From that hill there, Napoleon commanded the French forces at the Battle of Austerlitz and defeated Russian Tsar Alexander the First, and—'

'Oh yes, yes! Wait. Austrian Emperor, Francis the Second.'

'So, you *know* the history.' This delighted her. 'Slavkov is the Czech name for Austerlitz.'

Simone paused to let it sink in. 'The Battle of the Three Emperors. 1805. I can't believe I'm standing here. Miro, Slavkov, Napoleon. There is a plan in heaven, *isn't there?*'

They went inside the castle where the two vanquished emperors had signed the surrender papers and where Napoleon slept before and after the battle. Waiting for them was Milena's old friend, Dagmar Martinková, the castle's museum director.

'Come, Simonko, we have something to show you,' said Milena.

Dagmar walked them to a hall not open to the public. As the huge, hand-carved oak doors to the chamber were unlocked and swung open, Simone spotted an oil painting on the middle wall—a portrait of a gentleman with hair in white curls, sporting a handsome moustache and wearing a scarlet tunic with gold-fringed epaulettes and buttons.

Simone gasped. Memories tumbled out of the dream. *The King of Persia. He looks so much like him! That kind nose and the blue eyes. He's wearing Papa's magnificent suit, like in my dream!*

'That,' said Milena, pointing to the portrait, 'is Miro's great-great-great-grandfather, *Reichsritter*, Imperial Knight, Raimund von Mannberg.'

Simone's eyes darted back and forth between the two women. Dagmar smiled and nodded in agreement.

'And who do you imagine was a frequent guest at his home in Vienna?' added Milena.

Simone gave her a tell-me look.

'Wolfgang Amadeus Mozart. Raimund loved science and classical music, and Mozart would come to play for him at his Vienna residence. Would you like to see the von Mannberg residence?'

'What? In Vienna?'

'No. Not far from here.'

Dagmar drove them to the tiny village of Bohdalice. They stopped by a small church founded by Raimund. A granite slab engraved with the names of Raimund's descendants hung from a wall at the back of the church. Raimund headed the list. Born 1723, died 1788. They scanned down the list, giving dates of birth and death, and came to Miro's great-grandmother, Countess Therese von Eisenstein, mother of *Reichsritter* Ernst von Mannberg, Miro's granddad.

'Look, Simone.' Milena pointed. 'She had your middle name. As a bachelor, her son Ernst was in no hurry to get married. Seems he was quite a womaniser.'

They both glanced at Dagmar. She nodded. She knew the von Mannberg history.

Milena went on. 'Slept with his chambermaid, Antonia Novotny, and fathered Miro's dad, our dad, Stanislav. It was said that Antonia was the most beautiful of the women employed at the von Mannberg estate manor. In the end, Ernst married the Duchess Magdalene von Langen, a descendant of one of Queen Victoria's siblings.'

'You mean Queen Victoria, the *British* Queen Victoria?'

'Um hm. They had three sons. The eldest one committed suicide. See, here, his dates?'

Simone released a short, sharp gasp. 'Why did he commit suicide?'

Dagmar jumped in. 'He was a lieutenant in the Imperial Reich's Dragoon Regiment. He wanted his father to buy him an automobile as a status symbol. But Ernst said no to that. One November evening, in 1912, he took his pistol and shot himself in his bedroom. The very next day, the car was delivered to their castle. It was supposed to be a Christmas surprise.'

'How awful.' The date flashed in Simone's head. 'Did you say, *1912*?'

'Yes, 1912.'

'That's the year the Titanic went down! And that's the year Scott and his men reached the South Pole and perished on their return journey. What a horrible year!'

Milena squeezed Simone around the waist. 'You know your history, don't you? They're all buried here, in the family vault. Would you like to take a short walk and see the mansion? Ernst's widow, the Duchess, still lives there. We'll go by and pretend we're not snooping.'

'*Ano, prosím.*'—Yes, please. 'Take me there.'

They passed by the mansion that had witnessed happier days. It was in need of repairs, but it was obvious that, once upon a time, it was a majestic place in which the nobility lived, and played, and entertained guests. The gardener saw them and waved from a distance. They waved back.

'Simonko, one more guess, before we head back to Slavkov. Who overnighted here in the mansion, way back in 1805?'

'I give up. Tell me.'

'Russian Tsar Alexander I. He was a guest of the von Mannberg family, the day before he went to fight the battle with Napoleon.'

'*Pravda?*' True?

'*Ano, bylo to tak.*' Yes, that's how it was. Milena waited for that look of impossible delight to surface in Simone's face. Now, it glowed from her school-girlish eyes.

When Miro came home, at last, and they lay in bed, Simone tapped her finger against the side of his kind nose, as if to admonish him for keeping things from her.

'Hey, mister knight, why didn't you tell me you have blue blood?'

'You've been talking to Milena, I see.'

'Yes, I have and I've discovered things about you.'

'Ummm, only half-blue. Grandma Antonia was just a commoner. Grandfather Ernst gave her a tract of land as compensation for making her pregnant—and leaving his employ to raise my father as a single mother. That's the land my brothers are now farming.'

'And she never married?'

'She never married.'

'But she was so beautiful.' Simone's upturned hand questioned fate's unfairness. 'You know something? There's a lot hiding inside you that I haven't discovered. You keep surprising me. I want to know *more* about you.'

As she lay there on her arched back, she began kicking the air with both feet high above her head. 'Moravian knight on a horse dashes into Palestine, rescues a distressed damsel from her nasty mother, and gallops away with her to Beirut.'

'You make it sound like you're Cinderella. In Czech, we call her *Popelka*.'

'*Popelka*?' Simone showered herself in mirth. 'Why *Popelka*?'

'Because *popel* means cinders, or ashes.'

'*Popelka*! I love it, I love it, I love it!'

'What is it you love so much, so much, so much?'

'I love the way our story is unfolding. Miro! Make love to *Popelka*, right now, while I'm still in heat. *Popelka* wants to give you a blue-blooded boy. Now, now, now!' she squealed. And with each *now*, her voice pitch went higher.

Miro turned to face her. 'Well, have you ever heard me say, "Not tonight, Josephine?"'

She softened her voice to a whisper. 'But I'd like it if you said, "Yes tonight, *Popelka*."'

Milena and Simone were chatting at the café *Veselá Vdova*, The Merry Widow. They were in the heart of Brno, Moravia's capital and a hotbed of Modernist architecture and art.

'Milenko dear, why does Miro not say much about his father or mother? He seems so secretive about his parents and his past.'

'I know what you mean. He's probably ashamed that

Stanislav was born out of wedlock. Lubor and I don't care about this. We are simple folk and we know that life on the land can get terribly boring. You desire someone, you sleep with this person. Sex and desire go together like bacon and eggs. You inject some excitement into your humdrum, country life.' She made a dismissive gesture with her hand. 'It's all a hush, hush façade, but a lot of this goes on. The who's who of extramarital affairs has a lid on the pot.

'We, country folk, milk the cows, feed the pigs, harvest the potatoes, marinate the beetroot, distil fermented plums, and stink of garlic. I never liked the farming life. Lubor and I are city people. Look at my hands. Are these the fingers of a farm girl?'

Simone grinned and clutched Milena's hand. 'You're just like me. City girl.'

Milena floated a touch of urbanised satisfaction. 'But Miro is different. He's more proper about such things. He's very principled. High standards of self-discipline. I think it bothers him that Stanislav was a bastard. Even though, let's appreciate, he was blue-blooded.'

'Tell me more about Stanislav.'

'When he was at school, the students would tease him: "Where's your dad? Come on. Tell us." His mother, Antonia, would say, "Don't mind them. Ignore them. You've got strengths they don't have. You're a gentleman. Polite, well behaved. And you're very precious to me."'

'Did Miro grow up carrying this stigma?'

'He kept this family secret to himself. He is a self-made man. Very strong, very determined. For him, the world here was far too small. He went on to higher studies and his destiny was to leave his native land and travel the world. Germany, Austria, the travels for Kolo.'

'And Stanislav?'

'He married Francesca, who was quite well educated. Her family was from Brno. Miro was Francesca's only child. When she was twenty-four, Stanislav took her dancing at a village winter festival and, returning home in an open carriage, she caught a chest cold and developed pneumonia. She never recovered. Miro was just a year old when he lost his mother.'

'Gosh. I didn't know.'

'Miro is the gentleman tiger in our clan. He has his father's bravery and his mother's brains. And he is such a charmer. He had lots of girlfriends here swooning over him.' She caught herself. This was spilling beans in front of a new bride. 'Let's order some *Apfelstrudel*, shall we?'

'Yeah! Topped with yummy whipped cream. But I'm paying,' Simone smiled. 'And Stanislav remarried, yes?'

'Yes. And had five more children. Miro's stepmother, Marie, raised him as if he were her own and he returned that love in every way he could. Three of us became farmers and not one of us has ever left Czechoslovakia.'

'And what did Stanislav do for a living?'

'He was a travelling salesman. Worked for a company in Vienna making soap and cosmetics. During World War

I, he joined the Czechoslovak Legion. It was a volunteer armed forces fighting alongside the Russian army to win the support of Russia for an independent homeland for Czechs and Slovaks.'

'Ah, yes.' Simone raised her index finger. 'France, Russia and Britain joining together to defeat the German Empire and Austria-Hungary.'

'He was part of the Czechoslovak Rifle Brigade when they attacked the Austria-Hungary trenches near Zborov on the Eastern Front. His small group of legionnaires was equipped with grenades and broke through the enemy trench line. During the battle, the Legion captured *lots* of enemy soldiers.' Milena collected her thoughts. 'Stanislav was unlucky. During the Battle of Zborov, he took an enemy rifleman's bullet in his neck and fell.'

'And he died?'

'No, it wasn't a fatal wound, but the surgeons in a military hospital did not want to remove the bullet because they feared the surgical procedure might paralyze him for life. So, it stayed embedded in his neck. But the metal jacket was made of lead and slowly poisoned him.'

'And then he died?'

'Oh, no.' Milena smiled. Put her hand on Simone's shoulder and gave it a squeeze. 'He lived many years after the war ended. He set up a small button-making business in Slavkov.' Simone burst into laughter. Milena nodded. 'Yes, it's true. With cutting and drilling machines he purchased in Vienna, he would carve perfectly round disks from mother-of-pearl, then drilled either two or four holes where the button could be stitched to clothing. He would go out and peddle his buttons to shirt makers and dressmakers who wanted to achieve a bit of class by capturing the iridescence of mother-of-pearl buttons. It helped him make a modest living as an invalid.'

'And he survived to see the creation of Czechoslovakia!'

'Um *hm*. That was his dream. That's what he fought for.'

'The button maker from Slavkov. How charming.' Simone touched Milena's arm and played with the thought: 'I wonder if my Papa would tailor a suit with his mother-of-pearl buttons.'

'It would look classy.' They invested the idea with sister-like chuckles.'

February, 1939. Miro is called to an important meeting at Head Office. The chief executive of the Kolo Company assembles all senior and middle managers to make a major announcement. Store controllers are included in the gathering.

'All of you are aware of the political developments shaping up in Europe. These will affect the way we do business. You also know that we've begun production in the two new tyre factories in Africa. We are now nearing completion of our third factory, in Nairobi,

Kenya, to make motor car tyres. My policy always is to place employee welfare and safety above everything else. Many of you will be sent to staff and support these new operations. We have Jewish families working for us. They are in danger if Nazi Germany decides to invade and annex the Czech lands.

'One of my priorities is sending these employees to our locations in Africa, out of harm's way, as early as possible. Your supervisors will be informing you who has been chosen to go and where they will be posted. I advise those of you affected to discuss this matter with your spouses and families and to prepare them for such a move.'

Three days later, Miro came home with the news.

'Simone, get ready to pack. We are moving to Kenya.'

'You're just teasing me, aren't you?'

He locked her in his arms and touched his nose to her forehead. She liked it when he did that. It was comforting. 'No, I'm not.'

'Oh, my gosh. More change.' She pulled back from his arms and sucked a sharp breath. 'When?'

'April.'

'April? But ...'

'Now, I have another surprise. Turn around. Close your eyes. Do you trust me?'

'I've always trusted you.'

'Good. Give me your hand. Now open those lovely eyes.' She looked down at the postcard in her hand.

'What's this? From whom? It's from Beirut! It's from Marek!'

My Dearest Simonko,
I have kept my promise. Now my right leg is bulletproof.
I'm sure you recognise this place in the picture. In the
right corner, is the restaurant Le Paris. I send you kisses
and best wishes from a place that will prepare and serve
you many delicious memories. Give an extra hug to
my dear friend, Miro. We will stay in touch.
Much love from Beirut,
Marek

Miro had business to finish off in South Moravia. He would be gone for two weeks and return to prepare for the journey to Africa.

March, 1939. With Bohemia and Moravia putting up no resistance, Hitler's troops push across the German border and spill into Czechoslovakia. First Pilsen, then Prague, and then they press on towards Brno. Nazi Germany annexes the Czech lands and creates the Protectorate of Bohemia and Moravia.

Like the black spider's legs on the Nazi flag, further news spreads outwards in all directions: scouting ahead, German soldiers reaching central Brno fan out across the city in search of houses with vacant rooms. They hunt for temporary lodgings for the bullying troops, until permanent accommodations are built.

Milena took Simone to her lodgings. It was safer than leaving Simone alone in her house.

'When darkness comes, we turn off all the lights, lock the doors and stay quiet. Yes?'

Simone understood.

Two days later, when night came, they shuttered the windows, and darkened the house. They heard the sound of approaching boots and huddled in the kitchen. Three loud bangs on the door, in rapid succession.

'*Auf machen!!*' Open up!

Index finger at her lips, Milena glanced at Simone. Simone nodded.

Three more loud bangs: '*Auf machen!!*'

Simone's heart was thumping. They could hear the voices of several soldiers.

'*Niemand da.*' Nobody there.

'*Versuche noch mal.*' Try again.

Four bangs, this time, slower and more forceful.

'*Ja, komm, wir gehen weiter.*' Come on, let's keep going. And then they moved on.

Simone felt a new kind of fear. This wasn't being thrown into the sea and gulping water. It was the dread of being hunted, then discovered, in a dark hiding place and whisked away. They spent an uneasy night, cuddled together in Milena's bed, like mother and frightened child.

Miro came home with the papers needed to leave Czechoslovakia and board a cargo ship in the Italian port of Trieste. Its final destination: Mombasa, Kenya. There were tearful farewells in Slavkov and *au revoirs* in Brno. Milena and Lubor came to see them off at the Brno train station.

'Come join us in Kenya.' Simone cupped Milena's face in her hands. 'You and I have become devoted sisters.'

'I can't, sweetheart, this is my home.' Milena burst into tears. They stood on the platform hugging for a long time.

The train trembled a little and began to creep along the platform. Through the open window of their compartment, Miro and Simone waved. In his arms, Lubor held a distraught sister who couldn't look up and wave back.

Change has an ironic way of making things permanent. Miro and Simone would not see them again for an unknowable time. It was Allah's will and one could hear the words uttered: *It is written.*

Chapter 6

The train took them south to Trieste on the Adriatic Sea. While passengers boarded the half-cargo, half-passenger Italian ship, m.v. Madonna, dock workers were loading the 7,000-ton vessel with weapons and ammunition, hidden inside barrels. These were destined for Italian-occupied Abyssinia, in preparation for war on the African continent.

Leaving Trieste, they sailed south, on their way to the first ports of call in Sicily. Approaching the southern end of the Adriatic, Simone was out on the deck of her cargo ship, testing the sea air. Miro joined her a while later.

'Miro, I don't like this Adriatic Sea.'

'You're not feeling seasick, are you?'

'No, no. There's something about this Adriatic. Something evil.' She grasped the railing and clutched his hand. The skin on her knuckles stretched taught. 'Something will happen to our family here. Something terrible.'

The Shrine was in her thoughts.

'I don't understand. *What* will happen?'

She saw small islands going by. They were treeless and rocky and looked parched by the Balkan sun. 'There! On an island like those ones. That's where it will happen.'

'How do you know this? You're not telling me!'

'I know it, I know it.' She caved in and held on to him. 'I don't know what, but it will. It will!'

Miro looked and saw foreboding in her face. She went silent. A puzzling expression had eclipsed her usual composure. *To hell with these bad omens and premonitions!*

He took her inside. He summoned the steward. 'Champagne, please. Two glasses.'

Approaching Messina, Simone was not feeling well. She was overcome with an unfamiliar sensation. Nausea in the morning and loss of appetite. The doctor examined her and asked a few questions.

'Mrs. Novotny, I believe you are pregnant. Is this your first child?'

Simone nodded. She did not know whether to cheer or cry. Ahead of them was a long voyage and she was becoming seasick. She kept the news from Miro so she could surprise him when the time was right.

They crossed the Mediterranean to Egypt's Port Said, at the entrance to the Suez Canal, and anchored. It was getting hot.

'Port Said pilot, Port Said pilot, Port Said pilot. This is m.v. Madonna. Come in, Port Said pilot ... Over ...'

That was the radio officer, calling the canal's pilot to come on board and guide them into the north end of the canal. The radio crackled with static, and the call was repeated many times. A reply came at last, in a British-sounding voice.

'Madonna, Madonna, Madonna. We have the pilot coming on board at fourteen hundred hours. Have the ladder ready on starboard. Over!'

'Roger, Port Said pilot. Confirm pilot on Madonna at fourteen hundred, ready on starboard. Standing by. Over and out.'

They began the first leg of the Suez Canal passage. The sun was nearing the horizon and the water was like oil in a millpond. Simone felt better. Her cargo ship was no longer pitching and rolling. She came out on deck and saw, for the first time, the sands of Egypt that Napoleon had conquered and occupied. Her mind wandered. *This is where Lawrence of Arabia stood, after he had taken Aqaba and silenced the guns of the Ottoman Turks.*

Her spirits soared until the thrill was unbearable. Splendour in the dunes, victory in the sands. She floated with the ghosts of the past. They could never arise like *this* from yellowing pages in history books, stinking with the inherited odour of mildew and dust.

Miro put his book aside and went up to join her on deck as the sun began to set. The desert sand on both sides of the canal was glowing reddish-pink.

'Miro, look, your past and my past!'

He gave her a big squeeze.

'Ouch! Not so tight, you'll get my baby upset.'

'Really? Fragile cargo, handle with care.' He felt liberated by this fulfilment.

She kissed him first. 'See? I had secrets, too.'

Miro used voyage time to catch up on the Greek myths, Alexander's conquests, and the Roman Empire. He had a fondness for antiquity and things Latin. It came from school and the liturgy of the Catholic mass.

May 1. The chef prepares a special dish for May Day. They are now in the Red Sea and the passage becomes rougher. Simone is seasick again. No gyro stabilizers to settle matters in the stomach.

She made a noble effort to attend the captain's dinner, featuring *canard a l'orange* and champagne. Halfway through the meal, squeans were dancing over her head. She bolted outside onto the adjoining deck, leaving a cloud of briffits. Leaned over the railing. Fed the fish of the Red Sea.

The ship continued south, unloaded its cargo of

weapons in Massawa and Assab, strategic Red Sea ports in Italian Eritrea. Then, rounding the Horn of Africa, they sailed into the Indian Ocean towards Mogadishu in Italian Somalia, stopping there to unload more cargo.

As they neared Mombasa, Simone and her unborn baby made their first equator transit. The crew put on a silly shipboard ceremony for her crossing of the line. Out on the main deck, they made Simone sit on a stool, fully clothed and holding Neptune's trident fashioned from plywood. Then they emptied a bucket full of water over her head. The captain stood facing her and made some Neptunian incantations in Italian. In one hand, he was holding a pineapple, in the other, a large breadfruit.

'Signora Novotny, do you weesh a boy *bambino* or girl *bambina*?' he asked.

'I want a boy,' she spluttered and wiped her eyes.

'*Bene*; pineapple eez for boy.'

A crew member handed the captain a large kitchen knife. He cut the pineapple in half. He carved out the inside to make a little cap and plunked it on Simone's head, with the green stalk sticking up as if growing out of her head. The deck full of onlookers cheered.

The voyage spilled into early-June and they arrived in Mombasa, Kenya's lifeline seaport on the Indian Ocean. Simone had offered eighteen body-pounds of Italian cooking to the denizens of the sea. Next day, she and Miro took the fourteen-hour train journey to Nairobi. Leaving lush, tropical Mombasa, the steam locomotive puffed through the night, pulling its cars upward until it reached the plateau, 5,500 feet above sea level. They were in the heart of Kenya. With the lower air pressure, champagne corks would pop much higher into the sky. At sunrise, the hissing and panting train slowed and braked to a grinding, squeaking stop at Nairobi Central Station.

As wispy steam escaped between the gargantuan black wheels of the locomotive and filled the air with a heady railway smell, a racket of opening carriage doors spread along the platform. Porters ran back and forth, canvassing the passengers stepping down from the carriages and soliciting in their Indian or Swahili accents.

'Your baggage, *sahib*? I carry your baggage, *Memsahib*! Yes, *Memsahib*?'

Simone stood on the station platform of her new home in East Africa and smiled at them. They took it as a 'yes' and scurried off with her suitcases. Simone began running after them, yelling, 'Wait, stop!'

Miro knew. 'They're not going far. Off to the entrance, to hail a taxi for us. We're on British soil. The Brits keep things orderly.'

Nestled at one-degree South, the capital displayed

the British hand: clean, tidy, well-managed. Gardens manicured by native hands, a comfortable size of 60,000 denizens. The police wore white uniforms and tall pith helmets, and sported white truncheons which they would use to regulate traffic at intersections. Simone was in a Crown Colony of the British Empire and George VI was king of the realm. His decapitated and bodiless head, neatly combed and clean shaven, graced postage stamps, East African shilling coins, and permits issued by Government House.

It didn't take long for Simone to feel safe. Not a Nazi uniform in sight. And Nairobi was far from big water.

September 1939. Kenya is now officially at war with Germany. Without warning, the British authorities swoop down and arrest Miro and confine him to a downtown Nairobi church. His arrival from a country occupied by the Third Reich transforms Miro into a Sauerkraut-eating espionage suspect. Simone needs a police permit to visit him, but the guard never takes his eyes off the couple. Two weeks pass. Miro is tired of mushy, white-bread sandwiches smeared with that ghastly British spread they call Marmite, invented by an evil German scientist.

The British mandarins discover that Czechoslovak combat pilots have joined RAF bases in England and are training to defend the shores of Britain from a possible German invasion. The bureaucratic stiff upper lips give Miro the benefit of the doubt. How could he be an enemy of Kenya when his countrymen are in the cockpits of Hawker Hurricanes, radioing their squadron members in thick Czech accents? The British penny drops inside the British head.

Miro is cleared and made a private in the Kenya Defence Force—Nairobi Battalion, a volunteer force of white settlers based in Kenya. The dashing young man from Slavkov looked quite impressive in his outfit of rifle, khaki uniform, shiny brown boots, and Boer War-type bush hat with upturned brim.

As the war spread beyond Europe, Kolo closed its operations in Lebanon. Earlier, Marek Svoboda had resigned, left Beirut and disappeared.

Spring's approach brought a perplexing Christmas to Simone. Catholic Moravia, with its dark, wintry days, firewood burning in the hearths and fir trees blanketed in white, was a world away. Here, the flame trees of Africa were in splendid bloom, their red-and-yellow blossoms in flamboyant contrast against the canvas of a brilliant, deep-blue sky. Everything around her was tropical green. She could smell the fragrance of the papaya tree blossoms. And the clustered white and yellow petals of the frangipani flowers captured the air and saturated it with a therapeutic scent. The jacaranda tree in her garden had exploded into an impossibly purple foliage. At the back of their Riverside Drive home, the aromatic Spanish Flag lantanas were splashed with yellow, orange and red flower clusters. There were no long winter nights or summer days that ended at ten. Like planetary clockwork, the sun made the day a six-to-six affair, all year long. *I'm in such a strange land!*

There was no Christmas card from Marek. No news of him at all. *That war, over there, has commandeered him! There won't be any more kisses by postcard.*

She sat on the veranda of their farmhouse and cradled Theo in her arms. He was there to lower the curtain on the golden years of the Thirties. Simone's own golden years as a girl were fading into memories and her twenties beckoned, as though they must go on till the end of time. Now, there was an extra beating heart to look after. Simone had flown from *Mademoiselle songbird* to *Madame la mère*.

Chapter 7

Life in Africa shifted into high gear. The new Kolo tyre factory in Nairobi neared completion. Miro got the task of looking after the defence force's tyre needs during Britain's East African military campaigns against Italy, in Italian Somaliland and Ethiopia. He would also need to make occasional trips to Southern Rhodesia and South Africa.

Kolo had given Miro a loan to purchase a ten-acre plot of land four miles out of Nairobi, on Riverside Drive. On it sat a tiny farmhouse, built from stone and topped with a corrugated iron roof. Their water supply was three corrugated iron tanks which collected rainwater draining from the roof. They hired two manservants, Njomo and Kabiru, and a nanny, Wangui, all natives of the Kikuyu tribe. Only Kabiru spoke English. Simone got the hang of Swahili in a hurry. Basic words, nothing fancy. For Miro, English was everywhere: road signs, billboards, the BBC Overseas Service on Nairobi's radio station, motion pictures in English, and *The East African Standard* daily paper.

After Theo was put to bed, Simone and Miro would go for long walks with Teddy, their Old English Sheepdog, testing the boundaries of their wild surroundings. When Miro was away, she would plunge into books borrowed from friends or the Nairobi Public Library. Everyone knew what to give Simone as a gift. She read and stored everything in a book depository conceived and catalogued in her mind.

Miro was in Southern Rhodesia. Simone put away the book she was reading and retired to the bedroom for the night. The light of a full moon shone through the open windows. On the brink of falling sleep, she heard a very faint hissing noise, a constant, quiet hiss that wasn't fading away. She couldn't recognise the sound, so she sat up in bed and looked towards the window. In the dim light, she could make out the shape of a black ribbon moving towards her bed. She flicked on the night table lamp and let out a scream.

The black ribbon was an army of flesh-eating driver ants, marching in a file about six inches wide, and the hissing noise was the sound of a hundred-million feet tramping along the floor. She shot out of bed and pinned her back against a bedroom wall, staring at the advancing horde. An electrical storm of horror played out in her brain and sent a current of fear throughout her body. It flowed through a circuit of terror and disgust. She stood there petrified. These ants would devour every creature in their path. Instinct told her not to flee the bedroom because she would have to cross the path of their relentless advance. They continued coming in from the open window, the band of black becoming ever longer and moving across the floor, up the bed and down the other side, in a very disciplined straight-line march which headed for the opened window at the opposite wall. The marching ants created a barrier, walling her into a corner with no doors or windows.

'Don't come this way, pl-e-e-e-z don't come this way.' She stifled the groan, afraid that if they heard her, they would swerve towards where she stood. Even if they didn't have ears, it was pointless to scream for Wangui. She would enter, step on the horde and be eaten alive.

The black mass turned to grey, as the last of the ants brought up the rear. And then they were gone. Out the window and into the woods. Simone's heart was pounding again. *Where the hell is Miro when I need him? Why does Africa have these savage creatures?*

April brought the showers and thunderstorms. The rainy season was in full force. Richness returned to the land. Parched riverbeds sprang to life. Water flowed and drink holes overflowed. The land grazers and browsers gave thanks—elephants, buffalos, impala, wildebeests and zebras.

Wangui would do the washing and hang the laundry on the clotheslines outside. They were strung between two trees and the Kenyan sun did the rest. Theo began to cry and no one knew why. When his wailing continued, Simone took the bus into town to get gripe water, thinking he might have intestinal pains. She came home with the shopping and a concoction from the chemist. But Theo was no longer crying.

'*Memsahib, angalia hii!*'—Madam, look at this! Wangui showed Simone a small, clear-glass bottle with some whitish things writhing inside.

'*Nini hii?*'—What's this? quizzed Simone.

'*Nimeona minyoo wadudu saba.*'—I found seven insect worms, Wangui declared.

Simone's eyes narrowed, 'Found them *where*?'

'In your baby's arms and back.'

Simone stared in horror at the tiny worms wriggling inside the bottle.

While Theo's clothes were drying outside, insects had laid eggs in the shirts and, when he wore the shirts, the eggs hatched, the worms emerged and burrowed under his skin. Wangui discovered the worms feeding on Theo's flesh, took a needle, dug out the worms one by one, and put them in the bottle.

When Theo was a year old, Simone took her son to Tanganyika. Miro was away in South Africa, and the prospects of finding diamonds in her own backyard were slim. She went looking for them elsewhere. They boarded a train in Nairobi, crossed the border into Tanganyika and travelled by bus to the sleepy village of Marangu, nestled at 4,500 feet in the lush rainforest carpeting the lower slopes of Tanganyika's illustrious Mount Kilimanjaro. Marangu and its surrounds were peopled by the Chagga tribe who worked the fertile volcanic soil to cultivate their maize, bananas and coffee. Simone and Theo stayed with a Czechoslovak couple, Filip Krupa and his wife, who owned and ran the Marangu Hotel, a modest lodge for holiday makers from Nairobi. The Krupas organised climbs for hikers wanting to tackle the 19,340-foot dormant volcano. Krupa, a towering volcano himself, with a bald, Freudian lava cone, goatee beard and immense girth, had an impish sense of humour.

At 5:50 a.m., the faintest of glows was tinting the equatorial sky. The pings of small pebbles, tossed at her bungalow's window panes, went unanswered. Then came gentle but insistent knocks on Simone's wooden bungalow door.

'Simonko. Simonko.' That deep, composed voice outside betrayed a pinch of excitement. 'Come take a look. Kilimanjaro is clear today.'

Krupa had kept his promise. On the very first morning when clouds were not shrouding Mount Kilimanjaro, he would awaken her to view the first rays of sunrise bathing its majestic summit. The early part of the day was best, before the warm, humid air of the valley rose up the sides of the volcano and formed into a thick, blanketing cloud.

'We have to hurry. If you don't come now, I'll put a snake outside your door.'

'You're joking, aren't you?'

No answer.

'Well, aren't you?'

A chuckle was heard outside.

She opened the door, just enough to poke her head through and scan the ground, to make sure.

'Where's the snake?'

Krupa pointed to himself. 'I am the snake. Bring your camera. I have a good viewing spot.'

They spent a month in Marangu. Theo had a young Chagga nanny with a missing front tooth. She always wore a bright orange, cotton print headscarf and wrapped her legs, from the waist down, in a floral-patterned kikoi. Her upper body sported a short-sleeved shirt. Its V-neck was a cut too high for Theo's inquisitive fingers. Krupa gave Simone a tour of the hotel's fruit and vegetable plot. Their Tanganyikan Garden of Eden supplied the hotel's needs. Everything from avocado to zucchini—a horn of plenty to set before the guests and to cultivate the kitchen's culinary creations, under the watchful eye of his wife.

He led a short hike and they got to twin waterfalls, hidden inside the rainforest. There, Simone disappeared and re-emerged wearing a one-piece swimsuit that was almost sheer. Standing beside a rock pool, with the falling water gurgling around her, she stretched into a sexy pose. Krupa reached for Simone's camera and took a picture. Later, he pasted the print over a paper reproduction of Botticelli's *Birth of Venus* so that Simone's body was superimposed where Venus had been standing in the scallop shell. He hung it on a wall in the lodge dining room for all to see. Beneath it, he had penned the caption, *Birth of Simone*.

Covering this wall were several dozen framed certificates of people who had climbed Kilimanjaro in earlier years. Krupa's daughter was the climbing expert. Having scaled the snow-capped volcano many times, she pioneered the route and ideal timings for successful attempts by the lodge's mountaineering clients.

Simone got home. Miro was already back. She felt a surge of joy to see him again. *He's turning into a stranger.* He stood at the farmhouse door and she ran up to him and gave him a tight embrace.

'Wow! What's in your pants pocket? Is that a souvenir you bought for me, or is that Miro, my hero?'

And, having missed it for a while, they both shared those moments of ecstasy which the French call *la petite mort*.

They left Theo with Wangui and went into town. There was a dance party at Torr's Hotel, and Miro arranged to meet his Kolo colleague and close friend, Josef Stepanek, and his girlfriend for a dinner-and-dance evening out.

Back at home again and lying in bed, Simone put her head on his chest and fingered a toccata on his keyboard chin.

'Miro?'

'Hm?'

'Would you mind having a second child?'

'No, I'm Roman Catholic, remember?'

'Well, even if you did mind, it's too late.'

He raised his head off the pillow. 'Another one coming, huh? You've got good connections with the stork. How do you do it?'

'You're the stork, my Kolo knight. Only, you don't fly. You come on a horse.'

'Do you think Mother Angelica would be happy?' he probed.

She smiled and closed her eyes. 'Um, hm. So would Mother Popelka.'

Chapter 8

April 1944. The Allies score major victories against Germany and the air offensive is paralysing Germany's arms production. The fabled Dam Busters of the RAF's 617 Squadron, flying their Lancaster bombers, smash key dams in Germany's Ruhr district, with the resulting flooding doing even more damage downstream. Fittingly, 617 Squadron's adopted motto becomes *Après Moi le Déluge*: After me, the flood. Italy loses its territories in Eritrea and Somalia to Britain. Italian East Africa no longer exists.

But one spectre loomed on the horizon: Soviet forces were advancing on the Eastern Front, pushing back German positions and holding fast onto their newly won territory of influence. Once again, foreboding clouds were rolling in towards Czechoslovakia.

A letter arrived.

My Dearest Simonko,
I cannot write much. This brief note has passed

the censor's eyes. I have been out of touch, for which I apologise, but my situation demands that I keep a low profile. I am reasonably well and one day, when life returns to normal, I will write again. Please forgive. I send you kisses. Please give Miro a nostalgic hug from me. Much love from Palestine,
Marek.

Simone began to cry. *At least he's alive.*

Miro was speculating. 'I guess he's no longer in Beirut. Who knows? The Brits might be using his magnificent brain to intercept or translate enemy communications. He knows German and Italian. And French.' He kissed her on the back of the neck.

'I can't write back. There's no return address. Miro, is there someone at Kolo who might help us find him?'

'I asked, hoping to get a morsel of fodder.' He swung his palm towards his head. 'Door in the face. No one has a clue. He's no longer with Kolo.'

Michael Novotny was baptised at Nairobi's Church of the Holy Family, which came under the Apostolic Vicariate of Zanzibar. Theo stayed at home with Wangui. Miro had taken Simone and Michael to the church in their white, two-seat convertible, a Morris Eight with wire-spoked wheels. Godparents Josef Stepanek and his girlfriend

Helena Kubik were at hand as Father MacNamara performed the baptismal ceremony at the fountain and Helena poured the holy water on Michael's forehead.

Outside the church, Helena held the baby. 'You know what they say about pouring the water. If the baby doesn't cry, it will take to water like a dolphin.'

Simone smiled. 'He will come to love the ocean. Unlike me.' Then her face changed. The Adriatic Sea thought came back. Cheeks turned bloodless. She looked away and tried to forget. A lump of coal formed in the throat. Coal is fathomless black, a dark, sudden colour of death. Shivers, like the ones at the Shrine near her secret thinking place on Mount Carmel.

Miro was teaching her to drive. They used the back roads behind Riverside Drive. She trained alone on weekdays, grinding the sports car's gearbox with clumsy shifting. Rulebook by her side, she would stop to study a road sign. Memorise its meaning. Once, she forgot to check the fuel gauge. The car ran out of petrol and snorted to a standstill in the middle of a plantation road. Simone walked seven miles to get home. Seven miles of watching for snakes, left, right, up in the trees. They could stalk and ambush her. This was Africa. More shivers.

When Theo and Michael were older, the family took to holidaying on the Indian Ocean coast. Malindi was their beach resort and they became the lodge's privileged return guests. October and June skirted the rainy seasons and sent them off on the Nairobi-to-Mombasa overnight train. Descending from Nairobi's high plateau, the steam train puffed through semi-arid grasslands and savannah. As dusk approached and the train sped across the plain, Miro would alert the boys to the wildlife they were passing: a giraffe loping in the distance, its towering neck undulating rhythmically with the animal's long strides, or impala darting in all directions as if racing their train. And always, there were lots of zebras and wildebeest.

'Papa, look! Ellifunt!' Michael spotted the elephant herd kicking up dust as it marched across the parched plain, oblivious to the metallic clickety-clack of that elongated black thing, smoking its way through their waterless grazing ground.

Reaching the coastal lowlands early morning, the train rolled into Mombasa's station. Miro and Simone gave the boys time on the platform to inspect the giant locomotive and its huge wheels with fat spokes. The oily, black behemoth seemed to ooze steam from every crevice, hissing with anger. Dwarfed by this monster-sized boiler on twelve wheels, Michael held onto Theo's hand while the rumble of the coal-fired furnace shook his chest. The train's engineer in oil-stained overalls smiled and beckoned. He helped them up the grille steps. They stood there, faces glowing from the roaring furnace, and imagined a hell controlled by levers, valves and pressure gauges.

Driving north along the coast on their way to Malindi, they stopped for a picnic lunch at Kilifi Creek. On the gently-sloping sandy stretch, Simone spread out a mat and Miro fetched the picnic hamper and plates. As the boys tucked into the sandwiches and samosas, Simone poured the iced tea into cups.

There was a splash at the edge of the water. A Nile crocodile heaved itself out of the creek and onto the muddy banks, then crawled on its belly towards the grassy embankment and began to bask with its jaws open.

'Mama, a crocodile!' Theo pointed towards the dark-brown, scaly creature. Simone spun round and let out a yell. She grabbed the boys' arms and raced to the car.

'Boys, you stay inside and keep the doors and windows closed!' She got in front and shouted. 'Miro, get into the car. Its jaws are wide open. Quickly!'

Miro walked back. 'No immediate danger, really. Crocs bask on the banks with jaws open to cool off in the hot sun. They can die from overheating. This one's probably a mature female.'

'Miro, it will smell the food and come this way,' she fretted.

'I'll pack things up. We'll finish our picnic somewhere else.' They drove north along the coast towards Malindi.

'How come you know so much about crocodiles?'

'One of our Kolo colleagues has a crocodile farm on the Tana River and keeps a pet croc at home.'

'Papa! Can we get a pet crocodile?' That was a beaming Theo.

'Over my dead body, Theo,' Simone jumped in.

'Mama,' said Michael. 'Will the crokdile make you dead?'

Malindi's palm-lined beaches were fine coral-pink sand, softened by eons of wave pounding. Along the beach, were inviting lagoons where the ocean became still and there were no waves. The boys were wading in a shallow lagoon. Like a fearless helmeted diver, Michael disappeared below the surface and opened his eyes. He spotted a cluster of milky-white strings dangling from a shiny, blue object floating on the surface. Thinking it was a pretty shell, he surfaced and scooped it up in his hand. A sharp sting made him recoil and he jerked his arm away from his body, sending the creature flying through the air. It landed on Theo's bare chest.

The tentacles of the moon jellyfish injected a malicious venom under Theo's skin, setting his chest ablaze with pain. He was in agony for six days, chest inflamed, bright red. Simone and Miro were helpless. They tried ice packs, papaya skins, coconut jelly. Nothing worked. Theo's body needed time. Healing is the daughter of time.

April came round and brought autumn with it. And then the heavy rains started. Back at Riverside Drive, Theo and Njomo were checking on nature's activities and doing the rounds of the property. Theo was wearing his father's gumboots, but they were too large and he hobbled in clumsy strides. He spotted movement in the tall grass. He saw the monster and froze.

'*Njomo!*' he screamed. '*Kuja hapa! Haraka! Kukimbia!*'— Come here! Hurry! Run! Njomo hurried over and saw the African rock python. The beast looked a good five metres in length.

'Wait here,' Njomo said. 'Stand back. Don't move. Keep your eye on it. I'm going to fetch the snake stick.'

He came back with a long-forked branch and, creeping up behind the snake, jabbed the stick directly behind its head, pinning its neck to the ground and making it immobile. He pushed the stick into the soil with all his strength and held it there.

'Go call Kabiru. Tell him we have a big python.'

Kabiru came running with a large gunny sack and they eased the python's head into the open end. With Theo holding the sack open, Kabiru and Njomo worked the rest of the heavy, writhing snake into the sack and tied it up. Kabiru was going back to his village on the weekend and would take the live python home on his bicycle.

Theo was awed by the speed of the capture. 'What will you do with it?'

'Skin it and eat it. Then, I'll bring you the python's skin,' Kabiru promised.

Weeks later, he laid out the dried and treated skin for Theo and Michael. They measured its length: 4.6 metres.

Michael imagined it was alive. 'Can it eat a person?'

'It could swallow you whole,' smiled Kabiru.

'All of me?'

'In one gulp.' Kabiru rolled his big, white eyeballs in an arc that gave his shiny, black face a story-telling expression. He could have been Uncle Remus, telling Theo and Michael the story of Brer Rabbit an' de Tar-Baby.

Kabiru offered the python skin to Miro. The snake's scales were small and smooth and had an exquisite pattern of lustrous blotches that varied in colour between brown, olive and buffy-yellow. Its head had a distinctive V stripe on top that resembled the tip of a spear and made it look even more fearsome.

'A gift from my village, for Bwana Noboti,' said Kabiru, unable to pronounce Novotny.

'Can I pay you for your troubles?' asked Miro.

'*Ni furaha yangu*'—It is *my* joy. 'You have been kind to us,' Kabiru smiled. His huge grin displayed teeth whiter than his sun-bleached shirt.

'Simonko, let's hang it, unrolled, across the living room wall.'

'Uh-uh. Not that thing. It frightens me.'

They rolled up the python skin and put it away. But it was a source of endless awe for Theo and Michael, who spread it on the floor and measured its length in child-sized paces, then took a broom and pretended to spear the creature, like brave Masai warriors.

Easter came. Simone had Miro to herself for a few days. They sat at the dining table.

'Miro, do you think we will stay in Africa?'

He put down his fork. Finished munching the mouthful of bread dumpling topped with vegetable gravy. 'Why? Don't you like it here?'

'Things are changing in Europe. Don't you want to go home?'

'Eventually, yes.'

'What does *eventually* mean to Bwana Noboti?'

'Well, the company isn't sending me anywhere, so *here* is our home.'

She got up to get the paprika shaker. Poked her finger into his shoulder. 'No, Miro. Czechoslovakia is our home.'

'I know that, but the boys are getting an amazing education here, so close to nature. Think what an experience Africa is for them. Look at it through a child's eyes.'

'Muh! I'm looking. Snakes and worms and jellyfish and army ants.'

'And crocodiles,' Miro added.

'Yes, those too.'

'While we're in Africa, let them have these. They may never return after we've left. What stories they will have for *their* children!'

He has a point. She tried to digest it, without the paprika. *I've got to do my part. The boys may never come back here.*

Simone drove the boys to Thika in the Morris Eight. August nights were cold and needed an extra blanket at this altitude. They stayed in a lodge at Thika Falls and began to explore their surroundings. She put on her knee-high leather boots.

'Gumboots, Michael. Where are they?'

'In the car.'

'Go get them. Put them on.'

'Mum, they hurt.'

'Where do they hurt?' She pressed down the toe cap, felt his toes. 'Okay, take them off. Put on your plimsolls. But don't you take a single step if you see something moving in the bush.'

'Why?'

It was pointless to scare him with a snake warning. 'It could be a beautiful butterfly!'

They took a short hike not too far from the lodge. The cloud forest was dotted with outcrops of African violets. Giant fennel plants, with their bright-yellow flowering umbels, filled the open spaces where the sky could offer sunshine. Sucking on the hollow fennel stems yielded a tangy, succulent juice.

'It's like toothpaste,' said Michael. Theo agreed.

Tree lizards had climbed to safe viewing spots and a chameleon up in the trees clung to a branch, aiming to snare a hapless praying mantis with its ballistic tongue. Meal captured in a flash, it pivoted its odd telescopic eyes to watch the three visitors passing, below.

'Michael, your birthday's coming soon.' Simone sat him on her shoulders for the return to the lodge.

The dry season approached. Back in Nairobi, Michael's godparents toasted with endless sundowners and put on a party until midnight. They had brought Michael two pet rabbits, which were kept in a cage, outside the house. The boys would stroke the soft, translucent ears that glowed pink. These were docile animals, so unlike Africa's nasty creatures. They were shy and quiet. Michael would get lettuce leaves from the kitchen so he could watch them nibbling the edges, their noses quivering up and down like the needle on Simone's sewing machine. At the back of the house, Theo cut papaya leaves for the rabbits.

One night, Miro was working late at home, finishing reports. Kabiru came in, looking distressed.

'Bwana Noboti,' he pleaded. 'Please come.'

Miro and Kabiru went outside and Njomo was there with a torch, shining it on the rabbit cage. Miro stared at the scene. An army of driver ants was crawling up and into the cage, eating the rabbits alive. The two animals were squeaking. There was little they could do. The ants were already into the flesh of the rabbits and they could not be saved.

On the ground, the band of ants that had fed on the rabbits continued marching into the forest.

'Njomo, bring kerosene,' instructed Kabiru. 'We'll set alight the forward flanks of the ant column.'

Njomo fetched the fuel and they lit the ground. As the flames rose, Miro was astounded. Some of the driver ants veered to the side and, like traffic policemen, were directing the band of marching ants around the flames to avoid the fire. Miro ran upstairs and woke up Theo.

'Come,' he urged his sleepy son. 'You have to see this.'

Theo took a while to comprehend the situation. He stared at the black band of ants marching around the flames and disappearing into the woods.

Next morning, the boys saw skeletons of the two rabbits inside the cage, polished bare of flesh. They grew up a little more that day, grasping the two faces of nature: beautiful and cruel.

February 1946. Miro is summoned to Kolo Africa head

office, in Nairobi. With the demise of World War II, Kolo wants a presence in the Middle East. Miro is asked to relocate to Tehran to begin developing a market in Persia.

He did not like the idea. His heart was set on returning to Czechoslovakia. Kolo promised that the move to Persia would be for just two years. After that, they would relocate him to his homeland. He did not tell Simone right away, mulled over the implications. Persia was a complete unknown for them. They did not know Persian and had no idea what schools were available for their sons. He took a while to break the news to Simone.

'When do we need to leave?' She inhaled to brace herself for the next twist of destiny.

Chapter 9

A shiny Junkers Ju 52 monoplane glistened in the Kenyan sun, as it sat on the tarmac at Nairobi Municipal Airport. Its fuselage was fashioned from corrugated duralumin sheets, riveted together into a square-looking, ugly bird. Nose pointing to the sky and lowly tail wheel resting at the back, it looked as though its three radial engines (nose-mounted, left wing, right wing) could take it anywhere but to heaven. Kenya in June, 1946 was still basking in its designation as a Crown Colony, glittering among the globe-girdling possessions of the British Empire.

Simone and the boys approached the parked aircraft. The perfume of 100-octane aviation spirit infused the morning air. As Michael and Theo clambered up the flimsy aluminium ladder to enter the belly of this ungainly people-swallower, Theo clutched his cotton teddy bear and pressed Simone for an answer.

'Mummy, where are we going?'

'We're going to heaven,' she announced. Simone was saving a fuller reply until they were inside and settled in.

His seven-year-old brain flooded with anxiety. *Only dead people go to heaven. This is not a good idea!*

Their aircraft had served as a troop and cargo transport for the German *Luftwaffe*, fighting the Allies in North Africa. When the German campaign collapsed, the Royal Air Force seized the plane and refitted it for passenger transport. The sixteen passengers sat facing each other on benches running along the walls of the fuselage. The toilet at the back of the aircraft was little more than a tin hut with a hinged door. There was no air hostess. Simone was the cabin crew for their maiden flight.

The three noisy engines tugged the airplane down the runway. It shuddered and rattled like a tin of biscuits on roller skates, until a final hop unglued the wheels from the ground and lifted the plane into the African sky. After seven years in a wild and enchanted land, they were leaving Kenya for good, and Cairo was their first destination on the way out of post-war, colonial Africa. They flew northward, following the Nile River.

Every now and then throughout the flight, the co-pilot would step out of the doorless cockpit and use a hand pump to pump oil into the engines. They broke their journey in the late afternoon for an overnight stop in Khartoum. When the aircraft touched down and the exit door was flung open, they were greeted by a blast furnace of Sudanese air, superheated to a temperature of 46°C.

The following day, they landed in Cairo and the boys waved goodbye to that heavenly plane. Ahead, lay the beginning of a long, hot summer north of the equator. Scanning the night skies north of Earth's great dividing line, the boys would need to farewell an old friend: *kwaheri*, Southern Cross, and make new ones: *salaam*, Big Dipper, Cassiopeia's Chair, and Polaris!

A week later, they were on a train to Palestine. They sat in the dining car and Simone was buoyed by the thought.

'Miro, when we get to Haifa, let's drive to Beirut and look for Marek.'

'Let's start by visiting Malouf. See what he knows. If that's a dead end, we'll try Beirut.'

'Papa! My dearest Papa!' Simone flung her arms around him. He had been awaiting them at the railway station.

He caught sight of Theo and lifted him up to plant a kiss on his cheeks. Theo winced. His grandpa had not shaved for several days and Avram's whiskers were as thorny as a Negev shrub. The fez was gone, replaced by a grey felt hat, and the moustache was now white.

They took a taxi. Esther was waiting at the open door, sitting on a kitchen stool, cotton hankie clutched in one fist. Her hair was greying and she wore a band below the hairline to keep the sweat out of her wrinkled face. The stern mother of yesteryear paused for a moment, absorbing the actuality of a daughter she hadn't seen for eight years. Then, her expression dissolved into sobs and she hugged her child.

'Danni, you haven't changed much. Bring me my two grandchildren!'

Esther sat there, legs apart, her apron creating a tent between the knees, and stared at Michael and Theo. They looked so European to her. The permanent frown stitched to her brow intimidated the boys as they stood before her, not knowing what to say. She pulled them closer and enfolded them in chubby arms, a boy on each side.

'Mummy, does granny speak English?' asked Theo.

'No, dear.'

'Can I talk to her in Czech?'

Simone smiled and gave a regretful shake of the head.

'How about Swahili?' he tittered, his eyes emitting mischief.

Esther turned to Simone. '*Qu'est-ce qu'il demande?*' What's he asking?

Simone told her and Esther put her hand on Theo's head and rocked it like an infant's cradle. 'You must learn *Hebrew!*'

Simone's brothers Moshe and Yigal came to see her. Yigal was married but not Moshe. The three yakked in a mishmash of languages, throwing in words and phrases from different tongues whenever it seemed handier. They kept calling her *Danni*. It felt alien, after being Simone

Thérèse to the whole world. Moshe asked whether she remembered Lev Gavish, the man that Esther and Avram had chosen for her as a husband.

'Of course, I remember him. That slimy creature. What's he doing now?'

'Well, he married someone else and they are already divorced,' smiled Moshe.

'It's a good thing I eloped! You see? There is a plan in heaven.'

Plans were made for visiting old friends, Mount Carmel, the Haifa beaches, and Nassim Malouf at the Kolo tyre store. They would be in Palestine for two months, Miro's stay, shorter. He would scout out Tehran to find an office and set things up for their arrival.

Malouf was dead. Killed in a bus accident. As for news on Marek's whereabouts, it was a dead end. A cul-de-sac. They would need to travel to Beirut.

Simone and Miro walked up the path lined with cedar trees and entered the Convent of the Redeemer. Simone spotted a young nun inside. 'Would it be possible for us to see Mother Angelica?'

The nun cupped a hand to her mouth but couldn't hide a smile. 'Mother Angelica, my dear, has gone to be with the Lord.'

'I'm so sorry. I mean, I'm not sorry. I'm happy for her.'

'Would you like to speak to Sister Scholastica?'

'Oh, yes please!'

'May I tell her who is visiting?'

Sister Scholastica hadn't aged a bit, as though the holy water font in her chapel had been filled from the fountain of youth. She wanted to know all about Simone and Miro's movements since their wedding in Beirut. But she had no idea what had happened to Marek.

'After your wedding, we received a letter thanking us, but that was the last we heard from him.'

Another cul-de-sac.

'Miro, let's try that Restaurant Le Paris where we celebrated after the wedding. It's a long shot, but Marek was a frequent patron. Someone there might know where he went.'

'Could be.'

Following cul-de-sac number three, they ran out of ideas and stayed to have lunch there. *Canard a l'orange* was the menu special. Simone recoiled at the thought: feeding the fish of the Red Sea with her mouthful of orange duck, on *that* cargo ship.

'I don't think so.' She put the menu down. 'I'll stay with champagne.'

'Champagne?'

'Yes, champagne.'

'On an empty stomach?'

'Ah, Miro. If only you could climb into the mind of a woman. You would see a girl, escorted by two suave

Czechoslovak admirers on the loveliest day of her life, and getting all bubbly about being invited to dance until dawn.'

'Oh, alright. I'll dive with you into champagne.'

'You're such a gentleman. And remember, it was you who introduced me to those fizzy bubbles. Pity there's no band music to dance to.'

'Um, not at lunch time, I'm afraid.' He chuckled. 'We're in Beirut. People take naps at midday. Everything comes alive at midnight.'

'Obviously not sleepy Nairobi, is it?' she twinkled.

Simone wanted family time during Miro's last days in Palestine, before he left for Tehran. 'Miro, let's take the kids and go to the beach.'

They took a bus ride to Khayyat Beach, the one that stirred up memories for Simone. The lost engagement ring surfaced in her mind. It mattered less now. On one of his trips to South Africa, Miro found her another ring with a solitaire diamond and now she wore that only on special occasions. When they arrived, the two flags were white and white. The boys whooped with delight: she allowed them into the water alone, watching them from the beach. It wasn't Malindi with its pristine coral-pink sands, but they didn't care. Seaside beaches are wet and splashy everywhere.

'Miro, this is where we sat when you proposed to me.'

'Was it right here?'

'Propose to me again!' Simone parodied an eyelid flutter.

'I can't remember what I said.'

'Come on. I'll help you.' She looked into his face and lip-synched the words, *Chère Mademoiselle Daniela, will you marry me?*

He repeated those words.   Simone looked delighted. 'You're a good lip reader. Now kiss these same lips, like you did before.' Miro looked around to see if anyone was watching.

'You're embarrassed,' she giggled. She grabbed his neck, pulled him close and did it herself.

Michael ran out of the water and up to them. 'Mama, why are you kissing Papa?'

Simone grabbed Michael around his waist and spun with him like a merry-go-round. 'Because I love him and because he's leaving us tomorrow.'

'Does he have to go to Persia?'

'Um, hm.'

'Is Persia a nice place?'

'You'll see soon enough. Where's Theo?'

'He's still in the sea.'

Simone stood up and couldn't see him. She scanned the horizon and spotted him far out. 'Miro, he's too deep! He's *way* too far out.'

'He's quite alright. He knows how to swim. I'll keep an eye. The flags are white and white.'

'Please Miro, go get him!'

Miro went in just as a lifeguard blew his whistle and signalled to Theo to swim back towards the shore. When Miro caught up with him, they swam back together.

'Theo, don't *do* that to me again!' she scolded. 'I don't want you going out that far. You stay where you can stand up.'

Moshe showed up one morning on his motorcycle fitted with a sidecar. They would stop first at a petrol station and then head for Mount Carmel. Simone and Michael sat in the sidecar, with Theo in the saddle behind Moshe. After climbing uphill for a distance, Moshe pulled into a station to tank up. Theo jumped off to offer a helping hand. His bare ankle touched the end of the red-hot exhaust pipe. It seared a perfect burn circle into his skin. Theo was in agony. They had to turn back and head home. Night after night, he couldn't stand the pain and lay awake calling out to Simone to put something on the burn. She had no special burn ointment. Finally, they saw a doctor and the pain subsided. He got his first peaceful night in three days.

They made several trips into Tel Aviv. Everywhere, the signs were in Hebrew. Gone was the Arabic on street posters, billboards, and bus schedules. After an absence of eight years, the change was quite apparent to Simone.

The Jews of Palestine were hell-bent on creating their own nation. As Jewish migrants from post-war Europe poured into their promised land, they resolved to do whatever it took to regain it from the British.

Theo was in Moshe's flat, rummaging through the shed where he kept the motorcycle. He found a black rubber gas mask. He donned it and went out into the street, wearing the oversized, theatrical thing and fogging up the glass goggles. Alarmed neighbours spotted him and alerted Moshe. Theo got a good telling off.

Terrorism was now a fact of life and the authorities were on high alert for Jewish nationalist saboteurs who wanted the British out of Palestine. Encouraged by Zionist groups, the Jewish civilian population were rioting in the streets and accusing the British of Nazi-like, anti-Semitic policies. The British responded by dispersing crowds with tear gas grenades. House searches became draconian forays into people's private lives. If Moshe's gas mask were found, he would be arrested as a saboteur.

Simone and the boys landed at Tehran's airport. Miro was there to meet them. Under the hot Persian sun, they walked across the tarmac to the arrivals area for clearance. It consisted of three thatched-straw sun shades, each supported by four wooden poles. The primitive simplicity of this air terminus stunned Simone:

the entire airport was nothing more than a few, open-air counters resembling a dusty, windblown Persian bazaar.

The family was now in the world's oldest country—a kingdom dating back to 3,200 B.C., a legendary land of roses and nightingales, and kings with a kind nose.

Simone had arrived in the homeland of the Báb. The setting was foreign, yet inexplicably familiar, like stepping back in time and feeling awaited by an eternally silent incarnation. A revelation took place. The message from the Shrine of the Báb was delivered in whispered silence, a familiar hush: *Here began the voice of your thoughts.*

Her mind wandered to the words of Rumi, the Persian poet and Sufi mystic:

Why should I seek?
I am the same as He.
His essence speaks through me.
I have been looking for myself!

Chapter 10

Miro found a flat to rent but it wasn't ready for occupancy. They spent a week at the Peacock Throne Hotel, used by foreign business visitors and tourists on their way to elsewhere. Minutes after settling into their room, Theo went to the washbasin in the bathroom. He turned on the tap to drink from the spout. Simone spotted him and let out a scream, lunging into the bathroom and pulling him away just in time.

'Don't ever drink from the tap! Ever!'

Theo was dumbfounded. He couldn't fathom her reaction. He'd drunk this way countless times in Kenya. He didn't know where this water was coming from. He nearly became a desert Bedu, drinking from a poisoned well.

'Theo, this water is filthy. It's full of germs. They don't have piped water in this city.'

'Like in Nairobi?'

'Yes. Nairobi has safe water from the taps. This water

comes from canals in the street. People in the street are washing their clothes in it, their pots and pans, their dirty feet!'

'But I'm thirsty.'

Simone brought him the jug of boiled water standing in the room, making sure there was no perilous ice floating in it.

Tehran was dry, dusty. The streets were filthy. It didn't rain for nine months of the year. Summers were blistering hot. Winters had a cutting bite. In August, they moved into their flat on the third floor of a three-storey building. Their new home sat on the roof. Looking down, they saw the street traffic at the intersection of tree-lined avenues. There was no lift and shopping had to be hauled up the stone steps. The ground floor was occupied by a chemist and the friendly pharmacist would give the boys latex condoms to blow up into balloons.

Back in Africa, when Miro was packing their belongings, he had used four shipping crates and sorted the effects into two lots. Non-essential items and African souvenirs were packed in two crates to be shipped to Czechoslovakia, where the family would resettle in a couple of years. Two crates containing all their essential household goods were destined for Persia.

Simone opened the crates and a shock travelled up

her torso. The shipping company had blundered and reversed Miro's instructions. Squatting ankle-deep in packing paper, she glared at the soapstone hippopotamus, stamp albums, shoe boxes filled with photos, African wood carvings, and the python skin. Two precious crates offering a modicum of household comfort had gone to Czechoslovakia.

She sat on the doorstep of their flat and juiced the hopelessness into tear puddles. *How can we settle in an alien land where English isn't spoken, in a city without piped water, surrounded by abject backwardness and dirt, while our household goods from British East Africa are out of reach on another continent? How? How? How?*

Simone hated this place. She felt trapped in an isolated, vulgar spot, marooned in a dried-up wadi with just her children and Miro holding her hand. She wanted to return home to Czechoslovakia. Persia was supposed to be the illustrious land of roses and nightingales, of Persian poetry and Persian carpets, Persian lamb and Persian cats, Persian miniatures and Persian caviar from the southern shores of the Caspian Sea. But she, who had studied the Persian Empire at school, could see none of this in her surroundings. *Where is dear Papa, to narrate his fables about storied lands ruled by a kind Persian king?*

She buried herself in her books. They were her friends. They brought rainfall to the wadi and clean, life-giving water flowed once more.

As the days grew shorter and autumn's chill began

to colour the leaves, a very un-African atmosphere descended on the city. The greenery was gone. The leafless trees became dried twigs, sticking upright from a greying earth. Theo felt the melancholy of being stranded in a land so foreign to his earlier experience of year-round blossoms and a dizzying cocktail of wild, garden fragrances, and even wilder creatures. He was missing his native Africa. His sensibilities were shaken by the primitive conditions in a depressingly backward place, made sharper by their contrast against life in progressive, British-ruled Kenya. A bright-eyed child's version of geographical affective disorder, brought on by sensory deprivation, had distilled into the autumn of his discontent. It was an early milepost in the Persian saga.

They found a school for Theo. Tehran had only one for English-speaking children. Established by American missionaries on a shoestring budget, it grew until it could offer twelve years of schooling. Most of the second-rate teachers were imported from the United States and stayed just a few years. The curriculum was mothballed in mediocrity and manacled to Americana: American history, American geography, American literature, American music, American weights and measures, American values and mores, American holidays. Miro had considered the alternatives: better to have his son there, than in some Persian school that taught in a language they didn't yet know.

Theo's school was a continually reconstituted salad bowl of international and privileged students. These were the children of perpetually mobile foreign diplomats, American military personnel training the rudimentary Iranian army and gendarmerie, European contractors and engineers, White Russian émigrés, the Eurocentric and old-moneyed Persian upper crust, and native Armenians and local Iraqi Jews striving to obtain a middle-class foothold for their offspring. When most of the local and native students graduated, they were swallowed into America.

Winter came sooner than anyone expected. Freshly fallen snow blanketed the city. Like a big, white sound muffler, it dampened all the street and traffic noises. The boys had never seen snow: they picked it up with frozen hands, tossed the powder at each other, and stamped their boot prints into it. Munching on it made it melt in the mouth. In the street below, enterprising casual labourers took advantage of the day and turned themselves into snow-shovellers. Shouldering their large, wooden spades they roamed the streets, calling out to householders who needed to have their rooftops cleared before the snow melted and caused bedroom ceilings to collapse in a heap of straw-filled mud and plaster. These were the *barfi*, the snowmen of Tehran. Their cries carried far in the icy air.

'*Baaarfiiii! Barf pārū mīkonīm! Barfi!*' Snowmen! We shovel your snow. We are snowmen.

Winter squeezed moisture out of the air. Playing outside had its own cost: the skin on the boys' knuckles was cracked and bleeding. Simone would rub glycerine into their hands and it had a stinging bite. The other stuff they hated was the daily tablespoon of cod-liver oil. The green bottle of ominously-pure fish oil, imported from Norway, sat on the breakfast table each morning, and the boys prayed that Mama would forget to administer the ghastly liquid that day.

'Miro, can you remember where we put the silver picture frame from Northern Rhodesia? I can't find it.' Simone was fumbling through the irritating African souvenirs.

'It's on Theo's desk. He's got a picture of Captain Marvel in it. Why do you need it?'

'I want to frame Marek's postcard from Beirut.'

Miro came into the bedroom, holding a framed photo of their wedding. 'Why don't you use this? It's two sided, and Marek wouldn't mind if we turned our backs to him. Use both sides. When you're in a good mood, you can turn Marek to face you. When you're not so happy, you look at our wedding and realise how lucky you are.' He was grinning.

'You're in a good mood, I can see.' Resentment spiced the dry bedroom air.

'Um, hm. I am. I'm always in a good mood.' He returned to his work in the home office.

'Well, I'm not!' She bit her lip. Sat at her dressing table. Stared into the mirror. Began to weep, then sob. She tipped the wedding picture over with her finger. It clanged as the frame hit the glass top of the table. *Where are you? Why don't you write anymore? I hate this place. I miss you.* The bedroom window let in a greyish light. It wasn't the light of a golden Beirut wedding day or the eye-squinting brilliance of the Nairobi sun. Just the drab greyness of a half-hearted autumn, filtered through alien clouds. She took apart the frame and fitted the postcard, then stood the picture holder upright. Beirut was looking at her. The dressing table was happy.

Christmas Day broke into a brilliant, sunlit spectacle. The snow on the roads sparkled for a short while, then melted and turned to muddy slush. But the bare branches of the plane trees in the street carried their load of fresh snow without breaking. The air was cold but filter-clean. In the distance, towered Persia's majestic volcano, Mount *Damāvand*, Bride of the Gods, robed in white from headpiece to bridal gown and silhouetted against an azure-blue sky. Yesterday's snowfall had turned into her wedding day at sunrise the next morning. Nature in Persia could be beautiful, after all. And the buds of spring were almost around the corner.

Simone began emerging from her shell and sniffing the air. The advent of spring brightened her outlook, made it more elastic to adversity. When it came to welcoming a New Year, the Persians got it beautifully correct with *Nowrūz*, the new day. Their solar year began on the first day of spring, the vernal equinox. But the old year's final Wednesday was important too—Red Wednesday it was called, the ancient Zoroastrian Festival of Fire. The night before, Red Wednesday Eve, children and grown-ups in the streets and alleys lit small bonfires and jumped over the flames.

'Mama, they're jumping over fire down there!' Michael was watching the street scene below.

'Put on your shorts and plimsolls. We'll go down together.' She didn't want live cinders setting fire to his trousers. Skin regenerates like bamboo shoots. Pants on fire are hard to put out. 'You too, Theo! Theo? Where are you?'

Theo was already down in the street, jumping over a bonfire flame. The sight of him brought smiles and chuckles to the native kids and their parents doing the same. They watched this energised foreigner in khaki shorts going back and forth, flying over the fire and giggling when he should have been invoking the age-old words directed at the flames, to invite wellness in the New Year: *Your red glow of health to me, my yellow pallor to you.*

Again, and again, he accelerated down the runway and launched himself over the flames. Simone caught up with him and smiled at the amused crowd. They knew she was the mother of this jinni with fire in his belly. Some of the older boys were twirling a small wire basket, filled with glowing iron filings and attached to a long wire. As they twirled, faster and faster, a shower of yellow and white sparks lit up the darkness.

People had spent the weeks before *Nowrūz* spring-cleaning the house, buying new clothes, getting potted hyacinths, and filling vases with tulips. They visited family and friends and exchanged gifts: rosewater-flavoured sweets, chickpea-flour confections, and pistachio-filled nougat for the adults, silver or gold coins for the children. On the thirteenth day of the New Year, families chased the bad spirits out of the house and went on day-long picnics. It was unlucky to stay at home. Any mode of transport would do to get out of town and toss away the bowl of green barley or lentil sprouts that had been growing in the house and capturing all the sickness and bad luck. Eat, celebrate, play music, dance, throw out the evil.

Miro set up a Kolo office in the southern quarter of Tehran, near the city's labyrinthine main bazaar. The immense bazaar was a catacomb of corridors running in every direction, dozens of covered passageways where skylights illuminated the pedestrian traffic of shoppers seeking out merchants. Simone was fascinated by the atmosphere, reminiscent of her beloved open-air bazaar in Haifa, but busier and more complex. Like the aisles of a giant underground supermarket, each corridor was earmarked for specific goods: a myriad of gold bracelets dangling from horizontal poles, hand-painted miniatures, enamelled kitchenware, bowls with live goldfish, rows of smoked and salted Caspian White Fish, gunny sacks filled with rice, dried nuts, spices or black tea leaves. Carpet merchants in one corridor, artisans in another corridor. She could get lost in this Kafkaesque world.

Simone stopped to watch craftsmen creating mosaic inlay cigarette boxes and, in another workshop, hammering their finely-pointed chisels into silver trays to give them intricate motifs. She also discovered the delights of Persian cuisine which sprang from exotic ingredients. Here, imagination could fly, fuelled with saffron, turmeric, sumac, rose petals, *senjed*, and powered by pomegranate sauce, bright-yellow quince, vivid-orange persimmon, crimson-red barberries, dried Omani limes.

Chapter 11

Tehran had a large expatriate community of Czechoslovak citizens. They were the technical and engineering elite: civil engineers who had built the roads, bridges and tunnels needed during the wartime years and now devising textile factories, sugar refineries, and power stations. Leaning on his earlier experience as organiser of the Czechoslovak Circle for British East Africa, Miro got together with several expatriates and formed the Czech Club in Tehran. With this social network in place, club members and their families got to know each other through holiday season parties, Mother's Day gatherings, children's outings, puppet theatre, and National Day celebrations.

Among the club members catching Miro's attention was Battle of Britain flying ace and former RAF Spitfire pilot, Pavel Vrána. He had arrived in Tehran as an engineer trained in aircraft engine maintenance. Pavel was hired by the fledgling airline, Persia Airways, which flew Douglas DC-3s. He was licensed to fly twin, piston-engine aircraft like the DC-3 and would often fly a domestic route to pick up or deliver aircraft components, or ferry a fleet service mechanic to a worksite.

Pavel was phenomenally talented as a fighter pilot. He had the eyes of a falcon and the reflexes of a cat. He would spot an enemy aircraft in the sky long before his flying colleagues could see it. In 1940, during the early stages of the Battle of Britain, he joined the RAF as an allied pilot and was assigned to a squadron flown by Czechoslovak pilots. With his mechanical intellect he got to know the workings and capabilities of the Spitfire, inside out. And he shared that precious knowledge with his fellow pilots and the ground crew.

He impressed his RAF commanding officers and was made squadron leader. Pavel would lead his squadron into aerial battle and meet the attacking German planes head-on. His unit had the task of shooting down the *Luftwaffe*'s Messerschmitt fighter escorts giving air cover for the incoming bombers, thereby exposing the much slower bombers as easy targets. His wartime total of twenty-two confirmed 'kills' of German aircraft earned him Britain's Distinguished Flying Cross, with two Bars.

But there was a humanistic side. He would not fire his eight, wing-mounted machine guns straight at the cockpit of an enemy aircraft. Instead, he would go for the machine itself. A Messerschmitt 109, with its single engine knocked out, is just a metal glider with a swastika painted on its tail. When an enemy aircraft went into a flaming nosedive, permanently crippled. Pavel had a habit of glancing back and hoping he could spot the enemy pilot bailing out and deploying his parachute. In 1943, he was withdrawn from combat flying and assigned to the RAF's Maintenance Unit, where his skills were badly needed and he served until the end of the war.

Miro came home and announced, 'Simonko, I've got a special guest coming to our house on Thursday.'

'Oh? Who is it?'

'I'm keeping it a surprise. You will not be displeased.' He put his arm around her waist and she removed the apron. 'He's Czech and, for the occasion, I'd like you to serve *svíčková na smetaně*.' Miro was referring to the signature Czech dish, marinated beef tenderloin in sour cream sauce, served with big, fluffy bread dumplings. 'Would that be okay with you?'

'Well, well. This mysterious *he* must be a very important guest.' She handed him her apron as though he would be in charge of preparing the Thursday dinner.

Thursday evening came and Pavel Vrána was at the door. A bouquet of eleven, deep-red Persian roses was in his hand.

'*Dobrý večer, milostivá paní!*' Good evening, m'lady! He bowed and kissed her outstretched hand in the Viennese manner.

She took him in breathlessly. *Wow! All I asked for was a cargo ship and now all these gorgeous men sail into my life.* Not quite as tall as Miro, his dark, curly hair and his chiselled face gave the impression of determination, but the eyes radiated energetic kindness. The upright posture conveyed a hint of military discipline. They chatted in Czech over dinner and Simone's curiosity simmered.

'Pavel, tell me about your pilot exploits. Why did you want to fly?' To her, flying was escaping the pull of gravity, travelling far and away to new lands and nesting places, like a migratory bird.

'When I was a boy, I saw a small airplane flying above our house and asked my father, 'Why can't little boys have an airplane to fly?' He said it was because little boys were too small to sit in a cockpit and see over the top of the dashboard. So, I vowed I would become big enough for a cockpit and fly an airplane all by myself.'

Question answered, the laughs subsided, and Pavel continued.

'Before the war, I joined the Czechoslovak Air Force as a trainee pilot, and I got my wings. When Germany annexed the Czech lands, I fled to Poland. The Polish Air

Force invited me to join them as a reconnaissance pilot. After Germany invaded Poland, I had to flee again, but the Poles asked me to help them remove some of their aircraft to Romania, to keep them out of German hands. I did that and then escaped to the port of Constanta, on the Black Sea. From there, I took a ship to Beirut and—'

'To Beirut?' She glanced at Miro and he winked back. 'And then?'

'And then I caught a ship to Marseille and made my way to England. The British were desperate for pilots. They knew that Hitler was planning a ground invasion of Britain. The Poles and Czechoslovaks were seen as allies and the RAF created many squadrons of non-British pilots. We were already seasoned pilots, a bit older than the young British recruits. They trained us in Hurricanes and Spitfires. In my case, we became 341 Squadron when the Battle of Britain was already underway. The Poles were amazing flyers. Fearless! They would ignore Fighter Command's rigid rules for formation attacks and take off in their Hurricanes and fly straight up into the oncoming enemy planes. They had fire in their testicles because of what Hitler was doing to their country. And they had their own style of fighting. They made up 303 Squadron and their kill-rate was far above the average of the other RAF squadrons.'

'But you were one of those fearless ones.' Simone touched his hand.

Pavel smiled and lowered his head. 'In the end, we

did the British proud. We'd joke that the 341 Squadron designation they gave us held a fiery truth: three for one. Three enemy planes downed, for each one of ours!'

Simone reached for the dinner bell and gave it a vigorous tinkle. 'Touché!'

Miro broke into a chuckle. 'Heil Hitler! We'll give you one of our planes, for three of yours.'

She couldn't tame her impulsive craving for more. 'Do you have any flights you remember well?'

'Ah, yes. September twenty-seventh. An amazing day I won't forget.' He switched to easy-flowing RAF jargon as he relived the episode. Simone was swept into battle. 'It was late-afternoon and our squadron had already flown three sorties that day. The Germans were bombing London and, almost daily, there would be waves of bombers, escorted by Messerschmitt fighters, coming in from France, crossing the English Channel and headed for London. We were on alert because Fighter Command had received intercepted German radio communications that a third bombing raid on London was imminent that day. Soon, radar picked it up and then came the telephone call from Operations Command to our airfield. The station's brass bell was clanged and I yelled, "Scramble, Scramble, Scramble!" We were flight-ready and ran to our planes, I saluted my wingman, and we were airborne in less than two minutes.

'I was given Ops Command's estimated position of the detected raid. When our squadron was in the air, I radioed our pilots: "Crowman to squadron: vector One-Two-Five, angels One-Four." That meant we would fly southeast from our base and climb to 14,000 feet. My radio call-sign was *Crowman* because Vrána is *crow*, as you know. We used code names so the Germans wouldn't identify squadron members, or the airfields we flew from.

'At 14,000 feet, we were out over the Channel and I spotted a large formation of bombers approaching, escorted by about twenty or thirty Messerschmitt Me109s. It was like a cloud of black and grey filling the sky. I radioed our pilots, "Crowman to squadron. Tally-ho. Bandits at angels One-Six, dead ahead. Right, chaps. Let's show Gerry what we're made of!" Our aim was to surprise the formation, attack the escort of Messerschmitts, draw them away from the bombers, then close in on the bombers. If we could break up the formation, the bombers would become easy targets. We climbed to 18,000 feet.' Pavel pointed his straightened arm and finger upwards. Simone was in the cockpit with him.

'We flew in from the sun, so the enemy would have a hard time seeing us. As we closed in, our planes lured away the 109s and the dog fights began. The trick was to come up behind an Me109, get on its tail and open fire on its engine. Several bombers were shot down and it became a mess of smoke and vapour trails in the sky. I swooped in to approach a bomber from behind and get beneath him so the rear-gunner could not hit me. Our Spitfires had only machine guns in the wings, and the bullets did no more than make small holes in the bomber's fuselage. I needed to hit him in one of the two engines. That's where the bomber was vulnerable. All of a sudden, my wingman radioed me: "Ballet Tights to Crowman. One-O-Nine on your tail!" My wingman became frantic. "Ballet Tights to Crowman, I can't cover! He's on your tail! Break away!"

'I was very close to the bomber, less than thirty yards. I knew that the Me109 behind me wouldn't dare fire because the 109s had cannons in their wings and a cannon shell might miss my plane and hit the German bomber in front of me. I unloaded two bursts of my machine guns at one of the bomber's engines. Black smoke poured out and the bomber was crippled and began to go down. Then, I pulled a sharp left turn to get out of the Me109's sights. The Messerschmitts were faster, but the Spitfire could make much tighter turns. I made a tight circle and, soon, I closed on his tail and now the 109 was in my sights. I couldn't get a bead on his engine, so I went for the fuel tanks. There was an immediate flash and his right wing burst into flames. He went down and I lost sight of the plane. I didn't see if the pilot bailed out.

'The dog fights lasted twelve, fifteen minutes. The Me109s could stay airborne only one hour before their fuel ran out and they would be forced to ditch in the English Channel while attempting to return to their bases in France. This was the Achilles' heel of the Me109, its very limited range because it did not carry much fuel. We were now north of Hastings and the bombers were well short of their target. They began to unload their bombs over the countryside, then turned to head home across the Channel. The Me109s began to do the same. And our Spitfires were ordered back to base. Several of our planes had serious damage.

'But one Me109 was still around. I was determined to go after him, even though my fuel was low. We chased and circled trying to get each other in our gun sights and then he turned towards France. It was my last chance to get him. We flew past the cliffs and over the Channel. I nosed into a shallow dive to hide under the Me109's belly until I was 100 feet away. Aiming for his engine, I fired a short burst of gunfire. His engine cowling splintered and a big chunk of metal debris bounced off my canopy and hit the left of the tail plane. My Spitfire shuddered and became hard to control, so I eased back on the speed. The Me109 was leaking oil and smoking now, and went into a spiralling dive. I could see the pilot bailing out and his parachute open before his plane hit the sea.'

'Did you shoot the pilot as he was coming down with the parachute?' asked Simone.

Pavel went silent, as though he had been hit. Simone sensed she had asked a bad question. Embarrassment crept into her breast.

'No.'

'But he was a German.' She tried to save face. 'He could live to fly again.'

'No. That would be murder. Combat pilots are a silent brotherhood. We fly for different masters, in different planes, but there is a feeling of professional respect that goes beyond uniforms and nationalities. Every pilot has a love of his machine, and every machine knows its master. If a pilot loses his aeroplane but manages to get out, you leave it at that.

'Wow ...' She studied his expression. It radiated compassion.

'But here's what I *did* do. I flew past his parachute and rocked my wings, saluting his airmanship. Then nursed my crippled Spitfire back to our airfield. Approaching the landing strip, my engine cut out and I couldn't lower the landing gear. I managed a bumpy belly landing, sliding all over the grass. The Spitfire was damaged. Fuel tanks were bone dry.'

Pavel took a deep breath. 'End of a very long day,' he exhaled. 'All of us were exhausted, totally spent. It was a bittersweet day. Two of my colleagues did not return, we lost four aircraft, but Hitler lost ten of his planes that day.'

'Goodness, what a day. I didn't know pilots did such things.' She paused for a moment. 'Did you ever find out who that German pilot was?'

'I did! Years later, I discovered it was the ace, Helmut Geiger. He was my kill number fourteen. When he went down into the sea, a British coast guard launch spotted him and fished him out, then took him prisoner. He spent the rest of the war in a camp and could no longer fly. I tracked him down, we exchanged letters and he has invited me to visit him in Germany.'

Simone looked amazed. 'So, it's good that you *didn't* shoot him.' Her mind sifted through this tale written by air and fire and water and earth. 'Tell me, why was your wingman called *Ballet Tights*?'

Pavel chuckled. 'His name was Tomáš Horák, a handsome chap who looked very suave in his blue uniform with the RAF wings. He was quite successful with the ladies. One evening, a few of us were in the pub, knocking back pints of beer, and this staggeringly attractive peach comes over and sits down right next to him. Really close. Tomáš looks at her legs and sees that, under her skirt, she is wearing ballet tights made of fine wool. He asks her if he can borrow the tights to keep out the cold during high-altitude flying. She disappears for a moment and returns holding up the tights and gives them to Tomáš. "Make sure you come back. They're my only pair," she says to him. So, after that, I suggested he take the call-sign *Ballet Tights*. Later, he told us the tights were an aphrodisiac that gave him the will to return alive from a sortie and visit the owner of those tights.'

Simone's voice wore a wool-warm smile. 'You flyers had a tough time in the air, but you knew how to relax when you were not in your cockpits. I'm sure all of you dashing, young RAF pilots were attractive to the women.'

'I was one of the lucky few who survived. Battle of Britain pilots had very short lives. The RAF lost 544 airmen during this aerial combat. The Luftwaffe lost 2,500. It was very intense.'

Simone took a deep breath. 'What a waste of young lives.'

'Yes. I lost many friends. Combat pilots, like so many soldiers who dare the enemy and lose everything, are a different breed. But, you know, that English Channel is Britain's guardian angel. The Germans had to cross this body of water before they could do any damage. We didn't know it at the time, but the *Luftwaffe* were terribly understaffed and short of aircraft. The few good German pilots flying the shrinking pool of fighters were overworked and stressed out. They would get *Kanalkrankheit*, Channel sickness. Today, we call it combat fatigue. And, once across, they faced the fierce defenders of the English coast, the RAF *and* her Czech and Polish flyers. A tough combination for Hitler. His treatment of Poland and the Czech Lands, we were determined to destroy his ambitions in the air.'

Simone went silent. *How the world has changed. There is so much to digest.* But she was smitten with him. Pavel, the Spitfire pilot in blue uniform with RAF wings, had fixed her in his sights and gunned her down with irresistible magnetism. And he had the angels One-Eight gift of spellbinding storytelling. Just like Papa.

Chapter 12

Miro opened the envelope. The notification looked severe and the letterhead was emblazoned with the Czechoslovak twin-tailed lion on a red shield. The instructions from the Czechoslovak embassy in Tehran glared at him: the passports held by Miro and Simone were no longer valid and new passports would be issued to them. Miro was to return to Communist Czechoslovakia with his family as soon as possible. After seizing power in a Soviet-backed coup d'état in 1948, the Communist Party of Czechoslovakia held a political monopoly in the nation and a choke-hold on her people. Miro's homeland had been sacrificed to appease Joseph Stalin. A monstrous betrayal by the allies now placed Czechoslovakia under the Soviet spell.

He did not go to work that day. Pacing up and down, Miro weighed up the situation. With the collapse of the Third Reich, Churchill and Roosevelt had double-crossed their former ally and ceded control of Czechoslovakia to the Soviets. It was a brutal stab in the back of a nation whose pilots and soldiers fought on foreign soil, in the Battle of Britain and throughout the war, helping to defeat Hitler.

Leave Iran and return to a country run by a socialist regime which took directions from the Soviets? Infuriating! Sickening! Not on my bloody life! He knew the tools of Soviet-style communism: stifle people's initiative and rob them of every civilised right. *Better to be turned into a frog, than into a communist supporter.*

He spent a week thinking about the orders. He talked to friends in the Czech Club. They got similar letters. Simone tried to paint the ugly scene: implanting the family in a society where private property is taken away and given to the state, religion is anathema, and individual liberties are crushed.

Two weeks passed. Miro wrote a reply to the embassy letter. The family would not return to the homeland. The Czechoslovak ambassador's response was swift and ruthless: the embassy, as representatives of the Ministry of the Interior, were stripping Miro, Simone and the boys of their Czechoslovak citizenship. Their passports were annulled. A month passed and Miro was notified that Kolo was now a state-owned enterprise and he was no longer an employee of Kolo, nor a representative for Kolo in Iran.

They were stuck in Persia and Miro was out of a job. He tried to reassure Simone: the country's English-language daily paper, *Tehran International*, allowed him to keep an eye on economic developments and business opportunities.

It was Friday, the Muslim weekend and day of rest. The boys were out playing in the street and Miro was sitting in his favourite chair reading the newspaper. Simone peeled away the page he was reading and poked her head through.

Miro looked up. 'What?'

'Can I talk to you?' She eased the paper out of his hands and set it aside. She sat on his lap and put her legs around his waist, then rested her head on his chest. She flirted with the buttons on his shirt and slid one finger up and down, between two done-up buttons. The fingers were thinking. The buttons were the possibilities.

'You're not pregnant, right?'

'No,' she sighed, 'I'm not pregnant. Miro, are we going to be alright? Should I look for a job?'

'Your job is to look after your family at home, not out there in the work world. You have plenty on your plate.'

'Are we going to survive this?'

'Of course. Come on. It's just a temporary setback. We'll be alright.'

'Promise we'll be okay?'

'I don't want you to worry. We do have some money saved up to weather this storm, and then the sun will shine.' Miro had a good reputation among his clients. He knew he could count on some of them to lend him money. He wouldn't play that card unless things became critical, but it gave him added confidence.

She bit his nose softly, squeezing out a bit of kindness. 'And when the storm has passed, will you take me on a second honeymoon to Spitsbergen?'

'I'll take you to Spitsbergen, and Persepolis, and Isfahan, and the Caspian.'

'I want Spitsbergen.' Her eyes lit up. She took hold of his ears and stretched them apart from each other.

'Miro, Miro, where do you get all your courage from?'

'Where do you get all your ear-pulling charm?'

'Not from my mother.' She picked up the newspaper and gave it back to him.

'Then perhaps from Papa?'

'Papa is a storyteller, and when he begins his tales, he can pull ears too.'

Miro wasted no time. He fired off letters to tyre manufacturers that were once his major competitors. The German firm, Unireifen, was impressed with Miro's experience in Africa and the Near East, and showed an interest. They corresponded and negotiated until Miro became their agent for Iran. Unireifen's mainstay was passenger car tyres, and tyres for trucks and motorcycles.

They would pay him a minimal salary and he would receive commissions based on sales in his territory.

He wrote to the International Refugee Organisation, headquartered in Geneva, requesting the protection of the IRO, so that the family would not be deported to Czechoslovakia. The IRO sent a formal letter and certificate declaring that the Novotny family were refugees and had the legal and political protection of the Organisation.

Simone, Miro and the boys were now nationless, and their movements were restricted by the Iranian authorities. Even holiday trips to the Caspian Sea, a four-hour drive north of Tehran, would require police permits. A minor irritant that could never stop their intended pilgrimages to this blissful body of water.

As if throwing down the gauntlet to arid Tehran—sitting on a plateau at the edge of a great salt desert, the Caspian coastline was blanketed in thick rainforest. But getting there was a different challenge. The road was a 200-kilometre, gravel-surfaced ribbon twisted by countless hairpin bends and snaking its way through the Alborz Mountains with snow-covered peaks. The road had neither shoulders nor guard rails, only a sheer drop of 1,500 feet to the bottom of the canyon carved out by primordial rivers. A car and lorry graveyard, it was. The boundary between the barren landscape to the south and the lush, sub-tropical Caspian on the other side of the mountains was sharply demarcated by a tight, single-lane tunnel drilled through the mountains at the road's highest point. Built by Czechoslovak engineers during WWII, it linked the wartime supply route stretching from the Persian Gulf to the Soviet Union.

Now, this cave-like tube deep inside the mountains had become a bottleneck. Cars queued up with lorries and rickety buses at the entrance to the tunnel. When the one-way traffic, travelling in the opposite direction, had exited, it was their turn to enter. Miro had hired a long-distance taxi for this trip. Headlights turned on, they penetrated the leaky, potholed, diesel smoke-filled wormhole for an agonising six kilometres. Theo hated every metre of this pitch-dark pipe. *What if the whole thing collapsed on them?* Then, to everyone's relief, the post-tunnel descent towards luxuriant vegetation gave promise of bathing in the serene Caspian Sea.

For these summer escapes from Tehran, Simone stuffed a picnic basket full of books. Everything else took care of itself. The humidity was kind to complexion and turned long hair into a tornado of curls. They would stay a month and became regulars at the Pension Madame Arkanian, a holiday villa owned by an ancient Armenian lady who worked her staff to the bone so that guests would have a flawless stay.

Pavel was visiting Miro and Simone. He had become close to them and dropped by often.

'Pavel, you're not going back, are you?' Miro was probing Pavel's plans.

'Never. Those *sukin syn* Soviets are raping our homeland.' Pavel used the Russian words for *son of a bitch*. 'Why would I go back? To help them ruin everything we have built? They will brainwash everyone and the nation will go to the dogs, go the Soviet way.'

'So, what will you do, now?'

'I continue my work here, as aircraft maintenance manager, and then we shall see.'

'And then we shall see,' parroted Simone, her smile glowing with mischief. 'We need to find you a beautiful Persian bride and then you can stay here forever!'

Pavel became stoic. 'She would have to be impossibly beautiful. Because *nothing* is forever.'

Nothing is forever. Those words echoed inside Simone. There was a frightening finality to them. *Why do these Shrine-like words sound so irrevocable, so inevitable?* She got up to serve her visitor.

'Gentlemen, some tea.' Simone drew boiled water from the silver samovar spout and filled a teapot containing black tea leaves. She set down tea cups and a bowl with sugar lumps.

'If I'm not mistaken,' said Pavel, 'I should hold a sugar lump between my teeth and sip the tea through it. Yes?'

'You know the Persian way!' she beamed.

Another year passed. New Year's Eve came round. Pavel suggested they gather a few Czech friends and go partying at a hotel in the foothills of the mountains north of Tehran. Simone and Miro had not gone out dancing for a long time. For this occasion, they created costumes and masks. By now, they had a maid-servant and she would stay home with the boys.

They partied into the night. Miro and Simone danced. Then, traded partners with the other Czech couples. Pavel invited Simone for a dance. They were like magic together, her gown flowing to his polished steps as they swept across the ballroom. They swung as one, syncopated then rhythmic, and he carried her like a feather gliding across the floor. Miro looked on and there was jealousy. He, too, was a good dancer but his woman was in someone else's arms. Pavel had won yet another dog fight.

Weekends during the long, hot days of summer were spent hiking into the high country outside Tehran, where there were trout streams and big boulders and the water ran mountain-cold. Pavel would fish for spotted trout and they grilled the fish on skewers, after building a charcoal fire out in the open. They spread the picnic blanket in the shade of a grove of tall poplar trees.

Out came the potato salad, flat bread and river-chilled beer, and they would talk about future trips to interesting places, while the boys tried their luck fishing with improvised rods Miro had fashioned from a poplar branch, with hooks, earthworms and advice provided by Pavel.

Simone kept a special place for him in her heart and she did not try to hide it. He was her eternal gentleman aviator. The attraction was intense, but not fatal, as it would be for a gypsy moth flying into a flame.

Friday outings in late-spring found the family with Pavel picnicking on the lower flanks of Mount *Damāvand*, the iconic dormant volcano. The Bride of the Gods was asleep and no prince had come to awaken her. Even as she slept, the bride had a radiant beauty throughout the year, veiled in white from head to toe during the winter. Now, her skirt had erupted in florescence and was bathed in bright scarlet poppies that had sprung up—tall poppies, waving in the breeze, signalling her wish to remain asleep forever. As they hiked through the brush looking for a picnic spot, lizards froze in their camouflage to assess the level of danger, or scurried off to safety under rocks. The aroma of sage and thyme filled the air. Simone imagined the bride sharing her fragrance with visitors, her perfume of Persian hospitality.

They found a patch of level ground to eat. 'Simonko,' said Pavel, looking up at the summit and shielding his eyes from the sun. 'How high is the cone of *Damāvand*?

Give it to me as though you were squadron leader, radioing the coded number to your pilots.'

'Er, I've forgotten how it's done. I wouldn't be much use in the RAF.'

'What if I told you the summit is at 18,000 feet?'

'Um, angels eighteen?'

'Close. Not bad at all. Angels One-Eight.' He dug into the picnic basket. 'Here's your distinguished flying croissant with two bars of chocolate.'

She chuckled at the wordplay. 'Tell me, have you kept in touch with any of your squadron mates?'

'Many did not survive the war. But I have stayed in contact with my wingman, Tomáš Horák. At the end of the war, he moved back to his hometown, Opava, near the Polish border.'

'You mean Ballet Tights?'

'Ah, you remembered. Yes.'

'And what happened to that eye-catching owner of the ballet tights? His RAF girlfriend?'

'He returned the tights to her, she fell in love with him, they married and he gave her more than tights: two girls and a boy.' Simone burst into a peal of laughter. And the echo drifted up the mountainside to angels Who-Knows.

Chapter 13

Pavel was visiting. He was regaling Theo and Michael with his exploits as an ace pilot. Then he recreated the experience for them.

'Michael, your radio call-sign is *Mamba*. Theo, your call-sign is *Tango*. I am *Crowman*.' The three of them sat on the tiled floor in the hallway, instructed to do so by Pavel. Each sat behind the wooden-stick end on a rubber suction cup for unclogging drains, after three plunger's cups had been stuck to the floor. Then, he got them to imagine they were piloting a Spitfire and controlling it with their joysticks.

'Push forward, to dive your Spitfire. Pull back, to climb higher. Left push is to bank your Spitfire left. Right push, to bank to the right. Got it?' They nodded. Excitement was building.

Michael chirped up, 'Crowman, let's fly really high!'

'Okay, chaps. Follow me into battle. British radar has detected enemy aircraft coming towards the coast of England: vector One-Two-Five, angels One-Four. Scramble! Scramble! Scramble! Jump into your cockpit. Up we go, through the clouds and into the sun. Now we're over the English Channel. Crowman to squadron: Bandits at angels Two-Zero, vector Zero-One-Zero. Here come the Messerschmitts!'

'Yeeee! Here come the messy shits!' Michael echoed, ready to unwind like a tightly coiled spring.

'Crowman to Tango. Messerschmitt right behind you! Dive quick!' Theo thrust the stick forward. 'Crowman to Mamba. German bomber ahead. Aim your guns at its wing. Give it a short blast with your machine gun! Down goes the bomber!'

And the boys would spout the noise of a machine gun as they rolled their bodies, banking left and right, and followed their leader. 'A-a-a-a-a-a-a! A-a-a-a-a-a-a! Got you! Voooooom!' They were spellbound.

Simone overheard the battle unfolding and smiled. When he got up to leave, the boys were begging. 'When will you come again? When? When?'

'Next time I visit, I'll bring you the inside of your airplanes.'

'Really? You'll bring airplanes into our house?' said Theo.

'You'll see.'

Simone embraced and kissed him as he left. She always did this after a visit. He was still an active pilot and this was her way of steering him away from danger. But those words, *nothing is forever*, troubled her.

Pavel brought the surprise. Using discarded cockpit instruments from an old aircraft being cannibalised for parts in his maintenance hangar, he had one of his service workers cut out two plywood sheets, so Pavel could create two sets of instrument panels. After cutting out holes in the boards, he fitted several indicators to resemble the instrument panel of a Spitfire. When the boys got their cockpits, they were speechless. Now, they were really going to fly.

'Right, chaps, let's get those toilet plungers out.' They stuck the rubber suction cups to the floor and Pavel propped up the Spitfire instrument panels in front of each boy. Then, as they sat in their cockpits, he explained what each instrument told them as pilots, and what to look out for. 'Now, remember. We never, never want our air speed to fall below eighty miles per hour. Yes?'

The boys looked at him with worried faces. 'What will happen, Crowman?' said Theo.

'Your Spitfire will stall. It won't stay up if we fly it too slow.'

'And then I will crash?'

'And then you will kiss your Spitfire, goodbye.'

'Crowman, if I crash my Spitfire, will I go to heaven?' chirped Michael.

'No, Michael. Heaven is that way.' Pavel pointed to the ceiling. 'Don't crash your Spitfire, keep it at the correct speed. You need to fly up through the clouds, to the blue skies. Because flying a Spitfire is heaven,' he smiled.

Michael relaxed and returned the smile. 'Can we keep our Spitfires, please?'

'Of course. They are yours now.'

After Pavel left, they studied each gauge on the panel. Flying in the cockpit was beautiful. When Miro got home in the evening, Simone told him to pop his head into the boys' bedroom. There they were, under the covers and fast asleep, huddled close to their Spitfire cockpits.

Theo was not doing well in school. He was bored, uninspired, under-challenged. He wanted more science, world geography and especially astronomy. His creative mind yearned to give classroom talks on the animals he had encountered in Africa, his exploding experiments in his lab at home, or how the radioactive decay of radium could be observed with a spinthariscope. He was always in some sort of trouble with the mediocre teachers and the principal, that tyrannical man from the American South, The Reverend Berkeley Ulysses Grundy. Theo resisted going home straight after school so he could play with a friend or watch the older kids during their after-school activities. Grundy made a walking inspection of the school grounds at the close of each day, his forest of keys dangling from a large loop and the whole apparatus tucked inside his pant pocket. As this Presbyterian tormenter from the Bible Belt, lord and master of his realm, did the rounds, he would jingle the keys in his pocket with vigour. It became a reliable signal that he was approaching. Theo would slip away to hide, praying that the battleship, USS Mississippi, would sail past with its radar turned off.

Theo sat once on a corrugated tin roof, using it as an inconspicuous perch to watch a handful of boys playing a friendly game of basketball. Grundy spotted him. His booming voice filled the open-air court. 'Theo Novotny, go home!' he bellowed in his deep Southern accent. Going home meant facing the dreaded homework.

One afternoon, during a fourth-grade class in session, Grundy marched in without first knocking, spotted a comic book sticking out from under a student's textbook and swooped down on the offending piece of literature, tearing it up for all to see. Theo's class was hushed into terror while the sound of the ripping seemed to make the walls reverberate. Comic books and bubble gum had no place in Grundy's kingdom. It did not dawn inside his hardboiled brain that, in a school where half the students didn't have English as their mother tongue, reading comics might create an English foundation for further reading development.

Theo was fascinated by his hero, Captain Marvel. Each month, he would use his pocket money to buy the latest issue of Fawcett Comics featuring the exploits of Captain Marvel. He would imagine he was the boy, Billy Batson, Captain Marvel's alter ego, who would transform himself into his idol by shouting out *SHAZAM!* acronym for six immortals—Solomon, Hercules, Atlas, Zeus, Achilles, and Mercury. This would turn him into a super-powered adult in bright red costume with gold trim and a yellow lightning bolt emblazoned on his chest. Captain Marvel fights injustice and evil and his arch-enemy is the mad scientist, Doctor Sivana. Theo could easily imagine Grundy as the evil Doctor Sivana.

Wednesday afternoon was Movie Day and the punishments on that day were legendary. Just before the school-wide screening of Donald Duck or Mickey Mouse cartoons in the assembly hall, Grundy would call forth all who had misbehaved during the previous week. He would have them line up in a single-file phalanx facing the seated students, then make them turn around, stand behind the projection screen and face the wall, while the remaining pupils watched the fare of cartoons imported from the United States. Theo was a frequent visitor to the wall of shame in the hall of infamy.

End of each term, Theo would come home with a dismal report card. Michael was now attending the same school, and his report cards put him ahead of his older brother. But Theo had an ace up his sleeve. His strands of DNA had copied Simone's ability to soak up languages. Winning English spelling bees and reading or writing Persian came easy.

Language aside, French class ripened into Theo's crush on his Swiss-born French teacher who had the head of Athena and the figure of Aphrodite. Mademoiselle Labelle.

She was testing the class, one day, on conjugation of verbs. Each pupil got a different verb.

'Theo, conjugate the verb, *to love.*'

A golden gift landed in Theo's lap:

'Je t'aime'—I love you; *'tu m'aime'*—you love me; *'elle m'aime'*—she loves me; *'nous nous aimons'*—we love each other.'

'Theo-o-o! *Qu'est-ce que c'est ça?'*—what is this? 'This is not the way to conjugate, *to love.*'

Inside, Theo twinkled with mirth. The class erupted in fits of giggles.

'I want to see you after class.'

'Oui, Mademoiselle Labelle,' he grinned.

'Simonko, would you and the boys like to fly to the Caspian for a few days?' Pavel was visiting. He needed to get to an air strip there to fix an aircraft with engine problems. 'I'm taking two mechanics with me and I got the company's approval to fly you as passengers.'

'You really mean it? Will this cost us a lot?' she asked.

'The flight there and back will cost you nothing. Three or four extra bodies make no difference. The cost comes with having a grounded aircraft sitting idle at the Caspian. Can Miro come too?'

The boys were over the moon. Their chance to fly in a DC-3, with Crowman at the controls! Miro was too busy to take time off, and he thanked Pavel for giving them this opportunity.

As they flew north from Tehran, over the mountains, Simone pointed out the Bride of the Gods. It looked so different from this high up. Pavel's co-pilot got out of his seat so the boys could sit in the cockpit for a while. All the fabulous instruments were in front of them, working, showing what the aircraft was doing.

Theo piped up. 'Crowman, make sure we never, never let our air speed fall below eighty miles per hour.' Pavel broke into a very surprised grin. *Lesson well learnt.*

'Tango, you're a born pilot.'

'Me, too,' chimed Michael.

'You too, Mamba.' Pavel smiled. He could see that Michael was mesmerised by the working instruments.

Soon, they were over the greenery of the Caspian rain forest. It looked like Africa after the rainy season. Pavel made his approach to the grass landing strip, but there were cows on it. Pointing the aircraft parallel to the strip, he made a shallow dive towards the cows, hoping the engine noise would frighten them away. Some of the cows scuttled off, but a few that were chewing their cud didn't seem bothered. Pavel put the nose up and began a go-around to try another landing attempt. This time, he came in lower to make the engine noise louder to the cows. Still two animals would not budge. He climbed once again and began circling the air strip. At last, a cowherd showed up and used his stick to poke the cows off the strip. When they touched down and rolled along the grassy strip, Simone and the boys broke into a loud cheer and clapped.

She hired a long-distance taxi and took the boys to the Caspian seaside. Three days was all they had to get back to the air strip. Pavel had fixed the engine problem and made a test flight to check out the grounded aircraft. Then, they flew back to Tehran in their DC-3.

Michael and Theo came home before school ended for the day. They had taken a taxi.

'Mama! Theo broke his arm!'

'What?' Simone came running.

'Mum, it's not broken,' Theo insisted. 'I just sprained it. It's nothing. See?' and he gave the arm a gentle shake. It was a grotesque sight, a broken tree branch. He had fractured his radius. She went out to the street and hailed a taxi, then hurried with Theo to their family physician.

'What exactly were you doing?' she asked Theo.

Theo was high jumping at the school playground and landed on his wrist. His arm broadcast an audible snap and the gym teacher sent him to the principal's office. When they got to the doctor, the nurse laid Theo on a surgical bed, placed a wad of cotton wool on his air passages and sprayed it with ether. He felt a choking sensation and wanted to tear the mask away, but his hands had been tied down. Soon he was in an unconscious world and when he woke up, a plaster cast was on his arm. They went home in a taxi and Theo vomited on the floor of the car.

In early November, Miro took a telephone call in his office. A member of the Czech Club was phoning. Miro listened to the news and said very little. He hung up and hurried home. The ride home seemed to gobble time. His mind was struggling, his thoughts jumbled.

Simone was surprised. 'You're home early! Guess what. Michael got his school grades today and you'll ...' She looked at him. 'Miro, what's wrong?'

He wore an unrecognisably disquieting expression that sent chills through her body. She had never seen this on him. It was like the stare of a zombie.

'Come outside with me, please.'

'Miro, is it bad news?'

'I don't know how to say it. Pavel had to fly down to Shiraz to deliver aircraft spare parts. His plane never made it. They got into a sandstorm and crashed just a few minutes from landing. He and his two passengers and co-pilot were killed.' His lips began to quiver. 'He's gone. We've lost him. Our friend is...' Tears formed.

'What?' she screamed. 'This can't be true!'

Simone's face went to stone. The blood in her cheeks seemed black. She burst into a passion of sobs, launching herself into Miro and pounding his chest with her fists a dozen times. 'No, no, no. It's not true! Tell me it's a lie, it's a lie!'

The Czechoslovak community held a funeral service at the Roman Catholic church. Even some of the communist Czechoslovak expatriates attended.

'Do you want to come to the burial?' Miro asked Simone.

'No. I don't. I don't like burials. There is evil in the air and it descends on the next person to die. I begin to think, "Who will it be? Who will be next?"'

'Should I take the boys?'

'No, Miro. Please don't. Let them remember the good times with him.'

'Out of respect, do you mind if I go?'

Simone began weeping. She shook her head many times. 'No. You go ahead. You're our brave one.'

It took her a long time. Her spirit had been sucked out and the vacuum was excruciating. He was gone. Her dashing Battle of Britain flying ace, her raconteur, masterful dancer, picnic partner, entertainer and private boyfriend was gone. Her soulmate had left life, unmarried, no children, all turned to nothing. Like so many in his 341 Squadron, his luck had run out, shot down, not by a Messerschmitt, but by a sandstorm. *Pavel was right. Nothing is forever.*

Chapter 14

'Miro, I want to move out of here.'

'Move out of this home? Where to?'

'Please, a small house, away from here. Somewhere close to downtown.'

'I'll try. But it will take time.'

She hugged him a tight hug. 'Miro, sweetheart, don't leave me. Never, never leave me. Please?'

'Why would I leave you? I don't understand.'

'You know what I mean. Do you promise?'

He realised that Pavel had left. He tried to take her mind off all this. They soon found a tiny house to rent, with a small garden and a lone persimmon tree, and tiny decorative pool that every house seemed to have in its courtyard. It was in an older, established neighbourhood, on a very quiet street lined with mature plane trees. On one side, their neighbours were an Armenian family and, on the other, lived a general in the Shah's army. They were well protected. Theo and Michael could walk to school.

Theo was thrown out of school. It was a violent expulsion. During class, one morning, a student's pencil had rolled off her desk, fallen to the floor, and kept rolling towards Theo. He reached down, picked it up and handed it back. She thanked him.

'Theo Novotny! I've had enough of your talking. Come to the front.'

The homeroom teacher, Mr. MacAskill, was yelling. He was the school's one-armed bandit. As an American soldier, he had lost an arm during WWII. It was replaced with a steel one, and the fake hand was covered with a grey, leather glove. His badge of glory was a nervous temperament, decorated with intolerance and angst.

'Take this Blue Book and go see the principal!'

Theo reported to the principal's office. Grundy wasn't there so he sat down and waited. The huge grandfather clock on the office floor had an ominous tick-tock, its swinging pendulum stretching out every frightened second before Grundy would appear and judge. Theo heard his heart pounding on the door, howling to be let out. The clock hands crept unstoppably towards the moment of punishment. *Execution will surely be swift.*

'Theo Novotny, why are you not in class?'

'Mr. MacAskill sent me down to see you, sir.'

Grundy opened the Blue Book and read the pencilled comment from MacAskill. Theo had no chance to explain the rolling pencil. Grundy slapped him across the face and sent Theo flying to the floor. As he struggled to stand up, Grundy kicked him hard, then pushed him through the office door and into the hallway.

'Get out of my school! Bitchin' trouble maker. Out. Go home and don't come back.'

He kept kicking Theo as the boy walked backwards towards the school portal, trying to shield himself from further blows. Theo's back collided with the screen door behind him. He swung it open and fled the punishment. He did not go home right away. He wandered the streets, plucking up the courage to ring the house doorbell and give the bad news.

'Mum, I wanted to be a gentleman. You told me to be kind. I was trying to help her. I wasn't talking in class.' Simone understood. She gave him a hug. 'You're not angry?'

'I'm not angry. But I think Dad will not take this well.'

'Mum, you remember the book you showed me, *The Boy Who Breathed on the Glass*—'

'*In the British Museum*? Um hm, I do.'

'They are punishing me the way they punished that boy, just for breathing on the museum glass.'

Miro was angry. Trying to explain the rolling pencil was pointless. He had been kicked out of school. That was shame enough on the family. Theo was confined to his room for ten days, bicycle taken away. He had gone to prison, it seemed to him, for breathing on the glass.

Simone let things linger for a day. Then, 'Miro, I need to talk to you.'

'About?'

'About Theo.'

'And what's on your mind?'

'Miro, you're being too harsh on him. He is a gentleman, but you don't see it that way. You're always praising Michael because he comes home with good grades, but you're being too focused on grades. Theo has good qualities, too.'

'And he got expelled from school.'

'He is brilliant in languages, you know that. Persian, Czech, French. He's talented in writing. He wins English spelling bees, he won a class prize for writing a—'

'Yes, I hear you. He gets his language talents from you, but that doesn't excuse his bad behaviour in school.'

'He thinks you don't like him. As much as you like Michael.'

'Of course, I like him. I love him.'

'You don't show it. Show him the love of a proud father.'

'What, I got him a Meccano set so he could build models, and I always praise his inventive constructions. He built a replica of the Eiffel Tower. It teaches patience and persistence and manual dexterity.'

'You bought him Meccano because you wanted to keep

him busy and stay out of trouble. That's practical stuff. That's not love.'

'And what is *love*?'

'Love him the way you love me. *Show* him some fatherly love. He looks up to you, but he's scared of you.' Miro went silent. Simone cut into his thoughts. 'Hug him, kiss him, praise him. Not only when he has achieved something. Show him constant fatherly love.'

'Constant fatherly love. Hm.'

'Czechs show emotion, don't they? I saw it all the time when we were living there.' She laid a soft hand on his shoulder. 'Don't make him go to that principal by himself and apologise. Go with him and talk to the man. He was treated very unfairly.'

School friends showed up, tapping on the window pane of Theo's room which faced the street.

'Hey, Theo. How are you?' The hushed voice belonged to a classmate.

'I'm not supposed to see anyone. I can't talk to you.'

'When are you coming back to school?'

Theo shrugged. He feared Miro would make him go to the principal, apologise and beg to be readmitted. The thought of grovelling to the Presbyterian dictator with the deep, Southern drawl was so humiliating that he banished it from his boyish shoulders. *Why should I apologise? I was punched and kicked for helping a classmate.*

Eventually the day came. Theo was in the principal's office. 'Mr. Grundy, sir. My father said I'm sorry.'

Grundy burst out laughing. 'Your *father* said you're sorry. What about *you*?'

'Mr. Grundy, sir. Do you hate me because my parents came from a communist country? Because you hate communists? Don't Christians preach forgiveness?'

Grundy was stupefied. Wavering embarrassment washed across his face like a spent wave drenching a littered beach.

This was the McCarthy era in the United States. Senator Joseph McCarthy was conducting demagogic witch-hunts for suspected communists inside America that reached a paranoia of accusations and blacklisting.

Grundy penned a note for Theo's homeroom teacher and signed it with his initials, BUG. Having dealt with the evil Doctor Sivana, Theo was readmitted and sent off to his classroom.

When he showed up in class, the entire room was floating in welcoming smiles. Theo was wearing a bright red pullover with the yellow, *SHAZAM!* lightning bolt knitted on the chest. Captain Marvel was back.

While Theo was grounded at home, Setareh would steal into his room and bring goodies she had baked for him. She felt sorry for the boy. He could have been her own son. The Novotnys had hired Setareh as a live-in maid and she was a genius. She taught Theo and Michael to speak Persian, and learned to cook the Czechoslovak dishes that Simone prepared, even the cakes and desserts. She was a chain-smoker of the cheapest, unfiltered cigarettes produced in Iran, but nobody seemed to mind.

Setareh had been married off at the age of nine, to a man five times her years. But when she was in her late-teens, her husband dumped her and went looking for another child-bride. He said Setareh had become too assertive, too smart. Her name was the Persian word for *star*. She had twice his intelligence but ended up with no children, no future, no family. She had hardly known her parents and didn't know whether they were still alive.

Setareh was illiterate, committed everything she saw and heard to memory. When signing an official document, she would use her inked thumbprint. Nobody knew her exact age. She had no birth certificate, no identity documents. To the Novotnys, she looked forty-something. On Thursday evenings, Setareh would leave for the weekend and go home, two hours away by bus, and be back on Saturday mornings at 5 a.m.

Setareh approached Simone one day. 'Khānom, an American family has asked me to work for them. To be their live-in maid.'

Simone's cheeks went pale. 'How sad for us.' Her mind was struggling with this news. 'But it will be good money for you. The Americans pay very well and they—'

'Khānom, I told them 'no.''

'You said 'no' to them?'

'Khānom, I don't want to leave you.'

'Uhhh.' She heaved a merciful sigh. 'You are so sweet. We want you to stay.'

Christmas came and Theo's misadventures had boiled away in the cauldron of the past. Miro took Theo to midnight mass at the city's Catholic church. They walked the five kilometres in sub-zero temperatures, and Theo could feel the sting of winter biting his ears. Miro was a great walker, strong legs, long strides, hurried pace, honed by years of twelve-kilometre walks through the morning ground fog that veiled the wheat and potato fields of Slavkov to get to school and back. Every few blocks, Theo would have to shift into higher gear in order to catch up with his dad.

Simone found four hard-cover books under the tree. Miro and the boys had gone to a street behind the British Embassy where enterprising vendors sold freshly harvested pine trees to Christian expatriates and Eurocentric Persian families during the festive season. Their spruced-up tree was a forest of dangling, crescent-shaped vanilla rolls and gingerbread hearts, baked by Setareh and decorated with icing.

The boys got roller skates. They skated up and down every street and alley in the neighbourhood. They played with the White Russian boys whose parents had fled the Soviet Union, and Theo soon learned enough Russian to understand his street pals and tell them about Africa. It made for a safe game of multicultural comradeship. Theo would come home and tell his parents about Russian tanks, and Russian warplanes, and soldiers with fixed bayonets standing on a dead German in uniform and planting a red flag on a pole through the German's skull. And Simone and Miro asked where he got all this.

'The Russian boys invited me to their home and showed me their children's books.'

Chapter 15

Spring was jump-started by the Persian New Year and Setareh invited the family for tea to her shabbily furnished, one-bedroom dwelling in the south of Tehran. When Simone, Miro and the boys showed up, they could not believe what they were offered. Setareh had baked a huge cake according to a Czechoslovak recipe and it was covered in a chocolate icing topped with pistachios and walnuts. How she had managed this was discussed in the family for months afterwards. That was the chain-smoking, illiterate genius with a phenomenal memory.

Some nights later, the skies were clear and Miro took the family to the outskirts of Tehran, up in the foothills away from city lights. 'Okay boys, tonight we name a constellation after Setareh. As we know, *Setareh* means *star*, so, very appropriate.'

The boys were thrilled about an excursion into astronomy, led by their stargazing dad.

'Right. Theo, Michael, can you spot the Big Dipper?' The boys found it. 'And you know that the two bright stars on the outside of the pot are Merak and Dubhe?' Miro pointed the narrow beam of his torch to the two stars.

'They point to the North Star,' said Michael.

'Yah! They locate Polaris,' added Theo.

'Good. Now let's keep going in a straight line from Merak and Dubhe, past Polaris.' Miro scanned the torch beam in a straight line towards the constellation Cassiopeia. 'Recognise this group of stars?'

Simone piped up to help the boys. 'Looks like a capital *M* or, the other way around, like a *W*.'

'Isn't that Cassiopeia?' wondered Theo. Simone patted his back and then turned to her other son. '*M* is for Michael and *W* is a double *you*! You and you.' She poked a teasing finger into Michael's neck.

'That's right,' said Miro. 'And if we continue just a little bit further, still in a straight line, we get to ...'

The three of them went silent.

'That is Andromeda, Cassiopeia's daughter!'

They laughed. 'Do constellations have mothers and daughters?' asked Michael.

Miro smiled. 'Those names come from Greek mythology and Cassiopeia was Andromeda's mother.'

'Dad, who was Andromeda's father?' Theo was curious.

'Andromeda's father was Cepheus, an Ethiopian king. Andromeda was very beautiful and married Perseus, who fell in love with her after he found her naked and chained to a sea cliff and rescued her. They're all up there as constellations, thanks to Poseidon, god of the sea. But, let's get back to astronomy. Between Cassiopeia and Andromeda, we have a galaxy, like our own galaxy, the Milky Way. It's faint, but you can just make it out. See?' He pointed the beam on that spot and wavered it a bit.

'What's that called?' Michael held his breath.

'That's the Andromeda galaxy. It's more than two *million* light years from Earth.'

They gave a gasp of astonishment. 'It took that many years to reach us?' wondered Simone.

'It took the light from the Andromeda galaxy that long to get here. And we know that nothing can travel faster than light. Right, Theo? So, imagine how far away it is. If something happened in the galaxy, this moment, we wouldn't find out for another 2.5 million years.' They took it in and heard each other's breaths.

The stars were twinkling brighter than ever, now. 'That's a long, long, long time,' sighed Michael. *Would I have enough patience to wait that long?*

'And another thing. How many stars in the Andromeda galaxy? Theo? Michael?' They both shrugged.

'Shall we start counting?' teased Simone. 'Tell us, Miro.'

'You ready for this? Take a deep breath. One *trillion* stars.'

'Wow! How many zeroes, Dad?' Theo tried to imagine the number.

'One, followed by twelve zeroes. A million million.'

Simone smiled at the boys. 'Big numbers!'

'Now, take a look here,' continued Miro. 'There's a group of stars between the constellations Andromeda and Cassiopeia. See?' He pointed to the group and used the torch to trace an outline of them. 'Looks like a poodle with a long nose.' The three of them giggled.

'Shall we call it the Poodle?' snickered Theo.

'Ah, no. We will make it into a new constellation in honour of Setareh.'

'And what do we call it, Miro?' Simone's brow lifted like a wispy cloud.

'We'll name the constellation *Setareh Borealis*!'

The joy of approval was palpable. Simone could poke her teasing finger into it. They sent a boisterous cheer into the night air, and it carried up to the stars.

'While we ponder all this, let's think about the stars,' Miro expanded. The occasion was right. 'They say, "nothing as true as the stars above." Why do they say this?'

Silence followed. 'Tell us, Dad.' Theo wanted the answer.

'They are true because they are unchanging. You can rely on the stars. They will be up there in the sky, when you look tomorrow and next year and in a thousand years. And they have been there for thousands of years. They guided the sailors and explorers who sailed at night without a compass. And if you get lost on a clear night you will always know which way is north, or south. True north, true south, true as the stars.'

'What if there isn't a clear night?' chirped Theo.

'Then you will need a compass.' And they all laughed.

Simone was exploring her new neighbourhood and soon became a regular patron at the local butcher, greengrocer, dairy shop, and chemist. She expected honesty and good service and if she didn't get it, the Esther gambit would be deployed. The grapevine took care of things: 'Don't cheat *Khānom* Simone, or you will face her wrath.' Simone came in one day to buy beef. The butcher began to slice the meat off a cow carcass hanging from a meat hook in his shop.

She shouted at him. 'No! You are giving me too much fat with those cuts. I don't want this.'

Once a local merchant could be trusted, Simone didn't buy anywhere else. *Keep the corner store and small shopkeeper in business.* That was her mantra. Loyalty is a two-way street.

Theo came home from roller skating in the street. He was too lazy to remove his skates at the door, so he decided to come downstairs to the kitchen, wearing his skates. It didn't work. He slipped and fell a full flight of stairs, hitting his forehead on the steel-reinforced edge of a concrete step. There was blood everywhere, but he didn't say a word and got himself up to skate to the kitchen. Setareh almost fainted when she saw the blood pouring from his brow and down his face. She grabbed a kitchen towel and called out to Simone, who rushed him to the doctor, where he got five stitches over his eye and a good telling off for trying to negotiate concrete stairs in roller skates.

'Theo,' said Simone, trying not to scold too much because he was already hurt. 'How, *ever*, did I manage to lay an egg like you?'

'Is that what Grandma Esther used to say?'

'No. That's what *I'm* saying to you.'

Another Friday. It would not be long before school was out for the summer. For Theo, time to learn new things that didn't get graded on a report card. A blissful reprieve from The Reverend was around the corner. The battleship of the Bible Belt would be at anchor for the next three months.*If only a Catholic commando frogman would read my thoughts and foul up the ship's propeller shafts with bubble gum!*

Michael and Theo were listening to short-wave radio

on the family's Swedish-made Radiola. It was a square wooden box, plywood veneer, with a Cyclops eye that glowed green from a radio tube inside. The tuner had a dial with a needle that swept across a glass screen in this wave band and the screen was imprinted with station names that seemed so exotic: Minsk, Helsingfors, Malmö, Omsk, Rostov, Tallinn, Uppsala. They knew nothing of these places. Warbles, hisses, squawks and radio static came out of the speaker as the tuning dial was turned. Suddenly, there was nothing. Total quiet. Then, a signal shattered the silence:

'Di-di-dit, dah-dah-dah, di-di-dit ...Di-di-dit, dah-dah-dah, di-di-dit ...Di-di-dit, dah-dah-dah, di-di-dit ...'

Michael froze. He had no idea why the radio was doing this. Theo was fascinated. He knew Morse code from Boy Scouts. He dashed upstairs.

'Mum, someone's sending a distress signal! Come quick, listen. It's an SOS.'

The SOS in dots and dashes was repeated several dozen times. Then, it was followed by a stream of code, too quick for Theo to decipher it.

'What do you think it is?' she asked.

'Someone's in trouble. Maybe a ship that's sinking, like the *Titanic*.'

'Poor souls. I wonder where they are. I hope they're not over deep water somewhere. I hate deep water.'

'Why?'

'It's too deep.'

'But you know how to swim.'

'Never mind, sweetheart. Keep listening. Maybe we can figure out where they are and what happened. Why don't you teach Michael the Morse code? Then the two of you can send each other coded messages on Dad's typewriter.'

'Mum, Dad's typewriter doesn't have a dash, it's Czech.'

Simone fished under the desk in the living room and took off the typewriter cover. 'Yes, it does. Look. See?'

'Mum, that's not a dash. That's a hyphen.'

'Grruhhh!'

On went the radio: '*Di-di-dit, dah-dah-dah, di-di-dit ... Di-di-dit, dah-dah-dah ...*'

Summer approached. A long weekend came up and the Novotnys decided to hire a long-distance taxi and spend the break at a mountain resort. They gave Setareh the three days off and she went home. When they got back, they were appalled to find the house had been ransacked. Chests of drawers had been looted, empty drawers were everywhere on the floor, Persian carpets were missing, locked cupboards had been broken into, the gramophone was gone, knives were missing from the kitchen, Simone's jewellery box was empty, Miro's stamp albums were on the floor, the British colonial stamps from Africa scattered across the living room.

Everything had been tampered with except for the wooden voodoo carvings from Kenya. The bust of the Madagascar woman, carved from teak, stood there on the bookshelf, staring at the scene of the crime. She must have frightened the burglar.

Marek's framed postcard was still on the dressing table. Beirut was staring at Simone. The wedding photo was missing. *Bizarre! Is he still alive?*

Miro went to the police, next day, accompanied by a business associate who could translate for him. He reported the burglary and the police said they would come the following day to inspect the scene and look for evidence. Next morning, a police officer showed up and questioned Simone and Setareh. Did anyone else have keys to the house? Had Simone mentioned to anyone that they would be away for three days? How did Setareh come and go? Where was she during those three days? How many house keys did she have made? Setareh replied that she had two keys cut for her own use, but she could not remember what had happened to the second one.

The officer said that Setareh would have to come to the police station for further questioning. Setareh began to tremble.

'She's not going anywhere without me. I'm coming with her.'

At the police station, the officer continued grilling

Setareh. She was intimidated by the accusatory tone of the interrogator. She began to cry.

The man turned to Simone and said, 'Your servant will have to remain in custody. We will not release her until we have questioned her further.'

The police wanted to show they were keen to find the culprit in the burglary. It was easy to pin something on a defenceless, illiterate woman.

'Not while I'm alive will she be put behind bars!' snapped Simone.

The officer replied, '*Khānom*, if you want us to pursue this case, we have to hold your servant until we find out more.'

'If that's what you will do, then I don't want this case pursued any longer,' said Simone.

'*Khānom*, we cannot proceed if you do not cooperate.'

'I want you to drop this investigation. You are suspecting the wrong person. She had nothing to do with the burglary.'

'You will have to sign a declaration that you want us to release your servant and drop this case. Do you understand this? We can no longer try to recover your stolen goods.'

'I will sign. Right here and now. She's coming back home with me.'

They got up to leave and Setareh fell to her knees and wrapped her arms around Simone's legs. 'Thank you, *Khānom* Simone,' she sobbed.

Embarrassment churned inside Simone's breast. She reached down and lifted Setareh off the floor. 'Setareh, please, there is no need for this. I don't suspect you. You are a wonderful person.'

Chapter 16

Miro came home and trumpeted, 'I've applied for Iranian citizenship. We've done the required residency of eight years, so we qualify.'

'You mean, we can get passports again?' a smile began its curl round Simone's lips.

'I can't see why not.'

'Woweeee! We can start travelling!'

During the early years, Miro relied on the Unireifen people to visit Iran and help with market development. They were keen to road test various Unireifen designs on the widely dissimilar surfaces and conditions of Iranian roads: snow, ice, mud, sand, gravel, asphalt, and extremes of road surface temperatures. Miro had mastered the matching of tyres to surfaces, but Unireifen aimed to upgrade his skills and knowledge on the technical side of tyre construction and design. As soon as he could travel, they wanted him to visit the German plants and learn how tyres were lab-tested for specific road conditions and surfaces.

The family got their citizenship papers and passports. When school was out for the summer holidays, they packed and headed for Europe. Setareh was asked to live in the house and look after the daily household tasks. Simone gave her sufficient cash to keep the place running and feed herself. Setareh wrapped the money in a newspaper and buried it inside a pile of charcoal behind the kitchen door. There, at the bottom of the dusty, black pile, she found that second house key. Closed her fist around it and began to sob.

A very different world opened up to them. After eight years in post-war Persia, visiting Europe seemed like entering a storybook about fanciful castles in a modern fairyland. Public parks and gardens were rain-washed to a luxuriant green. The electric trams, trolleys, and high-speed trains made everything compact and accessible. There were coin-operated telephone booths in the street. The roads were a forest of traffic signs. The gothic cathedrals had outlandishly tall spires. The marble or bronze statues of horses and naked human torsos erected in city squares were sculpted marvels. And the water that flowed out of taps was safe.

Geneva came first. The family called in at the headquarters of the United Nations High Commissioner for Refugees, successor to the International Refugee

Organisation, to pay their respects. Miro never forgot a group or person who had helped his family in difficult times. Later, they took a steamer cruise around Lake Geneva and travelled by coach, through the Alps, to Zürich. There, they visited the Zürich Zoo and met Heini Hediger, the father of zoo biology and director of the zoo. His ideas had a world-wide impact on the design of zoos and wherever animals were kept in human care.

The boys told him about their wild animal adventures in Kenya. The driver ants, the jellyfish, the python, the poor rabbits, and the herds they spotted as they travelled by train. And that crocodile at Kilifi Creek. Hediger smiled broadly and listened with great interest, then gave each of them a *Special Visitor* pin to commemorate their zoo outing. The boys wore their pins to show off their daring African escapades.

They were now so close to Czechoslovakia. Distance-wise, it would have been nothing to get there. Simone yearned to see Milena again.

'Miro, let's go there and try to find Marek.' Her heart skipped a beat at the sound of his name.

'Who knows if the poor fellow is still alive.'

'I know he is. I can feel it. It wouldn't be hard to find him.'

But Miro was firm. He gave Simone his catalogue of reasons: they would not go there and spend their tourist Swiss francs and German marks, precious foreign exchange needed by a socialist regime that was hanging the Czechoslovak nation with the rope of censorship. The Communist regime might find some twisted reason to hold him if they held files on him as a supporter of the underground Free-Czechoslovakia Movement. They could pin on him the accusation that he was a foreigner who had come into the country to stir up political trouble and engage in subversive activities. That would be reason enough to arrest and jail him.

'Miro, I think you are being paranoid. You hold a Persian passport. Czechoslovakia has good relations with Iran.' She waited for his reaction. Nothing came her way. He was playing backgammon where *his* dice were loaded.

While the family waited in Switzerland, Miro went off to Germany to meet with Unireifen management and receive technical training in their tyre-testing laboratories. When Miro came back, he had surprising news. Unireifen had offered him a position in Canada. They were impressed with his ability to develop a difficult market under trying circumstances, in a developing country. Unireifen was expanding its operations in Canada and building a tyre factory in Ontario. Would he be interested in moving there? There was a growing demand for truck and car tyres that could take the punishing Canadian winters and the wilderness roads, especially in Canada's Far North. They needed a technical person who would spearhead the tyre testing and tread design phases of production.

'Oh, my goodness,' Simone reacted. 'Canada is so cold.'

'I didn't commit myself. I told them I would need to think about it. It's funny how one gets attached to a place. I do love Iran, you know.'

'It's more exotic and foreign than Canada, isn't it?'

Miro smiled. 'Exotic. Good word.'

She continued. 'Europe is so tidy, precise and clean and organised. But Iran is so friendly, and welcoming, and fickle. And at ease. It's the saffron glowing on a plateful of Persian rice.'

They set off for England. At their Fox Hunt Hotel, in Kent, they saw a television set for the first time. It was July, and the black-and-white TV in the hotel lounge was tuned to the Wimbledon tennis final. A thirty-two-year-old Czechoslovak called Jaroslav Drobný was playing a nineteen-year-old Australian called Ken Rosewall. Miro had to watch. Here was his countryman who had defected from Communist Czechoslovakia and was playing for Egypt, because they had offered the stateless tennis player Egyptian citizenship. Drobný won the championship in a match that lasted two hours thirty-seven minutes, the longest final in Wimbledon's fabled history. Miro was delighted. Later, he came across

Drobný's recollections after the Russian soldiers of the Red Army had taken over the tennis player's hometown of Prague, in 1945: *They came to Prague like a plague of locusts, with the manners and appearance of tramps. Private property meant nothing to them.*

London beckoned and Simone saw her chance to make a historic pilgrimage to Trafalgar Square and the monument to one of her cherished heroes, Vice-Admiral Horatio Lord Nelson. At the huge plaza, made even larger by the two giant fountains, Theo looked up at the ludicrously high column and spied the man of marble standing atop it, sword in hand.

'Mum, who's that?'

'That's Lord Nelson, dear.'

'Who's Lord Nelson?'

'He's my hero.'

'Why is his one arm so skinny?'

'He lost his right arm in battle and that's just the hollow sleeve of his coat hanging down.'

'So, he couldn't write anymore?'

'He learned to write with his left hand. Remind me to tell you the whole story when we get back to our hotel. Yes?'

They walked to Piccadilly Circus and the broad daylight was made even brighter with dancing commercial signs blinking their messages and changing colours: PAL razors, and Gordon's London Gin, Wrigley's 'Healthful, Delicious, Satisfying' chewing gum, Player's cigarettes, and Martini vermouth. High-spirited fluorescence like this had not yet travelled to Persia.

Simone revelled in the bookshops. They went shopping at Swan & Edgar to buy colourful blouses, scarfs and skirts for Setareh. Visited Lilywhites, to get soccer boots for Michael and spiked running shoes for Theo's track and field.

The four of them entered Piccadilly Circus station on the London Underground. They were heading for London Zoo, at Regent's Park, just two stations away on the Bakerloo Line. Michael and Theo ran ahead.

'I know which way! Follow me!' cried Michael. The boys reached the wrong platform, and jumped into the waiting train, expecting Simone and Miro to be right behind them.

'Mind the doors, please!' called the platform guard.

The sliding doors shut and Michael and Theo stared at each other, dumbfounded. The train started moving and their parents were left behind. When it reached Elephant & Castle station, they knew they were headed the wrong way. They got out and studied the Tube map.

'Come!' said Michael. 'We'll switch to the Northern Line and go to King's Cross St. Pancras. Then we'll take the Piccadilly Line back to Piccadilly Circus.'

When they got to King's Cross St. Pancras, they

scurried off to another platform, but didn't check the signs. Off they went on the Piccadilly Line, in the wrong direction, northbound, towards Holloway Road, Arsenal and Finsbury Park. By the time they were back at Piccadilly Circus station, ninety minutes had passed.

'Let's go look for Mum and Dad,' said Theo.

Simone had turned sickly-pale with anxiety. She and Miro were waiting at the station entrance and the stationmaster had advised them to stay put.

'Your boys know how to read. They'll find their way back. The Tube's the best system in the world,' he declared.

'I'm sorry, Mum,' said Theo.

She didn't need apologies. She wanted her boys back, and they were there. There would be no Esther-style telling off.

Miro was ruffled. 'Theo, Michael. We stay together. We *always* stay together, understand?'

Back at their hotel, when the boys were asleep, Simone cuddled up to Miro.

'What do you think about that Canada offer?' she asked.

'I don't know. It's a huge change. I know the Iran market so well now. I wonder how useful to them I would be in Canada.'

'Will it affect the boys?' she probed, combing her fingers through his hair.

'Yeah, that's another thing. We don't need to decide right away. Come kiss me and do what you do best. You're the best wife in the world.'

'You too.'

'I'm a wife?'

She tapped her forehead against his. 'Silly, you know what I mean.'

Chapter 17

They came back to Persia, land of persimmon, pistachios, pomegranates, quince, roses, and pālūdeh, that divine dessert made from frozen noodles flavoured with rose water, lime juice, and sugar. Once again, the minarets were singing. The mullahs were calling the faithful to prayer and the loudspeakers spread the word as far as the soundwaves would carry. Brand-new, hand-woven silk and wool Persian carpets were spread out on city avenues to hurry their ageing, as thousands of car and truck tyres ran over them. Soon, they would become well-worn antiques and fetch a higher price.

The bazaars were alive with goldfish, goats and goat's cheese. The tea houses were serving chicken with long-grain rice pilaf, topped with barberry, *zereshk*, and saffron. The year's first crops of fresh walnuts were peeled to their white, jellylike flesh and held together with matchsticks and wood slivers. The walnuts sat there on ice, and the evening's shoppers and casual strollers would buy and eat for a few rials a bag.

The wine harvest was nearing, and the vintners and wine stores, owned and run by Armenians, would have their shelves stocked with Shiraz reds and Cabernets.

Setareh was delighted with the London clothes. She would try on each item, in turn, then stand in front of Simone and say, 'You are so kind. It suits me, doesn't it?'

Each time, Simone would answer, 'Yes. You look beautiful in it.'

But nobody outside the house would see her new clothes. When Setareh left to go shopping or travel home, she wore a body-length *chādor* which hid everything but her face, the Islamic dress code for women that emphasised modesty. Her *chādors* were light coloured with floral patterns. She didn't look like a walking crow, as some women did with their black *chādors*.

Setareh was sent to buy a watermelon. When she came home, they sliced it open and it was pinkish and not sweet.

'Setareh, where did you get this?' asked Simone.

'From our greengrocer, *khānom*, the usual place.'

Simone stuffed the two halves of the melon into a string shopping net and marched back to the shop.

'Shame on you!' she told the shopkeeper. 'Look at what you've sold me.'

'*Bebakhshīd, khānom*' forgive me, madam. To save face, he turned to his assistant. 'Why did you sell such a bad watermelon to the *khānom*? You should know better!'

He walked over to a huge pyramid of watermelons, displayed at the front of the store and proceeded to tap several with two fingers, while holding his ear close to the melon. The hollow sound would reveal the good one.

'*Khānom*, this one is very good. It is juicy, sweet and bright-red inside. May I open it for you?'

Simone motioned with her hand and he cut it in half. It was a beauty.

'*Khānom*, with your permission, I will return your money and not charge you for this one. *Insha'Allah*, if it is the will of Allah, you will forgive me.'

Simone was back in her element. Gone, were the department stores of progressive Europe with their fixed-price merchandise and cash registers. Gone, too, were the metered taxis, tall office towers, clean streets, telephone booths, marble statues of nudes in city squares, and rain-washed monuments of great admirals. Simone was happy. Here, she was the invincible arbiter of who would get her business.

The autumn leaves of yet another year appeared, and the boys were back in school. This would be Theo's final year, before graduation.

A few weeks later, Miro came home and announced that Unireifen wanted a decision about their offer of a job in Canada.

'Simonko, how do you feel about this?'

'Gosh, I don't know. I like it here. I don't know much about Canada.'

'Do you want a little more time to think about it, before I give them a reply?'

'I don't know if more time would solve the dilemma. How do you feel?'

'About fifty-fifty.'

Simone went to the Canadian embassy in Tehran and asked for materials about Canada. They gave her a handbook, published by the Canadian government. As she focused the microscope, surprises came into view. This progressive land was a magnet for immigrants. British Columbia seemed the most attractive to her. Days passed.

'Miro, Unireifen can't send you to British Columbia, can they?'

'Not right away. The job is in Ontario. Why?'

There was a smile in her eyes. 'I wouldn't mind living in British Columbia.'

'We'll need to wait. Perhaps after some years?'

'How do you feel about it?'

'Let's go. I'll take the job. It's a step up from what I'm doing now. And the pay is good.'

'Will they cover our moving expenses?'

'Yes, that was in their offer.'

She feigned a wince. 'No more python skin and African carvings going to the wrong address?'

Miro smacked his palm against his forehead. *Jamais une vraie merde comme la dernière fois*: No more fuck-ups like the last time.

Simone busied herself filling out the application form for Canadian Immigration and collecting all the requested documents to be attached. They were applying for Miro, herself, the boys and Setareh. The forms were sent off to the Canadian Embassy Visa Office, in Beirut.

Four months later, came the response: on the basis of Miro's job offer from Unireifen, the Department of Manpower and Immigration was approving their application for permanent residency in Canada. However, the application to include Setareh in the visas for admission to Canada was denied. Setareh would not be admitted.

Simone made an appointment to see the Consular Attaché, at the Canadian Embassy. When she arrived, she was greeted by Eric Gregory. To her, he would have been aged no more than twenty-eight or twenty-nine.

'Mrs. Novotny, sit down please. How can I help?'

He sat across from her at his desk, and she handed him the letter they had received from Canadian immigration. He leaned back in his chair and put both feet up on his desk, the soles of his shoes in her face.

Simone said, 'I don't understand why Canadian immigration authorities have denied permanent residency to our maid-servant, Setareh. She is a member of our household. We consider her a member of the family.'

Gregory reached inside his desk drawer and pulled out a sandwich. He began to munch on it, when his secretary entered the office.

'Mr. Gregory, you can't eat in front of a client!'

Gregory lowered his sandwich. 'Simone, you don't mind if I eat?'

Simone smiled, 'No, no. Enjoy the sandwich.'

'See?' said Gregory, looking at his secretary. The secretary laid down some papers for him and left the room.

'Simone, you don't mind me calling you Simone, right?'

'No, of course not.'

'You know, I really don't think your maidservant ... er, Setareh? ... would be happy living in Canada. She doesn't speak English or French, right?'

'No, that's right.'

'Can she read and write?'

'No, she can't.'

'How old is she?'

'Nobody knows. She is an orphan, and she has no birth certificate. We think she is in her late-forties or early-fifties.'

'Does she have children?'

'No, Mr. Gregory. She was married at age nine, a child bride, and her husband dumped her for another child bride when he got tired of her.'

'So, unless she works only for you, she's stuck, right?'

'She would always work for us. We would never let her go.'

'But, Simone, we have laws in Canada that make this illegal. She will have to be paid a minimum wage, she would have to remain a free agent, you could not stop her from leaving your employ and accepting something else. Do you see what I'm getting at?'

'What if we put her into a school? She could learn English while she's working for us, couldn't she? We would pay for her schooling.'

'Yes, but do you want that responsibility? And then risk losing her, later?'

'Yes, we will take that risk.'

'So, what would you like me to do?'

'I would like you to write to the Immigration authorities and make our case that she is a family member, and indispensable to us. I need your support on this. Please, Mr. Gregory, we need your help. She is a member of our family. We love her. I couldn't just abandon her and go to

Canada and leave her alone here. She has no family of her own. She is an orphan.'

Gregory said he would write to them. He cautioned Simone not to raise her hopes too high. Whichever way it went, the Manpower and Immigration decision with regard to Setareh would be final. But he would do his part.

Simone was at the Tehran passport office. She had the documents ready for all five of them. Iranian passports had only a single-use validity. One trip abroad, and they were no longer valid and were confiscated. Each departure out of the country required a new passport. The officer at Central Police Headquarters looked over all the documents. Was everything there? Had they paid all the separate passport fees and taxes? Did each applicant have a personal guarantor who would vouch for any unpaid expenses incurred while abroad?

'This Mr. Theo Novotny,' started the officer.

'Yes?'

'Where are his military exemption papers?'

'Military exemption? What do you mean?'

'*Khānom*, this man is twenty-two years old. Is that correct?'

'He is twenty-one.'

'He cannot leave Iran until he has completed his military service.'

'What?' cried Simone.

'*Khānom*, he is of military-service age. We cannot issue a passport to someone who has not completed military service.'

Simone took a taxi to Miro's office. She told him what had happened. Miro said he would make some enquiries. The truth hit hard. Theo could not leave the country before he had completed two years of military service in the Imperial Iranian Army. A thick gloom descended on the household. Simone said she would fight this.

'We're leaving Iran for Canada and Theo will be left behind, stuck with military service? Never!'

Miro tried to reason. 'What's wrong with military service? I had to do it, two times. Stanislav was a soldier in World War I. Have you forgotten?'

'Yes, but you were not serving in the Iranian Army.'

'So, think of it as character-building for Theo.'

'Character-building?' She exploded. 'What character? Ha? Tell me! Do you know what they feed those soldiers? Do you know how they treat them? Do you know the horrible conditions they endure? I've talked to my Persian friends and they've told me. Their uniforms are scratchy and stink. Their heads are full of lice. That's why they shave them bald. They are marched to wash at the *hammāms*, public bathhouses, just once a week. They go to the firing range and find unexploded grenades and get killed. It happened. A soldier's bloodied clothes were brought back to the barracks so his relatives could pick them up and bury them with him. How can you just accept this? Two wasted years of his life. I can't believe you're talking like this!'

They didn't speak for three days. He skipped lunches, she skipped dinners. Setareh took care of things.

Silence ended and Miro said, 'Simone, we've always been model citizens, haven't we?'

'What do you mean?' she tightened up, wondering what would come next.

'Wherever we've lived we accepted the laws, in Czechoslovakia, in Kenya.'

'And so?'

'Why would we break the rules here? It's their law, men of age serve in the Shah's Army. Do you want Theo to flee like a rat? Escape across the border, without a passport, into Turkey or Iraq or Pakistan? Do we want to move to Canada, knowing that our eldest child is a fugitive from Iranian law? This country granted us citizenship when we were refugees. You told me that Theo has my values and sense of honour. And now he should abandon these?'

Simone said nothing. Wiped away a tear. There was tidying up to do in her head: *He knows that freedom of choice lies on the far side of principle and self-discipline. It's in his blood.*

Chapter 18

Theo's Czechoslovak girlfriend was visiting him at the *Bāgh-e Shāh* army garrison in Tehran's South. She was allowed just inside the walled garrison gates to see him for no more than half an hour. Theo's head had been shaved. He was in a sandy-brown uniform made of rough wool and the cloth was scratchy and uncomfortable. His clumsily hand-stitched leather boots were a size too tight. He felt humiliated in Tereza's presence.

Tereza brought him a dozen globes of švestkové knedlíky her mother had made, plum dumplings prepared from potato dough, each stuffed with a single plum and topped with melted butter, sugar, cinnamon and poppy seeds. It was a scrumptious treat compared to the garrison diet of *āsh-e reshteh* that had to be stomached every day. This thick, porridge-like noodle soup, containing dried kidney beans, chick peas, brown lentils, chopped spinach, garlic and chives, was spiked with either potassium nitrate, saltpetre, or camphor, as an anaphrodisiac. Ostensibly, it was added to diminish the soldiers' sexual drives. The unappetising broth often had bits of stones or brick in it, so he took care not to break a tooth.

Tereza was a stunningly attractive blonde, with deep-blue eyes and a round face. Her perfect teeth and smile could levitate any deflated soldier. She was an air hostess for Lufthansa Airlines, based in Tehran but travelling between Iran and Europe. They had hired her because she spoke five languages, fluent as a gurgling brook frolicking over polished multicultural pebbles. Persian came from having grown up in Iran and graduating from a French school in Tehran.

She was the ideal airline stewardess, too: unmarried, aged twenty, certified in first aid, with legs that could launch a fashion revolution. Theo had spotted her across a crowded room during a New Year's Eve party at the Czech Club. She was standing alone and he glided to her side and asked her to dance. And that's how the enchantment started.

Theo was now a private in the Shah's army, 3rd Infantry Division, and undergoing his six-month basic training. The regimentation was a vitriolic concoction of formation marching under the scorching midday sun of summer, standing two-hour guard-duty shifts every third night, learning to fire, disassemble, clean and reassemble his World War II, American-made M1 rifle, and target practice while camped at the sandy, wind-blown firing range out in the desert, west of Tehran.

His platoon sergeant was a heartless disciplinarian. One morning, at 4:30, Theo had gone to shave at the barracks washroom. When he returned to his quarters to sweep the barracks floor, the sergeant confronted him.

'Novotny! Where were you?'

'I went to shave, sir.'

'Why are you lying?' he yelled. 'You went to have breakfast. I know.' The sergeant gave him a slap that sent Theo staggering backwards and landing on the floor. 'Do you think you're in your auntie's home? Get the floor swept, right now!' Theo's first tangle with such meaningless brutality left him wary of what might come next. *This is their version of six months of basic training. Primitive savages.*

Now they were being drilled in the workings of mortars. Sitting on gravel in the parade ground, they all watched as the garrison's weapons officer, an Army major, explained the purpose and parts of the weapon, the tube, the explosive round, and the sighting system. He demonstrated the firing procedure: set up the firing angle, drop the mortar round down the tube, plug the ears, phoooom!

He repeated the steps several times. 'Any questions?'

No hands went up. 'No questions?' He surveyed the faces. Dumb expressions, foggy stares like those of opium addicts, a sea of shaved heads looking like unplugged robots. Then, he spotted the blue-eyed soldier. His martial finger pointed at Theo.

'He understands. Look at him!' he bellowed. 'There, you have intelligence. It shows from his eyes. How can you mother-fucking recruits fight an enemy if you don't know how a mortar works? Learn something from him!' He paused. 'Soldier, what's your name?'

'Novotny, sir.'

'Novotny, huh? Not a Persian name. Teach these donkeys how it's done. Make sure they get it right, so they don't blow their heads off."

June delivered another milestone for Michael. He finished Grade 11 and would have to complete his final year of high school in Canada.

To mark the end of the academic year, his school had arranged a picnic in the mountains north of Tehran and each student was asked to bring some item of food. Setareh had promised Michael to put together a cold meal that could feed a handful of hungry classmates. Michael was up early on the day of the outing and went to the kitchen to check on his picnic takeaway. Setareh was nowhere. She was always the early riser in the house. He knocked on her closed room door. There was silence.

Michael ran up to his parents' bedroom. 'Mum, it's six o'clock and I can't find Setareh.'

Simone came downstairs and knocked. 'Setareh?' she whispered. 'Setareh, are you there?'

There was no reply. Simone opened the door and saw that Setareh was lying in bed, completely motionless. She approached and felt her hand. It was cold. She felt her forehead and cheeks. Cold, too, and dry. The dreaded touch spoke no language.

'Michael. Run to the pharmacy at the corner and ask the pharmacist to call a doctor.'

Dr. Azimi arrived at their house and listened for a pulse. There was none. He beamed a light at her pupils. No reaction.

'I'm afraid she's gone. She has been called by *Khodā*, God. It appears that she died several hours ago, in the early hours of the morning. How old was she?'

'Nobody knows,' mumbled Simone. 'Maybe fifty.'

Simone was too stupefied. Her mind anaesthetized, she sat on Setareh's bed for a long, long time. A family member had said adieu.

A letter arrived from Canadian immigration. Simone tore open the envelope. Setareh's application for permanent residency in Canada had been approved. Her hands began to tremble. The acrid smoke of unfairness was burning her eyes. Fate had turned her salty tears into a Great Bitter Lake.

Michael went to visit Theo at the garrison. He told him about Setareh. Theo had a hard time digesting it. His mind did a rewind of the years gone by: she would never bake another cake, never see another Persian New Year, and never experience a world so contrary to the humble life she had led in her native land. She was the illiterate governess who had moulded their growing-up days, scolded them for using Persian swear words, ironed their shirts with a charcoal-heated flat iron, taken them to the cinema to see serialized Captain Marvel films, urged them to get married soon, and hand-fed the goose that became the centrepiece of dinner on Christmas Eve. There could never be another *Setareh Borealis*. She was now a permanent fixture in the endless night sky.

Simone came to visit Theo for the last time. She and Michael were leaving for Canada in three days. Miro was already in Germany for more training and briefing. Everything had been packed and shipped to their new temporary address in Ontario. When she got to the garrison's meeting place for visitors, she begged the visitor guard to allow her an hour with Theo.

'*Khānom*, I'm very sorry, but thirty minutes is the maximum time allowed for visits.'

Simone slipped him a 100-rial banknote.

'Forgive me, *khānom*. You can have a *little* more time. It is not a problem.'

Theo turned to Simone. 'I saw that. You've just bribed the visitor guard. My, my, Theo's mother is into bribery.'

'Theo, remember this. Bribery is like garlic. It stinks, but it opens windows and doors. And for those who don't have much, it flavours their stale bread.'

She had brought Theo goodies to eat, a contact address in Canada, and details for touching base with Miro's former associate who was taking over the Unireifen business. All his essential personal belongings were stored for him and the remainder shipped to Canada. Simone was upbeat, in a bubbly mood. Her bones told her that all would go well. She began to sing:

He's got the whole world.
In his hands, he's got the whole, wide world …

'Mum, what are you doing?' Embarrassment flowed up his throat. 'They're all looking at us.'

'I'm singing you a song, sweetheart.' Theo buried his face in his shamed hands.

He's got the whole world.

In his hands, he's got the whole, wide world.

In his hands, he's got the whole world in his hands.

She hugged him, then dug into her canvas bag and brought out a table knife. With the blade of the knife, she tapped him three times on the shoulders: left shoulder, right shoulder, left again.

'I dub thee Imperial Knight, *Reichsritter Theo von Mannberg Novotny*. From this day forward, you may call your mother *Lady Simone*.'

'Mum. What, in *your* whole, wide world, did you have for breakfast?'

'I had Tootsie Rolls with a glass of milk and porridge. Now listen, Theo dearest—'

'That's it! It must be the Tootsie Rolls.'

'Theo, I have to tell you this. Did you know you have blue blood?'

'Blue blood? This is madness.' There was ridicule in his voice. 'I cut my hand when I was cleaning my rifle and the blood was red.' He pointed to the scab on his wrist.

'No, Theo, you do have an amazing ancestral history. Miro and I have never told you about this. But one day, when you get to Canada, I will tell you the whole story. Now, can you keep a secret? Just between you and me?'

'Here we go again. This *is* a crazy day. What kind of secret, Mum?'

'Promise me?'

'Alright. I promise. What's the secret? More blue blood?'

'Mothers are not supposed to feel this way, but you are my special one, my lucky star, my firstborn, my African blessing, my dearest little egg. I love Michael as a mother loves her children, but you were the one who took it on the chin while growing up. You were showing Michael the way to be brave. You set an example for him.'

Theo lowered his head. 'I don't know what to say, Mum.'

She touched his cheek. 'Lady Simone, remember?'

It was time for Theo to play tricky raconteur. He stared straight at her, in order to fix her gaze. 'Are you superstitious?'

'Sometimes.'

'Do lady bugs bring good luck to a person?'

'I don't know. Why?'

'There's a bug sitting on your collar.'

Simone screamed and jumped up.

Theo's belly jiggled. 'Relax, Mum, it isn't an army of African driver ants. Lady bugs are gentle creatures. They're cute, like you.'

She hugged him again, then held his face in her hands and kissed his lips. Theo was blushing. 'I love you sonny boy. Stay brave. Soon you'll be joining us in Canada.'

Theo's soldier friends, who had seen their own visitors and were waiting at the barracks, gathered around him.

'Theo, *khān*, who was that singing lady?' one of them asked.

'That was my mother.'

'What? Why didn't you introduce us? We could have spoken to her and wished her well!'

His fellow soldiers joked endlessly about the fact that he was a blue-eyed, fair-skinned foreigner among them. The questions rolled out, much like free advice given when flogging a dead horse: *What the hell are you doing here? Why didn't you find a way to skip military service, find someone influential to get you off the hook? Why didn't you buy your way out of conscription?*

Theo always wore a pendant around his neck. It was given to him by Tereza: a cloisonné medallion at the end of a fine, silver chain, with the relief image of the Virgin Mary, coated in a deep-blue enamel that almost glowed. When the soldiers discovered him wearing it, they would tug at it, pretending to tear it off his neck.

'Hey! Don't pull on it! You'll tear the chain and I will lose my girlfriend,' he pleaded.

They found this comical and teased him, 'Theo, *khān* needs *Hazrat-e Maryam*, the Virgin Mary, around his neck to keep his girlfriend.'

Chapter 19

There was a bright spot on the horizon. Theo could read and write Persian, so his Company's commanding officer, Major Mohsen Afsari, approached him one day and asked him to teach the illiterate soldiers in his unit to read and write. Theo was thrilled to get something meaningful to do.

Soon, Major Afsari approached him again. 'Novotny, I understand you know English. Is this correct?'

'Yes, sir.'

'I am asking you to help me learn English.'

'Yes, sir?'

'Are you willing to spend two afternoons a week to teach me?'

'Er, yes, sir. I am.'

'Good. Then we begin today.'

The major brought out his little English book and began to read. Every now and then, he would stop and ask, 'Is this how it's pronounced?'

He continued reading, then stumbled on the word *light*. 'Liiigt, ligat, leigt?'

'*Light*, sir. It means *nūr*, as in *nūr-e cherāgh, nūr-e khorshīd*, light of a lamp, light from the sun.'

'Thank you,' said Afsari. 'Light … light … light.'

One day, into their fourth or fifth lesson, Afsari looked up from his little English book. 'Novotny, why are you here?'

'Beg pardon, sir?'

'What are you *doing* here?' he emphasised. 'What is an intelligent, well-educated foreigner doing here as a soldier?'

'But sir, I'm doing my military service.'

'Why aren't you in Officer College? You know so many languages. You could be teaching army officers another language. Why are you a private at this godforsaken hole of a garrison?'

Theo was thunderstruck. 'Er, I never thought to apply at Officer College, sir.'

'Is there anything I can do for you, during basic training? Do you *need* anything?'

Theo saw his chance. 'Well sir, I would very much like permission to have a two-week leave of absence.'

Afsari went silent, thought for a while. 'You have my permission, but it will have to be unofficial. I cannot make it a formal leave. I will speak to your platoon sergeant and we will turn a blind eye to your absence from the garrison. It will not be recorded. Is that understood?'

'Yes, sir. Thank you, sir!'

'When do you want to go?'

'End of this week, sir.'

A few days later, the platoon sergeant took Theo aside and told him he would have to escape from the garrison on his own. There would be no pass to present to the guard on duty at the garrison gates. He was warned: *if you're not back in two weeks, we will go after you, find you, and you go to jail.*

Theo asked one of his soldier buddies whether escaping like this happened before. He got an amused reply.

'It happens all the time. You get your friends to haul you up until you're standing on their shoulders, then you grab whatever you can reach and pull yourself up over the garrison wall. Once you're on the other side, you disappear and look for a taxi to take you wherever you're going. But don't get caught. It's doomsday for you.'

Theo asked about getting back in.

'Same thing, in reverse. Get an outside friend to help you up and over, very early in the morning. Then, you sneak back to your barracks and pretend you're asleep.'

Theo was up at 3:30 a.m. He woke two soldier buddies and they went together to the garrison wall. They helped him over and saluted.

Tereza got ten days off from work. Tereza's old schoolmate and Armenian friend, Armen, had a car and they drove to the Caspian Sea with Armen's Polish girlfriend, Sofia. They went camping and set up two tents on the sand dunes near a remote beach far from the nearest village. Evening came, and they cooked by campfire light. In their tent, Theo and Tereza had sex like never before. They had been sleeping together, but never like this. Her orgasms were quite unpredictable. Sometimes they were quick, sometimes slow and tortured. They always caught Theo by surprise. *Is she tormenting me with a timing game?* But this made it all the more exciting, second guessing what would happen with Tereza, the mysterious, the unpredictable.

'I heard you two last night,' smiled Armen. 'Wow, you lucky bastard. You Czechs have a real ball, with your crazy language that no one can understand.'

'Hey, Sofia's not a bad lay either, right?'

'Yeah, but she can't make love in Armenian. We, Armenians, we want to hear each other's sex words in Armenian. If a woman wants a lover in her pants it has to be on her own terms, and in her own language.'

'I guess you'll have to learn Polish, then.' Theo's face went impish. 'You've known Tereza for quite some time.'

'Yeah. When we were still in high school, I would take her dancing. I tried to get into her pants, but she was a firm *no*. "After the dance, I want you to drop me off at home," she would say. She always struck me as a touch puritanical. The impenetrable virgin. I don't know how you broke through that barrier.'

'I asked her to make love to me in Czech.'

'Home run!' Armen gave the thumbs up and smacked Theo's back. 'Women like her turn out to be very loyal, you know. You're lucky. Hang on to her. Don't lose her.'

Armen was a little older than Theo and Tereza. He seemed wizened by his extra years and Theo liked his flair for having fun. He was also the consummate, camping-ready cook. They built another campfire when darkness came. Armen had brought his butane-fired barbecue to make ground-beef *kabābs*, skewered with onions and tomatoes. He didn't forget the Armenian red wine and Armenian cognac and they all drank out of aluminium cups. Theo played on his harmonica and Armen had brought his guitar. They made primitive music but the rhythm was sufficient to get the girls to wiggle their butts and want to dance. They sat around the campfire. The flickering flames and the shadows they created danced like genies, licking their bodies with the rawness of nature. All about, the crickets were chirping. They, too, were courting the females.

One evening, at sunset, Theo and Tereza went skinny dipping in the Caspian. They left their clothes on the beach and tried all kinds of things in the water. Tereza said 'let's get married' and Theo said he was far too young to get hooked so soon.

'You just want to sleep with more women. That's why.'

'Hey. Give me some slack. I'll get it out of my system, and come back to you.'

'Well, I might not be there anymore. Who says I'll wait?'

'Come on, don't get all huffy. Maybe I'll change my mind and make you my bride.'

Armen stole their clothes and made off with Sofia, taking the car. Theo and Tereza ran back naked to their tent.

'The bastard. He's taken our clothes!' Theo chuckled away the situation.

'You don't need clothes to screw me, do you? If they never come back, we'll just hitch a ride to Tehran in our naked bodies.'

Theo flicked his head back and did a silent laugh. '*You* should have no trouble getting a ride.'

Tereza glanced at him, then her gesturing hands pointed towards her body. Theo played up on that. 'Gentlemen, start your engines! Who will be the lucky one to drive this absolutely gobsmacking torso to Tehran?'

Armen and Sofia returned, spilling over with mirth.

'Here are your clothes. You can come out of your sleeping bag. Were you worried? We went into town to get some bread and rice and eggplant. Tonight, I cook *khoresh-e bādemjān*, eggplant stew on rice.'

They ate and played music and danced by campfire light, until the moon was overhead. Theo said it was the best ten days of his life. A few days later, Armen drove him to the garrison at 3:30 a.m. and helped him scramble over the wall. Theo owed him one.

Major Afsari and Theo were having another English lesson. When they finished, Afsari switched to a more serious tone. 'Novotny.'

'Yes sir?'

'Our garrison commander, Brigadier General Sālehi wants to see you.'

Shock descended. 'Am I in trouble, sir?'

Afsari gave a sympathetic glance. 'No, you're not in trouble. He wants to talk to you about being an interpreter for the American advisors working with our officers in the vehicle maintenance units. I've put in a good word for you.'

'Thank you, sir.'

'Go see the General. He'll give you the details. It's a good opportunity, Novotny.'

'Yes sir. Thank you very much, sir.'

Theo went to see General Sālehi. He was standing in the waiting room when Sālehi emerged and Theo saluted in a tense way. He had never before met such a high-ranking officer and he was nervous.

'Novotny, I've heard good things about you.'

'Yes, my General? I am at your service, sir.'

Sālehi explained that the United States Military Assistance and Advisory Group was helping the Iranian Army by sending American army advisors to train and supervise personnel in various units and functions: vehicle maintenance, weaponry, terrain mapping, and radar. None of the Americans could speak Persian, and there was a shortage of interpreters fluent in both English and Persian. He was assigning Theo to a group of U.S. non-commissioned officers, to be their interpreter. He would be free to come and go, without a garrison pass, and would make himself available wherever the Americans needed him.

Theo was ecstatic. The cloak of imprisonment was being lifted. He could feel human again. Tereza visited him at the garrison and he told her the news. Her spirits soared to 30,000 feet, with the seatbelt unfastened. Now she could see him for more than half an hour at a time, whenever she wasn't flying.

Theo went to see his American contact, Sgt. Arnold, who introduced him to four other American sergeants in that office. They were impressed with Theo's fluency in English. Arnold was delighted they hadn't sent him yet another interpreter who spoke Persian, but very poor

English. Minutes later, Sgt. Wilson strode into the office, having finished his daily round at the garrison's motor pool. He was the expert on engine maintenance.

'Sergeant Wilson,' said Arnold. 'This is Private Novotny. He's our new interpreter guy. Ask him something in English.'

Theo straightened and saluted. Wilson grunted, 'Yeah, okay, that's good.'

Arnold persisted. 'Come on, go ahead, test him. Ask him something.' Arnold's smile now spanned his entire face.

'I don't know what to ask.'

'Come on, sarge. Try him. Ask him something, anything.'

Wilson yielded. Without looking at Theo, he muttered, 'Where's your piston rod?'

All heads turned towards Theo. The silence was saturated with expectations. Seconds ticked away. Finally, a reply.

'Well, sir, I can't show it to you here, but my girlfriend knows where to find it and she likes it well lubricated inside her cylinder.'

A flash of astonishment, then the room-full of sergeants burst out laughing.

'See?' said Arnold, 'I told you he knows English!'

'How come he's got an American accent?' asked Wilson.

'Because he went to an American school in Tehran,' said Arnold, breaking into an irrepressible chuckle.

Wilson shook his head. 'Well, I'll be god damned. This is Iran. How good is his Persian?'

Theo piped up. 'I teach the illiterate soldiers how to read and write in Persian, sir.'

'You do, huh?' said Wilson. 'Well, now we'll teach you engine mechanics.'

Theo's service time flew by. He was not required to stay overnight at the garrison, so he found himself a cheap flat in Tehran's north and settled in there. The Americans were paying him a modest salary for his services and the Iranian Army did not mind this. Tereza often slept at his flat when not in Europe.

Chapter 20

Theo was discharged. Two years completed. He landed a job as an editor for the features pages of the English-language daily, the *Tehran International*. He also took up photography and threw himself into it, buying a 35mm SLR camera, lenses, and filters. He photographed people wherever he could, candid shots of illiterate women squatting in the street, while dictating a letter to a post-office scribe. Close-ups of merchants selling gold bracelets in the bazaar, or women washing Persian carpets at a communal fountain, or a child with a bloated belly, licking a lollipop with flies stuck on it. His favourite subject was people, faces, expressions, poses, gestures, body language. And the close-range study of the naked human form began to creep into his artistic consciousness.

Theo's Senior Editor was discussing a new project with him, a feature article on a famous mountain guide living in the Alborz Mountains. He wanted Theo to write an in-depth story on Mashhadi Safar, who had guided many foreign climbers visiting that part of Iran and become something of a mountaineering legend. The editor knew Theo had climbing experience and was fluent in Persian.

As a climbing client, Theo had befriended Safar, having twice climbed with him to the summit of *Alam-Kūh*. Touching the sky at 16,000 feet, it ranked as Iran's second-highest peak after *Damāvand*, Bride of the Gods. This time, Theo would use Safar's services to explore the *Takht-e-Soleimān*, Solomon's Throne massif, to get his feature story.

'Tereza, you've got a two-week break coming up. Would you come with me on this assignment?'

'I won't climb with you all the way, but I'd like to see that part of the high country. What about taking Armen, would he be available? We could make it a threesome.'

Theo was on the phone to Armen. 'Hey, Mister Armenia. How would you like to climb a mountain that's almost as high as your national symbol for Armenians, Mount Ararat?'

'What, are we looking for Noah's Ark?'

'Not quite. We're looking for Solomon's Throne.'

'Theo-*jān*, I don't understand.' He switched to Armenian. '*Inch'e katarvum?*' What's going on?

Theo explained the project. 'Trust me, Armen. This one's a beauty.'

They leased a Jeep Wagoneer, four-wheel drive station wagon, and the three of them headed north, taking the *Chālūs* Road into the mountains. It was that same winding mountain road that Theo remembered from childhood, full of hairpin curves and sheer drops into the valley far below. But the road was now paved. They went through the *Kandavān* Tunnel that had frightened Theo as a child, and was now a memory to be laughed off. As they descended from the tunnel into a world of lush vegetation, they turned off the main road and headed westward along a gravel road, climbing ever higher into the mountainous country.

They were aiming for the tiny village of *Rūdbārak*, home of Mashhadi Safar and his family. They got to his adobe brick house finished with plaster and painted white. When the car stopped outside, the hens scattered and three of Safar's youngest children came running barefoot out of the house.

'A car has arrived! We have visitors!' they cried out.

Safar's wife, Azizeh, emerged and recognised Theo. Theo introduced Tereza and Armen. Safar is in the mountains, she said, but he would be home in the late-afternoon. Safar had taken his eldest son, Ali, up the climbing trail to inspect a footbridge across the *Sard-āb Rūd*, Cold-Water River. It had been damaged by the glacier melt-off in spring and needed repairs.

Azizeh invited them inside and served tea and sweets. They all sat on brightly coloured kilims, spread out on the floor.

Tereza was curious. '*Azizeh-khānom, shomā chand-tā bacheh dārīd?*' How many children do you have?

'I have seven. Safar's two oldest sons, Ali and Rezā, are helping their father with the mountain guiding. And how many do you have?'

'I'm not yet married.'

'*Masha' Allah.*' What wonders God has willed. 'You are still young and beautiful. You will find a husband and make him happy.' Tereza smiled and lowered her head in modesty.

Azizeh continued. '*Insha'Allah,* God willing, you will have many boys. They bring bread with them when they are born. They bring joy and good fortune to the home.'

All over the guest area, the walls were papered with photographs of Safar with his clients. They left no doubt that Safar had the climbing ability of a mountain goat. Plastered everywhere, were postcards and letters of appreciation from far-off places, written in French, Polish, Italian, German and English. There were ribbons and medals and certificates from the Mountaineering Federation honouring his service and his rescue efforts when climbers had been injured and needed to be evacuated. And there was a picture of him with Theo, standing on the summit of *Alam-Kūh.*

The sun's last rays were bathing the mountaintops when Safar appeared. Word had gone up the trail that he had visitors and he hurried home. He was a living monument to high-altitude adventure. His stocky build and five-foot-two-inch frame was pure muscle, skin and bones, not a sliver of fat could be extracted. The sun-baked crow's feet radiating from the outside corners of his eyes gave his face a cheery character. And his leathery complexion, aged and cracked by the years of wind, made him look wise and experienced.

He was wearing faded, corduroy knickerbockers, tucked into knee-high woollen socks that rose up from well-worn alpine climbing boots, gifted to him by some grateful foreign climber. His brown, flannel lumberjack shirt was worn thin at the neck and frayed at the cuffs. And his head was topped with a sweat-stained, olive-drab French beret. From head to the soles of his boots, he was outfitted in hand-me-downs from past mountaineering clients.

He removed his boots, came inside, and found everyone sitting on the floor.

'*Mūsio* Theo!' he cried out, his voice rumbling like a bulldozer traversing a bed of gravel. 'You have honoured us with your visit!' His *Mūsio* was his way of pronouncing *Monsieur*, the common French term of address for foreigners in Iran.

Theo jumped up and they gave each other a kiss on each cheek, the Persian way. 'Safar, I am so happy to see you.' He introduced Armen and Tereza. Safar bowed slightly with right hand over the heart.

'*Masha' Allah*, you have remained very young. I have waited a long time for you! Tell me your wishes. I am at your service.'

Theo explained the project and was hoping that Safar could guide them up for a four-day trek.

Azizeh was up at 4 a.m. making tea and breakfast for them. Ali and Rezā saddled up the two mules and loaded the saddle bags. It was a crisp, bright morning and they would set off before the warmth of the day rose up the valley. Tereza would accompany them on a day-long hike, then Rezā would return with her to Rūdbārak. She would wait in the village until Safar, Theo and Armen got back from the mountains. It was a glorious hike. Alpine flowers carpeted the grassy highlands. The clean, cold stream coming from the melting glaciers was gurgling, and the mountains' shadows in the valley gave the stillness an excuse to showcase the tall peaks in the distance.

After Tereza turned back, the team continued upward.

The green soon gave way to the harsher dryness of rocks, sagebrush and dust. Safar's sharp eyes spotted a wisp of rising dust, high up on the opposite mountainside. About a kilometre away, a lone man was descending rapidly like a skier down a sand dune. When the man was lower down, Safar recognised Nūrali, who had gone up for a few days to find fresh pastures for his flock of sheep.

Safar let loose with the throat-ripping mountain yell of an alpine warrior.

'A-a-a-w-u-u-u-u-u-u-u-u-u!' He waited for the echo to subside. Then, 'N-ū-ū-ū-ū-r-a-a-a-l-i-i-i-i-i-i-i-i-i!'

'Saf-a-a-a-a-a-a-a-r!' came the reply. Recognition achieved.

'Are you going home?' Safar yelled.

'Tomorrow,' came the echoing reply.

This was the mountain telegraph of the region's denizens. They had no radios or walkie-talkies. Deep throats were tuned to communicate vital information, simple, crisp, and only the bare essentials. It served to keep track of villagers whose livelihood was in the high country. If they were not back in the valley when they should have been, a search party would go out.

'*M-i-r-i-i-i-i-m b-ā-ā-l-ā-ā-ā-ā-ā-ā-ā!*' We are going up, Safar called.

'How many days?' called Nūrali.

'Four!' yelled Safar.

Evening came and they found a campsite. The water from the Sard-āb Rūd was now just a trickle. Next morning, they headed southwest and the climb got steeper. Several glaciers glistened above them. As they made their way up, Safar stopped for a moment and pointed to a tall, black rock spire that seemed to touch the sky.

'*Mūsio* Theo! *Angosht-e khodā.*' God's finger.

Theo took photographs. He got Safar to stand righteous before God's finger and clicked more. As they slowly gained altitude, Safar chatted with Theo.

'*Mūsio* Theo, is it true that in foreign lands men and women freely sleep with each other without having to get married?'

Theo winked at Armen, who fought to suppress a chortle. 'Yes, if a woman wishes, she can sleep with many men. Women can have as much fun as the men do. They don't have to wait until they are married to sleep with a man.'

'But what about virginity?' Safar worried. 'Doesn't a bride need to be a virgin when she gets married?'

'In Western cultures, a bride's virginity is not as highly prized as it is in Iran. As long as a wife is faithful, the man is not terribly interested in her past sex life.' Safar digested this bizarre state of romantic affairs. He had never been outside Iran.

'But how do the woman's parents allow this? Isn't she fiercely protected by her brothers?'

'In the West, women are not chaperoned when they meet with a would-be husband.'

'And do you sleep with *your* lady?'

'I do. And we both enjoy it.'

Safar rumbled a bulldozer laugh. 'And will you marry her one day?'

'I hope to. If she'll agree.'

'She will agree. I know it.'

Early afternoon came. It was time for Ali to turn back with the remaining mule. The trail was getting steeper and narrower and they had reached the point where the climbers would carry their gear in their backpacks. There would be enough time for Ali to get back to the village before dark.

'Ali,' said Safar. 'Make sure *Mūsio* Theo's lady is comfortable. If she needs anything, take care of it.'

They reached their final overnight camp at 14,000 feet. Safar confirmed, 'Tomorrow, we begin our summit climb to Alam-Kūh. Tonight, we limit our food and drink to dry bread and black, unsweetened tea.' They walked to the edge of a nearby glacier and scooped up snow to be melted on the Primus stove. Armen was hungry and could not resist opening the tin of sardines in his rucksack.

Safar set up a tent for the two climbers but he would sleep outside, under the stars, tucked inside his sleeping bag. When night fell, Theo and Armen were stunned by the clarity of the star-studded heavens. One could read by starlight. The Milky Way arched across the indigo sky, horizon to horizon, its galactic glow casting faint shadows on the stony ground. A meteor slammed into the upper atmosphere, streaked a fleeting glow across the sky, then vaporised. Theo set up the camera on a tripod and fed starlight onto the film plane.

But it was an uneasy night for Armen. The sardines were protesting against the high altitude and his stomach was bearing the brunt of their displeasures.

Dawn arrived, clear and cool. They hiked to the base of a glacier, then climbed slowly upward and along a ridge. Nearing the summit, the sounds of crashing rocks echoed around them. The mountains were alive, eroding right before their eyes. It was an eerie spectacle to see and hear rocks tumbling from the surrounding summits and cascading down the steep snowfields to the bottom of the Solomon's Throne massif.

At the summit of Alam-Kūh, Theo captured Safar and Armen in a friendly embrace of fists-in-the-air victory. Treading backward with care to get another angle for this shot, Theo stepped close to the edge. He slipped on a wobbly rock and Safar darted forward to catch him. The peak's sheer granite north face was a 3,000-foot drop to the base of the mountain.

They returned to their campsite and rested until the following day, before reaching the peak of *Takht-e Soleimān*, Solomon's Throne. Safar had his pet theory of how King Solomon came to have his throne installed on this remote peak. Theo smiled and listened politely to the story. Safar swore that the pieces of wood they saw at the peak were parts of King Solomon's throne. Armen was amused. He compared Safar's story to the phantom arks found by various climbers searching for Noah's Ark on the slopes of Mount Ararat. He turned to Theo and spoke in English. 'Reminds me of all those claims made about finding pieces of the ark, many of them baseless and outright fraudulent. Do people really believe that a wooden ark built 5,000 years ago would survive snow, glaciers, earthquakes, and volcanic eruptions?'

'Um. I know what you're saying.' Theo put his hand on Armen's shoulder. 'We humans love our stories. They give meaning to an otherwise unfathomable universe. Who can comprehend the vastness of time and distance in the untouchable emptiness of space? We need something tangible to hold on to.'

Night had fallen. It was getting late. Tereza had expected them by mid-afternoon. Rezā and Hamid, Safar's third son, were up in the hills above the village, looking for the climbers. Then, far away, Rezā spotted hurricane lanterns slowly descending. The lanterns were rocking back and forth, as Safar and Theo each held one in their swinging arms. Hamid ran back to the house to get Tereza. They hiked up the village trail to meet them.

She hugged Theo, then Armen. 'You're a little late. What happened?'

'Armen sprained his ankle coming down. We had to descend more slowly.'

'Yeah,' chuckled Armen. 'I sat on Solomon's Throne and it collapsed right on top of my ankle.'

Tereza went to the car and got her first-aid kit. When Armen was helped inside the house, she put a rigid foam splint on either side of the ankle, then wrapped it with an elastic bandage. 'That should take some pressure off the ankle.'

Azizeh had made a rice and stew dish. It was a welcome change from the tea and dry bread of the past days. Azizeh said if the swelling in Armen's ankle did not diminish, she would wrap his ankle in goat's cheese.

After the meal, Safar brought out a bottle of Iranian vodka. He passed around the glasses and they chatted about the climb. For Tereza, it was a stripped-down replay of what the men had experienced. Next morning, they prepared to leave. Theo paid Safar and added generous tips for his guiding sons. He waited for the right moment and squeezed several folded banknotes into Tereza's hand, asking her to pass them discreetly to Azizeh for her hospitality. He promised a few copies of the feature article when it was published. Safar removed his French beret and bowed his head. *'Be omid-e didār!'* In hopes of seeing each other again, he fare-welled, in his bulldozer rumble.

Chapter 21

Armen came over and Theo showed him a photography magazine. It was a special issue on photographing the human form, using nude female models. The pictures were black and white and showcased only small portions of the body. Armen leafed through the magazine.

'Armen, what do you think? I want to do this kind of photography and have my work exhibited.'

'I don't know. Is the public interested? Is this art?'

'Yes! It's a form of art, seen through the lens of the camera. But you have to be creative, to find the right angles and lighting, light and shadows.'

'So, you want to do photos of nudes?'

'Don't you see? You don't photograph the entire person. Just a small area of the body reveals its form. Lighting is the key. You get right up close to get an effect. Fill the frame with just a thigh, or the curve of a hip. That's all. Or just a belly, the smoothness of skin, a breast, or long fingers resting on the neck. Never the genitals. People don't see the whole person, they see through the eye of the camera. Every picture becomes a creative statement of the human form and its details. The key factors are shadow, light, angle, focus.'

'And where will you get your models?'

'I don't know.'

'Would Tereza pose for you?'

'Nah. I don't think so. I'm afraid to ask. She might think it's pornography and say no. And she would never approve if I photographed other women. She'd question my intentions.'

'Yeah, a touchy subject.' Then he reflected. 'You would have a very limited audience. Mainly Westerners. Would Persians understand that this is art?'

'Why not? They love to watch belly dancers. The upscale holiday makers swim at the Caspian in bikinis. The young girls wear miniskirts. They love ballet and gymnastics. Why wouldn't they appreciate the human form?'

Tereza came to visit, one afternoon. Theo opened the door. He went into shock.

'Uh. Hi, I thought you were on your way to Germany.'

'They cancelled our flight. Schedules are being changed.' She noticed a pair of ladies' black, leather riding boots standing near the entrance. 'Are you with someone?'

'Uh, Tereza.' He began to stammer. 'Can we meet some other time?'

She pushed him aside and marched into the living room. Theo's camera was on a tripod, flood lights were blazing, a grey paper backdrop was hanging from the ceiling and there was a woman in a bikini, topless, posing on a high stool.

Tereza pulled Theo by the sleeve. 'I want to talk to you.' She towed him into his bedroom and shut the door.

'What the hell is going on?'

'Hey, I'm just photographing her. It's nothing. Isabel's the Argentine ambassador's daughter and she agreed to model for me.'

'What? How come you never photographed *me* in this way?'

'I thought you would . . . uh.' he struggled. 'It wasn't a hobby, then.'

'But now I'm not good enough to pose for you? And you go after other women? My body wasn't good enough for you? You wait until I'm out of town to do this? How can you *do* this to me?'

'Tereza, please. It's just photography. I like to capture the human figure, that's all.'

'Well, I'm ending my friendship with you! You're finished.' She stormed out of the house and into the street. Theo went running after her.

'Tereza! Wait. Please. I'm not *sleeping* with her. She's just a friend modelling for me. Honest. This is just a hobby. I love you. Please don't go.'

'Girls are your hobby! Naked girls. That's what. What will you do with those pictures, huh? Sell them to your friends?'

She was in tears, hailed a passing cab and jumped into the back. He ran towards it as it sped away. *How will I live this down? Mistake, not asking her to pose for me.*

He took Isabel back to her embassy residence on his Vespa scooter. When they got to the embassy, Mr. Ambassador was standing outside. He glowered at his girl as she dismounted. *More trouble!* It showed as she crossed the driveway and scaled the steps to the residence.

'I don't want you seeing that man again. *Entiendes?*—Do you understand? I don't want my daughter riding on a scooter in the streets of Tehran, *como una princesa morena gitana!*—like a brown-haired gypsy princess!'

Theo gave a half-hearted wave and scootered off.

He waited a few days, then called at Tereza's home. Her mother answered the door.

'Oh, Theo!'

'Is Tereza not in?'

'She's in Paris at the moment.'

'When will she be back?'

'I'm not sure. They've changed her flight schedules. She's mostly in Europe now.'

Theo saw Tereza less and less. She was avoiding him. A knife in the heart. The only way to catch her was at the Mehrābād Airport office, or as she was walking to board her flight to Europe. It was difficult to match her movements with his own non-working hours.

Agonising weeks passed. Theo was lonely and missed Tereza. He wrote to Simone that he would be coming to Canada soon. He asked Armen to help him get Tereza's flight schedule. Tereza's mother would not give it to Theo. The Lufthansa office did not release such information for security reasons. Armen had a friend at Lufthansa. Theo needed the days and flight numbers for Tereza's departures from Tehran airport.

Armen came by and gave Theo the list. 'How's the nude photography going?'

Theo threw up his frustrated arms. 'I've stopped doing that. I destroyed the few pictures I had made. Armen, I need to return your favour. Can I do something for you?'

'It's a pity you threw away those nude photographs,' Armen was smiling.

'I'd like to repay you in some way.'

'So, give me the addresses of your nude models.'

Theo looked embarrassed.

'Theo, I was teasing,' and they both saw the humour. 'Invite me to a cabaret show with belly dancers. How's that? And then we're even?'

'I want to ask you one more favour. I want us to compose a song. You play the guitar, I will do the singing.

We'll practice, then go to a soundproof studio and record it on tape.'

'A song?'

'Um, hm. For Tereza.'

Theo got busy making arrangements to leave Iran and move to Canada. He made sure to buy an air ticket on a flight when Tereza would be on board. When Tereza was doing a final cabin check before take-off, she spotted him in an aisle seat. He was sitting next to a woman in her twenties.

'What are you doing here?' Her surprise betrayed a pinch of excitement. 'Where are you flying?'

'I'm on my way to Canada.'

'Really? With this young lady?'

Theo wore a sheepish look and the female passenger chuckled. 'No, I'm flying alone,' he said. 'I'd like to talk to you when we're at cruising.' Afterwards, Theo moved to a row where the seats on either side were empty. When she walked past, Theo caught her attention.

'Tereza, sit down next to me. I need to talk.'

'I can't sit down in the cabin while I'm on duty.'

'Please, I need to talk to you.'

'Go to the back of the aircraft. I'll talk when I've finished with things.'

Theo made his way down the aisle, holding onto the

seat tops as he fought for balance.

'Turbulence, go back to your seat!' said Tereza.

'Tereza, I will, I will. But I need to tell you something.'

'You'll get me into trouble, please!'

Another stewardess came into the galley and, glancing at Tereza, pointed at Theo. Tereza gestured to her that he needed to use the toilet.

'Hurry up. What's on your mind?' Tereza snapped.

'Tereza, I love you. I want to marry you.'

'Oh! Now you want to marry me. I'm still very angry at you.'

'Please, Tereza, I don't want to lose you. I'm sorry about what happened. I've given up that nude photography shit.'

'Get down on your knees and beg.'

The tail section of the aircraft was wagging, as though the aeronautical engineers had designed the fuselage tube to do just this when things got rough while men proposed marriage. Holding onto a food trolley and lowering himself towards the bouncing floor, Theo knelt in front of her. 'Tereza, will you marry me?'

She flicked her head upwards. 'No.'

He didn't mind that reaction. *She's testing my resolve.* Now he was the drone and would have to chase after the Queen Bee, on her nuptial flight from the hive. They were landing in Beirut for a scheduled overnight stopover. After that, Frankfurt. As the cabin was prepared for landing, Tereza came by his seat and handed him a note, then continued down the aisle.

This is where I'm staying. Be there before six.

When she returned and walked past his seat, she gave him a glance. Theo fixed his eyes on hers. He lifted the note to his lips, and kissed it. *'Uvidíme se brzy,'* he breathed in Czech, we'll see each other soon. He tightened his seatbelt, closed his eyes, smiled. Mission nearly accomplished.

Theo found her hotel room and knocked on the door.

She opened. 'You're here early.'

'Can I come in?' She let him in. Theo wanted to invite her to dinner somewhere in Beirut.

'I can't. I'm joining the crew for dinner.'

'Allow me to invite you to a quiet, special place. Just the two of us. This is Beirut. Lots of wonderful cafes.'

'I know Beirut better than you do.'

'My parents were romancing each other here, when they were getting married.'

He convinced her and they had dinner together. *Why his sudden change of heart?* They went back to her hotel room. He wanted to talk. She wanted to hear.

'So. Now you find me on the plane, and you want to marry me. Why would I?'

'Tereza, it's your character. We're destined for each other. You are my type.'

'And what is your *type*?'

'Look, I wasn't ready then. Now, I don't want to lose you.'

'Ahh. I see. So, did you have your fill of all the girls you wanted?'

'Tereza, I didn't have any girls. You've been in my heart for a very long time. There was no room for other girls.'

Disbelief was engraved on her brow. 'With all those nude models of yours?'

'Photographing nudity doesn't mean you're having sex with the model.'

'Hah. You never slept with another woman. Is *that* what you're telling me?'

'Well, except with my mother, when she was breast-feeding me in Kenya. I've missed you.'

'I know you have.' Retaliation leaked in.

He edged up closer to where she sat on the bed, then struck the pose of a Shakespearean actor about to deliver a pompous oration, his arm outstretched in an affected manner. 'O goddess of the airlines, sovereign of the skies. Let me through the gates of heaven, into paradise!'

It made Tereza giggle. '*Tu es fou, toi, tu sais?*' You are crazy, you know?

Tereza allowed him to stay the night. But they didn't sleep. They caught up on many things, including wildlife.

Afterwards, Theo became curious. 'And how many men have *you* slept with?'

'Not counting you,' she punctuated the air with the

circle-sign gesture of thumb and forefinger, endowing it with the French expression for *nil*.

'But you're in the industry that's known for this—sexy stewardess meets handsome co-pilot and off they go to a hotel somewhere.'

'Nuh, uh. I stayed out of this. That was for the other girls.'

'I'm amazed. You're still an airline virgin.'

'So? Do I need to copy what they are doing? Don't you put me on a pedestal.'

'I won't put you on a pedestal. You already stand on a divine pair of pedestals. Now, tell me: after all that happened, why did you stay loyal?'

Tereza threw her head up in mock contempt. 'I was waiting for a certain soldier to catch up with me. But first, he had to do battle and show me what he's made of.'

'Armen was right,' he smiled.

'Armen?' Her eyebrows furrowed.

'Yeah. He said, girls like you turn out to be very loyal. Don't lose her. Or something like that.'

A smile spread across her face. 'Armen said that?'

'Um, hm. That's what he said.' He brought out his tape player, set it up and fed in a cassette tape. 'Now, listen to what your certain soldier was going through.' He hit the PLAY button. His voice filled the room:

The blue-eyed soldier with the shaven head
Lost the battle through his passion and his lady fled.
He tried so hard
To reconnect
But she had flown so far awaaay,
So far away, to a place where he couldn't reach her heart.
He tried to catch her at the airport
But the timing was wrong,
So, he bought a ticket, instead.
And there she was, there she was, on a flight he'll never forgeeet.
The soldier found his lover, he found her at last, and now he was touching her heart.
And that's when he vowed, now he made a promise, that they would never paaart.

She broke into a chuckle. 'I didn't know you could sing like that.'

The drone had caught up to the Queen Bee on her nuptial flight.

Chapter 22

Theo was in Canada.

'Mum, I'm getting married.'

'What?'

'I'm getting married.'

'How did this happen?' Simone's brow showed disquiet. 'When?'

Theo put on his serious look. 'Early. Tomorrow morning, at five.'

'What? I don't understand.'

Theo leaned forward and tapped the collar of her blouse with his finger. 'Lady bug, lady bug!' He chuckled, 'Hur, hur, hur.'

'Oh, Theo! You're impossible.'

'But I *am* getting married, the truth. There's still lots of time.'

'And who, may I know, is this lucky girl?'

'She has your middle name. Her name is Tereza.'

'Really? Tereza. Do I know her?'

'You know her from Tehran. Tereza, the Czech girl.'

'*That* Tereza? Theo! She's not right for you. She's just an airline hostess. Who knows how many men she's bedded with? Theo, you can do better than that. That's no good.' Jealousy flooded Simone's voice and Tereza was not a worthy competitor.

'Mum, it isn't about her job. It's her personality. You don't know her. She hasn't bedded with men. She's a very decent woman. I've known her for a long time. She is not a femme fatale. She's as true as a calibrated compass. I love her.'

'Every rose has thorns, Theo.'

'Well, I have de-thorned this rose.'

'Oh, have you? But you don't know who has deflowered her.'

'I know perfectly well who's deflowered her.'

'How could you know that?'

Theo pointed his thumb at his chest and smiled.

'You? You've just made that up. I don't believe you. When did that happen?'

'Secret, mama. You have to believe me.'

'Arrrhh! You're just like your dad, full of secrets.'

'That's because I keep them and don't let them out. Pretty soon, it gets full.' He was still smiling. 'Mama, *mādar jān-e man*, my dearest mother. Love is a million passions, but you know when you've found the right one. You sense it. It's a mystery, how you know it. Why does one feel like a balloon floating away and never landing?

They say it's chemistry. A hormone that kicks in when you meet the right person. Didn't you feel this with Dad?'

'Theo, she isn't right for you. You can do much better than that. What's your hurry? There are lots of good fish in the sea. Why would you marry that airline hostess?'

'Mum, you're beginning to sound like your mother, Esther.' He drew out the last words in a falsetto tone. Simone recoiled. Then, in the finishing touch of a gentleman striking a resonant chord in Simone's heart, his *coup de pouce*, as it were, '*Elle est comme toi, Simone. Elle m'a été fidèle. Elle a une loyauté absolue.*' She's like you, Simone. She's been faithful to me. She is absolutely loyal.

It was time to digest the developments.

Miro and Simone were living in Oakville, on the shores of Lake Ontario. The house overlooked the lake, with spare bedrooms for visiting guests. Michael was away in Vancouver, studying oceanography at the University of British Columbia. On a four-year scholarship, he was finishing his third year of studies. In his final year at high school, he had chanced upon Jacques-Yves Cousteau's book, *The Silent World*, which seized his imagination. The stories of the invention of the aqualung, the pioneering dives of Cousteau's team, and the later explorations in the Red Sea and Indian Ocean dominated Michael's aspirations. He would watch the underwater documentaries that Cousteau had filmed as he sailed all over the world on the research vessel *Calypso*. Michael wanted to do something similar. An unexplored and mysterious undersea world demanded to be investigated.

One late-spring afternoon, the doorbell rang and Simone answered it. Standing at the bottom of the entrance steps was an eye-catching woman, in her mid-twenties. Simone undressed her with her eyes, top to bottom. She was wearing a patterned silk blouse and miniskirt which revealed a divinely sculpted pair of legs. Her long, blonde, silky hair glistened in the sunlight. She was holding a brochure in her hands.

'Hello. I hope I'm not calling at a busy time. Could I take a moment to tell you about this fabulous—'

Simone smiled. 'Alright, dear, *what* is it you are selling?'

'I'm selling a lost diamond engagement ring that was found on the beaches of Palestine.' Simone's jaw froze open and she gulped her next breath. There was a moment of silence as she digested the weight of that.

'What!? Who *are* you?'

'I'm Tereza.'

'Tereza *who*?'

'*Je suis Tereza, fiancée de votre fils.*' I am Tereza, your son's fiancé.

Simone stumbled down the steps. 'Tereza, *C'est toi, vraiment?*' Is that truly you? She kissed her on both cheeks and gave her a quick hug. 'Where's Theo?'

Tereza pointed to the corner of the house, and Simone hurried round the back and found him standing there, face awash with a grin and holding a bouquet of carnations.

'Theo, you trickster! Why didn't you tell me she was in town? Putting her up to this act with the engagement ring. You scoundrel. Shame on you.'

They went inside and Simone made tea. As they sat there chatting, Simone had a hard time not staring at and studying Tereza. She found her manner and speech far more refined than she had imagined. The last time she saw Tereza was at the Czech Club in Tehran, when Tereza was in her late-teens. Simone was captivated. This woman was her future daughter-in-law. Her mind was in a whirl.

'Tereza, how long will you be in Canada?'

'I've taken a week off work, then I have to fly back to Frankfurt.'

'Wonderful. Then you stay at our house. Tomorrow, we'll do a little tour around this area and I'll make a special Czech dinner for us.'

Simone and Tereza were busy chatting and preparing snacks when Miro came home from work. 'We're in the kitchen!' sang Simone.

When he appeared, she said, 'Miro, we have a guest. Guess who?'

Miro gave her a studied gaze and hammed it up. 'Um, let me guess. Aphrodite, goddess of love and beauty?'

'This is Tereza, your future daughter-in-law. Do you remember her from Tehran?'

Miro was bowled over. He gave himself time to let things sink in and switched to Czech. '*Není možný, no toto je* překvapení!'—Not possible, well, this *is* a surprise!

He took Tereza's hand and kissed it. '*Enchanté, Mademoiselle Tereza!*'

'Miro, we go out for dinner, the four of us?' said Simone.

'Yes, yes. Of course.'

Miro took Theo aside and, beaming, gave him a mock punch to the chest. 'Well done! Theo has found a lovely lady. I'm very happy for you.'

'Thanks, Papa. I'm so relieved you like her. She's a star in the Andromeda galaxy. She took two million light-years to get here.' Miro laughed.

'Amazing that she and her parents were in the Czech Club and here we are together in Canada.' Miro squeezed Theo's shoulder. 'Small world.'

After dinner, they were walking along the lakeshore. Miro was with Tereza. He had a lot of questions for her about Tehran, about her parents, about the Czech Club, and about Beirut. He wanted to know how Beirut had changed in the intervening years.

Simone and Theo were walking ahead of them. 'Theo, she is a delight. I am so happy for you.'

'There you are, Mum. Not every rose has thorns. I see a lot of you in her.'

'You do?'

'Yes, I do.'

'Then you're a lucky man, Theo.' They synchronized their moulded-jelly giggles. 'Theo, I told you the story of how I got my middle name?'

'The Beirut nuns made you close your eyes and you put your finger somewhere on the page.'

'And isn't it amazing that you should happen upon a Tereza? Is there a plan in heaven?'

'I don't know,' he smiled. 'Would you like there to be a plan?'

A few days later, Tereza had to return to Germany. Before she left Oakville, Simone gave her the second ring with solitaire diamond that Miro had brought from South Africa when they were living in Kenya.

'I want you to have this,' said Simone.

Tereza was astonished. 'But why?'

'Because it seals the bond between us. I doubted you at first, but now I know better.'

'But . . . I can't take this from you.'

'You are not taking. I am giving. It is symbolic. Hold onto it, and let it not get lost in the vast ocean somewhere.' Then she added a bon mot. 'Now you can go find a buyer for that lost diamond engagement ring that was found on the beaches of Palestine.'

Tereza laughed. 'That was tricky Theo's idea.'

Chapter 23

Theo landed a job on the editorial staff of *Canada Today* magazine, a monthly general-interest periodical with national distribution. They had hired him as roving editor and would send him on assignments for feature articles. His writing and photography backgrounds were beginning to pay off. Tereza continued with Lufthansa, but soon took a job with Air Canada, flying the domestic routes. They had hired her as Purser, in charge of the cabin crew. It made a huge difference to Theo. She would now be home much more often, and with less jetlag. They lived a few miles from Oakville.

Miro's Unireifen lab was in Greater Toronto. As a senior design engineer in charge of tyre tread design and testing, he loved his work and found the daily challenges invigorating. He was the expert on aquaplaning, the event that causes so many car accidents, when driving on very wet paved roads. If the tyres don't channel the water out from under the tread and away from the tyre, contact with the road surface is lost and the car skates on a sheet of water, completely out of control. Designing treads with good water and snow removal was his specialty. Miro often reminded his young colleagues and test-track technicians: a good tyre design saves lives.

The seasons seemed to rush by on the railroad of life, pulling the years behind them as though they were attached like boxcars to a freight train. He was approaching mandatory retirement at age sixty-five. The stretches of hard work and long hours had worn him down. Miro was not as healthy as before and Simone was worried about his high blood pressure. She complained he wasn't spending enough time with her and convinced him to take a week off to visit Quebec City, where so much of Canada's early history had been shaped. There was the added charm of French-Canadian cuisine and a homey bed and breakfast to fritter away the mornings.

They had their first dinner, the evening was young, and their B&B had all the trappings of a nineteenth-century country lodge. Simone cuddled up to him on their bed and then rolled over so she was staring straight into his face. Her arm reached down and the hand did some exploring of its own. 'Mm. Homo erectus isn't extinct after all. He's migrated to Quebec City. Do you remember the first time we made love?'

'*Mais bien sûr!*' But of course. He said that with a chirrup. 'How could I forget? As I recall, you were a tiny bit sad.'

'Was I?'

'Um, hm. You had surrendered your engagement ring to the Mediterranean, and your virginity to me.'

'Yeah, that was good, no? Such a long time ago. I'm so glad it was you, not someone else. Thank goodness I didn't lose my virginity to that creep my parents had chosen for me. You know, every married couple should have a sign above their bed: *I was free to choose my partner and I shall preserve that liberty for my children.* When it comes to love, couples are smarter than their parents.'

'Um. You're light-years ahead of Esther.'

Chuckles bubbled up. She switched tones. 'But you know, Miro, now I've become a little dry. How time takes its toll. Age, age, age.'

'But there are some concoctions for that, aren't there?'

Her eyes widened and the words quickened. 'I remember how I would get all moist, down there, when I touched your lips and pushed my finger slowly into your mouth. And a telegram was sent downstairs. I was all wet! Did you know that?'

'Chemistry of the body. What magic a finger can conjure up.'

'Yes, chemical man. Mister tyre man. How come Unireifen never got into making condoms? They're both made of rubber, no?'

'Good question. Should I phone head office, next week, and ask them?'

'No, I was just playing with words, rubber words.' Then, she piped up with:

In days of old, when knights were bold,
And rubbers weren't invented;
They tied a sock around the cock,
And babies were prevented.

Miro's cheeks inflated and burst into a sputtered, 'Where, in Pinocchio's name, did you pick that up?'

'From Michael. When he and Theo went to Boy Scout Camp for two weeks. Don't worry. I won't repeat that in public. They came back with some scandalous rhymes and songs. The three of us would go into a room, shut the door and laugh ourselves silly with all the muck they had vacuumed while in camp.'

He was still chortling. 'I don't know *why* you collect these whacky yarns. Where do you store them?'

'Here, between my ears. Let's play another way, shall we? Miro, I *wish* we could do Kama Sutra.'

'Ho, ho! That calls for gymnastic flexibility, doesn't it?'

'Yeah. I don't know if my body can take all that twisting and arching. But there is the sitting position, where your *lingam* enters my *yoni* and we begin high congress.'

'You've been reading.'

'Um hmm. Kiss, kiss, fondle, fondle. Fuck a little,

then we cuddle,' she chirped. 'You like, Bwana Noboti?' And they enjoyed a few *petites morts* until the sun came through the window curtains.

Then came another soft day, another walk through the gardens of history. Another fragrant bouquet to banish the stresses of creeping age. Simone sensed it was exactly the elixir Miro needed.

Armen wrote to Theo. He and his Armenian girlfriend, Sarine, were going to visit Canada.

'Tereza!' he called out. 'Armen is coming to Canada!'

'Honest?' She gave a yelp and levitated a few inches.

Theo drove to Toronto Airport to pick them up. He was thrilled to see Armen again. When Tereza came home from flying the following day, she got the Armenian treatment.

'*Tereza, shāt sirūn!*' Tereza is very lovely! And you will need to take ten days off.'

'Really? Why?'

'Because we're all going camping.' Armen was beaming.

'For old times' sake?' Her eyes lit up the way he remembered they did.

'For old times' sake. Theo, what's a good place to go camping?'

'I know a place we will enjoy. It's called Mara Provincial Park, at the north end of Lake Simcoe. It has a wide sandy beach, we can swim there and rent canoes, and the campsites are inside a forest. The water is much warmer than Lake Ontario. Not quite the Masai Mara or the Caspian, but it will bring back memories. We can rent the tents there, and we can use the fire pits to cook. Sound good?'

'Sounds *shāt lāv*!' He used the Armenian words for *very good*.

'And one more thing,' added Theo. 'There will be lots of wildlife.'

'Is that so?' said Armen. 'What kind of wildlife? They have wild animals up there?'

'You and Sarine, me and Tereza, doing wild life inside a tent!'

Armen and Tereza dissolved in chortles and slapped each other a high five. Sarine was puzzled. She didn't know the history.

Next day, the girls went off to get supplies for the camping trip. Theo took Armen to a pub in Oakville dubbed A Knight in Gail. They sat at the bar counter, chatting about their days in Tehran and at the Caspian Sea.

'So, does Sarine make love to you in Armenian?' asked Theo.

Armen gave him a slap on the back. 'You remembered that. Hah!'

'You know, we haven't seen each other for years, but you're still my best friend! What ever happened to Sofia?'

'Ah, that Polish girl Sofia. Armen grinned. She crashed into an upright Pole and he took her to America.'

'During my early army days, there was that officer Afsari who allowed me to leave the garrison so we could go camping at the Casp—'

'Ah! You reminded me. Just before leaving Iran to come here, I saw in the papers that he was promoted to general.'

'No kidding! I'm so happy to hear that. He was so supportive.' He began to tap the counter with his fingers. 'Now, did you bring your Armenian cognac?'

Armen chuckled. 'No, but if you take me to a good liquor outlet, we'll find it.'

Theo turned to the bar girl and read her name tag. 'Angie, have you got Armenian cognac?'

'We have several cognacs. Let me check.' Her eyes roamed the bottle labels. 'This one has this funny writing on it. Is that Armenian?' She handed the bottle to Theo, who passed it to Armen.

'Mm, Arzrooni brand, since 1876. Bottled in Yerevan. Nice.'

Angie said, 'Would you like to try it?'

'Make it two,' said Theo. She went off to get the glasses.

'She gave you the eye,' Armen winked. 'How come?'

'Armen, people want to be recognised for who they are, not as employees with a name tag. The name tag is just an entrée to who they really are.'

'Theo's turned philosopher, I see.'

'Well, they're human. We all want *some* attention.'

'Um, hm. I agree. Look at my eyelashes. Aren't they beautiful?' They laughed.

Theo raised his snifter and Armen followed. They clinked. 'For old times' sake.'

'For old times' sake, old friend.' Armen sniffed and sipped. 'When it comes to brandy, leave it to the French. When it comes to cognac, leave it to the Armenians.'

'But you left your guitar at home, right?'

'No, I've got it with me.'

'Then, we're all set!' said Theo.

Next day, they drove off and entered their little Masai Mara-Caspian getaway in Ontario.

One night, when Tereza and Theo were into the wildlife inside their tent, she said, 'Theo, my periods have stopped.'

'Quite sure?'

'Yeah. I'm sure.'

'Okay.' Thinking wheels were spinning. 'Then it's time to set the wedding date.'

Tereza lay on her tummy and smoothed his face with her hand. 'Theo?'

'Hm?'

'When you were into the nude photography, why did you never ask me to model for you?'

He tensed up. 'Woah, I was hoping you'd never come

back to that. I don't know. Maybe, I was afraid you'd think I'm weird, asking you to pose naked might offend and turn you off and then I would lose you. Isn't it better if a model is not too personal with the photographer and keeps it formal, like an assignment? Why are you asking?'

'Because, one day, I *want* you to do that. I want you to play out your imagination with the body of the woman who's yours. But only for us. When you've photographed and enlarged, I want to see what you've done with, all that light and shadow. Um?' She paused. 'It will be our private thing.'

'You really mean that?'

'Uh, huh. Reveal my body in a way that nobody's ever seen it!'

'And you would be *happy* with that?'

'Yes! What does Theo's photographic eye see? Come close. Explore! Let me in on the visual enchantments my body holds for you. Do it, Theo.' She was breathing the words now.

'Hm. Tereza has interesting thoughts.'

Next day, Theo said, 'Armen, we are going to have our wedding while you're still in Canada. I want you to be best man.'

They walked to the shores of Lake Simcoe. There were dozens of children playing in the water, shouting and yelling little, high-pitched, look-at-this-and-that attention-getters to their friends and parents, the way kids always do, wherever land meets water.

'I like that noise,' Tereza said to Theo. 'It reminds me of my childhood. They are so carefree, and joyous, full of life. They don't have the burden of worries. The world exists just for them.'

Michael flew in from Vancouver and it was just the seven of them: the Novotnys, Tereza, Armen and Sarine. Theo found an officiant and they were married in the garden of Simone and Miro's house. Theo wrote his own vows. He wanted his own version of bliss, so he memorized them:

'Tereza, enter my soul and make it your home. Make me happy for everything that happiness stands for: loyalty, faithfulness, caring, remembering, honesty, sincerity, graciousness, doing one's best. And communicating openly, not judging, not taking things too personally or seriously, and appreciating what it is like to walk in someone else's shoes.'

And to make it easy for Tereza, she could say whatever pleased her. And she said, 'Theo, you are the best thing that happened to me. My heart is in your hands.' Then, she threw her arms around his neck and burst into tears.

And that was it. The drone had married the Queen Bee.

Chapter 24

Back in British Columbia, Michael would be starting the fourth and final year of his degree in oceanography. He was telephoning from Vancouver and he was laughing.

'Mum, Pierre Trudeau was here at the UBC campus yesterday, campaigning and making a speech. Everybody's got Trudeaumania! The students went crazy for him!'

'What did they do?' Simone wore a long-distance telephone smile.

'They mobbed him! They followed him everywhere, swarming around him every time he stopped to kiss a female student. It was crazy! The girls going up to him and begging for a kiss. And when he got to the hall to give his talk, he vaulted onto the platform. It made everyone cheer and clap. And when he finished his speech, he did a little boogaloo dance for them!'

'Do you think he'll be our next Prime Minister?'

'I'm sure of it. It will be a landslide for the Liberals. He's so different from the other candidates. And a sexy bachelor! Everyone seems to love him. I'm sure the girls get an orgasm every time he opens his mouth to say something.'

Simone giggled. 'Yes, he is the darling of the media.'

'Mum, I've got good news!'

'Tell me, sweetheart.' She pulled up a chair and sat.

'I'm joining a university team going to Yugoslavia to explore an underwater cave system. It's part of my research work on undersea caves.'

'You mean there are caves beneath the sea? I didn't know that.'

'Mum, it's amazing. Cousteau explored such caves in France, but that was just the beginning. There are thousands of caves under the sea that have never been examined. This is one of them.' Michael was working up a voice sweat, forgetting that Simone did not have a degree in oceanography. 'These caves have submerged caverns and shafts and passages. They have spectacular calcite formations, stalactites and stalagmites, prehistoric skeletons, ancient artefacts. These caves were once dry, inhabited by humans and animals 150,000 years ago, when the sea level was much lower on the planet. Now, everything is submerged. It's a diver's paradise!'

Simone tapped her pencil on the telephone notepad. 'And you need to study that for your degree?'

'Yes, I'm required to do this research, and report it as my

final paper. If I do well, my professors said I have a good chance of getting straight into the doctoral program here.'

'Where exactly is this cave?'

'It's north of Dubrovnik, on the island of Korčula, in the Adriatic.'

'Adriatic! No, Michael, I don't like it. Not the Adriatic.

'Why not?'

'Michael, you are *not* going to dive in the Adriatic!' The shivers began. The Shrine whispers were getting louder. 'Michael, I forbid it.'

'I don't understand. Why are you so much against the Adriatic?'

'Michael, you're *not* going there. No! Do you hear? I don't want to lose you.' She was almost shouting.

'Why do you think you'll lose me? Mum, we go as a team. It's a huge international project. We have anthropologists, archaeologists, a marine biologist, not only from Canada, but the U.S., Europe. Then, we have the exploratory divers, support divers, an expert in undersea cave systems, a surface crew.'

'Michael, I know you're a diver, but have you done cave diving before?'

'Of course. Anyway, I'm a support diver. I won't be doing the really difficult exploration inside the caves.'

'What does a support diver do?'

'Makes sure the equipment is functioning and all the air tanks are there, checks the underwater lights and cameras, checks the safety line attached to the exploratory divers so they can find their way back out. All that stuff.'

'How deep is this cave?' Simone had her hand on her forehead, pushing back the hair. The other fist was clenched around the receiver.

'Mum, I'm not deep inside the underwater caverns. There's a whole team of us near the entrance making sure that the experts are okay. We have a signalling system if something goes wrong with the explorers.'

'And if something goes wrong?' Tears were blurring her vision.

'We follow the safety line into the cavern, get to them and bring them out. If anyone has decompression sickness, we put the diver inside the decompression chamber. I'm in charge of that. We also have two doctors with us, both qualified in diving medicine. This whole thing is very organised.'

'No, Michael. You get out of this trip.'

'Mum, what the hell are you saying? Do you know how hard it is to get on such a research expedition? Do you realize how many students would give anything to be part of this research group? Come on, be serious. I've been chosen because my professors believe I have potential. I've had training in cave diving right here in British Columbia. We don't just go off without any experience. This isn't some kind of insanely dangerous stuff.'

'I'm not at all happy.' She wiped away tears. 'When do you have to be there?'

'We need to leave here in about three weeks. I may have to go sooner.'

'Michael, I hate this. Will you contact me when you get there?'

'I will try. I don't know what's available over there, but we are in touch with the Canadian embassy in Belgrade.'

'Do you have Dad's telex address at his office?'

'Yes, I do. I wish you'd stop worrying. By the way, afterwards we will visit Sarajevo, where you and Dad spent your honeymoon.'

'Sweetie. I love you,' she bubbled at the mouth. She let Michael hang up first, before putting the receiver down.

She knew nothing about cave diving, but she envisioned underwater labyrinths and all kinds of dangers lurking around corners, deep inside unexplored passages. *Why does Michael have to do this? And why the Adriatic? What's wrong with just breathing the air around us. Why does anyone need to go down into deep water and breathe compressed air, bottled in tanks, like trapped fish exhaling the bubbles inside a bottle of Perrier?*

Minutes later, the phone rang again. Simone rushed to answer.

'Mum, please, please don't worry. I beg you. I don't want you all distressed. This is very safe. Honestly, I'll be alright. This is important to me.'

'Michael, can't I get you to change your mind?'

'I promise to call you again, the day before I leave Canada. I promise.'

'Will you take extra care? For my sake and yours?'

'Michael, Mum's in an awful state.' Theo was calling from Ontario. 'You really need to do this cave diving?'

'Of course. It's part of my final research paper. If I get through this project, all kinds of research possibilities open up for my future career.'

'I know. You were always streets ahead of me in scholarship. I'm a fan of Cousteau's too. But I'm worried about Mum. She's got this bizarre sense that something will happen to you. It's all that Near Eastern stuff she grew up with. She won't talk about it. She's into omens, and bad signs, and I don't know what else. But when I question her, she clams up. Won't say a word.'

'Really?'

'Yup. Look, is there any way I can reassure her about your cave diving, give her some reassurance that what you will be doing is not that dangerous?'

'I've already told her all that.'

'I'm sure you did. But help me a little here. What's the key feature that makes it all safe? Something I can clearly explain to her, that she will understand and hopefully accept.'

'Tell her I'll be okay.'

'Tell her you'll be okay. That's it?'

'Yes. Simple as that.'

'Come on, man. Call her again. Tell her what you've already told her. Repeat the safety stuff. Is that asking too much?'

The team on Korčula needed to get all the equipment down to the sea entrance of the undersea cave. Dozens of heavy compressed air tanks and weight belts the divers would be wearing had to be carried from the above-ground cave entrance to the undersea cave hole, below. This is where the divers would enter the water and begin their explorations. At the cave hole, the sea was foaming with the swell. Power generators for the electric undersea floodlights, cameras, diving gear, stretchers, emergency equipment and supplies, all of this was being taken down along a steep and narrow path that ran adjacent to the cave wall.

It was slow and tedious and slippery. There was loose scree on the path that the team needed to descend. Like worker ants, each person carried a load to the bottom, then climbed back up for more. Most of the team members would descend with one or two air tanks strapped to the back, and a couple of lead weight belts around their waist. Some wore a miner's helmet with headlamp to see where they were going.

Blinded by the dazzling Adriatic sun outside, Michael didn't wait for his eyes to adjust to the low light in the cave. He was crab walking in the darkness without a headlamp. Carrying one of his many loads, with air tanks and weight belts strapped to his body, he lost his balance and tottered towards what he thought was a cave wall on the opposite side. He put his arm out, as if to steady himself against the imagined wall. His retinas, full of coloured stars and spinning pinwheels, were playing tricks. There was no wall, just empty space.

He plummeted eighty feet down the shaft of the cave, like a lead cannonball thrown over a cliff. The air whooshed by his ears as he gathered speed, a sky diver whose chute hadn't opened. He hit the rocky bottom of the cave with a sickening, metallic thud.

The expedition leader and two other divers clambered down to him, and he was motionless. Blood was pouring out of his mouth and ears and his chest had collapsed. They got him to the surface and a motorboat sped him to Dubrovnik accompanied by one of the diving doctors and the expedition leader. When Michael arrived at the local hospital, blood was still trickling out of his mouth and running down his cheeks and ears. There was no pulse, no breathing, his pupils were dilated and unresponsive to light.

The examining doctor shook his head. 'I'm afraid he is gone. Such a dreadful, needless waste of youthfulness,' he said in Croatian to the nurses around him. They crossed themselves many times. One of them was crying, a young girl, not yet toughened to the reality of the emergency ward and to a life in medicine.

The doorbell rang and Simone answered it. A uniformed sergeant of the Royal Canadian Mounted Police was standing there. She did not like the apparition. It signalled foreboding.

'Mrs. Simone Novotny?'

'Yes?'

'Morning, ma'am. Forgive me if I'm disturbing. I'm Sergeant Hewitt. May I come in, please?'

He removed his cap and Simone offered him an armchair in the living room. He had a portfolio with him. 'Mrs. Novotny, I've been asked by the Department of External Affairs to visit you and convey a message they received from the Canadian Embassy in Belgrade.'

An overloaded circuit started a fire in Simone's brain. 'Is it about my son?'

'Yes, ma'am. I'm afraid your son has had an accident.'

A primordial scream worked its wretched way out of a breast deepened like a dark, limestone cave blackened with hanging bats and full of sinister, cold-blooded creatures. It emerged as a soul-curdling shriek.

'How serious!? Where is he now?'

Hewitt broke the events slowly, in a practiced, restrained tone. She buried her face in her trembling hands, each piece of the story a thousand ice-pick blows to the bosom. He supplied his and the ambassador's meaningless condolences. The Canadian Government would offer assistance to repatriate the body to Canada.

Her mercurial spirit had plummeted to an all-time low. She picked up the telephone receiver and flooded the mouthpiece with salty water. Called Miro. Miro came home and found a heavy, wet shape crumpled on the velvet couch in the living room. He held her for a very long time. An alchemy of despair bubbled and boiled into thickening guilt.

'Miro, did I do enough to stop him?' Remorse gelled into blame. 'Miro, it's a curse. The lost diamond ring left a curse. It's there, it's there, in the Mediterranean. It won't let go. It'll haunt us.' The plea of a tortured soul got louder: 'Evil omen, let go!' Then dissolved into sobs.

Miro tried his logic. Panic needed to be coiled in and crimped. 'There is no curse. His dream was to go diving, to explore. These things happen. His heart and mind were in it. Don't you see? He had an unstoppable dream. No one could stop it. Take that away from him and he is forever unhappy. Simonko, no one could stop him.' Miro hugged her. 'We wanted him to be happy. He wanted to be an oceanographer.'

Soul-blistering weeks went by, hearts pumping the blood of loss. The tyranny of incessant suffering had delivered their decision on the tip of a reality-piercing knife. Simone and Miro were in Dubrovnik. They were talking to Father Stjepan Andric at Dubrovnik's Church of St. Blaise. Could Michael be buried at the cemetery of the Church of Sveti Nikola, on the island of Korčula, close to where he was killed? Michael, laid beside the silent world he loved and the undersea cave he didn't explore. Father Andric would make enquiries.

A week passed. The three of them took the ferry from Dubrovnik to Korčula. Michael was on board in a white coffin. A horse-driven hearse was awaiting them at the ferry terminal on Korčula. It was a rickety cart, pulled by a shabby, white horse that had seen better days and the local driver sat in front, with the coffin loaded on the back. Miro, Simone and Father Andric walked behind it for the short distance to Sveti Nikola Church. As they wound through the narrow, dusty, meandering streets of the town, men would stop and remove their hats and cover their hearts until the hearse had passed. They got to the church. Father Andric held a mass and then they buried Michael.

Simone held three deep-red roses. The petals were wilting, floral heads were now bowed over the thorny stems. She laid them on the grave, one by one.

'This one's from Pavel, this one from Setareh. They shepherded you as a boy. This one: from all of us. We'll love you . . .' She handcuffed the *forever* word and paused. That *thing* spoken by Pavel! 'We will love you always.'

Theo arrived the next day. The airline connections to Yugoslavia were convoluted, the times unreliable. He had missed the last boat from Rijeka to Dubrovnik, so he took a bus to Split and, there, boarded a boat to Korčula. Simone saw the signs in his red eyes. He had been spilling the tears of a crushed brother.

They stayed a week to bond with Michael's final backdrops. The island had a raw, Mediterranean beauty. The deep-blueness of the Adriatic did not match the rocky outcrop of the land. It was bleached dry and the plants and scrub were thorny and olive coloured. The air was fresh and clean. The scents of Beirut's and Haifa's shores had a calming effect on Simone after the turbulence of the last several weeks.

'You've been so brave.' Miro put his arm around her.

'But *you* are our brave one!'

'I'm so proud of you,' he added.

They made a last visit to the rock-strewn grave before leaving for Canada. By then, the headstone had been added. It was a quick job, hurriedly made, with poorly etched letters in the yellowish-white sandstone. A few Cyrillic characters stood out where the stone mason had erred.

Michael von Mannberg Иovotny, hero to his family.
Борn in Africa, taken by the Adriatic.
Died doing what he loved бest.
Gone now to join Poseidon.

Time passed. The dryness made things permanent. A hand reached down to the grave and left a bunch of calla lilies, clumsily tied together with hemp string. Pink freckles on this arm were swimming in a sea of sunburnt skin and the khaki shirt had its sleeves rolled up. Her shorts were frayed at the edges. It was late in the day and the long brown hair was glowing red. She stepped back, paused for a while to keep him company and her lips made inaudible words. Michael's girlfriend was on his expedition. Diving logistics, they called her job. Now, she took a precious moment to stay a while with all that was left.

It was eerily quiet around her.

Chapter 25

A brutal year had left its scars on a grieving family. Simone was immersed in human happenings. As Michael foresaw, Pierre Trudeau won the election. But the world was in turmoil. Americans at home were being torn apart by the Vietnam War. Rioting students in France were tearing up the pavements of Paris and ten million striking workers were shutting down the French economy. Martin Luther King Jr. had been felled by a bullet from a scope-fitted rifle and U.S. Presidential candidate Bobby Kennedy was gunned down at close range by a Palestinian kitchen worker in a Los Angeles hotel. The Vatican issued a pontifical 'no' to the contraceptive pill, angering many liberal-minded Catholics. Street-fighting student protesters and American *Black Power* sprinters—their black-gloved fists held high in defiance—were disrupting the Mexico City Summer Olympics. And Soviet tanks and troops rolled into Czechoslovakia to crush the *Prague Spring* and begin another winter of oppression.

Simone was tasting, touching, smelling (not reading) real history. Happening now. Blow by blow, image by image, paraded under raucous headlines. History collected in bits and pieces by correspondents and their camera crews, to feed future historians. Amid all this, a family member had left the world, his life cut short by a force of destiny and the silent voice of the Shrine. He had encountered a different enemy, an immutable law of nature, and lost the battle to gravity.

Spring was squeezing to get past the weakening grip of icy winter and bringing fresh hope. Tereza was in hospital. She had surprised everyone with the birth of twin boys. Simone came to visit. As she sat by her bedside, Tereza reached over and grasped her hand.

'Simone, do we have permission to name them Mickey and Paul?'

Simone took her hand and pressed it against her own temple. 'Of course. I have your name, and now you have their namesakes, Michael and Pavel. Let's take care of them.' She went silent. Her mind was a jumble. Things were missing in the harshness of uncertainty. Should she warn Tereza about the cruel sea, not letting the boys go diving, the dangers of water? Then at last, 'Tereza, you are the daughter I didn't have.' Her voice lowered to a whisper. 'Now, I have one.'

Tereza no longer did the airlines. Crazy working hours, glamour worn thin, days away from Theo.

Time flew. The twins became Miro's captivation. When Theo and Tereza were out of town, Miro and Simone took the boys and kept them busy. Miro was retired, his and Simone's final year in Ontario. They had bought a house in West Vancouver with a panorama of Burrard Inlet and a bay full of anchored cargo ships.

Miro took out the python skin and unrolled it across the living room carpet. The impossibly huge African monster had entered the house.

Paul jumped out of its way. 'Wow! What's it called?'

'What does it eat?' gulped Mickey.

'These rock pythons eat ducks and deer and pigs, and can even crush a crocodile and kill it.'

'Can it eat a man?'

'Let me tell you a story about the King of Africa.' He sat down. 'The king had a queen and he had two boys.' He used his own version and gave it the weight of a daring feat:

Sing a song of sixpence, now, don't you start to cry.
Four-and-twenty robin eggs were baked in a pie.
When the pie was opened, the chicks began to sing.
Oh, what a tuneful dish to set before the king!
The king was in his counting house, counting all his gold.
The queen was in the parlour, eating bread with mould.

The boys were in the garden, going for a stroll.
Along came a python, and swallowed them whole!
Now, see that nasty python, with its bulging belly.
If help didn't come quick, the boys would turn to jelly.
Kabiru came with kitchen knife and opened up the snake,
And there were the king's boys, alive, for goodness sake!'

They sat and listened, again and again, memorising the lines.

'Who killed *this* snake?' asked Mickey.

'Kabiru did,' said Miro. 'Your daddy discovered this snake in our garden when it was crawling through the grass.'

'We have snakes in our garden?' Paul recoiled.

'No. That's when your daddy was a little boy like you, in Africa.'

'Wow!' Paul turned to Mickey. 'Daddy found this huge snake!'

'And did it try to swallow him?'

'It could have. Kabiru came and they put it inside a sack, so it couldn't run away.'

'Grampa, who is Kabiru?'

'Is he a snake hunter?'

And so, it went. Miro had the stories, the boys fed their once-upon-a-timeless curiosity.

Miro had plenty of nostalgia for his old job at Unireifen. He visited often to see what was new at the division he once headed, and what was taking place at his onetime lab. Whenever he came by, his former colleagues would pick his brains and get his advice. You scratch my back, I'll scratch yours, unspoken words of everlasting camaraderie.

The telephone rang and Simone answered. 'Mrs. Novotny?'

'Yes?'

'It's David at Unireifen. I don't want to alarm you, but Miro is at Mississauga General Hospital.' Simone tensed up. She pressed the earpiece harder to the ear. 'While he was visiting the lab, we had to call an ambulance. Apparently, he's had a heart attack. They tell me he is being looked after at—' Simone's mind tuned out. Silent space opened up, expanding rapidly. *Not another tragedy in the family! I can't take any more tragedy.*

'I'm going there right away. Thanks for letting me know, David.' She dashed off.

'We call it congestive heart failure. It sounds worse than it is and he won't need surgery.' That was the cardiologist on duty, explaining to Simone. 'He'll need to stay a while, so we can monitor his condition and do the medical tests. I suspect constricted blood vessels, rather than blood volume, as the cause of his hypertension, but the tests will tell. I think we'll need to change the medication he is taking.'

'Doctor, aside from medication, is there a lifestyle issue here? Diet? Exercise? Eating habits? He's never been prone to stress, he's a non-smoker and he is retired now.' It carried in her voice. *Am I partly responsible for Miro's heart attack?*

'When we know more, I'll refer you to a specialist. Don't be anxious.' He put a kind hand on her shoulder.

Theo and Tereza were in Chicago. *Canada Today* magazine had sent him to do a story on Canadian ice hockey players skating for hockey league teams in America. Saturday evening came, and Theo took Tereza to a restaurant on the shores of Lake Michigan. The evening progressed and the wine had its way.

'Theo, I've got disco fever!'

He reached over and felt her forehead. 'Yeah, you *are* running a temperature.' His mock-serious look melted. 'You want to go dancing at a disco, right?'

'Yes! And I want to go all-night dancing.' Her eyes lit up the way only two men in the world would recognise, Armen and Theo.

As they were leaving the restaurant, a man approached and an expression of recognition crossed his face. 'Tereza! Remember me? Air France flights to Europe?'

She couldn't remember his name. 'Lufthansa, not Air France.'

'Oh, yes. Right. How are things with you?' Tereza shrugged and offered an anaemic smile. The entire time while he stood there yapping and filling his ego tank, Theo was invisible to him.

'Did we?' He formed a circle with the thumb and forefinger of his left hand and pumped the index finger of the other hand in and out of the circle.

'No, we didn't!' snapped Tereza. 'You've got the wrong person.'

He gave her a perfunctory farewell salute and marched off. Tereza glanced at Theo. A smile flickered across his face.

'Slimy narcissist,' she fumed. She glanced again at Theo and worried whether he was toying with suspicions.

Theo read her thoughts. 'That's airlines for you. I know you're an airline virgin.' He put his arm around her. 'Let's get to that disco.'

'What's the place called?'

'It's called Moravian Rhapsody.'

'You serious?'

'As serious as a disco can get. Chicago is full of Czech immigrants. They fled the communist takeover and gravitated to this city.'

They found the place where the rotating, mirrored disco ball sent spots of light spinning around the disco floor and flashing onto the writhing bodies with beams that resembled a psychedelic trance. A jet of ultraviolet light turned her white blouse into a sparkling purple and the throbbing music was amply loud. The dance floor was lit up with translucent panels that flashed their rainbow lights to the same tempo as the noisy beat. Disco, to her, was the greatest antidote to sensory deprivation. Tereza was in her element. They twisted and turned and pumped and wiggled to the beat of the incessant rhythm. It was a perpetual, never-ending orgasm on the dance floor. And it went on as if tomorrow would never arrive. The elixir of love was coursing through her veins. Just like the times when it was wildlife in the tent when they went camping with Armen and his assortment of non-virgin girlfriends.

They came back in the primordial hours of the day and waited for the lift at their hotel lobby. When its doors slid open, Theo scooped her up and threw her over his shoulders.

'Let me down!' she squealed in mock protest, kicking her legs and slapping his buttocks with both hands.

Up they went, to Room 341. He carried her into the shower and turned it on.

'It's cold!' she yelled.

'Take off your clothes.'

He brought her down. They both squirmed out of wet clothes and washed away the salt of the evening.

'Sometimes, I forget how gorgeous you are when you're standing naked in the rain,' he smiled.

Arms outstretched, she turned her palms upward as

if to catch some rain and struck the look-at-me pose of a Greek marble statue. 'You think so?'

'That's what I'm told by the lenses of my eyes and the mirror of my mind.'

Water poured down her head. She collected some of it in her mouth and squirted it in his face.

'Hey, what'd I say?' he spluttered. 'Turn around. I'll soap your back and survey the topography of your elegantly landscaped butt.'

'Did you bring your waterproof camera?'

'I have waterproof eyes. H-a-a, you've got goose bumps! Earth mounds carpeting the slopes of these undulating dunes.' His fingers took over the nude photography, frame by tactile frame. He ran his fingers in slow motion down her back and then they climbed, following the contours, up over her buttocks and down the other side, merging seamlessly with the sculpted legs below, to continue the perfection. 'Michelangelo could not have done a better job,' he whispered in her ear.

'Theo, am I still the same as when you met me?'

He grabbed her by the shoulders and spun her round to face him. 'What?'

'Am I still attractive to you?'

'What are you thinking?' he blurted.

'Well?'

'Tereza, what's this self-doubt shit?'

'You haven't answered my question.' She kept giving him the wistful look.

'Where's this coming from? Can't you *feel* our bond?'

'Then *why* haven't you photographed my body? Isn't it beautiful anymore?'

Theo caught up with those runaway thoughts and expelled a puff of droplets. 'Okay, okay, I understand. I will. I've been so busy. You know that.'

'So, this is not a priority for you.'

'I will make it a priority. Sorry.'

'You're such a good photographer. I want to see what *your* eye sees.'

'I'm not that good. But we'll wait for the chance. When the twins are visiting Miro and—'

'Okay, sexy shutterbug. Remember your promise to your naked wife.'

They used the last moments before dawn for wildlife.

Tereza was lying on her belly tracing the outline of his face with her finger. 'You handsome East African bastard. Where did you get your good looks?'

'Um. Don't remember. Oh, yes. I placed the order while I was still living in my mother's womb. When I moved out, my looks were waiting for me at the nursing home.'

'At your office, I saw Patricia giving you the eye. She must have roving thoughts about you.'

'Um. Didn't know that.'

'When we go shopping, I notice that a lot of women look

at you.' Her finger roamed to where the hair forest met the forehead plateau and chanced upon a scar. 'Hmm. I never saw this before. What happened here?'

'What happened where?'

'I've never noticed this scar. How did *that* happen?'

'I haven't told you the story? It was the year before we left Africa. We were coming back from a visit with friends who lived on a farm in Thika. Dad was driving our Chevrolet and it was dark. He didn't know the road well. He was driving too fast as we approached a curve in the road. All of a sudden, Simone yelled *'Look out, there's a man on the road!'* He was wearing dark clothes and, being black-skinned, was almost invisible. Dad swerved to avoid him and the car overturned on its roof. Michael was buried under the back seat and I was thrown forward and hit the windscreen. We got out of the car and I was bleeding from the forehead. Simone took a hankie to soak up the blood. There were some natives from a nearby village and they helped Dad turn the car upright, and then we continued home in it. That Chevy was built like a tank.'

'You've had *so* many accidents.' Her soft breath floated the words. 'Your guardian angel must be an archangel.'

'Um hm. She's decreed that my life be spared for you.' Cartoonified grin came and faded.

'And *how* do you know your archangel is a she?' The question formed at the pace of a snowflake falling from a quiet sky and settling on a Bohemian pine needle.

'Because her name is Tereza, and only a Tereza could make her lover get down on his knees at 25,000 feet and beg her to marry him.'

'Yes, in the galley of an aircraft when it hit turbulence.' Her grin was wide. Her beautiful teeth were on show.

He went silent for many moments. 'But there's one wound that never healed.'

'Oh?'

'Michael's death. It will never heal. No scar. Just a permanent wound. It's there forever.'

'I'm so sorry. Really sorry.'

Alarm went off. Far too early. They vacated their room to return home. Theo noticed the number on the door and pointed to it. 'That's funny. *341*. I didn't catch the coincidence until now.'

'What's the coincidence?'

'That was the number of the RAF squadron led by Pavel, 341 Squadron.'

Her eyes caught his expression. 'He had a big impact on you, didn't he?'

He smiled a diversion to deflect the touch of unmasking. 'You know, there's something quite unique about you.'

'My body?'

'Uh, that too. But something else as well.'

'You've got three floors to come out with it. Start telling.'

The lift doors parted and the elevator swallowed them up.

Chapter 26

The boys were with Miro and Simone. The idea of visiting Niagara Falls popped up.

'Wow, grampa, we saw a movie of Niagara Falls in kindygarden.' That was Mickey. 'Our teacher said the water pours down buckets and buckets and lets out steam, like clouds splashing. Pshhhhhhh!'

'A million, million, buzzillion buckets every day!' added Paul.

'Can we go?'

Miro drove Simone and the boys around the western shores of Lake Ontario, then along the Niagara River to the Canadian side of Niagara Falls. As they walked towards the Horseshoe Falls, water vapour was rising like a cloud from the foaming waterfall pool, at the bottom. They could see a boat cruising around the base of the fall, full of tiny people wearing bright-yellow, waterproof and hooded capes.

The twins were overwhelmed by the noise and the

sheer volume of water cascading over the edge. 'Granma, can we go down to that boat and get close?' said Paul.

'No dear. I don't want us to do that.'

The boys were now at the very edge of the river as it flowed past the last rocks before disappearing over the lip. They were straining against the barrier and leaning forward to get a better glimpse of the torrent of thundering water falling away to the roiling plunge pool, far below.

Another bête noire was surfacing in Simone's head. Anxiety was flooding her thoughts and washing away the bridges of reason. She grabbed both boys by their wrists and began to step backwards, pulling them away from the edge. She was squeezing so hard, her knuckles were white.

'Granma, you're hurting my hand,' yelped Mickey.

Simone, still holding onto them, made an abrupt turn away from the foaming water. What else could inoculate her against aquaphobia?

'Come. Let's go to a really wonderful ice cream parlour,' she said. 'Imagine. They have two hundred different ice cream flavours.'

Click! 'Tereza, turn just a little bit to your left. Yeah, hold it there.' Click! Click!

'Now, I'll adjust the light, point it away from your belly. I want you to take a breath and hold. You ready?'

'Um hm.'

Click! 'Okay to exhale now. I'm calling this one the sand dune in the Arabian desert.'

She giggled. 'Sand dune. Um. Never thought of myself as a sand dune.'

'Hold it. Don't giggle.' He moved just a bit. Click! Click! 'Hold your arm above your head. Elbow higher. Like this. Perfect.' Click! Click! Click! Click! 'Now, I'll move a little closer. I want you perfectly still while I focus on the belly button. It's a slight dip in the sand. Very delicate . . . Hold.' Click!

'Sandy belly button?'

'Good. I have to chill you just a little. I will be putting an ice pack just behind your neck, so be ready.'

'Why?'

'I need goose bumps.'

'What for?'

'Relax. There are no sinister motives.'

She yelled. 'It's freezing!'

'Sorry. Okay, now turn your body towards the light. Good. Just a little towards me. Little more. Great.' Click! Click! Click! 'Gorgeous! You're perfect at developing goose bumps.'

'What are you calling this one?'

'Goosebumps on pure, white snow.'

He loaded another roll of black-and-white film. Stepped back and shifted his position so the angle was low. He adjusted the lights and dimmed them so her pubic hair threw fine shadows across the belly. Click! Click! Click! Click!

He placed himself above her head. Repositioned the lights so they were well below her feet and lowered a black screen there. Now, her breasts and nipples formed starkly defined volcanos against the backdrop. Click! Click!

'Exhale as much as you can, and hold for a second.' Click! 'Okay to breathe, now.' Click!

'Now. Turn onto your belly. Um hm. Good.' He shifted to a low position. 'Legs together. Thank you. I'm standing in the valley, looking up.'

'And what do you see?'

'A valley between two smoothly-worn mountains leading to a high, pink plateau.' Click! He shifted a touch. Click! Click!

'So, give it a name.'

'Tereza's beautiful buttocks. TBB.'

Miro got permission to give the twins and Simone a tour of the tyre-making facilities and his old lab. Probably a last chance to do this, before moving to Vancouver.

They started by planting yellow hard hats on their heads. The boys were amused at the wobbly hats, too large for their heads, and held them in place with their hands. First stop seemed to fascinate them. There was this huge Banbury mixer, two stories tall, mixing the raw rubber with all kinds of chemicals. When the mixing was complete, the whole smelly, black gloop dropped down to the floor below and was kneaded on two, gigantic hot rollers. As this compound was being masticated, it made loud, popping noises like a school-girlish colossus of steel chewing a mouthful of black bubble gum and trying to impress her audience with the pops of the gargantuan bubbles. The twins giggled at this noisy spectacle and feigned self-protecting gestures each time a rubber bubble exploded. They wanted to linger, but Miro pressed on with the tour.

The boys were offered a dizzying mechanical extravaganza: calenders, cutters, coilers, extruders, and, finally, they stood at the presses that mould the tyre tread and vulcanize the tyre. As the lids on the moulds lifted, great clouds of steam and smoke rose to the factory ceiling and the twins let out a sigh of awe. Now, for the first time, they saw the finished tyre. Miro took them to the lab where, for so many years, he tested the tyres for all kinds of qualities, including resistance to aquaplaning. This is where he could teach the boys some valuable tyre-safety lessons.

Miro showed them sample tyre treads in various stages of wear. A bald tyre, a badly-worn tyre tread, a tyre with some tread left, a brand-new tyre. He pointed out the varying tread depths, the depths of the grooves. He took a car wheel, fitted with a tyre that had very little tread left, and mounted the wheel on a special drum that could be rotated at various speeds. Then, he lowered the drum until it touched a movable belt that simulated the surface of a road. He switched on the motor and the tyre began to spin over the moving belt. Hrrrrrrrr! And the boys made a similar sound of breathless awe. Then Miro opened a valve that sprayed water at the contact point between tyre tread and belt. Now, he increased the simulated travel speed: 40mph, 45mph, 50mph.

'Look boys, our car is traveling at fifty miles an hour on a rain-soaked road. The tyre is trying hard to let the water flow away.' He increased the speed to 60mph. 'It's struggling, it's fighting to squeeze away all the water, it's saying, "Out water! Out of my way. I need to hug the road!" But the water can't get out. It stays under the tyre.'

The boys were wide-eyed now. Suddenly, the tyre stopped rotating, but the belt kept rolling past. The tyre was floating on water. 'Look!' said Miro, 'The car is out of control. The driver can't stop! We're sliding on water. Help! Crash!'

'What happened, grandpa?' said Paul.

'The tyre couldn't push away all that water on the road. The tyre was bald, no tread left. So, the tyre said goodbye to the road and was floating. And the driver lost control of the car.'

'Did he die?' asked Paul.

'He could have,' said Miro.

Miro repeated the same demonstration with a

brand-new tyre. He got the speed up to 70mph and the tyre could handle all the water collecting under it and maintain contact with the road. No aquaplaning. They went back to the tyre tread samples.

'Okay! Paul, Mickey, who has a penny?' Miro said.

The boys looked puzzled.

'An American penny. Have we got one?' Miro began smiling. 'I've got one.' He held a U.S. one-cent coin in his fingers. 'Now we'll put Abraham Lincoln to work.' The boys looked mystified as Miro turned the coin upside down and inserted Lincoln's head into the groove on the tread of the badly-worn tyre. 'Can we see the top of Abraham's head?'

Simone and the boys nodded.

'Then, this tyre is no good. The top of the tread is not touching his head. Time to get a new tyre. Yes?' Miro made up a little Willy Wonka, Oompa Loompa act for them:

Top of the tread is not touching his head!
Top of the tread is not touching his head!
If you drive on old tyres,
You'll crash and be dead!

The twins and Simone giggled with glee and Miro moved to the tyre with some tread left and put Lincoln's head inside the groove. 'Can we see the top of Abraham's head, or is the tread hiding his head a little?'

Paul nodded. 'It's hiding his hair!'

'Um, hm. The tread is in his hair! So, this tyre is still okay, but we need to keep an eye on it. Because, soon, we'll have to change the tyre and get a new one. Yes?'

'Why do we need to get a new one?' asked Paul.

'Because, as we keep driving, the tread will get thinner, and thinner, until the tyre is bald. Like Abraham with a shaved head, Abraham with no hair! What's the golden rule, boys?' Miro put on his tiger look: '*Never, ever drive on bald tyres,*' he growled.

Mickey laughed. 'Throw away the bald tyres! Throw away bald Abraham!'

'That's right. Don't drive on bald tyres, because you might crash. But new tyres have deep grooves. They will let the rainwater flow away and the tyre will hug the road. We want the tread to kiss the road all the time, even when the road is wet! A wet kiss! Then we'll be safe. Let's have a rhyme for new tyres, shall we?'

Rain, rain, flow away;
Tyre tread hugs the road today!

Smiles came and they repeated the rhyme, giggling. Miro moved to the brand-new tyre and sank Lincoln into the tread. 'And here's a brand-new tyre. See? Lots of tread. Deep grooves. Plenty of room for the water to squeeze out when it rains. And where is upside-down Abraham, now? The top of the tread is touching his nose!'

'And now he'll go, *"Achoo!"* and then we will crash!' said Mickey.

They all broke up in chortles. Simone was in stitches. She dipped her knees and threw her head back: *Kids make the craziest connections.* Back at his old office, Miro whispered something to Simone and she dug into her purse and gave him two shiny, copper pennies in mint condition.

Miro put one in each hand and held his closed fists in front of the boys. 'Abraaa cadabra, what lies hidden in my hands?'

The twins looked at each other, then gave a *don't know* shrug. Miro opened his hands. 'One Lincoln for you, and one Lincoln for you!'

They both fleshed out a smiley face. 'Grampa,' said Mickey, 'who is Linkum? Is he a tyre man?'

Miro was in hospital for a few days to stomach a thorough check-up. Theo visited Simone during the weekend to keep her company. She craved taking her mind off the medical uncertainty and Theo's presence was a longed-for distraction.

'Theo, take me dancing.'

'You serious?'

'Um hm. Take me dancing somewhere. Anywhere. You have *carte blanche.*'

'Simone, I'm not a good dancer, all I know is rock 'n' roll.'

'That's good. You can rock me and I will roll you.' Her eyes invited a touch of mischief.

He felt embarrassed at the thought of rock 'n' rolling with his mum. *The age difference. Would others notice? Could he find a place where anonymity hid them? That place he went with Armen, the pub in Oakville, A Knight in Gail. No! Too many chances they would be spotted.*

Friday night came and Theo would be brave. His mother believed in him. This was not a time to chicken out. 'I'll take you to A Knight in Gail. They have a dance floor and hopefully the music will be good,' he told Simone.

Simone was beaming. When they arrived outside the pub, Theo offered her his arm and Simone took it. She paused, looked up at the pub sign, and chortled her surprise. 'Theo, I thought you said, "A Nightingale!"'

'I did.'

'You grew up in the land of roses and nightingales. This is not a nightingale. It's naughty wordplay!'

'Okay, you be the rose. I am the knight. I don't want you to be Gail.'

They danced to rock 'n' roll music. The band switched to slow music. Simone stepped closer to him, his arm went around her. The slowed rhythm befuddled Theo's jive-savvy feet.

Soon, he had the hang of the steps. Simone twinkled,

'There you go. You've got it.' She glanced at him. Suddenly, he looked like the Persian king of kings with the kind nose. Childhood memories rivered from the mountains of Ecbatana. She was dancing with the king. 'You know, Theo, if I hadn't met Miro, I would have married someone like you.'

'That's ridiculous,' he sputtered. 'How many champagnes have you had?'

'Just two glasses.' She rocked her head from side to side. 'I'm in a bubbly mood.'

'Then it must be the Tootsie Rolls you had for breakfast.'

Emanata sprang forth from her head: 'You remembered that! You're amazing.' She was ambushed by this ancient flashback and put her cheek against his. 'Do you recall how you would jump over the flames of the bonfires on *shab-e Chehār-shanbeh Sūri*, the eve of Red Wednesday?'

His mind did a quick rewind to Persian: '*Albateh. Khāterāt-e shirin-e zendegi.*' Of course. Life's sweet reminiscences.

'You had fire in your belly, and the kids in the street were amazed at this foreign firecracker flying over their bonfire.'

The music died down a bit. An announcement was made at the front. 'Ladies and Gentlemen, we have a surprise for you tonight. Please welcome the Kingston Blues!' The band moved on stage and began playing.

'Simone! It's reggae! Come, let's dance.'

'I don't know how to dance to reggae.'

'It's easy. I'll show you. It's Jamaican and you'll love it.'

She took to it very quickly, and let her hair down. Enjoyment began to flow, undiluted by the champagne and unfiltered by the music's newness. The steps came easy and her hips undulated to the *four-four* time of reggae. Her dance teacher from Lebanon would be impressed.

They sat down a little and Theo piped up. 'I've got a question for you. Are you a sybaritic dilettante, or a dilettantish sybarite?'

'I see. Theo is now waxing journalistic.'

'Well?'

'I don't know. What do you think?'

'Nah, nah. You must answer that.'

'I'm in a bubbly mood. This is self-analysis. Freudian stuff. Too deep to dance in.'

They danced more. Had more sips. Applauded the band. The fire in the belly subsided. Tired, they went home.

Chapter 27

It was on the road to Vancouver. Sharing the driving, Miro and Simone had the sweetness of time in their laps for savouring the vastness of the United States. Miro's mind would be teleported to their new home in British Columbia and Simone was thrilled to particles at the thought of having a relaxed Miro by her side. Awaiting them was the great lesson in geographic and regional lifestyles among America's inhabitants. They drove south from Oakville and passed through Buffalo before stopping for the night in Angola, New York.

'Simonko, this is our very last chance to visit Angola.'

Simone liked that. 'Do you think we can find a motel here?'

'We'll see. Let's keep looking.'

They stopped at a two-storey, Queen Anne style, wood-framed house with front porch, that looked like it might be a bed and breakfast. It was getting dark. Miro got out of the car and walked towards the entrance. There was a stone marker in front of the house.

'Well, I'll be damned,' he breathed.

He walked back to the car. 'You won't believe it. This is the house where Willis Carrier was born in 1876.'

'Willis Carrier?'

'Yeah, inventor of the air conditioner!' he snickered.

Simone saw the funny side too. 'We can thank him that our car has air conditioning. What an irony: born in Angola, invented air conditioning. Don't you love it?'

'I imagine we'll thank Mr. Carrier when we get to Arizona in July,' said Miro.

They found a tiny motel just outside the town limits. Next day, it was onto Highway 90 and heading towards the corner of Pennsylvania that touches Lake Erie. As they drove, Simone noted the bleakness of the landscape. It reminded her of Germany's Ruhr district, the heartland of the German steel industry, fed by coal. But, here, she could see shut-down plants, empty shells that were once thriving factories, rusting machinery and crumbling, ghostly housing blocks for industrial workers, and the grimy results of coal-fired production. Many of the public playgrounds were empty of children.

'Where is everybody?' Simone asked.

'Gone to work elsewhere in America. The loss of manufacturing jobs here has been devastating to workers and their families. Acid rain and smokestacks were a part of life, but it was nothing compared to the 400,000 industrial jobs lost in this part of the nation. Now they have urban decay, racial tensions and crime.'

'How sad for these people.'

Miro continued, 'Some journalists are calling this the *Rust Belt*. America wears many belts. After Chicago, we'll be heading towards the *Bible Belt* and shortly after that, the *Corn Belt*.'

'There's a *Sun Belt*, too, right?' she added.

'Umm, hmm. We'll touch it when we enter Arizona to see the Grand Canyon. But, you know, I do believe the *Rust Belt* will recover. They have one precious thing that many regions of America don't, lots and lots of fresh water.'

'Miro, do we have belts in Canada?'

'Well, for sure we have seatbelts,' he smiled.

'You're in a good mood, today, aren't you?'

'Of course. I'm always in a good mood.' His grin became more liberal.

'No, not always. I know when you're in a bad mood.'

'But I'm always in a good mood when we travel together.'

She caught the opportune moment. 'So, let's travel to Czechoslovakia!' She raised the volume on the last few syllables.

Miro stayed silent.

'You're not saying anything,' she said in a sing-song tone.

'You're right. I'm not.' He was smiling again.

'Miro, please. I'm dying to see Milena and Lubor. We can find Marek, your best friend!'

'You're my best friend.' He kept his hands on the steering wheel and swivelled his head her way.

'Well, he's *my* best friend. Don't you see? We need to go before it's too late. Before we can't travel anymore.'

'Then, go see them.'

Simone was appalled and it showed. 'No! I would never go there without you. They are your relatives and you need to see them too. It's your homeland.

They passed through Erie, Pennsylvania and approached the outskirts of Cleveland, Ohio. A highway sign read: *AKRON, RUBBER CAPITAL OF THE WORLD, 30*.

'Look, Miro, we're thirty miles from Akron. All the big tyre makers live there. Shall we make a small detour?'

'Nah. I'm all tyred out. Been there, a few times. Enough of tyres for a while.'

Several miles later, they stopped at a service station to tank up and get refreshments. At the entrance, Simone spotted a huge sign with bold lettering and pointed to it, laughing. It read:

Leave your car and we'll shock, tire and brake you, and check your underbody, too!

Miro chuckled as he started filling the car. 'That's English for you. Can't think of a language that lends itself so readily to wordplay and double entendre. It certainly wouldn't work in Chinese.'

'Or in Latin,' she added.

Miro was still driving. As they rode along the shores of Lake Erie, before crossing into Indiana, Simone saw a roadside billboard for the Case Erie Bank. Its prodding headline quizzed:

Is Your Husband Losing Interest?

She read it out for Miro and the verbal stunt made them chortle. 'Why don't we have clever bank signs like that in Ontario?'

'Am I losing interest?' he probed.

'Are you? I don't think so.' She took his free arm and clamped his hand between her legs, releasing it only when he needed to negotiate a curve in the road.

In Chicago, they visited the Science Museum and took a night cruise along Chicago's shoreline on Lake Michigan. The city was pulsing with nightlife. It was the first bright spot after so many miles of industrial Rust Belt, like an edible flower blooming between corroded girders in a mountain of scrap iron. They went to a night club and danced the evening away.

A few days later, they visited the grounds of the University of Chicago. Miro wanted to pay homage at the statue dedicated to Thomas Garrigue Masaryk, Czechoslovakia's founding father and its first president.

'He was a philosophy professor here. Did you know that?' said Miro.

'At the University of Chicago?' Simone was surprised.

'Uh, huh. For several years.' They walked along a boulevard neatly landscaped with hedges and trees.

'Why was his middle name Garrigue? That doesn't sound like a Czech name.'

'Back in the 1870s, Masaryk married Charlotte Garrigue, an American citizen from a Protestant family with French ancestry. He took her family name as his middle name.'

Simone sent mischief. 'You should have done the same. Then you would have been Miroslav Meir Novotny.'

'But there's more. Masaryk's mother was Terezie Masaryková. She had *your* middle name.'

As they stood before the Masaryk memorial, a thirty-foot-high equestrian statue of the Knight of Blaník, the legendary Czech saviour who emerges from Blaník mountain when his nation is under attack, Simone clutched Miro's arm and looked up at the knight on horseback.

'He wants you to come home, Miro. Listen to him before it's too late. This is your sign.'

They headed south to Missouri and entered the northern reaches of the Bible Belt. Simone wanted a few days in St. Louis, gateway to the American West. Once again, her spirit went soaring and flirting with the ghosts of history. Here is where the virgin Missouri River, born in the Rocky Mountains and meandering like a watery lost soul, finally meets the storied Mississippi River. The two join hands and marry, taking a vow to flow majestically towards Louisiana and spill hand-in-hand into the Gulf of Mexico, to drown together.

Standing at the foot of the gleaming, stainless steel Gateway Arch, Simone's thoughts migrated to her French hero. 'Miro, Napoleon sold the entire Louisiana Territory to the United States for fifteen million dollars. Can you imagine? All the land that France owned from the border of Canada, down to New Orleans, and from the Mississippi River to the Rocky Mountains, for *fifteen million dollars*! Miro, that's less than three cents an acre to double the size of the United States. What a bargain.'

'And what did your dear Napoleon do with all that money?'

'Well, he promised to use it to build five new canals in France.'

'And did he?'

'No! He spent the whole amount on his planned invasion of the United Kingdom. What a waste of money.' She was laughing and grabbed Miro's arm. 'Didn't we learn that, all over again, with Hitler? What did our dearest RAF pilot Pavel say about the English Channel? Britain's guardian angel against invasions.'

'So, what would you have done if Napoleon had built those canals?'

Simone's eyes said it. 'I would have taken more canal cruises with you.'

'Ah, that Corsican upstart. Full of chicanery and legerdemain. Look how he let you down with the promised canals.' Cheeky tongue pushed outwards.

They went out to try some of the local eateries. St. Louis was the home of the Anheuser-Busch brewing company, makers of Budweiser and Michelob.

Miro tried the Budweiser beer. 'What is *this*?' He put down the glass.

'Underwhelming?' she taunted.

'Breath-taking blandness. My colleagues at Unireifen would say, "Like sex on Lake Superior."'

'What does that mean?'

He leaned close and toned it down. 'It's fucking close to chilled water.'

She studied the bottle. '*Brewed by our original all-natural process using the choicest hops, rice and—*'

'Rice? You don't put rice in beer. This isn't Japanese sake.'

'Umm, yes. Czechs know their beer. Well, Miro, one more reason for you to visit Czechoslovakia.'

'Yes, my dear Simone. *In vino veritas*. But, greater words of wisdom are spoken around beer.'

'Who said that?'

'A Moravian philosopher named Miroslav Novotny.'

'Really. Never heard of him.'

Simone was driving, now. Taking Highway 70, they had crossed Missouri and were now in Kansas. The straight roads of the Great Plains were sending them ever westward. This vast and fertile prairie, with its rich soil nourishing America's heartland crops, was offering Miro and Simone, mile after seemingly endless mile, a visual diet of corn on the right, soybeans on the left. Soybeans on the right, corn on the left.

'Corn Belt, Miro?' she said.

'Yep. You're right in it. The breadbasket of America beckons.'

'Corn everywhere. But what's that green stuff on *this* side of the road?'

'That's soybeans.'

'Wow! How exciting.' Her memory flashed to Rodgers & Hammerstein's lines from *South Pacific* and she picked up the song:

I'm as corny as Kansas in August,
High as a flag on the Fourth of July!

And she jabbed a playful punch into Miro's shoulder.

They stopped for lunch in Salina, Kansas. Driving

along the town's tree-lined streets, they spotted the Big Nose Kate Inn & Tavern. Inside, they found an exposé of a legendary affair in the folklore of the American frontier and territories of the Old West. It was the illustrious Gunfight at the O.K. Corral, which took place in Tombstone, Arizona in 1881. Pictures and memorabilia from that chapter of Wild West history were splashed all over the walls of this tavern. There were larger-than-life, grainy photographs of Wyatt Earp, frontier lawman, gambler, saloon-keeper and brothel owner, and Doc Holliday, a dentist, gambler and gunfighter who was Earp's long-time friend. Three years before that gunfight, Holliday had saved Earp's life in a saloon in Dodge City, Kansas when a handful of gambling cowboys were out to kill Earp.

Among the murals, were pictures of Big Nose Kate, a Hungarian-born prostitute and long-time companion and common-law wife of Doc Holliday. Pictured too, were the three outlaw cowboys who were killed in the O.K. Corral gunfight.

'I can see why they called her Big Nose Kate. Miro, do you remember we saw the film *Gunfight at the O.K. Corral*, in Tehran? Burt Lancaster played Wyatt Earp and Kirk Douglas was Doc Holliday?'

'Um, hm. I remember.'

'But I can't recall who played Big Nose Kate.'

After lunch, Simone spread out their map.

'Miro, we are so close to the border of Nebraska. Why

don't we scoot up there and continue westwards for a while, through that state?'

They headed north on 81 and Simone buried herself in the map.

'Miro, let's go to Lebanon!'

'Ah, ah. I can hear the gear wheels grinding in your head, your way of smuggling me into Czechoslovakia?'

'No, dear. Lebanon, Kansas.'

'And what, exactly, is there in Lebanon, Kansas?'

'It's the geographic centre of the United States! Right in the middle of the Lower-forty-eight states,' she chirped.

'And this excites you?'

She looked up from the map and challenged. 'Yeah. It does.'

'And where is this amazing Lebanon?'

'Okay. Belleville is coming up, ahead. We turn left onto thirty-six.'

'Is there some kind of marker at this magical place?'

'Yeah. The map says so.'

They found the truncated pyramid of stone, inset with the bronze plaque announcing the special meaning of this spot on the planet. Miro explained that the marker was only approximate in locating the dead centre.

'Approximate? Why?'

'Because, my dearest Simonko, the thousands of miles of shoreline on either side of the continental United States are shifting all the time. How does one find a midpoint when we don't have exact end-points? Our stone marker, here, would have to be repositioned, every so often, in order to locate the true midpoint.'

'Miro! Go stand next to it and I'll take your picture.'

He did as he was told and stood ramrod-straight, as though the soles of his shoes were planted on the exact spot where the meaning of the universe becomes crystal clear.

'Ah, women,' he said, taking the camera from Simone and getting her to pose in front of the marker. 'They get so excited about being smack in the middle of nowhere.'

'Ah, men,' she snorted. 'They get so technical about a simple stone marker.'

Chapter 28

Soon they were in Nebraska, and heading west again. Farm after farm, the countryside was dotted with silos, with the land as flat as a pancake.

'Miro, stop, stop, stop!'

'What now?'

'Back up a few metres. I need you to see this.'

They came alongside the town's welcome sign at the side of the road and Simone rolled down the window. They both gave a gurgle. It read:

Welcome to Hildreth, 388 Friendly People and a Few Old Crabs.

'These people have a sense of humour,' she smiled.

They stopped in Hildreth and bought some Oh Henry! chocolate bars and soft drinks at a small grocery store.

'Hi there! Where y'folks from?' asked the cashier.

'From Canada,' said Simone.

'Canada! Golly, yur long way fr'm home. Luv yur maple syrup an' you got terrific wool blankets up there. Best blankets ah ever had in all m'life. Ma sistur was up in Canada, an' m'niece 'n' 'er husband. She got me couple o' them blankets, umm hmm. You folks got tornadoes, up there?'

'Not as many as you do, down here,' Simone smiled.

'Yeah, plen'y wind an' storms, that's fur shur. You folks have plen'y snow. I know. Hard drivin' through awl that snow comin' over, ah betcha?' She did the snowplough with her hands.

'No, dear. We don't have snow in June.' Simone did the patient tilt of the head.

'So, where ya headin' to now?'

'The Rockies,' said Simone.

'Oooh, yeah, the Rockies.' She did the hand climbing into mountains. 'One day, we gonna go vaycayshun there. Ma husband's workin' on the house now. His dad's helpin.' Gonna have a great big porch, up front. So, mebby nex' year we'll go, fur our twenny-uth.'

She could see that Simone wanted to get back on the road. 'Well, y'all have a great time, now, ya hear!'

They continued westward, driving past Lebanon, Nebraska.

'Another Lebanon,' she noted.

'Yeah,' chuckled Miro. 'I was inspecting the back of our Toshiba TV set and saw it was manufactured in Lebanon, Tennessee.'

Simone checked the back of the road atlas. 'Fourteen Lebanons in the United States. Wonder why this Lebanon fixation. Why not throw in a few Beiruts, to break the monotony?'

'They run out of place names, so they have to repeat them. Check your gazetteer. How many *Troys* are there?'

'Goodness.' Her fingers did the counting. 'Seventeen.'

'It's a big country, many immigrants, many towns. So, they borrowed: Nazareth, Pennsylvania; Moscow, Idaho; Ontario, California; Venice, Utah; Cairo, Illinois.'

'Angola, New York!' she piped up.

'But you know, sometimes they get very creative.' Miro was building mischief.

'Oh?'

'Yeah, like Truth or Consequences, New Mexico.'

'Seriously?'

'Um, hm.'

'Truth or Consequences, New Mexico,' she giggled. 'Poor people, when they need to write their return address on anything.'

Miro put on his mock-serious persona. 'And where do you hail from, kind sir? *I'm from Truth or Consequences, New Mexico. Really! What's it like there? Well, to tell the truth, the consequences of living there are breath-taking boredom. And where, may I ask, are you from, sir? I'm from Prague. Prague, Oklahoma? No, Prague.*'

'Miro, it's all wheat everywhere. Where did the corn go?'

'We're in the Wheat Belt. Runs north to south, more or less, from our Prairie Provinces all the way down to northern Texas. There's still some corn, but it's mainly wheat now.'

Simone began to sing again:

O-o-o-o-o-klahoma! Where the wind comes sweepin'
down the plain,
And the wavin' wheat can sure smell sweet
When the wind comes right behind the rain.

Simone continued, 'You know, I love the works of Rodgers and Hammerstein. They're America's answer to Gilbert and Sullivan. But they're better at it. I know of no country, in any language, that can get its musicals to be so magical. Americans are just so good at it. They take a very simple story and set it to music, and lyrics, and choreography, and stage work and—'

'And what?'

'And then it's magic. It all comes together into beautiful entertainment.'

'And they throw a lot of money at it,' he added.

'But that's okay, why not? That's why we have such jewels, and not only from Rodgers and Hammerstein. The musicals become ageless. They never lose their appeal. Think of it: *The Pajama Game, Guys and Dolls, West Side Story, Carousel, My Fair Lady, Show Boat, South Pacific, The King and I, Fiddler on the Roof,* you name it.'

'Is there a musical called *You Name It?*'

'You'll get music over your head, you!'

'No, I did enjoy *Oklahoma!* when we saw it on Broadway. I really did.' He put his hand on her neck. 'But operas, too, become ageless, no? Anywhere you look, there's a *Rigoletto* playing somewhere on this planet, every season. Or *Don Giovanni*, or *The Magic Flute*, or *La Traviata, La Bohème, The Barber of Seville*.'

'But unless you're fluent in Italian, or German, or Spanish you won't understand what they're singing. You enjoy the music and the arias, but you have to guess at the words. So, the only way out is to know the story beforehand, to get the whole plot, and try to enjoy the singing without knowing all the words.'

'And what's wrong with that?' Miro was frowning. '*Chacun à son goût*.' Each to his own taste.

'Well, it takes something away from the enjoyment, no? Miro, part of the pleasure in the musicals is to catch the beautiful words and see how they were crafted to rhyme and also fit the music. And then all the movement is choreographed. But in opera, even the exchanges in between the arias, are sung and it disrupts the flow. The non-speaker in the audience can't follow the dialogue and has to wait for the next beautiful aria.'

'And that doesn't happen with musicals? A Japanese goes to Broadway to see *Guys and Dolls* and doesn't know English. Same problem.' Miro's irritation swirled. The agitrons were palpable.

'Yes, but in musicals the dialogue is spoken, not sung. It's crisper that way. More creativity is possible on stage.

There's action during the sung pieces. Picture it with Sky Masterson delivering his *Luck Be A Lady Tonight* at a crap game with a bunch of gamblers inside a New York sewer. In opera, the choreographer can't do much when the singers have to stand fairly still and face the audience, in order to belt out a difficult aria in splendid costumes. It looks more wooden.'

'Nonsense! In *Carmen*, the gypsy girl glides all over the stage while singing. *The Barber of Seville* is packed with choreographed dancing and clever use of props. Not wooden at all.' He went all quiet, views belittled.

'Miro, there's a grove of trees coming up ahead. I need to go pipi.' He pulled over and stopped. 'No toilet. I just want to hug you. Please don't be upset.' He stayed silent. 'Please, *say* something.'

He spoke up, his voice tinged with admonishment. 'Just keep in mind what Plato said.'

'What did Plato say?'

'Wise men speak because they have something to say, and fools because they have to say something.'

'Well, I'll say it for you. You are the shining Moravian knight who rescued a dreamy damsel in Palestine and rode away with *Popelka* on a horse.'

'Hm. Where to?'

'To Czechoslovakia, of course!' She winked at him.

She leaned over. Held him a long time. A huge semi-trailer truck travelling in the opposite direction approached their car and gave a loud blast on its air horn.

Startled, they turned to look. As the truck was passing, the driver put his lips to the driver-side window and planted a kiss on the glass.

'Sex in the car, I'm sure he was thinking that,' said Simone. 'Must be a French Canadian.'

'Better than sex on Lake Superior,' he reminded.

'I like that quote from Plato,' she reflected. 'It reminds me of something from *South Pacific*:

Who can explain it; who can tell you why?
Fools give you reasons; wise men never try.'

They drove on and pondered the earthy friendliness of the locals they had met during their drive through the Midwest. Broad smiles, an easy chattiness, a willingness to lend a helping hand, and an unpretentious air of realism marked their manner.

Miro pointed out, 'Most stable, conventional group in the nation, I think. Basically, they're contented people, at peace with themselves. They certainly don't initiate social change and are the last ones to adopt it. You know what I mean? They're conservative and typically vote Republican. I believe many have German ancestry, as well as Scandinavian and Central European. It shows in their community pride.'

'And they're so much into farming and farm-related businesses,' added Simone.

'Um, hm, their livelihood. You can imagine how

dependent they are on agriculture. When things go bad in the Breadbasket, they have nowhere else to turn. You know the situation they faced in the 1930s, when this whole region became the Dust Bowl. Eight years of drought, top soil blown away by winds, dust storms so thick you couldn't see anything. And here we are, exactly where all of this was happening.'

'Umm, terrible. Like in Steinbeck's *Grapes of Wrath*. Poor people. They lost everything. Families migrating to California, looking for a way to scrape a living.'

Crossing into Colorado, everything looked drier. The Great Plains lifted its shoulders and the elevation mounted. Flat gave way to hilly, and hilly turned into winding roads carved through the imposing Rocky Mountains. They were in the land of spirit-lifting vistas, air so clean that, through it, one could see land features a hundred miles away.

Simone began humming a chirpy little ditty, softly at first, then set the tune to words:

I'd like to know what your
Thoughts have to say;
Have you found the woman
Who can still make your day?
Whatever you do,
I'll be thankful for you.
You were destined to be my lucky find.
My lucky find.

Miro was curious. 'Haven't heard that one. Where does it come from?'

'My head.' She twirled her wrist as the hand rose above her head.

'Just now?'

'Yeah,' she mused, as though this were an impossibility.

'Eh, heh! You really are a songbird, aren't you?'

'I've always thought of myself as your dance partner in Beirut.'

They overnighted in the tiny town of Eagle, Colorado. They were now at 6,600 feet above sea level. The night was clear. They went for a short walk in the chilly air. It was a moonless night and the sky was studded with diamonds, but they were not twinkling. There was no warm air rising from the valley to make them dance. They seemed to be frozen in time, begging to be fathomed in the total silence. Lit by a billion more silent stars, a carpet of pale light arched above them like milk splashed across the black canopy.

'Look, Miro,' Simone breathed. 'The Milky Way galaxy, our own galaxy. Have you ever seen it like this?'

'A humbling setting. It helps when there are no city lights and the air is so clear. I hope they won't spoil it and keep it like this.'

'Do you remember when you took us out into the hills

and named a constellation after Setareh? The boys were so thrilled. You were their stargazing dad. Their private guide to the heavens.' Her smile radiated enough to keep both of them warm in the night chill.

'I do, indeed. Constellation Setareh is holding Andromeda's hand and shining down on us. Can you find her?'

'I don't know. Let me try. Give me your torch.' Simone hesitated. She drew the beam in a straight line and got to Polaris, then lost her way. Miro's hand grasped hers and corrected the bearing, moving the beam until it found the Poodle. He traced the outline of the stars in that cluster.

'There. That's Setareh.'

Simone jumped an inch with joy. 'Hello, dear Setareh. You shine everywhere. Now, you're in North America! You made it, after all!'

She switched off the light and gave Miro a tight hug. Setareh smiled down on them.

They journeyed deeper into the Southwest. The dazzling mountainous topography dished out a banquet for the soul: Utah, Arizona, Wyoming, and Montana. They stopped for a two-day rest in Coeur d'Alene, Idaho.

Simone had sketched a few words for each natural wonder they had visited and read her notes to Miro. 'For Arches National Park, I put: Million years of wind and rain erosion gave these sandstone arches their amazing shapes.'

'Nice. Add: And their colour varies by time of day, best time, early morning or sunset.'

'Bryce Canyon, Utah. I wrote: Hundreds of tall, fairy-tale-like hoodoos, inside natural amphitheatres. Like going to an open-air opera in nature's wonderland.'

'Ahh, for me, please write: The greatest erosion story I have ever seen in one place. To me, this is the geological spectacle of water.' He closed his eyes and punctuated the air with his fingers, as though carving and shaping the hoodoos himself.

Simone scribbled as fast as she could. 'Wait, wait I can't keep up.'

He continued. 'Think of it, water chemically and mechanically scouring, abrading those vertical columns into bizarre hoodoos.'

She laughed as she jotted. 'Wow! You do technical justice to Bryce Canyon! Grand Canyon: I have: Millions of years of deep carving by the Colorado River. Canyon is 277 miles long, up to eighteen miles wide, and over one mile deep.'

'Mmm, good. Please add the comment: And thereby exposing almost two billion years of the Earth's geologic history.'

'Yes, technical man. Now, for Zion National Park, I wrote: Mountains, canyons, monoliths, and cream, pink and red sandstone cliffs. In Zion, you go to the bottom of the canyon and look up.'

'Sounds perfect. No further questions for the travel witness, Your Honour. I rest my Zionist case.'

'Miro, for Craters of the Moon National Monument, I put: Immense lava fields, volcanic cinder cones, lava flows with cracks, utter black desolation.'

'Good stuff. For me, you can add: And the lava field punishes soles that walk across it. Lava shreds the soles, or something like that.'

'Thank you, Miro.' She finished jotting that comment and sank a friendly punch into his shoulder. 'I lava you more than the lava does. And your soul is unshredable.'

'You think so? I wonder.'

'Why do you wonder?'

'Shall we move on to the next wonder?' His smile wore the emblem of escapist amusement.

'Okay. I have here, for Grand Teton National Park: nineteenth-century French trappers called three of the peaks *Les Trois Tétons*, the three teats. To me, the Teton Range looks like a long row of shark's teeth, not like the teats on a woman's breasts.' She flashed a toothy grin and her belly jiggled. 'How they saw nipples in those sawtooth peaks is beyond me. They must have been starved for sex.'

'Okay, shark's teeth it is. Nipples like that could only mean razor-sharp breast feeding.'

'Yellowstone National Park: Huge hot springs and geysers, geothermal wonderland sitting on the caldera of a gigantic active volcano that could explode one day.'

'Nice, but please reassure us that the next cataclysmic

eruption may not happen for another 700,000 years.' Miro paused and smiled. 'That should give you plenty of time to write your riveting novella about our great American odyssey.'

They crossed the Columbia River and entered British Columbia.

'Three cheers! We're almost home!' he said.

Simone broke into song, once more:

When Johnny comes marching home again,
Hurrah! Hurrah!
We'll give him a hearty welcome then,
Hurrah! Hurrah!
The men will cheer and the boys will shout;
The ladies they will all turn out;
And we'll all feel gay when Johnny comes marching home.

'World-War-One song?' he glanced at her.

'American Civil War.'

Chapter 29

Simone and Miro were getting to know their new hometown of Vancouver.

They spent a whole day at the University of British Columbia, meeting Michael's former professors at the Institute of Oceanography where he had studied. This was a pilgrimage offering a slice of his UBC experiences: the Student Union Building, where Michael had meals, the Main Library, where he devoured the literature on oceanography, the Japanese Garden, with its transcendent ambience for those who amble through the garden's sublime harmony of brooks, bridges, reflecting pond, waterfalls, stone lanterns and Tea House.

Miro took a picture of Simone standing next to the 123-foot-tall Clock Tower, the iconic centrepiece of the UBC campus. Engineering students, in one of their annual pranks during Engineering Week, used their technical prowess under the cover of darkness to place a Volkswagen Beetle on top of the Clock Tower. The university hired a huge crane to remove the car from the top. Over the years, the Clock Tower endured several indignities: engineers once shrouded the entire tower in translucent plastic film to make it look like an erect penis, sheathed in a condom. For months, afterwards, students on campus would refer to it as the Cock Tower.

Miro and Simone made an outing to Vancouver's Chinatown. As noon approached, Miro became hungry, and their guide book led them to the Heavenly Pearl Chinese restaurant: down a narrow alley, left at the Chinese laundry, up a flight of stairs and there they found it. A very noisy place it was, too. Packed almost full, this was where the Chinese locals ate. The two of them sat down at a table. The plastic tablecloth had a bamboo tree motif and there were wooden chopsticks wrapped in a tissue. A waitress gave them a menu and it was in Cantonese and bad *Engrish*. While Simone studied it, Miro was playing with his chopsticks to master the skilled movement in one hand, like a fencer ducking in and out with epee and surging forward to score a point against a steamed vegetable. There was a slip and one chopstick fell to the floor.

Simone noticed the mishap. 'You know what the Chinese say about a lost chopstick, don't you?'

'And what, pray tell, is that ancient Chinese wisdom?'

'Man, with one chopstick, go hungry.'

Miro chuckled. 'I know you read a lot, but where do you find all these jewels?'

'Man, who no read, know blank page,' she quipped.

When the waitress reappeared, Miro put on a sad-face mime, holding one chopstick upright and pointing to the floor with the other hand.

'Berry solly,' she smiled. 'I bling naddah chopstick. You wan' order, now?'

They placed their order, calling out by menu number. As they ate, Simone noted how delicately the Chinese treat their vegetables.

'Miro, the Chinese know how to prepare and cook their vegetables. No? They are so delightfully crispy and full of flavour and colour. They have character. They have soul.'

Miro nodded, 'Um, true.'

She continued. 'So, why must the British overcook their veggies and ruin them? Everything comes out limp and soggy and boiled to death. Don't the Brits have teeth? Or does water boil at a higher temperature on the British Isles? Or do they put the pot on the stove, then forget the time while they watch telly or gossip with the neighbour?'

'We must do our research and find out,' he smiled. 'Isn't there a Chinese saying for that? Man, who overcook vegetable, need new battery for kitchen clock?'

They returned to the streets and alleys. Simone had an urge to visit a Chinese fortune teller. Ducking her head under a tent-like entrance, she spotted an old woman fitted out in rural Chinese garb and sitting at a wobbly table, covered with a purple silk cloth. Her teeth were yellowed by tea and tobacco. Soon, the woman was exploring Simone's hand, and face, and her and Miro's dates of birth. She lit a half-dozen incense sticks with a rather pungent odour and began to tell her in broken English:

'Yo' man *Tigah*. You *Horse*. You match in Chinese Zodiac. Hum? You berry good matching couple. Yes? You berry lucky lady.'

After the astrology, Simone got herself deeper into fortune telling through face reading, palm reading, and the shaking of the bamboo cylinder. Almost an hour passed, and Simone emerged from her psychedelic session with a Chinese gypsy. Her head was spinning from the incense smoke. It was spiked with marijuana. She found Miro wandering down an alley, exploring this microcosm of China.

'Miro! Guess what. The Tiger doesn't hunt the Horse and the Horse doesn't eat the Tiger, so we are best friends.'

'What have *you* been smoking?' Miro propped her up before she fell over.

'I've been sniffing the air and it is g-o-o-o-d. You are brave. A tireless fighter, because you're a fearless tiger. Tigerless fighter. Fireless tiger. Tearless figer. It rhymes, don't you see? Miro, agr-e-e-e-e with m-e-e-e!'

He took her home to recover.

October, 1973. A fuse is lit and the Middle East explodes. Israel is at war again with her Arab neighbours. Egypt and Syria launch a surprise attack against Israel on Yom Kippur, the holiest day in the Jewish calendar. For the first time, the Arabs stage a pre-emptive strike that catches Israel with her panties down.

Simone was listening to CBC Radio. 'Miro! Israel has been attacked by Syria in the Golan Heights and by Egypt in the Sinai!'

'Looks like another firestorm in your part of the world.'

'I hope Marek is not involved in this one, too.'

Days later, President Richard Nixon authorizes a strategic airlift to resupply Israel with weapons. The Arabs are furious. They use their 'oil weapon' by putting an embargo on oil shipments to the United States and other nations friendly to Israel.

Over the next four months, the effects became painfully evident. In America, gasoline was rationed. Motorists faced long lines at gas stations. Twenty percent of stations had no fuel at all. By February, Simone knew her lucky break. *What good timing they had made their trip across America when they did. Stations would not sell gasoline on Saturday nights or Sundays. Would they sell gas to a car with Ontario licence plates? The speed limit was now fifty-five miles an hour, across the entire country. What a mess!*

Spring arrived and Vancouver's streets turned pink. They were dusted everywhere with cherry blossom petals that had been blown away by fresh breezes caressing the cherry trees. Miro and Simone were sitting on the veranda at home, looking out over English Bay. The air was a little chilly, but clear, and one could see Vancouver Island in the distance. Sailboats were everywhere in the bay. The ever-green Coast Mountains still had old snow on the peaks, but the skiing season had ended.

'Miro, why do you think American men are so weak when it comes to love and relationships with women?'

'Are they?' *Where is she going with this?*

'I see a pattern among the bits and pieces. Look at their behaviours. Listen to their rock and roll music. The lyrics in the songs are filled with postured masculinity, but underneath all that bravado is an undercurrent of insecurity that stretches from their teens into adulthood. Don't songs reflect a culture's anxieties, as well as its ideals?'

'For example?'

'They complain that their woman has left them. They wail and moan about the woman they cannot find, or who ran away from them and picked another lover. Roy Orbison captured this in his songs about broken-hearted men. He brought out the fact that they're running scared. He and others, like Buddy Holly, showed that men were vulnerable in matters of love, emotionally weak, or escaping to dreams.'

'But these are young men. Not much life experience.'

'Yes, but this weakness carries over into adulthood, leads them to worship the physically tough men. Nothing to do with love. Like the coal miners, the Paul Bunyans, John Henry, the iron-fisted boxers, Joe Louis, Rocky Marciano.'

'Okay, okay, I get the picture. But why do you think they do this?'

'I think it's because they're impatient. They want instant results. For them, time is too precious to wait for results. They have not been trained to be patient. And so, they don't have the patience to put in the effort when wooing a woman if she takes her time to decide. They do not see patience as a virtue. You and I have seen it where we lived, this oriental quality. Be patient! Give it time. Put in the effort and you will see results. Part of the Eastern culture. Children in the Orient are raised to be patient. Even the Czechs have this. You've said this so often: time has many daughters.'

Miro scanned the horizon. The brilliant sun shining in a spring-blue sky bleached the sails of the yachts and dinghies even whiter. Sails catching the breeze were bloated into graceful contours. 'And you don't see this in America?'

'Not much. It's not an important part of the culture. But I do see it in the animal kingdom. Love needs work. You need patience to attract your desired one, to show that you're the best one for her. The female is thinking, "You have to convince me. I'm looking for the best genes and best carer available for my offspring. Given that I bear the brunt of childbirth and rearing, convince me that you are the one I should devote myself to, and mate with, and that you'll stay and be my helpmate."'

Miro scratched his head and took a breath of sea air.

'But American men don't always put in the effort to convince her. They give up too soon. It's as though they feel entitled to the woman of their dreams. And this makes them weak. So, they cry, "Why did she leave me? Why did she turn to some other man? Why won't she come back? It's not fair." Perhaps they think democracy will solve all their problems, even their love problems.'

'Whoa! Those are pretty bold conclusions.'

'Miro, look at us. Didn't you need to convince me that you were the right one?'

'And did I?' He began a faint smile.

'The times you said, "I'm going to take care of you, I can take you to another world and look after you. Don't worry, we will be alright."'

'I don't remember saying those things.' He shuffled his feet, hoping the friction would clear the sticky plaque in memory.

'You did, but even if you can't remember, your signals were there. You were giving the message. Your behaviours were telling me these words, "I will stay by you, help you, be faithful to you, support you. I will be the tiger warding off adversity, protecting you." It's not always spoken. It's there in the actions. You are radiating the message the woman wants to hear. That's what will convince the woman. Then they know for sure, and they feel secure. And then they will stay!'

'My, you've become quite philosophical since we moved to Vancouver. Could it be the sea air?' His grin was alive with sarcasm.

Practical, rational Miro. He sees everything as a pragmatist. But he radiated his message to me. Simone wondered about *his* views.

He read her thoughts. Years together do that. 'But isn't it a two-way street? Doesn't the woman also need to put in the effort? To open up and show that she cares about his needs? Isn't it also a question of the woman using her charms, her social skills, intuitive talent and, to borrow Franz Kafka's words, become the axe for the frozen sea within the man? In an evolving relationship, that's the feminine half of the equation. No?'

'You mean, "You help me with my things, and let me help you with yours?"'

'Um, hm. Mutual back-scratching, while recognising that women and men have different needs and a different set of skills. Why not bring these together in the mating game? As the Hindu proverb goes, "A hundred men make an encampment. One woman makes a home." Or as Gandhi put it, "Who can make a more effective appeal to the heart than woman?" That should tell you something.'

She went silent. Downshifted to a lower gear. Took a

deep breath of the iodised, salty air. 'Yeah. It must be the sea air.' She got up to make some coffee, then returned.

'Now, I have a question I've been meaning to ask you for quite some time.' He assumed a tenor of great interest.

'Oh?' Her voice undressed a touch of suspension.

'If all the books in the world were taken away from you, but you were allowed to keep just one, which book would it be?'

'You mean I could never access any other books?'

'Right. You're serving a life sentence for reading too much, and your jailers allow you just one book, and never another one.'

'How cruel.' She went into thinking mode. Then a smile ran its fingers across Simone's library, and stopped and retrieved the title. '*Tales from a Thousand and One Nights*,' she warbled, and jumping to her mother tongue as if to reinforce her choice: '*Alf Layla wa Layla*.' Thousand nights and a night. '*Hezār o yek shab*,' she offered, by its Persian title.

'*Any* translation of *The Arabian Nights*?'

'Oh, no, no, no only Sir Richard Burton's translation would do. I want the words of Shahrazad telling her tales to King Shahryar, the way she would have related in Arabic, with all the sensuous delights of eye and ear and touch. High-bosomed damsels with breasts firm as a cube, bathing their skin in fragrances and Hammam-baths. Her stories, peopled by Wazirs and Sultans, Caliphs and Persians—jinnis, eunuchs, and deflowered virgins. Language enflowered with all the *by Allah*'s and *Inshallah*'s and *Bismillah*'s. Ah, what a storyteller she is. Papa would be happy that her life was spared. Shahrazad reveals that it's a woman's world, after all. Man is smart, but woman is smarter.'

By this point, Miro was giddy from all the imagery his question had conjured up.

'And what about you?' Simone probed in a testing manner.

'My book would be *The Greek Myths*.'

'Robert Graves's magnum opus?'

'Um hm. A more Western tale of gods and mortals than in the oriental life captured in *Arabian Nights*. The human elements of sexual passion, greed, revenge, anger, pride, jealousy, ambition, and deception are also embedded in the nature and behaviour of the Olympian deities. In this way, I see a similarity with the characters in Shahrazad's tales. Stories about people with their age-old problems and needs, and even gods and spirits endowed with human foibles and desires.'

Chapter 30

They travelled east to explore the Canadian Rockies. June brought impossibly long days: eighteen hours of daylight and twilight. Their drive would take them through towns with Anglo-Saxon and Native Indian names: Hope, Princeton, Kamloops, Keremeos, Similkameen, Penticton, Kelowna, Sicamous, Vernon, Armstrong, Revelstoke.

Progressing along Okanagan Lake, Simone pointed out, 'This is where the legendary aquatic monster, Ogopogo, lives. It's British Columbia's answer to Scotland's Loch Ness monster, Nessie.'

After driving through Glacier National Park, they made their way south to Radium Hot Springs. A few peaceful days of bathing in the hot water pools reminded Miro of the legendary thermal springs of Karlovy Vary, in Czechoslovakia. He mentioned it to Simone, then realised his mistake. Too late. The genie was out of the bottle.

'Yes, Miro. Radium Hot Springs never marinated the

bodies of Peter the Great, Empress Maria Teresa, Goethe, Beethoven, Chopin, Freud, Tolstoy, and Kafka. We need to join these luminaries by taking the waters at Karlovy Vary . . . in Czechoslovakia, Miro. You're not getting out of this!'

'You forgot one other celebrity, Princess Simone Thérèse.'

'You're throwing in a red herring. You just want to get off the hook about your homeland. So, ride with your Princess Simone Thérèse to Czechoslovakia. You're the shining Moravian knight, aren't you?'

They pushed on towards Banff, Alberta. Simone stopped the car. 'Look, Miro, there's Mount Assiniboine. It looks almost exactly like the Matterhorn, don't you think?'

'It is spectacular.'

'After the American Revolution, when Britain lost the American Colonies and a line was drawn across the map of North America, it was said that the British sovereign got stuck with the boring half.' Simone stiffened. 'What poppycock! No one should buy that piece of ignorance.'

'Well, you're the historian in our family, so you know what was said.'

'You know what's behind this remark? It's because the Canadian half has that pristine emptiness, that enormous, unexplored vastness, that divine quietness, the envy of India or South Korea or Netherlands and all those crowded nations. Get lost here, and no one will find you. People dream of visiting here because it's the true wilderness. Mountain after mountain, there is not a human in sight, only wildlife. Nature dominates here, not factories, or freeways, or flashy cars, or skyscrapers, or shopping malls. Does that make it boring?'

Miro put on his smiley face. 'Which scoundrel said it was boring? I'd like to show him Truth or Consequences, New Mexico.'

'But there's another thing.' A forest fire was blazing in her bosom. 'The sheer vastness of Canada, the second biggest country. When you have that size, how can you possibly fill every square kilometre with majestic vistas and heart-stopping landscapes? Physically impossible. A Canadian Prime Minister said it, I think it was Mackenzie King: "If some countries have too much history, we have too much geography." Even America, with all its attractions, can't do this. Americans drive through so much tamed and developed territory before getting to the Rockies, Grand Canyon, Yellowstone, or the Three Teats.'

Miro smiled. 'You have a great atlas in your head. But don't forget Singapore, no room for a Grand Canyon. Too many people.'

'We humans,' she gulped the rarefied mountain air, 'are so miniscule on the scale of the planet. But it makes us that much more in awe of places like this.'

'Umm, I like your philosophy.'

'Miro, you're such a down-to-earth person. But why not let your imagination soar?' Her voice dropped. 'Think what Napoleon might have uttered if he were standing right here witnessing this spectacle.'

'I'll let you pilot me on your flights of fancy. How's that, for a good travel arrangement?' He paused. 'I think Napoleon would have said: *They've stolen the Matterhorn from my empire and planted it over here. I'm going to conquer Canada and make it a part of my empire.* Wouldn't that be more practical than shipping the Matterhorn back to Europe?'

She reached over and gave his earlobe a tug. 'You.'

'More pulling of the ears?' he exhaled. 'Let's drive on to the next town. I'm hungry for that great, juicy, Canadian wilderness steak. Agree?'

'Uh huh. I hear my stomach rumbling. And it's not an active volcano.'

They wound through the mountain passes and crossed into Alberta. Miro's mind wandered. He reflected on their experiences since arriving in Canada. A dozen years had evaporated. 'You know my favourite quote about Canada? It was penned by John Robert Colombo. He said, "Canada could have enjoyed English government, French culture, and American know-how. Instead, it ended up with English know-how, French government, and American culture."'

Simone sucked in the clear, cold air. 'Clever. It is a very

self-effacing nation. Its people are far too modest and quiet. Canada still has no officially proclaimed national anthem. Can you believe it? No official anthem for a country that's 107 years old? That must be a world record. For all its huge size, Canada is a gentle nation. They're not the trouble-makers of the world. And they're always so polite, so Canadian.'

'Whoa! Just a minute. Except on the ice, in a hockey face-off. Then, watch out. Goodbye, modesty and politeness. The Canadians will try to slaughter you and hang you up on a meat hook. We, Czechoslovaks, also have ice hockey in our blood. When Czechs and Canucks fight it out, national pride is injection-moulded into the puck.'

As the spirit of summer flourished under the northern sun, it was time for the twins to visit Granma Simone and Grampa Miro. Tereza brought them to Vancouver.

Miro was reading on the living room couch, hidden behind the pages of the *Vancouver Sun*. The boys tiptoed towards him. Paul tapped on the hand that clutched the paper. Miro put on his dragon face and, lowering the paper, made a frightening snarl that sent the boys screaming and scattering in opposite directions. He laughed at the success of this ancient tactic.

The boys recovered and came back. Paul whispered, 'Grandpa, did you bring the snake?'

'Ahh, the snake,' Miro breathed. He got up and, doing the pantomime, put his forefinger to his lips. 'Shh. The snake is sleeping. Let's go take a look.'

The boys followed behind to the guest bedroom. Miro swung open a closet door. 'Still asleep, but let's wake him up.' And he flung the python skin across the room so it unrolled on the floor.

The twins started jumping up and down as if the slain dragon had come alive. 'Grampa, grampa. Tell us the story.'

'Would you like to see real, live crawling snakes?' Miro's face made the offer tantalising.

'Yes! Yes!' they shouted.

Miro, Simone and Tereza took them to the Vancouver Zoo and Aquarium, in Stanley Park. There, Miro showed them the snake exhibits in the Hall of Reptiles. The boys were quite spellbound and it was hard to get them away to view the other attractions: crocodiles, piranhas, scorpions, lizards, Komodo dragons, and Galapagos iguanas. By the time they headed home, the boys were fast asleep on the back seat of the car, with a picture book on snakes sandwiched between their exhausted bodies.

The years rolled on. Boxcars attached to a long freight train. Miro had suffered another heart attack. Simone felt the pressure of time running out for him. Would the train not reach its destination?

Then came the Great Iranian Revolution. The fuse that was lit was very short. Ancient Persia detonated. The Pahlavi Dynasty had been blown up with it. Simone, Miro, Tereza and Theo were reeling in amazement at the speed of the unfolding events. The Shah, his Queen and their children had fled the country. A hugely popular Shia Muslim cleric had flown into Tehran from Paris, aboard an Air France plane, and the mob that was there to greet him stretched twelve kilometres from Mehrābād Airport to the gates of the city. The scenes on television were incomprehensible to the Novotnys. They had known an Iran only under the Shah. He was friendly to the West and loyal to the United States and its allies. He had been a bulwark against communism and a source of stability in the Middle East.

'Miro, America has lost a major ally,' lamented Simone. 'In such a volatile part of the world. It's a good thing you took the job in Canada with Unireifen. Imagine if we were still living in Iran.'

'That's geopolitics for you. Now, comes a domino effect. I expect it.'

The mullahs and their fanatics were everywhere, spreading hatred of America. Agitators marched throughout the capital waving anti-Shah placards and chanting, *Death to America!* and *The Shah must return to face justice!* Soon after, the executions by firing squad began. Government leaders and army officers loyal to the Shah were labelled as traitors, arrested and herded through hastily set-up tribunals, then taken away to be shot. Around Tehran, corpses were hanging at the end of ropes attached to extended construction crane booms to remind the public that old-regime supporters received the ultimate sentence.

Theo was listening to a news broadcast on *CBC* radio. Several key generals in the Shah's army had been executed by firing squad. The announcer read out the names:

'Lieutenant General Manuchehr Khosrowdād; Major General Abbās Sālehi; Brigadier General Ali Rezā Yazdānpūr; Brigadier General Mohsen Afsari.'

Theo iced over. That was his former commanding officer, Major Afsari.

'Tereza!' he yelled towards the boys' bedroom. 'Do you remember my Company commander at Bāgh-e Shāh Garrison?'

'The one learning English from you?' she called out.

'They've killed him! The bloody bastards have shot him.'

Tereza and Simone were talking about travelling to Czechoslovakia. Miro was still resisting. The land of his forefathers remained in the grip of communism. But relations between Canada and his homeland were improving: increased cooperation, bilateral trade, easing restrictions on travel, and improved diplomatic ties.

The two girls prepared their battle plan. It came as an explosive flash of inspiration. Reinforced by verbal artillery when support was needed on the front lines, they would begin their assault to defeat the resistance. If needed, Tereza would provide the airborne backup, parachuting in ambush forces equipped with logic-fuelled flamethrowers.

The attack would use stealth to infiltrate the barrier built by years of Miro's intransigence and mistrust. The opening salvo: his failing health signalled a last chance to see his relatives. This would be followed by a second barrage: the Czechoslovak regime would not risk spoiling relations with Canada by holding a seventy-something Canadian for things he had never done. He was not an escapee, he had not fled from the communist regime, as many had done in 1948 after the communist *coup d'état* and again in 1968 when the *Prague Spring* was crushed by Soviet tanks. He didn't owe the state any money, he had no criminal record, he was not politically active, he was a bona fide retiree, an old-age pensioner.

They all sat together at dinner one evening and Simone declared war. 'Miro, we are all going together to Czechoslovakia.'

Miro was taken aback. 'Who are you referring to as *we*?'

'All of us. The entire family, including you.' She fired the first salvo, then followed it by a second barrage.

Miro tightened up. 'Where did this come from, all of a sudden?'

Simone loaded a shell in the howitzer and set the trajectory. 'Remember what Victor Hugo said.'

'And what did dear, old Victor Hugo say?'

'He said, "In all the world, there is no greater force than an idea whose time has come." The time has come, Miro.'

'And whose idea is this?'

Time to call in reinforcements. 'Listen, Miro.' Simone gave him that killer stare. 'Victor Hugo also said, "When a woman is talking to you, listen to what she says with her eyes."'

'Your eyes tell me you want me to go. Right?'

Tereza surrounded the resistance with her airborne troops. 'Miro, you are being paranoid about visiting your homeland. You hold a Canadian passport. I've contacted the Czechoslovak embassy in Ottawa and there would be no problem issuing you a tourist visa.'

It was hopeless. He was encircled and outgunned. The battle had ended and the conqueror's banners were planted. Signing the surrender papers was the only option available.

They all flew into Frankfurt and hired an eight-person Volkswagen Kombi van. It was mid-July and the days were long. They drove eastward across the southern half of West Germany and slipped into Czechoslovakia. They headed for the thermal spa of Mariánské Lázně, *Marienbad,* by its other name. They bathed in the sulphur-rich hot waters, Simone and Tereza in the women's section, the men and boys in a separate half.

Milena and Lubor were awaiting their arrival. Slavkov had changed very little. Miro and Simone recognised the houses and alleys and churches. And they were still painted outside in the same colour. They found Lubor's house and together drove with him to where Milena lived. Both siblings were living in two-bedroom, government-owned flats and paying rent. Simone gave her sister-in-law a forty-one-year hug. There was so much catching up to do.

Chapter 31

They sat around Milena's kitchen table while the twins played outside in the tiny yard at street level. Lubor brought out their best, home-made *slivovice*, plum brandy, and they toasted the visit. Milena was divorced from a captain in the Czechoslovak army and her daughter was working in Prague as a hotel clerk. Lubor, likewise, was separated and hardly ever saw his former wife. Milena fetched a string of tiny blue and grey beads, with a silver cross hanging from it. She laid it in front of Simone.

'What's this?' Simone's brow furrowed as her fingers caressed the delicate chain.

'It's your rosary. It came inside those crates from Africa that had been shipped to us by mistake.'

'Goodness, that was a long time ago.' Simone turned to Miro. 'Look Miro, the rosary given to me by Sister Scholastica at the Beirut convent. Is this a sign of things about to happen?'

Miro had a pensive look. 'Perhaps there's one bead for every year we've been away.'

Simone looked into Milena's eyes. They tunnelled to her soul. 'I want you to keep it.'

'But it's yours.'

'I want you to turn it into our unbroken bond.' Simone spread it out on the table, her fingers nimbly shaping the chain into a heart. Milena enfolded her and embedded a kiss on her temple.

'Now, you must see this.' Milena brought out a pile of letters. Letters she and Lubor had received from Miro, written on his Czech portable typewriter, while he lived abroad. 'Miro, look here.' Page, after page. In almost every letter, sentences, whole paragraphs, blacked out by a censor's ink. 'We don't know what you wrote here. They didn't want us to know. Isn't it awful, what a regime we live under?'

'This is communism for you.' He gave a shrug. 'News control, thought control, mind control. Our motto on the national coat of arms says, *Pravda vítězí*, truth conquers. But we should remember, *veritas temporis filia*, truth is time's daughter. People here haven't had enough time to discover the truth.'

Lubor chimed in. 'We know the lies and we know what's true. Friends and neighbours who can be trusted talk among themselves. The older ones know how things were in the Republic, and how bad things are now. At heart, none of us is a communist. We are radishes, red on the outside, white on the inside.'

Miro had a heavy voice. 'Alas, if people believe in something, it doesn't seem to matter whether others know it is not true. They are happy believing in, what you and I know, is a myth. But the deeper question of belief has to do with trust. Trusting in something, or someone, breeds loyalty. The tragedy comes when that loyalty has been squandered, traded away in order to gain something else. We Czechs trusted that our allies during the second World War would always support us, because we were helping to get rid of Hitler. We did our loyal best to help the Allies win. And then came the great political betrayal. Roosevelt and Churchill sold us down the river in order to keep Stalin happy. Our trust in these two allies was traded away. Our loyalty was expendable. We preach forgiveness, in the Catholic faith. I can never forgive those two political scoundrels for trading us to Stalin. In my heart, they lost their honour.'

Milena could sense that Miro was seething and his blood pressure rising. She tried to divert the discussion.'Miro, you are our dearest brother. You have wisdom. You have travelled. You are a man of the world. You see things from the outside, things we cannot see. Do you sense that things here will change? That communism will collapse?'

'Well, I don't have a crystal ball, but things are going downhill for the Soviets. They are stagnating. Their technology is outdated, they have no management skills. They are out of touch with people's needs. This is what happens in a command economy. Every decision is centralised, nothing happens without the State's approval. They do not understand the function of supply and demand. They set pointless industrial production targets without knowing what the people really need. To stay progressive and foster innovation you need private capital and competition, and freedom to make market decisions.'

'Do you see ahead that the Soviet masters will lose their grip on Eastern Europe?' Lubor probed.

'I see a dragon losing its head.' Miro gave the table top a chop. 'The Soviet Union is headed for disintegration. Their agriculture is a shamble. The economy is being drained by unaffordable military spending. Their propaganda is hollow and people have no incentives to be productive. Yes, they have people with sharp brains, engineers, scientists, mathematicians, but they are not being used effectively. See how the Soviets waste human resources, money and engineering know-how on the space race against America. For every Yuri Gagarin or Valentina Tereshkova, America has a dozen highly-trained astronauts and space scientists. Superior technology and engineering and good management got America to the moon. And they had the needed budget.'

Milena was desperate for a horizon. 'Miro, when? When do you think this Soviet collapse might come?'

He sensed that she wanted an answer. 'It won't be much longer. Give it another seven to ten years. It's coming.'

She beamed a lipstick-free smile. 'And then we will witness a free Czechoslovakia! Like the one Stanislav fought for and beheld in 1918.'

Lubor painted the local scene scripted by the Communist puppets. 'You are so fortunate that you did not end up with Kolo. The State nationalised it and ran it into the ground. The management was told by the State how many tyres to make, and which ones to make, and what price to sell them at. They know nothing about the market's needs and requirements, and they know even less about customer service. But you were smart. You found success elsewhere. We're proud of what you achieved. To us, you're the hero.'

The twins came inside and Lubor and Milena marvelled at their command of Czech.

Lubor shook his head in delighted amazement. 'How is it possible that they speak Czech so well? Milena and I don't speak any other language.'

'Well, it's thanks to Tereza and Theo,' offered Simone, glancing at the two boys. 'They continued the tradition that Miro and I had: at home, only Czech will be spoken. Outside, they can speak Hindi, if they wish.'

Mickey did a pantomime. He pulled on the skin under his chin and made goggle eyes. He stared straight into Paul's face and switched to English with a Hindi accent.

'You want Hindi, man? I talk to you Hindi.'

Tereza said in English, 'Where did you get that accent?'

'We have an Indian friend in our class, and he talks like that,' said Paul.

Tereza explained to Milena and Lubor. She turned to the boys. 'What's his name?'

'Sarandeep,' they both answered.

'Is he from Ceylon?' she asked.

'No, he's from India,' said Paul.

'He's not,' said Mickey. 'He's from Sail-on.'

'He's from India.'

'No, he's not, he's from Sail-on!'

'Okay, boys, we'll find out when we get back home and school starts. Why don't we invite him to our house?'

'For our birthday?' the twins sang.

'Why not? Or for *his* birthday. Let's give him a party.'

They would stay several weeks to absorb a country that offered them an alphabet soup of Central European life: acid rain, beer, castles, dumplings, early-risers, folk festivals, grottos, and hot springs. And wherever they went or ate, Miro and Simone always invited Lubor and Milena, never allowing them to pay, not even for their groceries. Miro was in his culinary element. Foods he had always liked were available in every cafe and restaurant. His favourite was *Svíčková na smetaně*, marinated beef tenderloin in sour cream sauce, served with white-bread dumplings and topped with cranberry sauce. He ordered it at every opportunity and always accompanied by a pilsner from the local brewery, tapped into a tall glass shaped like a buxom Aphrodite, with an inch of foam on top to trap the flavour.

For a while, Simone and Tereza stayed in Milena's flat. Miro and the boys slept at Lubor's place. Theo was happy to sleep on the floor. Lubor kept the windows open; it was hot, even at night. The visitors moved to a hotel in Brno. Now, it was time to visit Slavkov Castle and later the von Mannberg estate in Bohdalice.

'Simonko,' said Milena. 'I'm afraid you will be disappointed with the manor at Bohdalice. It is in terrible disrepair. When the communists came to power, they wanted all vestiges of nobility eradicated. The State has turned the manor into an elementary school. The tiny church that Raimund built is in a shocking state. The granite slabs, with the names of all the members of the von Mannberg family, you remember? The clever priest in charge of the church hid the two slabs in the family vault which he keeps locked, out of sight of prying communist eyes.'

'And the widow, the Duchess?' asked Simone.

'She died at the end of the war. She was dirt poor. Their estate was sold during the war to the owner of the sugar factory in Vyškov, so she could pay off her debts. She was allowed to stay in the manor until her death. It was said that she lived and slept in the laundry room.'

Simone cupped her hands around her cheeks. 'What a terribly sad ending.'

'Yes. Ever since her eldest son shot himself, the family's fortunes went downhill. The third son fled to Austria when the Red Army was advancing, and the second son was captured and put in a prisoner-of-war camp and given hard labour. He died there and nobody knows where he is buried. The widow, the Duchess, is the last person buried in the family vault.'

'That's the sad thing about blue blood,' Simone pondered. 'If it isn't regenerated with fresh blood, it goes stale. All these noble landowners intermarried, and never got fresh blood. They became degenerated village nobility, holding on by a thread. They had no strength of mind or character, no vision. They could not handle adversity. Generation after generation, they were imploding until they became helpless. France had that problem, too, before the French Revolution. So did Russia with its last line of Tsars.'

'Ah, of course!' Milena dredged up that ancient discovery. 'You know your history! But there was a final tragedy. When the Red Army marched into Moravia, several soldiers came to Bohdalice. They ransacked the manor. They stole all the oil paintings, the antique Persian carpets, the gilded furniture. They tore down all the chandeliers. Then, they found a cupboard full of the finest Meissen porcelain. They didn't know what the value was, so those spiteful beasts took all the plates and dishes and cups, the entire dinner service, and threw it all from the top floor window, smashing everything to pieces.'

'Horrible,' said Simone. She could hear all that porcelain smashing to bits. She heard the raucous laughter of those vengeful, greedy troops. *The savages were laughing at themselves.*

'Those Russian soldiers smelled awful, their breath stank. They were unshaven tramps. And they behaved like vulgar pigs. They tried to rape the maid looking after the manor. But she was clever and took an antique battle axe, hidden behind the piano, and started hitting one of the soldiers and cut his hand. Then, she escaped his clutches, got away and hid under a trapdoor until they left.'

Simone put her arm around Milena. 'It's been such a long time.'

'Do you see all the things that happened while you were away?' Milena turned her face and loaned her feelings to Simone. Her eyes gave away the synthesised mixture of regret and gladness.

When they got to Slavkov Castle, Simone wondered,

'What happened to your friend, I forget her name, the castle's museum director?'

'Dagmar Martinková,' replied Milena. 'When the Soviet tanks rolled into Prague, in 1968, and crushed the *Prague Spring,* she fled across the border into Austria and later ended up in the United States. Somewhere in Massachusetts. We wrote to each other, and then I lost touch. She was teaching the history of the Czech people, at some college, but that was a long time ago.'

After touring the baroque chateau in Slavkov, with its badly neglected landscaped gardens, originally styled by Italian masons and architects, they drove to Bohdalice.

'Miro, your grandfather's residence!' Simone stopped the van and they all got out.

'Grandpa!' shouted Paul. 'Can we test the tyres with Lincoln's head?'

'Sure,' said Miro. 'Did you bring your copper penny?'

Paul and Mickey looked at each other and shrugged with outstretched arms.

'Lincoln didn't want to come. He stayed at home,' said Mickey.

Tereza rummaged through her handbag and, in the coin pocket, she found several U.S. pennies. She said nothing, but hid one penny in her hand, then stretched out her arms with both hands closed.

'What's in my hands?' she asked the twins.

'A snake,' said Mickey.

'The king of Africa!' said Paul.

'Come on, Mom, open your hands,' said Mickey.

'Not until you've guessed.'

'Give a little clue.'

'Something round with a head on it?' she said.

'It's Lincoln! It's Lincoln! Yes?' cried Paul.

The boys went around the car checking the tread depth on each tyre.

'Number One, *Achoo!* Number Two, *Achoo!* Number Three, um nearly *Achoo*,' Paul took a look and nodded. 'Last one, *Achoo!*'

'Grandpa! It's all achoo. *Rain, rain, flow away; tyre tread hugs the road today!*'

The Bohdalice school was shut for the summer. There were seals on the door locks. The estate was ghostly quiet. They walked to the majestic linden tree, its imposing umbrella stretching to the mansion's portal. It had given shade for almost 140 years. When they were driving from Slavkov, Simone told the twins about their ancestry and that their great-great-great-great-great-grandfather had established the castle in Bohdalice in 1783 and planted orchards, invested in market gardening and agriculture, and built the little church. The boys got a kick out of all the *great-great-greats*, making a game of it by repeating the *greats* and sounding like a diesel engine being started and coughing into life.

Now, it was Simone's turn to play the game. When they had all gathered around the linden tree, she announced the ceremony. She had primed the adults gathered around and when she signalled to them, they chanted in unison, *Long live the Queen! Long live the Empress!*

She stood the boys in front of her, shoulder to shoulder, and switched to English. 'I am Queen of Bohdalice and Empress of Moravia. You will bow before me. Mickey Novotny, step forward and kneel in front of The Empress to be knighted!'

Mickey knelt and Simone took the knighting sword. She had removed the engine-oil dipstick from the Volkswagen van, wiped it clean and with arm outstretched, held the flimsy sword straight in front of her. She laid the blade of the dipstick on his right, then left, shoulder.

'I dub thee *Knight Imperial*, and invest you with the title *Sir Mickey de Melon*. Arise, Sir Mickey.'

'Mickey the Melon?' Mickey questioned.

Paul started giggling and couldn't stop himself. 'He's a melon. Will I be a cucumber?'

'Shhhh. This is all very solemn,' said Simone. 'Paul Novotny, step forward and kneel in front of The Empress!' She took the knighting dipstick and laid the blade on his right and left shoulder. 'I dub thee *Dame Imperial*, and invest you with the title *Lady Paula de Strawberry*.'

'Yum. Strawberry!' said Paul, still on his knees. Then, his smile faded. 'Gran'ma, Lady is a girl.'

'Your Majesty, not Grandma.'

'Your Majesty, can't I be *Sir Strawberry*?'

'Very well, my loyal subject. I re-dub thee *Knight Imperial*, and invest you with the title *Sir Paul de Blueberry*. Arise, Sir Paul.'

The whole group laughed. Paul and Mickey threw ghost punches at each other.

'Melon!'

'Blueberry!'

'Melon!'

'Blueberry!'

'You're a watermelon. Let me slice you.' Paul gave him a chop with the hand.

'Sir Blueberry, is your blood really blue?' quipped Mickey. 'I am Dracula. I want blue blood. Come, dear blueberry, come close.' He gave a toothy snarl. 'Closer, come to me.'

They drove back to Brno through the countryside, passing tiny villages, and stopped to see several of Miro's relatives. And everywhere they stopped, the glasses were filled and refilled with homemade plum brandy and the tables were laden with pork cuts, sliced ham, sausage rolls, and fruit-filled dumplings, topped with quark and melted butter and dusted with cinnamon or homemade cottage-cheese.

Chapter 32

Miro stayed a week with Lubor. It gave him a reverse periscope on life, to see below the surface and gauge the changes to his old homeland, sort out his feelings about the current social reality. Reading the local newspaper, he shook his head at the politically slanted tone of the articles, so transparent in Communist correctness. Factory workers were praised for increasing productivity, yet they had absolutely no say in production matters. These were all in the hands of managers who were simply yes-men to the State.

And the State kept churning out dice that, when a pair was rolled, would always come up snake eyes for the luckless mother working at the bakery, or the wretched father laying bricks. There were no product advertisements in the paper. Miro saw the long queues to buy fresh meat, dress shoes, nylon stockings, refrigerators, or transistor radios. The wait list for ordering Czechoslovak-made cars stretched to fifteen years before delivery. Everywhere he looked, he saw that demand exceeded supply. Goods stolen from the public sector ended up in all sorts of black markets. The land was a shamble in economic management, enough to make a beer drinker cry in one's mug of pilsner.

When evening came, he and Lubor would go to the local pub near his house. They sat at Lubor's customary table, tucked away in a corner of the tavern. They chatted in low voices. The walls had ears. A bouncy waitress in her forties, wearing a fraying chequered apron and a black leather money pouch, reached over to her tray and plunked down two mugs of beer on the stained, cardboard coasters with faded lettering of the tavern's name.

'*Chcete hned platit, nebo později?*' Do you want to pay now, or later?

'Later,' said Miro. She marched off without smiling. Smiling was forbidden in a communist state.

As Miro began discussing what his periscope revealed, two men in shabby suits sitting across them at another table kept eyeing Miro. He asked Lubor why they were so interested in him. Lubor lowered his head. 'They've noticed you are wearing imported clothes. We can't find jackets and shirts like yours here. You've given yourself away as a foreign visitor.'

'Are they plain-clothes police?' wondered Miro.

'Don't know. Might be. Or just curious locals, starved for quality goods.'

Miro's tiger nature leaped out of its cage. He turned

towards the two men. '*Dobrý večer, pánové!*' — Good evening, gentlemen!

They were somewhat startled. One of them said, 'We didn't think you spoke Czech. Are you visiting from abroad?'

'I live in Canada. I am visiting my brother here.' Miro pointed to Lubor. Lubor gave a polite nod.

'Canada! You have travelled very far to visit us,' said the other man. 'What do you do for a living?'

'I am retired. I used to work in a tyre factory.'

The two men chuckled. 'We are both tractor drivers. But our tyres are no good. They wear out too soon. How much does a tractor tyre cost in Canada?'

Miro said he could not remember.

'Well,' said one of them, 'I am sure Canada makes top-quality tyres. Allow me to buy you chaps a beer.' Miro and Lubor joined them at their table. 'It's a difficult life here,' he continued. 'We work on a collective farm and the pay is not enough. My wife is helping, but we keep chickens and rabbits, and a few pigs, at the back of the house. Nothing is available in the shops. How is it in Canada? Much better than here, I suppose.'

Miro chuckled. 'We don't keep chickens and pigs at the back of the house.'

And so, it went, sad-jovial chit-chat, until the pub's closing time. Miro footed the bill for all four and left a generous tip for the unsmiling waitress.

Miro was not feeling well. He said he was going to bed early. His brother was worried. Miro did not look well. Droplets of sweat had collected on his brow. His hands were cold.

At about eleven o'clock, Miro sat up in bed. He was gasping. 'Lubor, can't breathe, chest pain. It's the heart.'

Lubor jumped out of his bed. Holding Miro, he threw a bathrobe over him and helped him downstairs, then bundled him into the car. They drove to the nearby Vyškov Hospital. Lubor telephoned the hotel and Simone and Theo rushed to the hospital.

'I'm sorry madam, we cannot accept visitors, after hours,' said the receptionist nurse.

'I am not a visitor. My husband was brought here tonight and he's had a heart attack.'

'Madam, the hospital has strict rules. Your husband is in good hands here.'

Simone reached into her purse and pushed a twenty-dollar banknote into the nurse's hand. The air stank of garlic. The nurse stared down in disbelief. Simone dissolved the tension and put her finger to her lips. 'It's a secret between you and me,' she whispered. Then, looking all flustered, the nurse glanced left and right to make sure she wasn't seen and slipped the money into her pocket.

'Follow me, quickly,' she whispered. 'They mustn't see us.'

Lubor was at Miro's bedside. He jumped up and hugged Simone and Theo. Miro was unconscious but still had a heartbeat. Every so often, a nurse would come by to check his vital signs. They had given him heart stimulants.

Simone sat at his bedside, holding Miro's hand. Lubor and Theo went outside and waited in the corridor. By three o'clock, Simone had laid her head on the edge of the bed and dozed off. It was the sleep that, too briefly, banishes tragedy and forbids its existence. When the nurse of the ward came by again, she detected no signs of life. She hurried off to find the duty doctor and he confirmed the lack of vital signs. He tapped Simone's shoulder to awaken her and told her he was gone. Simone was still holding Miro's hand and bit into his cold fingers, her lips quivering as she buried her face in his arm.

'Miro, you promised. You promised me!' She sobbed until the bedsheet was wet. 'Hold my hand. Help me make it through. I don't want to be alone.'

Lubor came back in and enfolded her in his arms, then he and Theo lifted her away and towards the door. Simone tried to turn around and return to the bed.

'No, don't,' Lubor said. 'It will deepen your sadness. From this day forward, life will be different. Our strength comes from our hope.'

Miro had his funeral sometime later. Simone wanted the news to permeate his home town. News is the daughter of time. When the day came, she asked Lubor to bring a small bowl of coal cinders to the burial site. They buried him in Slavkov, close to where his father, Stanislav, lay and near to the mother he had never known.

As the coffin was being lowered, the priest spoke quietly. '*Memento, homo, quia pulvis es, et in pulverem reverteris.*' — remember, Man, that dust thou art, and to dust thou shalt return. He asked if Simone wished to sprinkle earth on it. She turned to Lubor and he gave her the bowl of cinders. She dipped her hand in and scooped up some ashes.

'You were my shining partner on a Beirut dance floor. Take *Popelka* in your arms, now, and let's dance to the Andromeda galaxy, light years away.' She tossed the cinders.

Theo held the boys in each hand. Standing with their father, they looked so still and upright. Tereza stepped forward and, stooping down to the base of the stone marker, left a deep-red rose. The boys looked up at the marble slab. The epitaph had been written by Theo.

Ancestral roots run deep
In the soil where I now sleep.
Time gave me spaces to have seen.
Random branches stretched far out,
Bent by winds of chance and doubt,
But, oh, what a journey it has been!

Miroslav Novotny
Nec male notus eques

'Daddy, what did you write on the bottom?' asked Paul.

'I wrote, "A knight of good repute."'

'Was he *really* a knight?'

Theo looked down at him and gave his hand a squeeze. 'In shining armour.'

Simone was astounded at the size of the crowd that attended the funeral and burial, perhaps two hundred, she guessed, generations of relatives and friends of relatives, some of whom had never met Miro, but had heard of his travels and adventures. Miro was something of a minor celebrity in and around Slavkov. He was the only one in his extended family who had left Czechoslovakia and made his future elsewhere.

As Lubor and Milena were leaving the cemetery with Simone on their arm, they saw a man running towards them.

'Simone! Simone!' he shouted. She stopped and he caught up. 'Do you recognise me?' He was out of breath.

Simone was astonished to hear English and looked puzzled. His neat, trimmed beard was greyish and his thick hair crowned a rugged, bony face. His ice-blue eyes were very intense. He had a cultivated, debonair look about him.

'I'm terribly sorry, sir. I'm afraid I don't.'

'Simone, do you remember Marek Svoboda? I was at

your wedding in Beirut.'

A sharp gasp. Stunned speechlessness. Eyebrows burdened with disbelief. She had forgotten his looks.

'Marek? No, not possible.'

'Yes, Daniela Meir. It is.'

Shock took its time. She didn't know what to do. Then she threw her embarrassed arms around him. 'How did you find us?'

'My neighbour in Brno saw the death notice in the paper and it mentioned that Miro had worked for Kolo. He came over to see me and asked if I knew anyone by the name of Miroslav Novotny.'

A wave began to form, gathering height and power, until it could crest no higher and came crashing down over her, like no other wave she had known. The foam bubbled inside and she broke into an emancipating, cathartic laughter of joy. 'Marek, Marek, Marek. I can't believe you are standing in front of me! Is this really, really you, really?'

Marek stayed quiet. He knew the momentousness of it all. He gave a huge smile.

She began to tremble. 'I thought we had lost you. Please don't go away. Please join us.' She translated all this to Milena and Lubor, and now Marek was the surprised one.

'You are fluent in Czech!' he chuckled with delight. 'How . . .' His look radiated amazement.

Three weeks later, they were all at the restaurant *Veselá Vdova*, The Merry Widow, in downtown Brno. Lubor had booked a large dinner table for eight. Simone was wearing a silk chiffon dress, with a small black ribbon pinned to one shoulder strap. Theo sat next to his Mum and, on her other side, was the guest of honour, Marek Svoboda. For Milena and Lubor this was a special treat. Such classy places were beyond their orbit. Tereza and the boys were deciphering the menu, trying to decide from among the Czechoslovak specialties.

Marek and Simone chatted in English, filling the vacuum created by the transit of time. He had resigned from Kolo during the war, then came home from the Middle East. He was embittered by what the State had done to his old company.

'Miro would agree,' said Simone. 'If only you and he had found each other. You know, we thought we would never see you again.'

'I'm so sad I didn't reconnect with Miro. How much I wanted to see my dear friend. As they would say in Lebanon, "Allah did not will it."'

'Do you still play football, scoring with that bulletproof right leg of yours?'

Marek laughed and hung his head. 'You remembered that! I am touched.'

'You may not believe this. I still have your postcard from Beirut framed and on my dressing table at home. It was my way of praying we would find you.'

'This is almost mystical.' *That was such a long time ago!* 'Yes, I'm still quite fit and play on weekends. We have formed a small football club, some my age, some quite a lot younger than me.'

Marek kept eyeing Theo. 'He looks a lot like Miro.'

'And he doesn't look like me?'

Marek took her hand and gave it a Viennese kiss. 'That too, but more like Miro.'

Simone ordered champagne for everyone and the bottles were opened.

'To you, Marek.' She raised her glass and they clinked. 'I have special memories of the last time we did this.'

'At Restaurant Le Paris, yes?'

As they ate dinner, a trio of rotund men with cherry-red faces and wrinkled smiles played folk music, polkas, and occasional waltzes and foxtrots for those inclined to dance. Two of them had accordions and the third one, a concertina.

When they had finished eating, Simone turned to Marek.

'Do you remember the last time we danced together?'

'Of course! Our evening at Le Paris, after your wedding.'

'Are you still such a great dancer?' she smiled.

'I shall let you be the judge.' He rose and leaned forward over Simone's chair. 'May I have this dance, *milostivá paní?*' M'lady?

Marek held out his elbow and Simone took his arm as they walked to the dance floor. Several couples were already dancing.

'Isn't that the Novotny widow?' asked one of the two men at another table.

His friend replied, 'I believe it is. But who is that man with her? She does look the merry widow, doesn't she? What is the point of mourning something that can never be changed? The sadness cannot bring back the dead person.'

'I agree,' said the first. 'Let's drink to her health and happiness.' They clinked their beer mugs and chuckled.

There, was Simone, in the arms of her other dancer in Beirut. During their third dance, Marek led her to the edge of the dance floor, away from the other dancing couples. He took on a serious tone.

'Simonko, I want to leave here and escape to the West. I have been planning this for a long time and, as luck would have it, you show up again in my life. I need to talk to you and perhaps you can help me.'

'How can I help?'

'We need to talk. In complete secrecy. Are you free tomorrow?'

'Why don't you come to my hotel and we discuss what's on your mind?'

'No. The walls there have ears. Let's go for a walk in the park. What time would suit you?'

They met outside her hotel. Simone was discreet and dressed in very ordinary clothes so she wouldn't look like a foreign tourist. As they strolled along a forested path in the city's historic park, he held her hand.

'You don't mind we do this?' asked Marek. 'If anyone is watching, it looks very innocent, a couple taking an afternoon walk and holding hands.'

'Of course not. I like it.' She looked up at him and squeezed the warm, dry hand. *There is sincerity in it. He hasn't lost his aura of confidence, or his Moravian charm.*

'And if anyone stops us and questions us, say nothing. I'll handle the answers,' he added. She gave his hand another squeeze.

'Marek, are you under suspicion?'

'No, Simonko. But I need to bring you up-to-date on a few things. When I was living in Palestine during the war, the British armed forces were very interested in my language abilities and hired me. They assigned me to signals and trained me as a signals engineer in wireless communications, intercepting enemy radio messages, passing them on for decoding, then translating them, that sort of thing. After the war, when I returned to Brno, the Communist officials found out about my training and earlier work. They ordered me not to go back to Kolo, but to work for them. They wanted someone with my language skills to monitor foreign communications for their own twisted purposes.'

'And you had no choice?'

'I knew there would be a lot of pressure: "You work for us, or we'll find ways to make your life difficult."' He took her hand, kissed it, and a smile of apology took shape. 'That's why I couldn't stay in touch with you and Miro. First it was the war, working for the British, then came this cloak of silence thrown over my soul.'

'Are you still working for them?'

'I retired some years ago. Now and then, they call on me to pick my brains.'

'So, why don't you simply leave and settle in another country?'

'I can't. The Ministry of National Security and the Ministry of the Interior will not issue me a passport. They fear I know too much and would become an agent working for some foreign intelligence service.'

'And that's why you need to escape.'

'Will you help me, Simone?'

'Does this mean you will need to slip across the border, undetected?'

'Yes.'

'It sounds dangerous. Can I get Milena, Lubor and Theo to help me in this?'

'Can you trust Milena and Lubor, absolutely?'

'Yes, of course. Miro's sister and brother would do anything to help me. If I put my faith in you, they would support me by helping you.'

'And you are quite certain they have no connection to any Communist authorities or party members.'

'Marek, they hate the communists. They are just like Miro was. They resent what the system has done to this country.'

'Alright then. The five of us need to meet somewhere in absolute secrecy. We need to discuss the strategy and the details. I've been planning this escape for two years and I have a lot of information about the border situation and setting. I need to escape into Austria. I need you and Theo to await me on the Austrian side, when I get through the barriers and fences.'

'Marek, when you get across, do you want to come to Canada? I can help you get settled there.'

'You are very generous, Simonko, but let's take it one step at a time. Right now, I have to get away from this horrible regime. They are bastards. The communists are committing crimes against humanity. It becomes so obvious at the border with West Germany and Austria, too.'

Simone stopped walking. Smiling, she looked up at him.

'You know something? You sound so much like Miro.'

'I do?'

'Umm hmm.'

Chapter 33

Tereza and the twins returned to Canada. School was about to begin. Theo stayed with Simone.

'Milena, why don't you come join me in Canada? We could be close together and I would help you get settled.' Simone and Milena had taken a walk and were resting on a bench along a forested path in Brno's Špilberk Park.

'I can't, *drahoušku*'—my dearest one. 'Much as I love you, my roots are here, my home is here and I am at ease in my surroundings. Canada would be so strange for me. I don't speak the language. I would have to start all over again. I don't know anyone there.'

'But you have *me* there,' Simone reminded.

'Yes, but you are free to come and go. You could visit me here more often. We wouldn't be separated for so many years.'

Simone let her in on the fresh development. 'Marek Svoboda wants to leave here and come to the West. He told me they will not issue him a passport because he knows too much about Czechoslovak communications secrets.'

Milena glanced over her shoulder to make sure nobody was within earshot.

'Then how will he get away?' Milena whispered.

'We have to keep this absolutely secret. I need you and Lubor to help us plan his escape across the border. He has to be very careful, because if he gets caught, it's finished for him. Theo and I would help in the planning, and then wait for him on the Austrian side of the border.'

Milena was getting nervous. 'Let's take a walk. I don't like the thought that someone has bugged this park bench or has spotted us and will be following.'

'We need to get together somewhere, the five of us, you, Lubor, Marek, Theo and me. A place to go over every detail. Can you think of a secure place to discuss the escape plan where we can be sure no one is listening?'

'I'll think of something. Can you give me time?'

'We have a little time.'

Milena looked over her shoulder again. No one was following.

They met at Milena's house. Lubor, Marek and Theo were there too.

Milena started, 'I have a place where we can discuss *Fearless Leo*.' That was their code name for the operation.

'There is a tiny Catholic chapel in a small village near Slavkov. I know the priest in charge and he is a trustworthy friend. I did not breathe a word to him. He will choose a time when there are no worshippers. He will let us in, leave us alone and lock the outside doors.'

In a country officially atheistic, no socialist official, soldier or paranoid member of the local Communist Party would dare attend a religious service or be seen entering a chapel or church.

They were gathered at the chapel. The doors were shut for their *Fearless Leo* meeting. Marek spoke first.

'I am here among dear friends, and new friends. I feel a safety of trust that I have not felt for a long time. I know what this means to you and the risk you are taking. I wish I could express the gratitude I feel and the favour I owe you.' He got down to the details.

'I have been thinking about my escape for a long time. And it has given me a chance to inform myself of the situation I face. I have visited the border region at several places and know the set-up at certain parts of the frontier with Austria. The frontier is heavily guarded. Let me give you a picture of the set-up. There are six-metre- and nine-metre-high watch towers. Each border sector can communicate with other sectors and with ground patrols by radio-telephone. Most guard units have trained attack dogs and guard dogs which are a crossbreed of male German shepherds and female Carpathian wolves.'

There was shock on Milena's face. 'How can you avoid being tracked down by the dogs?'

'But that's only the beginning. The watch towers have spotlights which can be aimed at trouble spots. On the ground, it gets a little more interesting: alert patrols respond to escape attempts that have been detected electrically at a signalling fence. Search patrols go looking for an escapee who was shot at, but not apprehended. Ambush patrols hide in concealed bunkers and await a would-be escapee in sections where many attempts to cross the border have been made in the past. All of these foot patrols are armed with sub-machine guns and pistols. They also have signalling pistols which fire flares, to alert another patrol that they are chasing someone trying to cross the border. The flare is red if they are signalling that a would-be escapee has been spotted.'

Theo spoke up. 'What is the border itself like, Marek?'

'The watch towers have been erected at the top of steep embankments. At the bottom, running along a ditch which follows the border, is the first barrier, the signal fence. It is a three-metre-high, barbed-wire fence strung with low-voltage wires. Any attempt to get through the signal fence, either over it or by cutting it, activates an alarm at the nearest border command post. They have a panel of lights which tells the tower guard exactly where the fence was breached, and an alert patrol is sent to that alarm area. After the signal fence, there is a fifteen-metre-wide clear strip of land which must be crossed to get to a second, barbed-wire fence. If you can get past this second one, you head for the woods or thick undergrowth until you get to the inner border of Austria, which is marked with border trace stones.'

A gasp from Milena. 'Jesus, Mary, Joseph! You're taking such a risk.'

Lubor was curious. 'I heard there are high-voltage electric fences around our borders with Austria and West Germany. People trying to escape have been electrocuted.'

'Those electrified fences are gone. Many escapees died this way trying to flee to the West. A jolt of several thousand volts will kill. This brutal way of stopping a desperate refugee is a crime against humanity. The fence had a total length of 1,400 kilometres and was costing the regime too much money and endangering the border guards, themselves. So, the bastards dismantled the electrified fences. A refugee's life is cheap but the fence was expensive.'

'Marek, do you have a date in mind?' said Simone.

'This has to be done under the cover of darkness. A moonless night is best. We have twenty-two days to the next new moon. Third week of September is a good date. Are you and Theo available?'

'I can spend some time in Vienna, until then,' she said.

'I will have to return to Canada,' added Theo. 'But I'll work something out to be back in Austria.'

Marek continued. 'Theo, Simonko. The three of us will wear black clothing. On my side of the border, I don't want to appear as anything but a silhouette. The border guards are under strict orders not to shoot at silhouettes. Some years ago, they killed one of their own guards at night when a young soldier panicked and thought the moving silhouette was an escapee. I will bring barbed-wire snips. Theo, you will have wire cutters, too, just in case there is some other barrier along the Austrian side. The Austrians welcome people who have escaped across the border and try to help them. They know how the Communists treat border violators who have been spotted or caught.'

Marek brought out a map showing the border region for the planned escape spot and taped it to a wall, directly below a wood-framed painting of Jesus being crucified.

'Milena, you and Lubor and I will wear ordinary, everyday clothes so as not to arouse suspicion. I will change to black, later. Put nothing in the car that might look as though you had driven someone close to the border. I will wear gloves so I don't leave any fingerprints in your car. We will drive south to Mikulov, which is the main border crossing if one is driving to Vienna. But, well before reaching this, we will turn and head east to Valtice, very close to the border. Then, there is a narrow local road which passes through vineyards and leads to the Austrian border. See, here?' He pointed out the spot on the map.

'Yes, we know Valtice quite well,' said Lubor. 'It's very close to the border.'

Marek went on. 'Now, at this fork here, can you see, which leads to the village of Úvaly, I will get out of the car, change clothes in a clump of bushes, and walk to the border. Please do not make any attempt to wait for me. Drive straight back to Slavkov as quickly as possible. There are soldiers and plainclothes police who check on people around villages close to the border.'

'And if we are stopped and questioned?' asked Milena.

'You raise rabbits at home, don't you? Put several of them inside their cage, put the cage in the car, and say that you were looking for a rabbit breeder in the vicinity of Valtice. Try to find a potential rabbit breeder in advance, in that area, so your story is airtight.'

Theo spoke. 'Marek, how do we find the exact spot where you will be coming through?'

'Take a look here. You see this tiny Austrian village of Schrattenberg? It's just one-and-a-half kilometres from the border with Czechoslovakia. On the arranged day of escape, you will be driving north from Vienna and will come to the village of Poysdorf. Here, you turn right and head northeast to Schrattenberg. Our meeting point will be east of the road which crosses into Czechoslovakia, so you will turn off and follow the track, heading east, for about 600 metres. I will give you a very small, hand-drawn map and diagram to take with you, so that everything will be clearly marked for our meeting at the escape spot.'

Theo and Simone studied the large map. Marek continued, 'Now, when you leave here to drive to Vienna until the arranged date, you will be crossing the border at Mikulov. At the border crossing, they will check your car, under the car, in the boot, around the engine, under all the seats, to make sure you are not smuggling a person out of the country. They may even ask to check your luggage and handbag for anything suspicious. So, well before you get to Mikulov, I want you to take the little map I give you, roll it up tight, seal it inside a condom, and ask Simone to hide it in her vagina. You must not get caught with the map. Yes?'

Simone smiled and Theo understood and they all chuckled.

'Do not attempt to use the toilets at the border checkpoint. The guards must not lose sight of you while they are checking the car and your passports. It makes those bastards suspicious. If you have a need to go somewhere, hold it until you are safely inside Austria. Otherwise, drink less and do it before you arrive at the border.'

Marek drew Theo's and Simone's attention to his large map.

'One more thing. When you leave here to go to Vienna until the rendezvous date, I want you to make a short practice reconnaissance of the place around my escape point. After you've crossed the border and entered Austria, head fifteen kilometres south to Poysdorf, make a left turn and drive back to Schrattenberg, towards the border you have come through. Then, continue right up to the Austrian side of the border, hide the car behind some trees and practise using the little map to walk to the escape spot. There are border stones and signs in German tracing the inner Austrian border and these appear about every 100 metres. See, here, on the map? So, you'll still be on Austrian soil. It's best if you do this orientation practice at twilight, but do not use the car's headlights or any hand-held torches. You will feel more at ease once you've seen the surroundings at my escape point.'

'And what about you?' asked Simone.

'I will find a way past the first signalling fence, cross the narrow strip of land between, get to the second barbed-wire fence and cut my way through, then make a dash through the tree cover, still on the Czechoslovak side, and reach the marked border of Austria. Theo should be able to spot me there. Remember: no headlights, no torches.'

'Marek, what if something goes wrong?' said Simone.

'Simonko, park your car close to tree cover a few hundred metres from the border and stay in the car. Do not get out. The guards sometimes shoot across the fence at escapees, even after the refugee has reached Austrian soil. Please, if you hear any kind of commotion, guards shouting '*Halt!*' or anything, shots being fired, dogs barking, floodlights being aimed, quickly drive the car back several hundred metres, and wait there with the headlights off.' He turned and put his hand on Theo's shoulder. 'Theo, do not try to be the big hero. If you hear shouts or warning shots on my side of the fence, get away quickly and return to the car.

I will take whatever happens. No taking crazy risks. You have a loving family to support and they need you.' His eyes were gimlets aimed at Theo. 'Do you promise me this, Theo? Do you hear me?'

Once again, a room went silent and all eyes turned towards Theo. He pictured the situation that might occur. 'You have asked for our help and we are giving it. More I cannot promise.'

Simone looked distraught. *What if things went wrong for him? Could I forgive myself?*

Marek took on a humbler tone. 'I want to say two things. I want each of you to know how much I appreciate the help you are giving me. I probably will never get a chance to return this favour. You are all taking a risk and I thank you from the deepest corner of my heart. But let me be clear on this: if any one of you feels the risk you are taking is too high, please don't hesitate to bow out. I will understand and perhaps I will give up on trying to escape.'

Is this my chance for getting him to change his mind? She didn't say anything. Her thoughts reeled back to the day she first met him in Beirut. The voice of the Shrine merged into her thoughts. *This man is a fearless lion. He's like Miro. Nothing will stop him. I sense the power. He will fight for what he cherishes. He knows what he wants. Help him, Daniela. The imprisoned soul needs its freedom. He is yours now.*

They met one more time in that chapel. Firmed up some remaining points. Theo needed to return home and work out a way to get back to Vienna. Simone wanted to wait in Vienna. She didn't tell Marek, but she intended to visit the Canadian embassy there to find out what paperwork was involved when people wanted to emigrate from Austria to Canada. No mention of an escaped refugee would be made at the embassy.

Milena spoke. 'Marek what will you do with all your personal belongings and possessions? If you are escaping, you will have to leave everything behind.'

'Yes, I know. It's the sacrifice for freedom. Once they discover I am gone, the State will come to my apartment and confiscate everything and make it State property. I would love to leave everything to you and Lubor, but that would incriminate you in the State's eyes and you would be in trouble. They would suspect you had something to do with my escape. I will leave you the key in any case, but be· very careful. They have informers everywhere. If anyone saw you entering my apartment, it would be reported.'

Lubor and Milena nodded.

'It is a tragedy. What can be done?' said Lubor.

'I'll be happy to bring small things out of my apartment and give them to you: books, stationery, personal items, small kitchenware, that sort of thing. Things that would not be noticed if I did that, little by little. Any removal of furniture or appliances would be risky because I could be spotted by informers who might report I am moving out.'

'Marek,' said Lubor, 'How will we know that you have made it across into Austria?'

'I have thought about that. Remember our code names when we send you a picture postcard from Austria: Simone is Sister Magdalena, Theo is Sister Angela, I am Father Erik. The names will be your signal that we are safe in Austria. The message itself will be a decoy. If you give Simone your priest friend's address, it should be okay to receive such a postcard.'

Marek turned to Theo. 'When you get back home, do not mention anything about *Fearless Leo* to anybody, not even to your wife. Do you follow? Find an excuse to return to Vienna. And do not make any telephone calls to Simone from Canada. Let Simone telex you from Vienna if there is any change in plans. The two of you should have some coded way of communicating dates, places and plans. The name *Czechoslovakia,* or any places here, must never appear in a telex. Use the code name *Geneva* if you need to refer to our land.'

'I understand.'

Marek put his arm around Simone. 'I need to emphasise to both of you. Never discuss anything in your hotel rooms, the hotel lobby, or in restaurants or cafes. Go for a walk in a public park if you need to talk about things related to my escape. Do not take written notes. Even when you are in Vienna, never mention any names, places or dates related to the escape. The Soviets have spies planted in countries bordering the Iron Curtain. Go for walks if you need to talk. Simone nodded.

'Simonko, I will give you final instructions just before you and Theo leave for Vienna. Remember what I said about hiding the map. Let me have your telex number in Vienna. When you check into the hotel there, tell them you are expecting a telex for a Madame Magdalena. I will send a telex directed to Madame Magdalena. It will confirm the date and time of our border rendezvous. My message will read something like this:

Have been enjoying the wonderful city of Brno. This is a beautiful country. Wish you were here. I drive back to Geneva on the 9th. I need to be home for my son's 27th birthday.

Love, Bernard.

'Pay attention only to the numbers. This means you and Theo need to be at the escape spot at twilight on the twenty-seventh of September and I should be coming through at about nine p.m. Yes?' They nodded.

'Now, if the last part of my telex reads: *I have to drive to Prague before the weather changes. Love, Bernard,* something has gone wrong and the planned rendezvous is off. We will have to try some other way and another day. Is this understood?'

'Marek, I'm a little scared about all this. What if something happens to you? You are the bridge to my past. You knew me when I was nineteen. It took such a long time for us to reconnect. I don't want to let go of it. I'm so afraid to lose all this.'

'Nothing will happen to me. Everything has been planned in detail. But please bring a first-aid kit with you. My hands and arms will be cut by the barbed wire. I will get a tetanus shot before the escape, just in case.'

She looked at him and mouthed the words, 'I love you.' He smiled. Stayed silent. Put his hand under her chin, then lifted it softly and angled his head sideways, as though comforting a child. 'All is well. I've known you for a long time. No reason to change that.'

Chapter 34

Simone sat in the car, waiting. Theo was pacing outside, glancing at his watch every few minutes.

'You know, there's something special about the twenty-seventh of September,' he said.

'Really? Why?'

'It's the day Pavel led his RAF squadron into battle and they shot down ten German planes.'

She sucked in a sharp breath. 'Goodness! Was it on that day?'

Simone compressed her fingers in her fists, grasping air that wasn't there. She lowered her head, then closed her eyes and whispered to herself. *Pavel, please, please, please shepherd him across. He is your countryman. He helped us win the war.* She bit her lip hard.

Nine o'clock came and went, and still there was silence. Disturbed by a light breeze, only the rustling of the leaves at the edge of the forest could be heard. Nine-thirty, and nothing.

'Theo, are we at the right place?'

'I'm pretty sure we are.'

Ten o'clock. Nothing. All at once, a bright flare shot into the sky, illuminating its surroundings for several seconds. The flare was red.

'Damnit! Damnit! Damnit! They've spotted him! This is bad, Mum.'

They heard shouts several times. '*Stuj!*' Halt! Then, warning shots cracked through the air.

'Mum, get into the car and drive down the road.'

'I'm not leaving here.'

'Mum, please! You know what Marek said.'

'I'm not going!'

Marek had cut through the signal fence, setting off the alarm at the border command post. Border command radioed the alert patrol. 'Signal fence breached at Zone L-6. Be ready to apprehend a border violator.'

The alert patrol reached the signal fence and saw the snipped wires. They spotted Marek fleeing across the strip of land leading to the outer barbed-wire fence and gave chase. He was about 200 metres ahead of them.

'Halt!' Then came the warning shots, a short burst from a sub-machine gun, fired into the air. 'Halt! We will shoot!'

Marek continued running towards the barbed-wire fence. He glanced back and saw the guards gaining on him. Two gun bursts in succession exploded the silence. A bullet tore through the cool, night air, creating its own shock wave and finding its target in Marek's left thigh, just above the knee, where it smashed into the thigh bone. He felt the searing pain and fell to the ground, picked himself up and continued his hobble towards the fence. He fell again and, using his elbows and right knee, crawled the remaining few metres to the horizontally strung barbed wires. Marek began snipping the lowest two rows of wires trying to wriggle through on his belly. He heard the guards shouting alerts to each other.

'Watch out! He may be armed.'

'Cover me. I'm gaining on him. We need the bastard alive.'

Out of the black, Theo appeared. 'Give me your hand! I'll pull you through.'

'Bloody hell! You sh, sh ... not ...'

'Come on. Quick. Hang onto my hand. I'll pull you through.'

Theo snipped a few more strands of barbed wire and stretched Marek's arm, almost tearing it from its shoulder socket, then grabbed onto his jacket collar and got him through the barbed wire fence.

'Let's go. I'll carry you over my shoulders.'

'We're still on ... Cze ... Czech soil.' Marek was panting, his voice weak and trembly. 'Must ... get ... to forest ... fore ...'

They got to the edge of the grove of trees and entered the woods. The guards lost sight of them and were still giving chase. Simone showed up. She had crossed over onto the Czechoslovak side. If the border patrol spotted them, they would open fire. She put Marek's arm over her shoulder, while Theo did the same with the other arm, and they supported him to take some weight off his legs. Marek's left leg was dragging along the ground and he made short hobbles with his right leg.

'Simo … you bruh … you bro … broke …' his gasping whimper got feebler. His jacket was ripped at the back and his arms cut and bleeding. He had a barbed-wire gash in his neck.

Distance stretched into boundlessness getting him through the woods, across to the Austrian side, and laying him down on the back seat of the car. Simone jumped in behind Marek and stretched him out with his head on her lap. His left pant leg was soaked in blood and blood was dripping onto the car floor. Theo swung the car round and headed along the narrow path leading back to the road towards Schrattenberg.

The blood of freedom was draining fast. 'Marek, did you get your tetanus shot?'

No reply. She couldn't reach the first-aid kit, so she tightened her free hand around his thigh, above the wound, to stem the bleeding. Then, she ripped off her scarf and wound it around the left knee. As they approached the village, Theo saw a house with the lights on and a man standing outside. He stopped the car and the man walked up to them.

'Maria!' the man shouted in German towards the

house. 'We have a wounded refugee!'

His wife came running and saw Marek lying there with his leg all bloodied. She ran back into the house and returned with bandage rolls and a blanket. Simone began to tie the bandage around the upper part of Marek's left thigh, creating a makeshift tourniquet. Marek's face was white. He could barely speak.

'Hospital,' Marek croaked in German, to the man.

'There is no hospital in Schrattenberg. There is a twenty-four-hour clinic in Mistelbach. I can take you there.'

Marek mumbled something and Simone said, 'Yes, please! Please. Take us there. Thank you so much.' Theo motioned for the man to sit in front.

'Franz,' he nodded, and shook Theo's hand.

'Theo.' Theo turned and pointed to the two on the back seat, 'Simone, Marek.'

'*Angenehm!*' Pleased to meet you.

They got to the clinic and the seriousness of the wound became apparent. In the morning, Marek would have to be taken to a hospital in Vienna. They gave him morphine to ease the pain and disinfected the wound. A temporary splint was made for the leg. Simone stayed up all night at his bedside. Theo took Franz home, and Maria gave Theo dinner and a basket of freshly baked rolls for Simone. He returned to the clinic, and slept in the car.

'We will have to operate on the leg. The femur is shattered. But it can be fixed. It will take some time to heal. I hope you are prepared to be very patient.' That was the surgeon talking to Simone in perfect English.

'Operate on the leg?'

'Yes, it has to be done.'

'Doctor, will he be able to walk?'

'Of course. And, ah, we removed the single bullet from his leg.' He fished into his white coat pocket and held up the shiny copper projectile. 'You might want to keep this as a memento of his bravery. A man of his age, we know the risk. Many younger men didn't make it across.'

Marek was receiving a blood transfusion and being fed intravenously. Simone stayed until the afternoon, then went with Theo to their hotel. Theo sent Tereza a telex message and ended it, *Simone has earned the Order of Maria Theresa for valour. Will explain when I get home.*

'Mum, you've taught me that strength comes from character, not from flesh and bones, and you are living proof of that. You took a huge risk.'

'Well, so did you! He owes his life to you.'

Theo stayed a few days visiting Marek in hospital. Before he flew home, Simone said, 'Can you give me half a day?'

'What's up?'

'I want us to drive up to Schrattenberg and thank Maria and Franz. I have a special gift for them.'

Simone remained in Vienna, visiting Marek every day. He was getting better and his strength was coming back. 'Simonko, do you realise what a stupid, dangerous thing you did? Do you have any idea how risky that was? How many young men and women were shot down where you—'

She pressed her finger against his lips. 'Shhh, no more of that. You made it through. That's the most important thing in the world. Now, can we let Milena and Lubor know that you got across?'

'Of course. We promised it.'

'So, what should I write on the postcard? You're the expert on cryptic messages.'

'Write, "We have visited Vienna. One day, we wish to visit Czechoslovakia, too. We have never been, but we have read about your beautiful castles and the Tatra Mountains. Blessings from, Sister Magdalena, Sister Angela and Father Erik."'

She shook her head. 'Quite amazing! You're a master at spraying subterfuge into the prying eyes of those communist cockroaches.'

'Well, I learnt something from them. Now they are getting it back.'

Simone's mind hovered over unfinished business. 'Marek, what were your thoughts as you stood at the pier in Beirut and were waving to me? You stood there for a long time after the ship left the dock, still waving.'

'Oh, that was an eternity ago. Probably something like, "I wonder when I'll see you and Miro again." It was a touch sad, but I never imagined that you would end up in Africa and Iran. War has a cruel way of changing lives. Why do you ask?'

'Because I had a heart flutter for you and I didn't want to wave back. It felt too much like a permanent parting, a never-see-you-again wave that might last forever.'

'Did you stay on deck for a long time?'

'I did. I thought about how I ended up on that ship going to Alexandria with Miro. All the hidden forces that propelled me to Miro, and then you. And my Catholic conversion at the Convent of the Redeemer. And then my wedding with a new name. Having to elope because my parents did not want me to marry Miro.'

Marek chuckled. 'Did you think that Allah had willed it, and it was written?'

'I don't know. There was a force driving all this.' She looked at him. Her eyes melted with compassion and she leaned over him. Left a kiss. 'It was written.'

Chapter 35

The weeks of stress and trauma unloaded with abruptness on Simone. Her appetite vanished and took her body weight with it. Dark circles under the eyes. A sallow complexion. Tremor in her pale hands. Absent minded moments. Loss of balance when she arose from sitting next to him. Marek could see what her offer of help had done to her. *How dare I hope to repay this time-tested loyalty?*

'Why don't you give yourself a break and go someplace quiet?' Marek was trying to inject a bit of joy into her state.

'No, no. I really don't want to leave you here and go somewhere. I'd be worried all the time.' She held his hand as if to transfer compassion to his healing wound. 'I want to see you healing.'

'Do it, Simonko. Even a short getaway will do you good. I'll be okay here until you get back. These people are real professionals.'

'I don't know.' She hated the thought. 'Where would I go to? Not being next to you depresses me.'

'Maybe a short visit to Salzburg by coach?'

There was surprising speed in his recovery. His physical fitness was paying off. Hope poured into the bucket of expectation. Simone was buoyed by it: *he will soon be out of hospital.*

'I hate to do this, but I'll take your advice. When I get back from Salzburg, I'll start looking to find you a place to live. Leave any messages with the hospital receptionist. Yes?' His hand was dry and warm. Like those smooth pebbles in the palm of the teenager sitting down and singing on Mount Carmel.

He smiled. She felt a roller-coaster flutter in a heart saved for the man she hadn't seen for much of her lifetime. It was a strange reunion. Not at all the way she had imagined. So, unlike the postcard image she had built up at her dressing table. The longing to see him had waited an eternity and here he was, in a hospital, recovering from a bullet wound. Lying there, was her other dancer in Beirut, waving to the bride as she sailed away to discover her own world. She bent over and allowed herself a kiss on his lips.

She returned from Salzburg. Visited the hospital. Crashed through a wall of shock, like a lorry whose brakes had failed. Bricks of pain rained down, shattering spirit and expectations.

The surgeon was explaining to her. 'There were complications after the surgery. We had to amputate his leg. The left leg is gone. We need to watch his progress hour by hour. I wish I could have prepared you for this.'

The days became short, the nights unbearably longer. The last of the autumn leaves were clinging to their branches. Vienna's rains had washed the rest away, down ditches and drains, cast off after the labours of spring and summer. The early morning mists threw a cloak over the city and made the streets seem darker. It felt like the year was coming to an end in a whimper and spring and its radiance would never return. The pain of decisions past, and the emptiness of untaken ones fused into a meaningless aftershock. *What do cargo ships matter anymore? They take you to this.*

Weeks oozed by like an iceberg of despair floating towards its ocean doom. She stayed at his bedside as many hours as she could squeeze out of each dismal day. No change in his condition was apparent. *At least he is holding on.* She prayed she could gift him what remained of her own élan vital, and its life-long wish to reconnect.

Marek died in February. A tiny bone fragment, a piece of undetected shrapnel, had emigrated to his heart. It crushed a breast full of hope, extinguished the flames of future joys. Her mind went numb with the smoke. She buried him surrounded by an alien silence, no family members by her side. The crimes against humanity would never again trouble him. A tiny, useless morsel of satisfaction leaked out: the heartless engineers of human suffering could not touch him anymore.

Pavel was gone. Miro no longer by her side. Now Marek, too. The trio of Daniela's dancers, gone. She listened intently, but The Shrine of the Báb remained silent. Life, hollowed out, had taken away the raspy advice of that old woman on Mount Carmel: 'Listen to it.'

She took the ferry from Dubrovnik to Korčula. Sun-bleached, bare, dusty the island was, as always. Nothing ever changed much in this part of the world. The autumn tourists were long gone. The pathetic whiff of withered sage rose up and lingered as she drifted through the meandering streets of the town, to Sveti Nikola Church. There were no men stopping and removing their hats as she passed. They didn't read her mind. Yet the long, afternoon shadow she cast had written it out plainly for them. They could not read her destiny.

She got to Michael's grave and sat to rest at the foot

of the granite headstone. How soft and undisturbed his eternal sleep, it seemed to her. *Was Michael hidden in Papa's untold story?*

'You're the only one I didn't dance with,' she whispered. She tried a half-hearted smile for him but the grimace was crippled. She hugged the granite and pressed a cheek against it. 'Why didn't you hear my heart?'

An hour passed. She made her way over the rock-strewn path to the edge of a parched cliff overlooking the Adriatic. The sea looked dark and angry. The flags would be black and black. She held the shiny copper projectile in her hand, looked down at it with eyes of lead, twirled it around in her fingers.

Her lipless mind spoke. *You did their dirty work for them. One leg was bulletproof, so you went for the other. Go, damn you! Go find that lost engagement ring and drown together.* She flung it towards the sea. The imprisoned soul had received its freedom.

Turning back, her footsteps clumsied by the wobbly stones, she felt a lifting of the hazy burden. A lizard catching the late sun flicked its neck and fixed the intruder in its gaze, the glint in its eye giving her the lizard stare and snaring her attention. She tossed a thought its way: *What do you know about life?* Mumbled words, without the cough, of that old woman on Mount Carmel.

A few steps onward, she spun round. The lizard was still staring at her. Fury stirred a touch. *So, how many dancers have you lost? Tell me! How many? What's your destiny?*

On the dusty steps of the church, she sat down, buried her face in hands filled with emptiness. No intrusion by the Shrine of the Báb. Only silence. A disturbing hush.

He came out of nowhere. Sat down beside her, the King of Persia with the kind nose, shiny black hair and eyes of blue. He was wearing Papa's suit jacket, scarlet with silk lapels and buttons of glistening mother-of-pearl and gold-fringed epaulettes. He put a kind arm around her and she swallowed the shock. His Eternal Majesty, King of Kings, was belittling himself. She dared not look up. He had not aged since the dream. He said nothing. Vanished from her side and took the memories with him.

A stubborn disquiet held on: *nothing is forever.* It hovered like a wounded gypsy moth, then flew into the flame.

www.ingramcontent.com/pod-product-compliance
Lightning Source LLC
Chambersburg PA
CBHW060727190726
48285CB00001B/101